Percy B. St. John

# The Countess Miranda

Percy B. St. John

**The Countess Miranda**

ISBN/EAN: 9783743344761

Manufactured in Europe, USA, Canada, Australia, Japa

Cover: Foto ©Andreas Hilbeck / pixelio.de

Manufactured and distributed by brebook publishing software (www.brebook.com)

Percy B. St. John

**The Countess Miranda**

# THE COUNTESS MIRANDA.

---

By PERCY B. St. JOHN.

---

WARD, LOCK, BOWDEN AND CO.,
London: WARWICK HOUSE, SALISBURY SQUARE, E.C.
New York: EAST 12TH STREET.
Melbourne: St. James's Street.   Sydney: York Street.

LONDON :
RANKEN, ELLIS AND CO., LTD., DRURY HOUSE,
DRURY COURT, STRAND.

# THE COUNTESS MIRANDA.

## CHAPTER I.

JEAN TORTICOLIS.

It was the evening of the 1st of March, 1789, and darkness had already veiled the face of nature; heavy clouds rolled their huge and unwieldly masses along the turgid sky, amid faint and dull flashes of far-off lightning, when a man on foot, a bundle on his shoulder, and wearing a rude costume—that of the working classes of society—broad-rimmed felt hat, blue cotton frock, dark trousers, and heavy boots—stopped before the auberge of the *Dernier Sou.*

This inn, situated on the roadside, about a dozen miles from Paris, was of mean appearance, but large in its premises, for over the door was written, in almost legible characters, with nearly correct orthography—

*" Ici one logg a pied est a chevale."*

The traveller, whose back was turned to Paris, paused ere he entered to listen for sounds from within; and as if satisfied with the result of his scrutiny, he prepared to pass the threshold, when another wayfarer presented himself.

This was a young man of better appearance than the other, though not a member of the upper classes. He wore, it is true, a sword, but his dress left it in doubt whether he were a simple citizen, or a student aiming at one of the learned professions. There was a careless mixture of both in his costume, but he, too, had a stick and a bundle. Like the artizan, he paused, looked up, and then followed the other into the auberge.

It was a large room which they entered, with a huge fire-place, a few tables and chairs, and a sideboard, on which were displayed bottles and glasses of varied shape, size, and contents. Near this table stood a woman, and by her side a man, apparently in active and earnest conversation—active, because both were lively—earnest, because the subject-matter was not of the slightest importance.

Of small stature, with a loose brown coat, a red cap, and huge boots, which had evidently seen service on salt water, this man, whose head was very much on one side, as if he were always in the act of listening, cast an uneasy and uncertain glance upon the pair as they entered. His eye rested an instant on the younger traveller, but nothing there seemed to him to require further notice; when, however, he caught sight of the other, he turned pale, and for a minute his whole form, the very sinking of his knees, betrayed an abject sense of fear. Without noticing the scrutiny, or the alarm which succeeded it, the object of so much terror asked for some bread, wine, and a *saucisse à l'ail.* He then seated himself at a table, and placed his bundle on the ground.

"And what shall I serve for you, Monsieur?" said the woman, addressing the young man.

"Have you materials for an omelette?" he replied, in a voice which made both men look up and examine his appearance, so richly musical were its tones, falling as it were with a metallic ring on the ear.

Of middle size, with long dark hair, pale and oval face, eyebrows pencilled like a woman's, a forehead high and smooth, a straight nose, and a mouth which seemed made to utter none but gentle things; there was a fire flashing from his eye, however, which belied this gentleness. He was evidently one of those who could be mild or stern as the occasion required.

"Monsieur shall have one in ten minutes," replied the hostess with a smile, for on her woman's heart his good looks were not lost, and away she hastened to perform her promise.

Meanwhile, the man with the wry neck and the other traveller had been eyeing each other with some little curiosity and anxiety. At length the former, whose first terror was now passed, but who was still uneasy at the pertinacious glances which the stranger, after once catching a glimpse, seemed to throw upon him, made an effort and spoke, though his tongue with difficulty performed its office.

"You seem to know me?" he said in a thick voice, which appeared to make itself heard by a struggling effort, and came rather from the ear which rested on his left shoulder, than from his throat.

"Oh, no!" cried the other, turning pale, and as if fascinated by the speaker's look, "not at all."

"Excuse the liberty; I thought you did; but as I was mistaken, let us drink to our better acquaintance, *sotte animale* he who swills alone," and taking up glass and bottle, he came and seated himself opposite to the stranger.

"You honour me vastly," muttered the other, who looked as if he only wanted courage to refuse; he was, in fact, though not a man easily daunted, in a state of the most intense agony of mind.

"But now I know *you*," whispered the wry neck, bending across the table, and looking full in his companion's face, upon which he lavished a most malicious wink—the other's alarm having acted on him as a cordial; "I ought to."

"Really!" faltered the little man, whose face was livid; his eyes rolled uneasily in their sockets, as if about to burst their bounds, and he trembled violently.

"You look uncomfortable," continued the man with the wry neck, still speaking confidentially; "have you the cholic?"

"No, no!" replied the other, "I am perfectly at my ease," the big drops of perspiration coursing at the same time down his cheeks.

"Well, I should think it strange if you were not. You are no chicken, but are as brave as a dragon. True, ain't it?"

"Ye—e—e—s," said the unfortunate, with a ghastly grin, his throat swelling as with a choking sensation.

"You have done too many deeds of note to be suspected," repeated his merciless tormentor.

"Deeds of note," repeated the other mechanically.

"Ah! there was the affair Latour," continued the wry neck.

"Ye—es," replied the man, peering cautiously round, as if in search of something with which to defend himself against the questioner.

"Ah! ah! you are modest, you won't unbosom your-self, but secresy is of no use. I knew you, Maître Duchesne," said the other, half maliciously, half in disgust.

"Hush, by all the saints; but who are you?" replied Duchesne, looking, despite himself, at the other's feet.

"Oh! I am Jean Torticolis," continued the other, pointing to his wry neck by a jerk of his thumb.

"Is that your only name?" inquired Duchesne curiously, but somewhat reassured.

"I have no other," replied Torticolis, somewhat sadly; "no name, no existence."

"Ah!" exclaimed Duchesne, again becoming uneasy, "and why?"

"Because I have a wry neck, and I am called Torticolis," answered the other moodily, his whole frame not only sombre, but terror-struck.

"But you have always been thus deform—, thus twisted?" continued Duchesne.

"Not always," said Jean, glaring almost savagely at the other.

"Since when then?" faltered Duchesne.

"Since the 1st day of March, 1784," replied Jean, striking his fist upon the table.

Duchesne turned pale again, moved his chair a little from his companion, and, strong man though he was, appeared ready to faint.

"You are then?—" he again faltered.

"I was—Paul Ledru," replied Torticolis, fixing his eyes hard upon the other, "but he is dead, the law has said it; and I am now as I just told you, Jean Torticolis—Maître Duchesne."

"*Mordieu!*" cried Duchesne, drinking off a draught of wine, and drawing at the same time a long breath, "this is too much. None of your *coq à l'anès* for me. You Paul Ledru! Why, I saw him dead—ah! dead, as my great-grandfather, if I ever had any."

"So you thought," said the other, half savagely, his face awfully distorted as he recollected the horrors of that day, "so you thought, *Monsieur le Bourreau de Paris.* But it was, I said, the 1st of March, 1784, and the execution of the assassins of the Count le Bague gave you work. When it came to my turn you were drunk. You hanged me, but you did it badly. Science, not from humanity, but love of experiment, restored me, and the name of Torticolis is all that remains to remind me of your good intentions."

"Bah," said Duchesne, with a grin, for he was now quite recovered; "this is too bad, to have one's subjects meet one in this way five years after death. Faugh! you smell of La Greve."

"You don't approve of it," grinned Jean, "but I do; there we differ."

"We do professionally," said Maître Duchesne; "but come now, shake hands and bear no malice; and as you are the first of my *pratiques* whom I meet *after*, just tell me what it is like; novel sensation, eh?"

"Brigand," exclaimed Jean, furiously, "don't speak of it, breathe not the question—it kills me."

"If Monsieur be delicate on the point, I will not press him," said the *Bourreau*, deprecatingly.

"You had better not, if you wish peace," continued the other, wildly.

"Agreed," said Maître Duchesne. "So the Doctor—I sold you to him for twenty livres—took the liberty to bring you back. So much the better. I did my duty, he did his."

"You were both very attentive, I must confess," said Jean, grimly; "but let us drop the subject. On what duty are you now bound?" he continued, as if the other matter was not pleasing to him.

"Duty, Mordieu!" cried the other, savagely, "none. It's all up with me; no more business. The *Etats Generaux* are convoked."

"Ah! but I am not strong on politics," said Jean. "Excuse me, therefore, if I inquire how this will affect you?"

"I am told, one of the first intentions of this meeting is to abolish death."

"Altogether?" inquired Torticolis, with a *naïveté*, which was, however, but assumed, to conceal his natural cunning.

"No, *farceur*, but by hanging," replied Duchesne, with a sigh.

"I wish they had passed it six years ago," said Jean, moodily.

"Do you? You are very hard," exclaimed the *Bourreau*, with a sneer.

"Yes; I should then have a straight neck, and not be called Torticolis, because my wife was handsome and a noble saw it."

"By the way, what is become of Madame Ledru?" said the other, affectionately.

"She is dead," replied the wry neck.

"And the young Count?"

"Lives; but there is time for revenge. My wounded honour, my legal death, because I chastised a scoundrel, and her decease, all call on me. Trust me, I bide my time. But whither are you bound?"

"For my village; I have saved a few hundred livres, and now for Picardy, where I hope to spend my old age in peace."

"You are wrong," said the young man, who had just commenced his *omelette*.

"Why Monsieur?" inquired Duchesne, turning round sharply.

"Because there will be more work for you than ever, though not of the same kind," replied the youth, a strange and wild fire shining in his speaking eyes.

"More work than ever?" cried Duchesne, incredulously.

"Man," said the other, with considerable excitement of manner, "we are on the threshold of wondrous days; great things are about to happen; all men should be ready, for all men are interested. Who knows," he murmured to himself, "my republic may turn out other than a dream."

"You said," observed Duchesne.

"Return to Paris—it is the place for men," replied the young man; and then, as if recollecting the horrible vocation of him he spoke to, a burning blush overspread his cheeks, and he resumed the consumption of his half-forgotten meal.

"You are going to Paris," said Jean Torticolis, meekly, his little grey eyes fixed piercingly on the youth.

"I am," coldly said the other.

"You are a deputy to the States-General, perhaps," continued the man with the wry neck.

"Perhaps," replied the other with a smile.

"At all events," insisted the other, "as you say great things are to happen, you may, perhaps, advise us when the time comes."

"If it be in my power," said the young man, quietly.

"Where shall we find Monsieur?"

"Oh! if you want me, on asking at *Rue Grenelle St. Honoré, No.* 20, *au Troisième,* for Charles Clement, you will find me."

"Good, I thank you, Monsieur," said Jean, drawing forth a greasy pocket-book, and with difficulty making note of the address and name.

"I shall face about," cried Duchesne, awaking from a reverie, and then addressing Jean in a whisper, " The youth has set me thinking.  Who knows what may happen? *Tonnerre,* but Paris is, after all, the place for a man to get an honest living."

"Did I know where to perch," said Jean, in reply, " I might join you."

"Until you settle," replied Duchesne, with a grin, " I will give you a berth, and not the first neither."

"Bah! no more of that; where do you quarter?"

"If my room be not let, I have a sky parlour ; it is rather high, on the sixth storey, but there is a good view of the tiles."

"What part?"

"Rue Grenelle."

"St. Honoré?"

"Yes."

"What number?"

"No. 20."

"Bah!"

"Why?"

"Why, that's where *he* lives," pointing with his thumb to the young man.

"You don't mean it?"

"Didn't you hear him say so just now?" continued Jean Torticolis.

"No, but this is lucky, we shall know where to find him, *en cas.*"

" Exactly; but I should like to know what he means by great events," mused Torticolis.

" Why, wine at two sous a bottle, bread at one sou a pound, meat the same, what else could he mean?" said Duchesne.

" Thunder, that would be great," continued Jean, " one might live without working."

" Not exactly," said Duchesne, who, for the first time in his life, perhaps, began to think; " but one might work a little less like animals."

" You might punish the insolence of a few nobles," whispered Jean, as if half afraid of the enormity of his proposition, " that would suit me."

" Impossible!" said Duchesne, alarmed, " they are too powerful."

" They are very few," mused Torticolis.

" My God," exclaimed Duchesne, " that never struck me before."

" And we are many," continued the wry neck, caressing his chin.

" Who, we ?"

" THE PEOPLE."

---

## CHAPTER II.

### THE STORM.

AN hour passed, during which time Charles Clement luxuriated in the study of a well-thumbed pamphlet—one of those leaves which, scattered as by the wind, and pregnant with seed, sowed everywhere the germs of the terrible future—his eye kindling as he read, and his whole mien revealing the emotion which agitated him; for he was an enthusiastic and ardent republican, dreaming of a state of things where the happiness of the people would be the first and only consideration of government, and dreaming, too, that democracy was to come forth in all its strength, quietly, calmly, and amid the joyous but peaceful acclamations of grateful millions.

Charles Clement, while wrapped in his ardent visions—

such as are ever those of talent and virtue—forgot the fierce passions, the brutal ignorance, the unbridled thoughts, the canker-worm of corruption, the rotten fabric of the State, the seeds of poverty, misery, and death, all plentifully sown by ages of debauchery, profligacy, and misgovernment, on the part of the kings and aristocracy of France; but concealed beneath the surface, hid by the spangled splendour of courtiers and court, veiled by the silks and satins of haughty dames, smothered beneath orient pearls, jewels, and gold; its cries stifled amid the resounding of great names, the glare of rank, and the laugh, the song, and the festival—but still smouldering—in places bursting forth and preparing to flood all bounds, to visit with awful retribution the authors of so much evil—was coming that terrible thing called public opinion.

But republicanism in France was but the splendid dream of a few noble, though erring spirits, who mistook hatred of oppression, impatience of suffering for love of liberty, and enthusiastic reception of it for fitness to enjoy it. They forgot that the despotic monarchy had not only impoverished, but corrupted the people, who were brutal, superstitious, ignorant, impulsive, incapable of reasoning, and that they must infallibly become anarchical, disbelieving, and not knowing what liberty really was, degenerate into license. A people passes not from slavery to freedom at a stroke without losing all self-control. A republic, being the perfection of human government, requires for its maintenance—and then magnificent, indeed, would be its career— that the monarchy upon whose ruins it is erected should have given the people a foretaste of freedom—that they should have exercised, without knowing it, most of the functions of democracy—that trusting in a religion which is cherished because heart and head go hand in hand with faith, they should not blindly follow mere ceremonies and symbols they do not understand—that they be educated sufficiently to understand the full difference between liberty and license—that they knew enough to distinguish between patriots and spouting quacks. The republic must come, too, gradually, but as the culminating stroke of a long line of reforms; in a word, they must have dwelt long beneath a constitutional government, not a despotism — be Protestants, not Catholics—an industrial, thinking people, not a passionate and military nation—have lived in the nineteenth, not the eighteenth century — and instead of Frenchmen be ———. History will conclude my sentence.

Meanwhile Duchesne and Torticolis, between whom a strange link had created a kind of fraternity, had spent their time in discussing over their bottle and glass the hopes which the few words of the ardent youth had awakened in their bosoms.

"*Peste*," said Duchesne, continuing his remarks, "if he were right, and the people were about to become something."

"It is time," replied Torticolis, gravely, for this his first political discussion seemed to weigh upon his mind.

"I rather think it is.  The nobles have skinned us long enough.  Their turn now.  I wonder if their hides are really so much softer," said the *Bourreau*-ready-made disciple of the reign of terror.

"*Fichtre,* you go quick," said the other, more cautiously. "our masters won't give way without a struggle."

" You are right," observed Duchesne, "therefore, 'quiet' is the word, and let us wait what turns up.  Be sure somebody will be *sappeurs*."

"Agreed, comrade, and now enough of history, it's dry talk," said Torticolis, pledging the other in a bumper.

"Enough—for the present."

And, unknown to himself, Charles Clement had secured for  the revolution two blind and devoted adherents, but such as served to ruin the hopes of its wisest advocates.

"But allow me to observe, M. Duchesne, that the weather is somewhat dark; I expect we shall have a storm."

"Two and two make four," said the *Bourreau*, "and thick clouds bring rain.  Madame Martin, we shall sleep here to-night."

"Very good," said the dame, complacently, "there is a double-bed ed room at your service."

"And for me?" inquired Charles Clement, raising his head from the pamphlet over which he had been musing.

"I have had a fire lit in No. 1," replied Madame Martin, with a smile and a curtsey.

"See what it is to be young and have good looks," whispered Duchesne, with a meaning wink; "I shouldn't wonder if she sent him away without asking for his bill."

"*Sapristi*," replied Torticolis, laughing, "it is the way of the world."

Meanwhile the weather had in reality set in with violence. The growling of thunder was heard in the distance, gradually becoming more distinct, while the wind shook the not very firm timbers of the *Dernier Sou*, making the travellers draw with additional pleasure round the fire, which Madame Martin had recently refreshed by the addition of several huge logs. Gradually, as the day quite faded, and no light illumined the room save the fitful flame of the fire, Clement closed his book, and, being in a dreamy humour, kept his eye fixed upon the blaze, while his ears drank in, with singular satisfaction, the sound of the storm without.

"It rolls on apace," he muttered, as the heavy booming of the thunder was heard overhead; "and, like it, will roll the anger of the people; much noise, much tumult, to leave the air all the more fresh and pleasant."

But Clement forgot, in applying his comparison, the devastating fire, which, previous to the termination of the storm, often does terrible deeds.

"It strikes me," said Torticolis, suddenly rising, "that I hear voices without."

"The wind," replied Duchesne, who was quietly loading a pipe, his *ultima thule* of happiness.

"Did you ever hear the wind say '*Sacré ?*'" continued Torticolis, somewhat contemptuously.

"Not exactly," answered Duchesne, raising a burning stick, and applying it methodically to the bowl of his pipe.

"Then don't contradict me," observed Torticolis; " and allow me to observe, without denial, that a voice just now said ' *Sacré !* '"

At the same time, the loud clashing of a postilion's whip, the rumbling of wheels, and the sound of horses' feet, were heard above the roar of the storm, which now came down in pitiless showers of rain.

" Travellers," said Madame Martin, advancing with alacrity to meet them.

Reaching the door, and throwing it wide open, the worthy landlady of the *Dernier Sou* peered forth into the darkness.

"Holy mother! a *chaise de poste!* Pierre! Pierre!" she cried in a loud and shrill tone.

"Hola! he!" replied a rough voice from the stable.

"Come round and attend to the carriage."

A vehicle, and one, too, of no small pretensions, to judge from its unwieldy though handsome form, with four horses and numerous outriders, had, in fact, halted before the little inn, while several men servants, descending from their horses, hastened, some to open the door of the carriage, while others advanced to the entrance of the auberge.

"Woman," said one of these, insolently apostrophising the worthy Madame Martin, "my master, to avoid the storm, has decided to honour your *cabaret* with his presence. Make way for the Duke de Ravilliere."

The various parties occupying the interior of the inn started, while each experienced sensations peculiar to their individual characters.

Madame Martin, true to the money-bag, like all faithful innkeepers—no longer the accomplices but the principals in acts of extortion—without noticing the too common impertinence of the servant, was overwhelmed with delight at the honour which fell upon her house, though a pang went to her heart as she remembered that her only decent room was engaged by the handsome young stranger.

The two men, Torticolis and Duchesne, were equally solicitous about their apartment, which they had little doubt would be summarily taken possession of by the lacqueys.

Charles Clement smiled. He, the republican aspirant, had possession of No. 1, and the Duke de Ravilliere was no doubt about to dispute it with him. Another sentiment evidently actuated him, as a blush passed rapidly across his intelligent face.

Meanwhile Madame Martin and Pierre busied themselves in hunting up and lighting several lamps, which, with the blaze of the fire, made the old room look more cheerful and sunny. Charles retreated into a dull corner of the apartment, to be as far apart from the new company as possible, and was nearly concealed by the curtains of the good landlady's bed, while Duchesne and Torticolis, their valiant resolutions and resolves made against the whole race of nobles vanishing for the nonce, like morning dew, rose, respectfully awaiting the entrance of the aristocrats.

Preceded by servants holding hastily-lit torches, and having on each side a young lady, the Duke walked with stately step, neither casting look to the right nor the left, and proceeded to dry his damp and spotted clothes by the now sparkling fire, in which he was imitated by his fair companions.

Tall, slim, and even gaunt, the Duke somewhat resembled, in his plumed hat, his powdered wig, his short mantle, and long braided waistcoast, with loose green coat, a diamond-hilted sword, and other courtly appendages, a skeleton dressed up in mockery of death, so thin were his cheeks, so shrivelled, dry, and yellow was his skin.

Presenting a marked contrast, not only with the aged nobleman, but one with the other, the two ladies formed a bright relief to the aspect, stern, proud, and cadaverous, of the courtier.

The one slight, delicate, and frail, the other of equal height, but fuller and more womanly proportions, without being a month older; the one pale, with a complexion of dazzling fairness, the other with a rich tint of summer skies on her scarcely less white complexion; the one with light graceful hair, worn powdered, in the fashion of the day, the other with a mass of heavy dark ringlets, falling as nature gave them on her shoulders; the one with liquid blue eyes, soft, tender, and fawn-like, the other with dark and speaking orbs, that spoke of passion, energy, and fire; the one with a delicate but somewhat low forehead, the other with a lofty, almost massive brow, all intellect; the one with a mouth made but to speak sweet things and give soft kisses, the other with beautifully-shaped lips, but ones on which sat determination and power; the waist of the former was thin, that of the latter disdained all artificial restraint, and exhibited the natural graces of form which woman generally does her best to mar.

Charles Clement had caught all these shades of difference at a glance, though his eyes, after the first impulse, rested, by virtue of the spirit of antagonism inherent in our nature, on the fair girl who so little resembled himself, it could be seen at once, either in appearance or character.  His attention was, however, only given to their native graces, omitting all search for the details of their costume, which he noticed not—in which particular, therefore, we shall follow his example.

" Germain," said the Duke, addressing his principal servant, after a brief pause, " can one dine here ?"

" No, monseigneur," replied the lacquey, positively, without waiting for the landlady's remarks.

" Monsieur le Duc, I beg pardon," exclaimed the irate cabaretiere.

" Germain, tell this good woman to speak when she is spoken to.  We cannot dine, I suppose—then we must fast."

" Faith, I hope not," said the dark-eyed beauty, laughing, " for the air and motion has given me an appetite."

" Countess," replied the Duke gallantly, " were you a man, I should remark that your observation was vulgar."

" But, as I am a woman," gaily continued the Countess, " it is truth."

" Monsieur," said the valet, respectfully, " forgets that the lunch is yet untouched."

The Duke recollected it perfectly well, but did not choose to know anything of which his servants could more properly remind him.  In those days inns were so ill-served that noble and wealthy travellers were constantly in the habit of taking all necessary articles with them.

" Then serve the lunch," replied the nobleman, solemnly.

" In the mean time, if Martin has a chamber, we will adjust our wet garments," observed the Countess, with a sweet smile.

" Madame," exclaimed the woman, in much confusion, and with a profound reverence, " I have but one room, and that——"

" Is perfectly at the service of these ladies, to whom I with pleasure cede my claim," said Charles, rising, and standing uncovered before the two ladies.

" We are much obliged," answered the Countess, surveying with some little surprise, and even confusion, the handsome youth who thus suddenly stood before them.

" For what?" exclaimed the Duke haughtily.

" For Monsieur's courtesy," said the Countess, turning, with steady mien, towards the nobleman.

" The courtesy of a *roturier*," sneered the Duke, with that characteristic disregard for the people's feelings which paved the way for so much bitter revenge.

" Monsieur," exclaimed Charles coldly, " you forget the times are changed, and that a bourgois is no longer a slave."

" This to me!" cried the Duke, reddening, while the painful conviction forced itself upon him that the words breathed truth.

" Yes, to you, Monsieur le Duc de Ravilliere, Marquis de Pontois," replied Charles; " I mean nothing impolite, but to remind you that we are no longer serfs."

" This comes of teaching the people; those vile pamphleteers are ruining the State," muttered the Duke; by pamphleteers the Duke meant Montesquieu, Voltaire, Helvetius, Rousseau.

Meanwhile the Countess and her fair companion, who had slightly coloured on the approach of Charles, whose manly, handsome form, and enthusiastic character, were no strangers to Adela de Ravilliere, retired, followed by their maids.

" Monsieur le Duc will perhaps allow me to observe," said Charles, modestly, " that there are others who have tended that way besides philosophers."

" Whom, pray?" replied the Duke, sarcastically, or rather with that profound impertinence which the ignorant rich sometimes assume towards the poor.

" The profligate, reckless, and ignorant men who have pretended of late to rule the State, to say nothing of the women."

" Young man," exclaimed the Peer, astounded and piqued—he remembered his own humble court to the seductive Dubarry—" this is rank treason!"

" You will hear much more," said Charles, " from the Tiers-Etat."

" Bah!" said the Duke, carelessly, " they may talk; all they will say will end in smoke. But have I not seen you before?"

" I believe my face is not strange to your family," replied Charles, bitterly. His mother had been a Ravilliere, who had married for love into a legal family, and died of a broken heart, in consequence of the persecutions of her relations.

"Ah! I thought so," exclaimed the Duke, vainly striving, however, to tax his memory.

"I am Charles Clement, son of Jacques Clement, counsellor, who married your sister," replied the young man, moodily, the memory of his dead mother's wrongs rising before him, and shedding withered thoughts upon his path.

"Hum!" said the Duke drily; "but I have not seen you since you were a child."

"You mistake, Monsieur le Duc; ten years back—I was then a lad of fifteen—I saved your daughter's life when thrown into the Somme," replied Charles, as drily.

Ah!" exclaimed the Duke, his better feelings at once prevailing; "and you never came forward to claim my thanks and gratitude."

"I knew you, Monsieur, for one of my mother's brothers, and, therefore, one of her persecutors," replied Charles Clement, coldly.

"Charles Clement," said the nobleman, taking his hand, "you wrong me. Perhaps I might have been—who knows? —had the opportunity occurred. But I was away with the army, and only heard of the matter a year after my sister's death. She was my playmate, too, in early days, and I am glad to meet her child."

"My Lord Duke," replied Charles, warmly, "this is to me an unexpected delight."

"You have the face of a Ravilliere," said the Duke, musing sadly, as he thought what he would have given for such a son; "and, were you noble by your father's side, might aspire to great things."

"Monsieur le Duc," exclaimed Charles, "you are mistaken. A time is coming when the factitious advantages of rank and birth will no longer have weight, and when merit, talent, energy, will be as ready a road to preferment."

"I believe," said the nobleman, sinking his voice, led away, he knew not why, by the charm of the other's voice, and forgetting awhile his stately pride; "I believe the state of the country to be more serious than the nobles suppose;

but the change you contemplate is an idle dream. A pretty state of things, truly, when a *gentilhomme* shall be no better than a *roturier*."

"And yet, my uncle," interposed Charles, quietly, "both are but men."

"Oh!" said the Duke, with an involuntary sneer, "you are one of the disciples of equality. But let us not discuss politics lest we quarrel. You are going to Paris?"

"I am," replied Charles.

"With what object?"

"To watch events. I have a small income derived from my late father, and hope that circumstances may arise favourable to the pursuit of my profession."

"You will find a friend in your uncle," said the Duke, sadly; "I have but one child left, with whom my name ends. Except yourself I have not a relative, save one distant one; and in these days a young head may be useful. Whenever you are at leisure you are welcome at the Hotel Ravilliere."

"Thank you, my uncle," exclaimed Charles, blushing crimson, while his heart's blood came and went with rapidity; "I shall avail myself of the privilege."

Meanwhile the busy valets, using the apartment as if it had been their master's property, had spread, on a white and snowy table-cloth, with plates of porcelain, silver forks, and other articles of luxury, a cold collation, which made the eyes of the two men glisten, and excited many admiring and envious whispers.

"I do not think that we have such very great reason to complain, Duke," said the Countess, returning, accompanied by Adela; "indeed, to have escaped the pelting storm is alone a luxury."

"Put another *couvert*, Germain," cried the Duke, resuming his stately tone.

The ladies exchanged glances, and then looked with no little surprise on the aged nobleman.

"Adela," he continued, "you have, doubtless, not forgotten your fall from your pony into the Somme?"

"Oh no!" said she, her cheeks crimsoning and her lovely eyes slightly moistened; "nor my brave cousin who rescued me."

"Humph!" remarked de Ravilliere, drily, but not angrily; "so you recognise him."

"Monsieur Clement and I have met once since," said Adela, recovering herself, "about ten days ago in the forest."

"Oh!" continued the Duke; "but allow me, at all events, to introduce to you," addressing the Countess, "my nephew, Charles Clement."

"Here, too," exclaimed the Countess, laughing, "you are too late—I was with Adela on the occasion referred to."

"Oh!" again said the old man; "but, nephew, know my noble and lovely ward, the Countess Miranda de Casal Monté."

Charles bowed, and, on the invitation of the Duke, seated himself on one side of the table, with his uncle opposite, while the ladies sat to his right and left. The meal commenced. The conversation was serious, but not sad. Charles, at the request of the Duke, spoke of his early life, of his orphan state, of his arduous studies in Paris for the legal profession, of his many courageous struggles against adversity, and those difficulties which encumber—though in the end they aid—the progress of the man who has to make his way in the world by the power of industry, talent, and learning.

"M. Charles," said Miranda, after listening with attention to his eloquent but somewhat bitter relation, in which his habitual sense of wrong and injury inflicted on his class burst forth—"M. le Duc has promised you his support and countenance; you will therefore scarcely want any other; but if my less weighty influence be of any use at any time, command it."

"I would owe my success, Madame la Comtesse," continued Charles, "to my own exertions; I would know that my pen or my voice—and if these fail me my hands—have made me whatever I am to become, and not to feel that I am rich, or powerful, or great, because rich, and powerful, and great people have taken me by the hand."

"But, Charles," observed the Duke, gazing at him curiously, "to your own relations you cannot object owing something."

"When I am the enemy of the class to which they belong," replied the young man enthusiastically, "however much I can love and respect them, I can owe them nothing."

The Countess Miranda raised her dark eyes with astonishment on the youth; Adela curled her pretty lips with a slightly-scornful air; while the old Duke, who apart from his courtier education had much good sense, replied calmly. "Confound not the class with its abuses," he said; "if indeed, such exist. That some disorders have taken place I grant, because certain men have looked rather to keeping their places and making money than to being upright ministers—a common failing with men in power; but I cannot descry in what the nobles are generally to blame."

"My Lord," replied Charles, warmly, "the present generation of the aristocracy are not wholly to be condemned; to the vices and immorality of the last reign we owe much of present misery."

"And are such the feelings," inquired the Duke, "of many besides yourself?"

"My Lord Duke," exclaimed the young man, "they are the cherished sentiments of thousands of Frenchmen, who hail the States General but as the prelude to a constitution and representation of the people, as in England."

And Charles Clement, whose keen and thoughtful mind had watched the progress of events, and who had pondered deeply on the probable consequences of the popular and universal ferment; upon the effect produced by the wide diffusion of political information; who knew—he, the law student, who had lived among the people—the excitable character of the Paris mob; who was well aware that thousands of men were hoping for liberty, and would risk fortune and life to win it, sketched, with almost prophetic power, much which was to come. His picture was dim; he dealt necessarily in generalities; his ideas of change fell far short of the reality; but his warnings were accompanied by so much that was cogent in reasoning, and were attuned with so much eloquence and animation, that his auditors were variously moved.

Vague sensations of alarm made the Duke shudder, for he saw that his old age, which he had so fondly hoped would have ended in peace, was likely to be a stormy one; and more and more he clung to the support which, in this time of popular tribulation, he might look for in a young and active relation.

Adela, though much struck by the words of the young man, was much more so by his manner, and the sparkling animation depicted in his eyes, which had become deeply imprinted on her heart.

Miranda listened coldly and critically, and not a trace of emotion of any kind was visible on her handsome, nay, beautiful countenance.

The ladies, the storm not abating in the least, retired shortly after the conclusion of the dinner to the room so gallantly ceded to them by Charles Clement, in order to repose from the fatigues of the day.  The Duke, too, determined to lie down on a bed made with cushions of the carriage, and other materials which the servants produced, in the double-bedded room intended by Madame Martin for Torticolis and Duchesne, but which now was ceded to the aged nobleman and our hero.

"Charles," said the Duke, soon after the two young women had retired, "perhaps you are not aware that I owe you 120,000 livres?"

"Monsieur le Duc," replied Charles Clement, startled, "I told you I could accept nothing."

"My friend," said the Duke, smiling sadly, "you would not surely refuse to accept a mother's gift?"

"A mother's gift!" exclaimed Charles.

"Yes, my nephew, for eighteen years my sister's portion has been accumulating in my hands; the arrears amount to 120,000 livres, while the principal is a farm near Paris, of which my *home d'affaires* will hand you the title-deeds in due form, with the amount which he has in his hands of the twenty years' accumulation."

"But, my uncle," said Charles, hesitating.

"M. Charles," exclaimed the Duke, gravely, "through culpable negligence on my part, and the fact that, pardon me, I had forgotten your very existence, this money has not been previously paid you, but yours it is, and M. Grignon will show you the necessary documents to prove this."

"I am deeply grateful, Monsieur le Duke, and can refuse nothing which was my mother's."

"It is then settled; good night, nephew,"—and in a few moments more the nobleman was asleep, leaving the young man to ponder on the events of the day.

---

## CHAPTER III.

### THE MAN IN THE CLOAK.

WHEN the ladies had retired, and been shortly afterwards followed by the Duke and Charles Clement, Jean Torticolis and Duchesne, who had hitherto kept aloof, drew timidly nearer to the fire, the front of which was almost wholly occupied by the lacqueys and ladies' maids, who, having no sleeping chamber, had agreed to sit up and enjoy themselves until towards morning, when a few hours' slumber could be sought on chairs and benches.

"Mam'selle," observed one of the domestics, addressing a lively brunette who officiated as lady's-maid to the Countess Miranda, "you have never been to Versailles, I think?"

"Never," said Mam'selle, as she was generally called; "but I suppose I soon shall."

"We are all bound to the Court," said the other, pompously.

"And a good many along with us," laughed the girl, thus displaying a row of perfectly white teeth, encased in a ruddy setting.

"*Mai-foi!*" said the domestic, shaking his head. "It will be a grand sight this meeting of the *Etats-Generaux*. All the nobles in grand costume—plumes, and gold, and white, and silver—messieurs the clergy in full costume—the *Tiers-Etats* in black cloth, *chapeaux clabauds*, and short cloaks. It will be worth the journey."

"That it will," exclaimed the other domestics, with profound and solemn looks.

"But what is this *Etats-Generaux*?" inquired the brunette. "I assure you, Maître Pierre, it puzzles me."

"Ah, there I am *flambé*, puzzled too," said Maître Pierre,

looking thoroughly so; "but I rather think it is a mode of showing respect to his Majesty."

"Bah!" interrupted the *maître d'hotel*, who, mixing more with his masters, was, of course, better informed; "you are in the wrong, Pierre; but that's no wonder, since this is a most weighty subject;" and the *maître d'hotel* shook his head knowingly, pursed up his mouth, and looked as profound as was in his nature.

"But what is it then, Monsieur Germain?" persisted the brunette, somewhat maliciously.

"Oh, yes! what is it then?" said Maître Pierre, a little ruffled.

Toticolis and Duchesne nodded their heads, not venturing to put in a word.

"Why, the fact is—" said the *maître d'hotel;* "but you know, Mam'selle, our first duty in this world is to our king."

"Exactly!" put in Pierre, quite triumphantly; "that's what I said."

"But I don't see it," said Germain, angrily, glad of the opportunity of being so, as he was somewhat nonplussed at his task.

"Never mind," muttered the valet; "we are waiting for your explanation."

"Well, then, that's settled," repeated the *maître d'hotel.* "Now, our best way of showing respect to his Majesty is by paying what money is necessary for his Majesty to support his army, his navy, his palaces, his household."

"Certainly," repeated the domestics, affirmatively.

"Then, why do not the *noblesse* pay their share?" said Mam'selle Rosa, carelessly.

"Oh!" exclaimed the horror-struck domestics.

"Recollect their outlays," said the *maître d'hotel.*

"Their horses," put in the negro coachman.

"Their mansions, their hotels," interposed another.

"Their dreadfully expensive habiliments," said Adela's maid; "their prodigious charges at court; their household."

"Ah!" responded Rosa, as if convinced.

"Well, it seems," continued the *maître d'hotel*, "that, in the course of time, people, perverted by a set of men my master calls philosophers, have got into the bad habit of not paying regularly, and there is what is called a *de—de—ficit.*"

"A *disette*," exclaimed the domestics, in chorus.

"No!" responded M. Germain, contemptuously, "a *deficit.*"

"And what is a *deficit?*" asked one; "something worse than a famine?"

"Much, I believe, since I heard Count Leopold say, a *deficit* is another word for ruin. It means a want of money."

"Oh!" again chorussed the domestics, visibly touched.

"So you see his Majesty cannot, for want of money, carry on the affairs of the State. His navy is without pay."

"Terrible," said the chorus.

"And his army!" continued Germain.

"Shocking."

"And his servants!" exclaimed Germain, with oratoric emphasis.

"Dreadful!" cried the domestics, with heart-felt energy.

"And the people who are starving, what of them?" said an exasperated voice, in a loud and shrill tone. It was the voice of the poor man, of what modern cant calls in France the *proletaire*, making itself heard in an assembly of the untaxed.

Scarcely had Torticolis—for it was him—given vent to his exclamation than he shrunk terrified into his chair, awaiting the result.

"Insolence! unworthy of notice! better not be repeated!" exclaimed the servants, with the true *insouciance* of power, holding the speaker too contemptible for serious attention.

"And the *Etats-Generaux* will bring his Majesty money for all these purposes," said Mam'selle, in affected admiration.

"Why," replied Germain "that's a question I don't exactly understand; but I think it's to settle about regular payments in future."

"And will the *Etats-Generaux* ask nothing in return?" said the favourite attendant of the Countess Miranda.

"*Corbleu,*" laughed Germain; "but Monsieur le Duke says they will ask for a great deal; from what Monsieur Clement says, I believe they will want some laws."

"Ah!" said Pierre, emphatically, "I know a good many which are much wanted."

" You do ! " exclaimed Rosa, merrily ; " and what laws are they ? "

" Why, laws against Savoyards, Swiss, Italians, exercising the *état* of domestic, and thus throwing Frenchmen born out of work," said the kitchen Solon.

"Most necessary," continued Germain, approvingly.

The discussion, however, was here prematurely closed, to the great loss, we doubt not, of society in general.

" Hola there ! *milles coulets rouges !* " thundered a voice from without ; " open ! "

The tone was so imperious that Madame Martin hurried across the apartment to open the door with even more energy than she had shown on the arrival of the Duke. The servants rose, startled at the intrusion, while Jean Torticolis and Duchesne consulted in a low tone their probable chances of sleep.

" *Sapistie !* " said the stranger, entering ; "this is a night ! Rain enough to melt a cannon ball. Oh ! oh ! a fire and company. Dame, a bottle of good wine ! By your leave."

With these words the man seized a stool which had previously been occupied by one of the domestics, and seating himself on it, proceeded to dry his clothes by the fire.

" A pleasant night for the rats," laughed the soldier, drawing his wet cloak round him, so as to bring it in front of the blaze ; " better cozy by one's fireside than abroad ; eh, pretty ones ? " And the stranger chucked the pouting Rosa under the chin.

" Hands off ! " cried the *soubrette*, with a laugh ; " faugh ! thy cloak sends forth no pleasant odour. Why not hang it up to dry ? "

" Ay, I will hang it up for thee," said Fournier, the black coachman, who had been curiously examining the stranger's countenance.

" Thanks, but 'twill stiffen off me," exclaimed the soldier, carelessly ; " and I have come to rest, not to stay ; I am bound on the king's service, and when my horse has eaten and I have warmed my jacket, I shall ride again."

" Thou hast ridden far ? " inquired Rosa.

" Far or near, it matters not," said the soldier, quaffing a huge draught.

" What ails you ? " whispered Duchesne to his companion Torticolis, who was pale as death, and sat trembling like a leaf.

" Nothing — but that voice ! " replied the crick-neck, with a shudder. " Come away ; let us go to sleep."

Duchesne, much puzzled, rose in company with his friend, and, after a few words with Dame Martin, they retired to a loft, overlooking the stable and the *remise* which contained the Duke's carriage.

" Plenty of clean straw," said Torticolis ; " too good for us ; as Foulon says, we shall live to eat hay."

" Plenty," repeated Duchesne, abstractedly ; " but what ails thee ? has the soldier given you a fright ? "

" Oh no ! " replied Torticolis, " only he reminded me of the past, when such gallants guarded me to the Grève."

" Not an over pleasant recollection, truly," said Duchesne, with a grin.

" Are you sleepy ? " inquired Torticolis, drily.

" Very," replied the *Bourreau*, with a yawn, and falling lazily on a heap of fresh straw.

" So am I," said Torticolis ; " wilt thou drink a *goûte* ere you snore ? " and the crick-neck produced his case bottle of brandy.

" Readily," replied the *Bourreau*, taking the flask ; " that's the stuff, it's devilish strong. Eh ? good night, Torty ; don't mind that *gens*—of a soldier—ah ! "

And, after a few more growling words, the *Bourreau*, who had almost emptied the flask, was fast asleep.

" Good," muttered Jean, putting the brandy away without tasting it.

With this one word he darkened the lanthern which had been given them, and having lit his pipe, put his head out of the window, with the air of a man who is about to watch.

The window at which Torticolis sat overlooked the yard. Facing him was a small door, which led into the principal room of the auberge, and through the cracks of which came occasionally the smothered sound of mirth and jollity. The servants, excited by the trooper, were evidently enjoying themselves, and giving way to as much merriment as was consistent with a due regard to the slumbers of their master.

Beneath was the stable. A trap-door, half over that and half over the coach-house, was close to Jean's feet, and he once moved towards this aperture, and made sure that there was a ladder to descend by.

In the corner of the yard is a snug shed, with a room over it occupied by the ostler, and beneath this was the trooper's charger, as well as three horses belonging to the servants, the stable itself being quite full.

The night, which was far advanced—it was past one—was dark and lowering. The clouds in ragged and black masses, hurried headlong by, charged with the storm and the blast. The low whisper of a summer's night was replaced by the blustering fury of the tempest.

Torticolis, however, paid no attention to the warfare of heaven. A tempest of hate, revenge, and mingled hope, was raging in his bosom, which blinded him to all else. This man, poor, unknown, humble, had endured unheard-of sufferings. Once happy with a young and cherished wife, who loved him as he loved her, his happiness had been destroyed by the illicit passion of a noble. Persecuted and followed unceasingly, the young wife had complained to her husband, then a tradesman, well to do in the world; and he, forgetting all prudence, had personally chastised the insolent aristocrat, who sought to rob him of his greatest treasure. But the law was strict. A noble was inviolate, and Paul Ledru was condemned to death. What became of the refractory wife was not known; the husband's fate has already been explained.

Inconceivable as it was, Jean Torticolis—thus in cynical remembrance of his escape, had he christened himself—had fancied that, in the ragamuffin of a soldier, he had recognised the voice, the tone, the face of him whom he hated with a hate which is impossible to be characterised, but which may be in part conceived in one who had, by an act of foul injustice, been robbed of life, of fortune, of her he loved, of legal existence, and even a name. But Jean hated not only the man, but his class, the system, the thing called aristocracy, which gave such monstrous rights to men over their fellow-men, to creatures of God over creatures of God.

Torticolis scarcely knew what was about to happen, save that the thirst for revenge was hot within him, and that the

words of Charles Clement had filled his mind with hope.
The soldier was armed, while he had nothing but an old
knife ; but in the hands of the man dead before the law,
whose wife had vanished from the earth, this weapon was
mighty.

And the night went on apace. It wanted but an hour
of morning ; and, had the weather been less tempestuous,
he would have discovered the first grey streak of dawn.
Jean listened attentively—the tumult within had some time
ceased—and yet the soldier had not appeared to pursue his
journey on the king's service. It was time to act—all in the
public-room probably slept. His first desire was to make sure
of his man. Taking his knife between his teeth, Torticolis,
without the aid of his lantern, descended the ladder into
the coach-house, groped about with both his hands, and
found the door. It was on the latch. He opened it and
stood in the yard. Before him was the side door of the
cabaret, to his left a high wall covered with grape vines,
and leaning against there a number of poles and a small
ladder.

Jean listened, scarcely drawing breath.

A slight noise fell upon his ear. It was the unbarring,
in the most stealthy manner, of the small door already referred to.

"He is going," muttered Jean, falling at the same time
behind the shadow of the poles, between which and the
wall his small and frail body was easily concealed.

At the same moment the door opened, and two men
came out, who noiselessly reclosed the issue behind them.

Jean Torticolis allowed a heavy sigh of rage to escape
his bosom, for the soldier was not alone. To kill was not
his only object. He had a secret to wring from his heart,
for which purpose it was necessary to take his enemy at a
disadvantage.

To be quite sure, the crick-neck peered forth into the
air, and looked carefully towards the pair.

It was the trooper and Fournier, the American coachman.

There are moments in a man's existence when, enlight-
ened by love, or hate, or both, his intelligence, usually
slugged and lazy—and it is oftener so than naturally dull

—acts with a degree of rapidity that seems to him at the moment almost prophetic.  The mind, sharpened by the passions, dives deep and brings up truth—not always, but often.  It was so with Torticolis.  The association of these two men was a shaft of light which pierced the dull husk and went to his very soul, infusing a terrible and savage joy.  He saw crime in their union, and for crime there was punishment.

Might not he live to see him receive that ignominious death which had so nearly been his lot ?  Such was the thought of this man, ignorant, debased, degraded ; but ignorant, not from his fault—debased, degraded, from the crimes of others.

He clutched his knife, and, more happy than he had felt for years, listened.

"Who was this man who joined the Duke here ?" inquired the soldier.

"How do I know ?" replied Fournier ; "I didn't listen. It's not my business to wait at table.  Germain could tell you."

"*Nigaud !*" said the other, fiercely, "but you say he retired with the Duke ?"

"He did," continued the negro, without paying attention to the other's tone.

"*Manant, coup-jarret,*" muttered the other, "you might be a little more respectful.

"And call you by your name ?" said the other, with low cunning.

"No.  But no more words," continued the soldier, apparently recollecting his part ; "who mixes in dirty work can scarce come out clean."

"It was your own choice, Monsieur," sneered the other ; "I should never have thought of it."

There was a moment of fierce passion on the part of the trooper, during which he drew forth one of his pistols, but it was soon lowered, though he still kept it in his hand.

"You are a rough customer," he laughed ; "show the way."

The negro, or rather the half-cast, was one of those hideous creatures who appear purposely chosen to give crime a repulsive aspect.  His forehead was so low as to seem scarcely to exist; his hair, half woolly and half silky, was thinly scattered over his dark-brown pate; his nose was flat, his lips thick, with an expression of disgusting appetite about them; while his heavy chin and goggle eyes, all surmounting a short thick body, made him the very incarnation of ugliness. To this, on ordinary occasions, he added a look of inconceivable stupidity, which deceived the most adroit. Save, however, to serve his various passions, on no occasion was his intelligence active.

This man, whose presence with the soldier, under such suspicious circumstances, had served to illumine the senses of Jean, led the way towards the coach-house. In his hand was a lanthorn which was very nearly betraying the presence of Torticolis, and would have done so to any less abstracted in their designs. The crick-neck trembled like a leaf, for he knew his man, and he, discovered there, would have served, he knew too well, to screen the true author of the crime, whatever it was, which was about to be perpetrated. He held his very breath, and by a super-human effort repressed the shaking of his limbs. He had once already, innocent, stood upon man's scaffold.

"Is there as much as we expected," said the trooper, as they entered.

"More than we shall be able to carry," replied the American, with a grin.

Torticolis' heart beat for joy. These men were in his power. For the negro he cared not, except as a means of denouncing the other, and having him condemned.

"Not a *livre* shall be spared, if our horses die," growled the other, who all along, from the habit of the evening, studied to disguise his voice.

"As you please," said Fournier, "but here it is."

Torticolis leaned forward, and saw the negro in the act of forcing, with a picklock, the padlock which secured the seat of the carriage, in the inside of which, it appeared, the Duke had placed his valuables. The black, however, did not appear very ready at his trade of thief, and the fastening remained good.

"Give me the *crochet*," muttered the other, impatiently, "you are but a bungler."

The negro yielded his instrument readily, which the

other seized, laying his pistol ou the step of the carriage, to have his hand free.  In another minute the top of the seat was open.

"*Peste!*" cried the trooper, joyously; "but here is a heavy load.  You were right, Fournier, we shall scarcely be able to carry it.  *Diantre*, there must be two hundred thousand livres in silver, and a jewel-box too.  It is fastened; but no matter, we shall have time enough, anon."

"We must lose no time then now," said the negro, his eyes glistening.

"Right," replied the soldier, whose back was half turned to the black; "go, draw out the horses, they are ready saddled."

The negro paused.  The lanthorn was full upon his face, and Jean Torticolis made ready to spring upon him, for he saw a horrid grin pass over the American's face, as he calculated how well the whole would suit him.  Jean feared his prey might perish too easily.  He did not wish him now to die so soon.  But the thought of the black was but momentary, and he moved away to the shed which covered the horses.

"These are the jewels of the Countess Miranda," laughed the trooper; "well, she must go to Court without, unless we sell them to her again, which is to be thought of."

"The horses are ready," muttered the black from the yard.

"I come;" and taking up several canvas bags of silver, the trooper passed within a foot of his mortal enemy.

"Here are the valises," said the negro.

"Bring them inside," replied the soldier; "the horses are trained and will not move."

The black did as he was directed.

"This is mine," said the man in the cloak, pointing to the large portmanteau; "you recollect our agreement—one-third for your part, which, with the passport I give you for England, will secure your fortune."

"I recollect our agreement," answered the black, with a slight tone of savage irony.

"Ruffian!" exclaimed the other fiercely; "you risk your carcase for what will make you for life; I risk life, rank, position, a brilliant fortune, for what will scarce carry me over my wedding."

" With La Grêve," muttered Torticolis within himself.

" I quarrel not with my part," said the negro.

The next of their task was performed in silence. The valises were crammed full. The jewel-case of the Countess Miranda the soldier placed in his pocket, along with a small and well-secured box, the contents of which he was ignorant of. This done, they left the stable to put on the horses' backs their heavy load. This was rapidly accomplished, and then, having well secured them, they mounted.

On the step of the carriage lay the soldier's pistol, which, in the hurry of his crime, he had forgotten.

It was now dawn. The criminals, shunning the light, hastened to unbar the door which opened into the road. Profiting by this moment of inattention on their part, Jean Torticolis glided into the coach-house, seized the neglected pistol, pressed it convulsively to his breast, where he concealed it, and then, with noiseless footsteps, mounted the ladder. Gaining the loft, the crick-neck rushed to the window, and leaning out, saw them about to depart.

" *Bon voyage !*" he laughed, hideously. " I hope your load is light?"

" Malediction !" cried the soldier, seizing his remaining pistol, and discharging it furiously at the crick-neck ; "away Fournier."

And giving spur to their horses, the robbers dashed away in the direction of Paris.

" Thieves ; murder !" roared Jean Torticolis, whom the ball had touched on the left shoulder. " Quick ! thieves ! murder !"

" Hang them !" said the *Bourreau*, sitting bolt upright.

" *Au feu !*" shrieked Dame Martin, who had been awoke by the pistol shot.

Jean, quick as thought, glided the pistol into his bundle, and then, without taking note of his wound, continued to bawl, " *Au voleur ! au meurtre !*"

In an instant the yard was filled with servants, while the ostler and Dame Martin hurried to examine the shed.

" Where ?" cried Germain.

"Gone," bawled Dame Martin, "without paying his score."

"The carriage burst open!" exclaimed the head valet, horror-struck.

"The soldier gone!" continued Dame Martin.

"And Fournier!" thundered Germain.

"Which way?" asked one of the servants of Jean, he having, his clothes all covered with blood, descended to join the domestics.

"What is the matter?" said the voice of the Duke, who, a sword in hand, and followed by Charles Clement, now entered the yard.

The worthy old nobleman, in a dressing-gown and night-cap, having taken not even time to don his velvet *culotte*, would, under any other circumstances, and in the presence of any but his household, have excited much merriment; but, as it was, a dead silence followed, all the domestics making way for Jean.

"But you are bleeding," said Charles, anxiously.

"It is nothing, *Monsieur*," replied Jean Torticolis, thankfully.

"But what is the matter?" inquired the Duke, petulantly.

Jean, who, for his own private reasons, chose to conceal that he knew all, quietly replied, that, awoke by a noise in the yard, he saw two men, the *reitre* and the coachman, on horseback, about to leave the inn. Judging from the hour, their suspicious manner, and the heavy portmanteaus they carried, that all was not right, he challenged them, when the soldier fired his pistol and rode off.

"Examine the carriage," said the Duke, who was pale, but whose face was rigid.

"The carriage seat is burst open," replied Germain, in a trembling voice.

"Have they then taken everything?" inquired the nobleman, in a faltering tone.

"Everything, Monsieur le Duc," said Germain, desperately.

Charles Clement, meanwhile, was obtaining from Torticolis some account of the appearance of the thieves. As for Duchesne, he had no idea upon the point save that they ought to be hanged.

"What *is* the matter?" suddenly exclaimed the musical

voice of the Countess Miranda, who, followed by Adela, now appeared on the threshold of the public room.

"That my negligence, in not taking our valuables into my room, has dishonoured me," replied the Duke, in a tone of deep grief. "I had charge of your jewels, and the deeds of your Italian estates, and they have all been stolen."

"You must buy me others; jewels are not rare in Paris, nor am I penniless; as for my papers, you must win them back through Ducrosne," said the Countess, laughing merrily. She was young, and could not grieve the old man by showing the slightest regret. "Come, come, no shakes of the head, my lord; but have you lost nothing yourself?"

"A trifle," answered the Duke, without flinching, "a month's revenue. Fasten up the doors, and prepare breakfast, it is useless retiring to rest again."

"But I will mount and chase them," exclaimed Charles Clement, who stood resolutely out of sight, his costume being far from complete; "give me two of your servants."

"It is useless, nephew," said the Duke; "the rogues have a fair start. That scamp of a Fournier, he looked like a cut-throat. By the way, dress that man's wound, Pierre, and give him a couple of ecus, if, indeed, the vagabonds have left us any."

"But who knows they are not accomplices," muttered Pierre, the barber-valet, pointing to Jean and Duchesne.

"Search us!" replied Torticolis, coldly, while his whole frame quivered.

"Do nothing of the kind," exclaimed Charles Clement, indignantly; "I answer for these men."

Jean gave him a look of humble gratitude. He still alone possessed the secret of the pistol. The servant drew back with an ill-suppressed growl.

"Go, finish dressing, ladies," cried the Duke to his daughter and the Countess; more, however, to get a clear passage for himself and Charles Clement, than because the young beauties required their maids.

"We go; come Rosa," said the Countess, smothering a laugh.

"Hush, Miranda," whispered the blushing Adela; "my father will be offended."

"But they did look so richly comic," replied the merry Countess, "especially your cousin of the long robe."

"Miranda!" said Adela, reproachfully; for this was reminding her of his inferiority.

"Tush! girl, I meant no harm," answered the other, faintly blushing; "I think better of him than you perhaps imagine."

"So much the better," exclaimed Adela, still pouting, for she had not disguised her affection for him from her friend. They had no mutual secrets—none. But we have all secret thoughts, which the breath of life has never fanned, and could they be exceptions?

"What manner of man was this?" inquired the Duke of Germain, who assisted him to dress, while Pierre bound up the wound of Torticolis.

The domestic described him minutely.

"Humph! a cut-throat thief enough. As soon as breakfast is over, put in the horses; then ride ahead without waiting for us. When you reach Paris, give information to the lieutenant of the police. Tell M. Ducrosne that I will give fifty thousand livres for the Countess' jewels, and as many for her papers."

It was the best plan: In those days the police served as go-betweens for thieves and their victims. The change has not been for the better.

In a few hours after, the whole party were on their road to Paris.

Charles Clement accompanied the Duke, his daughter, and Miranda.

Jean Torticolis followed on foot. After a brief colloquy, in which, without mentioning names, he told his history, Charles Clement had engaged him as a servant. With the young republican, his chief recommendation was his having been oppressed.

---

# CHAPTER IV

## THE FIRST SCENE.

AT no great distance from the Palais-Royal, and leading

from the Rue St. Honore to the Fromagerie, is a street known by the name of the Tonnelerie.

In this locality, where, at No. 3, in 1640, was born Moliere, we must now transport ourselves. Antiquated, dirty, with windows mended by paper, and tenanted by old-clothes-men, the houses project into the middle of the street on one side, being supported by huge square wooden pillars, black, begrimed, and soiled by the air of ages. Their duration had not added to their respectability; like the *noblesse*, they were rotten at the core. The pavement, at the time of which we speak, was broken and disjointed; while the front of the shops, where piles of old rags were displayed under the specious name of second-hand clothes, exhibited all the hideous features which appertained to one of the old quarters of Paris, in those days of utter disregard in relation to the comforts of the poor, the indigent, the humble.

In this street, and in a house which lay midway between the great and little *Friperie*, in a large room, almost bare of furniture, save a truckle-bed, a table, and a few chairs, sat a man, deeply engaged in the luxurious employment of drinking a *carafe* of brandy, and of smoking as black and ill-looking a pipe as could be found, even in that unwholesome establishment. If the walls of the room were dingy and repellent, with their plaister falling inwards—if the ceiling was clouded, the floor absolutely filthy—the whole was in excellent keeping with the occupant of the chamber. Not more than forty, there was yet in his puffed red cheeks, carrotty hair, bald crown, and unwashed visage—in his keen grey eyes, thin hands, and paunchy shape—in his shabby black hat, and coarse shoes—in his unshaven chin— a sublime whole, which spoke an age of crime or misfortune, or both. Those compressed lips and dilated nostrils, with eye fixed hardly or fiercely on the ceiling, showed that he was contemplating some object of deep interest. Whatever it was, however, it did not abate the perseverance with which he sent forth clouds of tobacco smoke, in the examination of which, as they rose upwards to the sky, he might, by a casual spectator, have been supposed engaged.

Suddenly the faint tinkle of a bell was heard, once, and then a heavy tread was distinguished on the stairs.

The man continued to smoke as impassably as if he had not heard anything.

"M. Brown," said a voice through a small loophole in the door.

"Come in," still without moving.

The man entered, and stood almost meekly before the dirty personage, whom he addressed by the name of Brown. In a plain suit of grey, with clean hands, clean face, clean shoes, he looked a marked contrast to the smoker, but not less with himself a few days previously, for under the garb of a sober domestic were the little piercing eyes and the crick-neck of Torticolis.

"Take a pipe and a seat," said the other, without moving.

Tortocolis looked irresolute and half indignant.

"Paul," exclaimed M. Brown, quietly, "you did not hear me. Take a pipe and a seat."

The crick-neck started as if he had seen the gallows of the Grève before him, but he did as ordered.

"You have been warmly recommended to me," said the man, taking up a paper from the table before him, but still continuing to smoke.

"Hum," half growled the other.

"By my worthy, by our mutual friend, Duchesne," continued Brown, eyeing the other with a horrid leer, which made him shudder.

"For what purpose?" said Torticolis, almost impatiently.

"Your name is now?" added his questioner, preparing to write his reply.

"Jean Torticolis is my name," he answered briefly.

"You are in the service of—"

"Monsieur Charles Clement. But why these questions?"

"Monsieur Torticolis," replied the other, "I am the secret agent of his Majesty's police."

"Oh!" said the domestic, curiously, and with another faint shudder.

"And your friend," continued the other.

"Ah."

"You wish to recover your wife?" threw out the other (M. Brown) carelessly.

"Man or devil!" cried Torticolis, with an indescribable look, "how know you all this?"

"And to be revenged on a certain aristocrat," said M. Brown, rubbing his hands.

"You are right," replied Torti, sombrely; "show me him, and I am your slave."

"Ah! I thought we should understand one another, and I am quite willing to assist you, if you satisfy me."

"I will do my best," said Torticolis, whose face was radiant with hope, for he hated, and revenge was at hand.

"Your master has inherited a portion hitherto unjustly withheld from him by his mother's relations."

"I believe so."

"His uncle, the Duke, fascinated by his talents and manner, aims even at giving him, through the king's letters patent, the right to inherit his title."

"I have heard it whispered."

"It remains to be seen," said Brown, peering at the ceiling, "if the king can do this."

"The king can do anything," replied Jean Torticolis, who recollected that the monarch was called "La France" by his courtiers.

"Can he?" continued Brown, who was French born, though of English parents, and who spoke both languages equally well; "then, why does he not without the States-General? But that is not the question. Your master loves Adela de Ravillicre?"

"I believe so."

"And she loves him," added Brown.

"I believe so," again drily observed Jean.

"To complete the romance, there is an impediment," chuckled the spy.

"An impediment?" cried Jean, anxiously—he already loved his master.

"A serious impediment, one which cannot be got over," added Brown.

The bell tinkled again; this time sharply.

"Ah!" exclaimed the spy, jumping to his feet, and laying down his pipe.

"Shall I go?" inquired Torticolis, rising.

"By no means." cried M. Brown, "but enter here, and

remain still until I call you.   You will find a bottle of brandy, drink it."

With these words Torticolis was pushed through what seemed a cupboard, but which was in reality a door into another apartment.

For an instant the crick-neck remained perfectly lost in astonishment.   He was in a chamber, half boudoir, half bed-room, that appeared to belong rather to some Madame Dubarry than to the dirty police spy.   In an alcove was a bed elegantly and tastefully laid out, while mirrors, sofas, velvet chairs, the unheard-of luxury of a carpet, little knick-knackeries, more suited to a woman than a man, a magnificent clock of Sevre China, with curtains to deaden the light, all added to the puzzled senses of Jean.   On a chair was a complete suit of clothes, of the most irreproachable character, which appeared to be those of M. Brown.   On pegs hung a number of suits of all kinds, suited to peer or peasant, but all of one size—that of M. Brown.

On a table in the middle of the room were the remains of a supper, at which two persons had been present, but not a sign was there of the second personage.   Numerous untouched bottles were on the sideboard, and to these Jean was advancing, when he suddenly paused as if a serpent had stung him.

"Monsieur Brown! Monsieur Brown!" said a voice, which made the crick-neck's heart leap.

It was that of the trooper of the *Dernier Sou.*

"Your servant, Count," replied the spy.

"It is he ; but Count, that is surely a mistake," muttered Jean, who, the wine now quite forgotten, was listening with all his ears through the door.

"Well," continued the new arrival, throwing himself on a chair, "any news."

"Plenty," replied the other, "the Court is allowing the people to get a-head."

"I know it, and this must be stopped."

"There is only one means," said the spy, coldly, "and I doubt your using it."

"What is it?" inquired the other.

"Win over the middle classes," replied Brown.

"Willingly, but how ?" asked the soldier.

"Concede some of your privileges, join with them heartily on the meeting of the States, divide the taxes fairly, let the nobles bear their part, the clergy theirs."

"I grant you the church," said the other, "having no interest in that venerable establishment; but for the rest, impossible."

"I know it; you have held too long your place to give up willingly," said the spy, with an expression of face impossible to be rendered or understood; "you have held it too long."

"But what then?" inquired the soldier.

"You must frighten the middle classes, you must separate them from the people."

"Whom call you the people?" said the puzzled trooper.

"The labouring classes, the porters, the hawkers, the little tradespeople, the beggars, the unemployed, all who work without employing others."

"And you think this *canaille* worth troubling our heads about."

"This *canaille*," said the spy, with lowering eye, "is hungry."

"Let them eat," sneered the soldier.

"To eat, they must have wages; to have wages, they must have work; to have work, there must be trade, commerce, credit; to have trade, commerce, credit, there must be a steady government; now we have none of all this."

"You are a politician?" said the soldier.

"I am a police spy, and know everything," replied the other, with perfect self-confidence. "Now, this people have their writers, their talkers, their plotters; and if the *Etats-Generaux* don't please them, and give them work and food, they will act."

"We must fill Paris with troops."

"You must have the consent and good-will of the middle classes."

"And how, pestiferous talker, can this be gained?"

"Frighten them, and they will consent to anything."

"Well," said the trooper, "of all this anon. The Abbé Roy and the Prince de Lambesc will be here presently, incognito, to confer with us. The Court is alarmed."

"The king?" inquired Brown, raising his head

" Bah ! his Majesty sticks to his blacksmith's shop, and comes out upon state occasions."

" You mean the Austrian, then, Monsieur, and the Count D'Artois ? "

" They are the rulers."

" They are," replied the spy, drily; " the more is the pity."

" As for that, it is none of my business; and now that I have sounded you, let us talk on my affairs, ere they come."

" I am ready, Count," said Brown.

Torticolis listened, his ear against the door ; what would he not have given to have seen.

" Well, and what says Ducrosne ? " inquired the soldier.

" That you can have thirty thousand livres for the diamonds, and the same sum for the papers."

" *Sapristie !* the lieutenant is generous. Nothing less than a hundred thousand for the two will satisfy me."

" That is exactly what he gets," replied the spy, drily.

" And he thinks to pocket forty thousand. I will treat with them myself."

" There is a slight objection to it," quietly answered Brown.

" What ? " inquired the Count, haughtily.

" The Châtelet," said the spy, looking at his empty fireplace.

" You would betray me ? "

" You would be no longer useful," continued the impassible policeman.

" Then my utility alone saves me !" said the Count furiously.

" And your generosity," smiled the spy.

" Well, never mind, I will wait; a greater reward will be offered, perhaps."

" Perhaps," said Brown.

Torticolis breathed more freely—the proofs of guilt were still in his enemy's hands.

" The Abbé Roy, I think you said," observed the spy, consulting a register.

" I observed so," replied the soldier, who was devouring

his rage at not being able to chastise the insolence of the policeman.

"A notorious intriguer and rogue," continued Brown, with perfect *sang-froid.*

Again the bell tinkled, this time with greater violence even than before.

"Our company," said the trooper carelessly, and seating himself, for hitherto he had been standing.

"I am your most humble servant," exclaimed M. Brown, as two men entered, the one in the rich costume of the Colonel of the Royal-Allemands, the other in the garb of a priest.

"Well met, Count," said the Prince; "have you come to an understanding?"

"Not at all," replied the soldier, "I leave that for you."

De Lambesc bit his lip, and took a chair, in which he was imitated by the Abbé.

"But what progress have you made?" inquired the Colonel.

The soldier explained what had passed upon the point.

"But what does this *canaille* want?" said the poor Prince, really puzzled; for what could such people possibly desire?

"They want equality of rights," replied the spy.

"*Peste!* nothing more?" laughed the Colonel; "and if we don't agree to so reasonable a wish?"

"There is talk—not loudly, but in corners as yet—of a republic."

"And what is that?" inquired the dragoon, elevating his eyebrows, and using his tooth-pick—he had just dined in the Palais-Royal.

"I refer you to the Abbé, Monsieur le Prince," said the spy, with a reverence.

"An atrocious system, which Montesquieu, Voltaire, Rousseau, and that gang, have devised," replied the priest, with an expression of horror, "in which there is a government without king or aristocracy."

"The devil!" cried De Lambesc; "but in France this is absurd; a monarchy of fifteen centuries, a powerful nobility, a—a——"

"Nothing else, Monsieur le Prince," said the spy, smiling; "the tradespeople, the merchants, the middle classes, all save the *petitte noblesse* of the robe, are against you."

" So it is said at court," exclaimed the Prince, haughtily; " but we have the army, and this herd of the middle classes must see that they, too, would suffer from the reign of the mob."

" More than they do now? " ventured the spy.

" And what do they want? " said the dragoon, impatiently.

" That, paying the taxes, they may have the voting of them; for this purpose they desire an assurance of regular States-General."

" *Peste* take that word! but supposing, this wish consented to, they were to take it in their wooden heads not to vote supplies? "

" When their will was baulked, they would do so," replied the spy.

" Then this shop-keeping *canaille* would rule——"

" As they do in England."

" Cursed example! "

" Unless middle classes and people united to rule, as in America."

" This comes of Lafayette playing the Quixote," sneered the Prince.   " But will the Paris *bourgeois* unite with the mob? "

" To gain their objects, as in the time of the *fronde* of Mazarin; the *canaille* will do the work."

" And the fat citizens reap the benefit."

" Exactly; your highness is a philosopher."

" *Ventre biche!* " cried the Prince; " not at all, I hate the race.   But the middle classes must be separated."

" There is but one means, Monsieur le Prince," said the spy.

" And that? "

" As I observed to Monsieur, just now, they must be frightened; the two classes must be placed in antagonism."

" How? "

" The mob must be roused to some violent act—they must commit some depredations, some burnings; they must pillage some shops."

" But how is this to be managed? '

" Nothing easier," said the spy, with a scarcely-suppressed sneer; " the people are ignorant, and easily deceived. They are hungry—persuade them that the grocers charge too high for sugar, the bakers for bread, that certain masters keep down wages, that there are forestallers, monopolists ; in a word, set labour against capital, its right hand."

" Can this be done ? "

" As long, Monsieur le Prince, as there is ignorance and hunger."

" But certain parties must be chosen ; we must not go to work blindly."

" Certainly not," said the Abbé Roy, with the look of a cat about to jump upon its prey.

" Have you any one to recommend as a victim ? " inquired the Prince.

" Your highness, I have heard of a certain elector, a friend of the pamphleteers, a man who wanted to have Mirabeau deputy for Paris, a certain Reveillon."

" The best master in the Faubourg St. Antoine," said the spy, drily.

" That will never do, then," observed the Prince.

" Nothing more easy," said the priest, warmly, his eye kindling as he spoke. " He is an atheist, a liberal, a friend to the working classes; their ruining such a man would rouse the whole *bourgeoisie* against the mob."

" But you propose a difficult task," exclaimed the Prince.

" I propose nothing which I am not ready to execute," answered Roy, with a savage leer. " I will myself go among the people, persuade them he is conspiring a general lowering of wages, and spread the feeling that the Tiers-Etats, which represents the masters, is all for themselves."

" Abbé, you are invaluable," said the Royal-Allemand, with a smile ; " your devotion shall be known at Versailles. For my part, anything to keep down all this *canaille*. But the police is sharp—Ducrosne will know all this in half an hour."

" He must have high orders to let things take their course," replied the Abbé ; " but the soldiers must come in at the end—it will make them popular."

" This is settled then," said De Lambesc, rising.

"But I must have some dozen or two aids, to assist me in rousing the mob—the Faubourg St. Antoine is large."

"And peopled like a bee-hive," said the spy; "once set moving, 'twill be hard to stop."

"I leave the details to you and M. Brown," continued the Royal-Allemand; "here are twenty thousand livres in an order on the treasury. Come, Count, will you to the opera? I have premised to meet La Volage."

"Willingly, Prince;" and the two soldiers went out, after plotting one of those infernal schemes which set the mob going, and taught them their power for evil.

"Monsieur the Abbé," said the spy, as soon as the other conspirators had left them, "you have a personal spite against this Reveillon. He lent you money when you were in distress."

"M. Brown," replied the priest, with lowering eye, "sufficient he is my enemy. More, he is a Rosseauite, talks *Contrat Social* by the yard, receives the enemies of the holy Catholic church at his table——"

"Bah!" said the spy, laughing; "no bigotry from you to me."

"You are strangely familiar even with princes," answered the Abbé, with a growl, "and I must not complain."

"It would be little use," said the spy, relighting his pipe.

"But my co-operators?" inquired the other, rising.

"At five to-morrow be at the cabaret, Rue du Faubourg St. Antoine, known as the Tour du Bastille—at five—I will join you."

"Agreed, and now may—" began the priest.

"Bah! no *orémus* for me," laughed M. Brown; "I'm half a heretic myself."

"Ah!" muttered the priest, retreating, "but duty before everything."

Then meekly folding his hands across his breast, this mild son of the church went out. Scarcely had he closed the door behind him than the spy rose. His step was stealthy and light: he was advancing towards the partition which led towards his inner apartment.

Suddenly throwing it open, he looked in. At a distance which rendered listening impossible sat Torticolis with two empty bottles before him, and a third just commenced, evidently in that happy condition when man, with justice, is doubtful whether he is an animal about to be led to the block, or a rational being in a state of temporary hallucination.

"Torti," said the spy, paternally, "you've made pretty free."

"Glad to see you, *preux che—che*—eh, what wants this dirty fellow in my—my—*boudoir?*" replied the crick-neck, acting his part admirably. The two bottles had been emptied out of the window.

"Jean," exclaimed the spy, laughing, and pushing him out at the same time, "go home, go to bed, and return to-morrow at four."

"Agreed," replied Torticolis, who floundered down stairs like a whale, nor walked uprightly until at some considerable distance from the house.

---

# CHAPTER V

### THE HOTEL RAVILLIERE.

In the sombre and stately Quartier St. Germain, and in the Rue St. Dominique, was the magnificent hotel in which dwelt the most noble and very puissant seigneur generally known as the Duke de Ravilliere. A *poste-cochère*, in the eentre of an elegant façade, led into a large square court, the mansion occupying three sides of a square; in the middle was a flight of marble steps, and through the open door could be seen, at the end of a noble passage, the leafy green of a garden.

Looking out upon this secluded and shady spot was an apartment with large bay-window and balcony.

To this we now transport ourselves.

Reclining languidly upon an ottoman, with all the exquisite grace and majesty combined which belonged to her, and conscious that no foreign eye rested upon her easy posture, was the Countess Miranda, her hair slightly loosened, and falling profusely upon her beautiful neck and shoulders. Her face was from the light, so that the expression of her eyes could not be seen; but she was apparently smiling.

Near her, sitting more demurely, in her stiff costume of brocade and silver, her hair all duly powdered, was Adela, evidently engaged in the matronly occupation of catechising her friend.

"Miranda," said she, pouting and half-blushing, "'twould seem, to hear you speak, that I was lowering myself much by accepting the affection of my cousin."

"And by returning it," exclaimed the Countess, laughing; "but by no means. I merely wonder that where so many noble knights have failed, this humbler suitor should have seen and conquered."

"Hush, Miranda," replied Adela, half impatiently; "who says he has conquered? See, when he comes, how proudly I will use him."

"It will not last five minutes, this heroic resolution before his candid smile. Charles Clement is not one who is to be played with thus."

"Why, how gravely you say this!" wondered the young girl.

"I am grave because I speak of one noble, generous, and with whom no woman who is loved by him should trifle," said Miranda, whose face now turned quite away, but who spoke seriously, almost gravely.

"But I will be as gentle as a young fawn, then, since you think it well," replied Adela, much surprised.

"Be so, not only now, but when you call him husband, Adela, for 'tis a sacred thing to have in trust the happiness, perhaps the life, of one who loves, and hopes, and trusts in us," and the young Countess was silent, as if much moved.

"Miranda," said her friend, gently, almost timidly, "how happy you would make such a noble heart as his!"

"Do you think so?" asked the young Italian, with a peculiar smile, so faint, it faded like the last breath of an evening wind amid the flowers.

"Do I think so?" exclaimed Adela, wonderingly; "were I worth half as much, I should be proud as Lucifer."

"You think," said Miranda, scarce conscious of what she was saying—she was dreaming though awake—"that I could vie with you—that I could give happiness where you could—that I have equal charms with thee?"

"Ten times more," replied Adela, quite innocent of any meaning which might apply to herself; "there is not in the land, peer or peasant, but would be proud and happy to call you his bride."

"You are a warm friend," answered the Countess, laughing, and again turning away, so that the expression of her face was hid.

"Not I, and much shall I wonder if you are a month at court ere you be an affianced wife."

"Never!" said the quick-emotioned Italian; "never, child. Thou wilt never live to see me a wife."

"Why?" asked Adela, strangely puzzled at her friend's manner, and a slight shudder quivering through her frame.

"Joy and merriness are not made for me, sweet one," replied Miranda, with a laugh, "nor wedded wifedom neither. Besides, I am young, I am rich, they say," she added, almost scornfully; "I am beautiful; why should I sell my sweet, sweet liberty to win the heart of any mortal man?"

"You are a wild, fickle being, and strangely changeful of late," said Adela.

"Then let us to the harpsichord," cried the Countess, rising, and turning towards the further end of the room, just as Charles Clement, whom she had heard coming, entered at a side-door.

"My Lord Duke," he said, half hesitatingly, "has sent me hither ——"

"Where you know, cousin, you are always welcome," replied Adela, with a sweet smile. "Friends are scarce now-a-days."

"Good evening, Monsieur Clement," said Miranda, almost coldly.

"Good evening, Madame," answered Charles, with a slightly-haughty tone.

Adela, too innocently happy to notice this, drew forth a portfolio, and, as was her wont, began to paint fanciful trifles, while her cousin spake to her, now admiring the labour of her fair hands, now gallantly lauding the exquisite fingers which were so gracefully employed, until gradually

4

his voice became lower and more impassioned in its tones, and then the Countess, gliding from her harp, moved toward the door which led to Adela's bed-room, and which was open.

On the threshold she turned round to look upon that pair, and her face was paler than the sheet of paper on which the blushing rose which Adela had painted lay senseless and immovable.

There she stood in the pride and splendour of her womanly beauty, a thing to be worshipped rather than loved.  Her liquid eyes were wet with tears—her colourless face quivered with emotion—her brow was contracted—for that happiness she saw before her could never be hers. A secret lay between the fruition of a woman's hopes; for her there was no rosy future tinged with the sweet thought of being an adored mistress—a cherished wife.

"And this is Miranda, Countess of Castel-monte, a princess in her own land, of high and noble lineage," she murmured, as she stood before a mirror.  "Perish these vain baubles; were I less noble, I had been more happy. But perish rather these vain and idle thoughts.  Down, thou soft heart," she added, pressing her hands upon her lovely and heaving bosom, "and know thou hast a mistress."

With these words the beautiful girl frowned upon herself, stamped her foot upon the ground, and then sunk into a large arm-chair which faced the mirror.  Involuntarily she cast her eyes upon the reflection of her figure, and her eye examined—not with pride—not with satisfaction—but curiously, with a scrutinising glance—every feature of her face.

Suddenly she rose, and snatching from her bosom a picture, a small miniature, examined it by the fading light of the garden.  Her eyes rested long upon it, and then again they fell upon the mirror.

And the mirror once more reflected a lovely form, but that of one pale and with an expression of sadness, strangely at variance with the merry creature who had so recently laughed with Adela.

"This picture is charming—is exquisite," she murmured, "but is she so much more so than I?"

And again her glance fell upon the mirror, which this time sent back a frowning and lowering brow, and Miranda started herself.

"Oh! to rest, my silly heart; take courage, there is one sure physician yet.   Time cures or kills."

And the miniature was warmly kissed and placed once more in her bosom, where it was gently hid away, nestling near her beating and aching heart.

The miniature was a medallion portrait of Adela.

Miranda then moved towards the open door which separated her from the lovers, and without being noticed by them, regained her seat before the harpsichord.

Charles Clement was speaking; he was commenting on the sufferings of the people, without work, without bread. He spoke with deep feeling, and eloquently, for he was in earnest.

"And do your philosophers hope to remedy all this?" suddenly inquired the Countess, in her driest manner.

"Madame," replied Charles Clement, waking from his charmed dream, while the fair Adela slightly pouted, "if the States-General do not provide willingly against all this misery, they must be forced to—"

"Forced to," said Miranda, with something of a scoffing air.

"Yes, Madame, forced to," answered the young republican: "Paris is in a state of fever which nothing but two things will allay, the assurance of their starvation being removed, and, more than all, that the Tiers-Etats will henceforth be a power in the State."

"And you think them right, of course, Monsieur Clement," said Miranda, in a tone of merry provocation.

"With me, Madame, there is but one power in the State, the people—with me they are rulers and ruled; and, until this principle be recognised, I can see no prospect of just legislation."

"But your people have been quiet enough under their kings and rulers hitherto," said the Countess; "methinks if they have been enslaved, it has been of their own accord."

"Which only proves that hitherto they have been as ignorant as debased, but excess of oppression cures itself.

Royal tyranny might have been borne, but the feudal system, with its monstrosities, has awakened the people."

"Think you, then," inquired his fair disputant, "that the States-General will ask a change in all this?"

"The constituents of the Tiers-Etats have required that their representatives should grant no supplies while one injustice remains to blot the fair face of France. May they nobly fulfil this glorious mission!"

"Amen!" cried Miranda, fervently.

"Madame," said Clement, with an involuntary start, while he looked astonished.

"Enough of politics," interposed Adela, with the pout of a spoilt child; "the weather is lovely, let us ride to Vincennes."

"'Tis not far from our dinner hour," replied Miranda, laughing.

"Never mind," said Adela, rising. "Monsieur le Duke has just gone out, and we can luxuriate in a forest picnic. I do so long for the air of the woods."

She might have added that her heart, all full of joy and happiness, her soul breathing the first fresh fragrance of young love, was too confined within their formal rooms, and she wished, she scarce knew why, for the free and open air of the woods. Miranda saw all this, though the lover was blind, and, with a smile, rose to second her project.

To order out horses—to command the attendance of servants—to horrify the family cook by countermanding dinner—to set the *maitre d'hotel* in a perfect flurry preparing a cold collation—and to order its being placed, all on a spare horse, was the work of a moment, and then away skipped the happy and wilful beauty to dress, accompanied by Miranda.

They are soon mounted, and reaching the quays, away they dash for the antique Pont Neuf, passing which, and the Hotel de Ville, they enter the busy Rue St. Antoine. In a few moments, for their speed is rapid, they are beneath the sombre shade and lofty towers of the Bastile, which frowned hideously over the hotbed of insurrection and revolution. The chief workers in all the great days of this mighty drama were those of the quarter of the Bastile.

"Gloomy spectre of despotism," said Charles, half-shuddering; "who knows what crime has been and is behind these walls!"

"Politics again," exclaimed Adela, holding up her riding-whip.

"Pardon," answered the young man, intoxicated at her glance of innocent affection.

"You are always easily forgiven," half-whispered his cousin, and then, as if alarmed at these few words, away she galloped.

"Happy pair," said Miranda, shaking her head; "but why reins in the lover?"

They were before a cabaret, over which, in large letters, was written, *La Tour du Bastille.*

It was five o'clock, and M. Brown, accompanied by Torticolis, had just disappeared through the door-way.

"My servant, who obtained leave of absence this morning to visit a friend, has just entered yonder ill-looking hole," he said by way of explanation; "but pardon, fair cousin, for bringing you to a halt, I am again at your service;" and away, once more, they sped towards Vincennes.

---

## CHAPTER VI.

### THE CABARET OF THE FAUBOURG ST. ANTOINE.

OCCUPYING the lower part of a house, in the Rue du Faubourg St. Antoine, the Tour du Bastille presented the ordinary features of a low Paris wine shop. Outside, on a red washed wall, all streaked with white, which ran down in smeary lines from above, were displayed blue bottles, beneath which huge figures of six and of eight showed that wine was sold at the moderate rate of three and four pence English per quart. Divers sausages, of a dubious brown, explained that there was also more solid refreshment. Ascending three worn and rough steps, you entered a room about a dozen feet square, of which half was taken up by the counter, and a small portion of the other half by the opening of the cellar. There was no bench before the bar— the landlord having no desire that his customers should sit down, as they would thus prevent the arrival of fresh thirsty visitors. The drinkers stood at the bar, or lounged about in groups outside, this being a popular and famous cabaret. where wine was generally good, and where Monsieur Du-crosne, lieutenant of police of the good city of Paris, permitted the engagement of workmen by their masters. For those who ventured on the luxury of a whole bottle, or who desired to eat with their wine, there was an inner room, a kind of tap, which owned two long tables, four wooden benches, a couple of dirty table-cloths, a pair of oil-lamps, a number of greasy candlesticks, and was waited on by a lad as dirty and repelling as the furniture.

At the very end of one of the tables, occupying each one side, sat two men, who remained apart from the rest of the company, and were evidently slightly superior in their social position.

The one was a stout, burly, well-fed personage, who seemed perfectly satisfied with himself, and with his own ruddy whiskers, and somewhat scanty hair, which he continually smoothed over the bald portion of his head, as if he thought these stray locks sufficed to conceal his real nudity. His costume was that of a tradesman.

His companion, who sat opposite, was a little more than five feet in height, but strongly built, and neither stout nor thin ; his shoulders were broad, his waist slight, while his legs were in some degree bowed. His strong arms were crossed upon the table. A thick short neck supported a head of vast ugliness, not, however, without features which, separate, were striking, and even handsome. His face was large and bony, with a nose aquiline and flat—the lower part extremely prominent ; his mouth was small, with thick lips, which were kept in continual motion by a nervous contraction ; a lofty forehead, eyes half-grey, half-yellow, lively, piercing, and naturally gentle ; an asumed bold mien, scarce eyebrows, a sallow complexion, with black beard, and brown neglected hair, completed the aspect of this man. whose shabby loose coat, dirty breeches, grey stockings, old hat, shoes without buckles—one fastened by string, the other not at all—gave him the air of a dealer in stolen goods, looking out for custom.

At some distance was a tall man, in more decent garb, about the middle height. There was nothing remarkable bore to a tiger who had the small-pox—(to use the energetic expression of Mirabeau).

This was the Abbé Roy.

Around were working men, drinking, smoking, and discussing the events of the day, principally the misery endured by the working-classes from scarce and dear food—the poor man's first scourge.

Among them were men whose sinister and lowering countenances were in a strange contrast with the generally honest and open expression which sat on those of the artizans, and which would always sit there, were this, the most important section of society, cared for as it should. These men, too, were, without and within, drinkly hardly, muttering low, in a strange *argot* of their own, casting, from habit, suspicious glances behind, and then laughing loudly, and clinking their glasses together in humble imitation of the higher *débauchées* of the past reign.

These men were thieves and robbers—vagabonds—some of the rich materials used by the enemies of the revolution to throw discredit on its progress. Warned by a hint from above that there was riot and plunder in the wind, they had hurried to the cabaret of the *Tour du Bastille*, ready for any act of violence or madness. They were amply supplied with wine, which they freely shared with the working-men around them, until these began to be merry and excited. As fast as their bottles were empty, they were refilled at the bar, an ill-looking fellow who leaned carelessly upon the counter paying for all. Strange as this was, the landlord asked no questions. The man was an officer of police.

M. Brown and Jean Torticolis sat apart, as if they had no connexion with the rest of the company. Near them was M. Duchesne, whom the crick-neck had readily enlisted in his enterprise.

The conversation was loud and confused, but the ugly man and his ruddy companion spoke without interruption.

"Ah, ah!" said the ruddy man, rubbing his hands, "I think, Doctor, your walk has done you good; you do credit to your bottle and to this matelotte."

"I satisfy the wants of nature," replied the ugly man, in a slightly-foreign accent—"nothing more."

"But you do not regret your long stroll in the wood,

*Nom d'un corporal*, but we crossed the forest rudely?" and the sturdy fellow stretched his legs, as if ready for another start.

"Certainly not," said the other, folding his arms, and reflecting.  He continued, after a pause, paraphrasing his own published expression, "At the sight of a beautiful country, which the sun shadows with the enamel of. its changing rays, I feel a secret delight I rarely otherwise experience.  The verdure of the field, the gentle perfume of flowers, the harmonious song of birds, and the fresh breath of the zephyrs, insensibly move the heart to gaiety. A soft sensation of peace glides to the soul; there comes upon you a species of enchantment, which few can resist. But as much as a lovely spot inspires me with joy, does a sombre desert shed melancholy upon my whole being. Arid plains, without turf or flowers, dead trees, dark foliage, enormous masses of rocks blackened by time, the noise of torrents roaring down the mountain-slope, mingled with the cawing of crows and the lugubrious cry of the eagle, fill me with sadness."

"Jean," exclaimed the other, with his mouth wide open, "I do believe you are preaching."

"I," snarled the other, with a strange smile, "it's not my trade; I leave it to yonder black crows," and he pointed to the Abbé.

"You are a philosopher," continued the other.

"I am a poor lover of my kind," replied the Doctor; "that is to say, of the humble, the poor, the wretched," he added, with an indiscribable expression of rage; "as for the rest, I hate them.  Aristocrats, merchants, tradesmen, money-dealers, go-betweens between dame Nature and the poor man, dealing out for every hour of blessed light devoted to slavery and drudgery, a hard morsel of bread and a handful of straw—giving with one hand, taking back with the other."

And this apostle of communism, though that sapient science had then neither habitation nor name, ground his teeth with intense fury.

"But," said the other, doubtingly, "there must be butchers, and bakers, and shoemakers, and capitalists to employ labour."

"Must there?" cried the other; "and booksellers to crush the free flight of genius within its bargaining soul. No, the world is my temple, and I would scourge out of it those who make profit of the subsistence and labour of others."

The whole room was listening, though the little Doctor was not aware of it. The Abbé Roy and M. Brown exchanged a glance, which was mutually congratulative. Unconsciously the stranger was serving their cause.

"But how would you have these men make a living?" suggested the bourgeois.

"Let them work," thundered the irate small man, who was foaming at the mouth with vehemence, and moving on the bench with strange contortions. "I would have every man who works not swept from the face of the earth as useless vermin. We were all born to live by the sweat of our brows, and *sang-dieu!* the *Tiers-Etat* will do little good if they do not bring us to that."

"But civilization?" cried the other.

"A sounding word," replied his friend, "never yet applied, but which is all for the advantage of one class."

"And great towns—Paris, Lyons, Marseilles?"

"Vast iniquities, where crime and vice are festering for the good of the few."

"And property?" continued the other, alarmed.

"Robbery. No man has a right to more than he can use for himself. Equally divided, all would have some."

"Tonnere!" cried Duchesne, "but the bourgeois speaks like a man. Long live the bourgeois!"

"Long live the bourgeois," cried the working men.

"Be patient," said the little man, rising, and now fully excited, "the time of the people is coming. You shall see, citizens, the hour when labour shall have its due, when the arms of the poor shall not be tired for nothing. But there must be rough work before then."

"*Peste,*" whispered Brown, "this man is dangerous. I must mark him."

"Eh?" put in the Abbé Roy, in an insinuating tone; "the artizan is daily more and more oppressed, bread is hourly scarcer, work is not plentiful, and wages fall."

"Whose fault?" said the little man, bluntly.

" I scarcely know," hesitated the priest.

" Of the thousand idlers, *mirliflores à la violclle*, who live but to tread on their scarlet heels, to advertise their tailors' goods, and watch for wrinkles on their erapulous skins; who consume the hard earnings of their miserable serfs; of pestilent lawyers, devouring the substance of the widow and the orphan ; of myriads of fat and lazy monks, stewing their huge carcases in dishonourable sloth and good living, true *sac-a-clous;* of hundreds of abbés, bishops, Malta-knights, spending their revenues and health in the dens of the Palais Royal; of heaps of forestallers and regrators, Foulons and Bertrands, who buy up the abundance of the earth and stow it away, that when scarcity comes they may drag the last *denier*, the last *liard* and *double*, from the entrails of the starving.   Whose fault ?" he half screamed, " we shall soon see."

The crowd, which never before had heard such words, and who now listened to them, yelled forth with a shrill and shrieking accent, flaming eyes, mouth foaming and distorted, hearkened breathlessly.   Each man held in his respiration, as if fearful of losing a syllable of the rude demagogue's harangue—he who just now had spoken so softly of nature ; and then, when he paused for breath, there followed a roar of applause, the orator's first oration—he as yet so despised, that all men slighted and shunned him.

" I hear," said one, duly tutored, when the noise for a moment ceased, " that there is question of lowering wages."

" Shame !" cried the mob, now well plied with drink, and still more intoxicated at the sound of their own griefs, savagely poured forth from sympathetic lips.

" We will resist," cried another.

" We will burn and destroy," said a third.

" But where heard you this ?" inquired one more cautious or less vinous.

" From a workman of Reveillen, the coloured paper maker, who will set the example," replied the other—a cunning rogue, who received his hints from the Abbé, himself scarcely yet recovered from the tirade of the dirty Doctor.

" Impossible," cried one.

" The best master in Paris."

"A workman once like ourselves."

"But the more upstart, perhaps," muttered the Doctor, wiping his forehead with a hideous cloth, which he drew from his pocket.

"True," said another.

"He is going to reduce his day wages to fifteen sous," continued the prompter.

"Starvation," cried the workmen.

"*A bas* Reveillen!" thundered the mob.

"Death to Reveillen," shouted the others.

"Come," said Duchesne, leaping up, "to the *atelier*."

"Come," repeated Torticolis, following his example.

"Where are you going?" exclaimed the Doctor, in his shrillest tone, and leaping upon his bench.

"To punish Reveillen, the blood-screw, the leech, who grinds men down to fifteen sous."

"Fools!" cried the Doctor, frantically, "you will be shot like wolves, skewered like frogs; the sword and the bayonet will slay you. What can ye do against soldiers?"

"Eat them, *à la croque au sel*," replied one, amid roars of applause, mingled with laughter. The mob was delighted at the notion of devouring soldiers, flavoured with salt.

The Doctor sank down upon his bench, a strange expression on his face. There was fear, fear for himself—he had roused their passions; fear for the people—the odds were against them; but there was a look of indefinable joy and hope in his smile, for he saw how the mob could be roused, and on that spot the man took measure of his materials. Still determined to prevent, if possible, the outrage which they were about to perpetrate, and of which he saw the danger, for the infant States-General, giving excuse, as it would, for military rigour, he again rose, but the room was almost empty. There remained but the Abbé Roy and M. Brown, the secret, but unsuspected, authors of the tumult.

The man, however, rushed forth to the step of the door, in front of which more than a hundred men were congregated, yelling, bawling, explaining to those without the supposed infamy of Reveillen, and recruiting new arms every minute. The Faubourg St. Antoine, quarter of labour, of industry, of poverty, of dirt, of ignorance, of crime, was becoming excited, the sullen roar of the tempest had attracted new faces from far and wide. There were painters and blacksmiths, coachmakers and shoemakers, wheelwrights and coopers, stone-masons and builders, and then fish-wives, rag-pickers, bone-grubbers, thieves, vagabonds, idlers, the *gamins*, who are here, there, and everywhere, neither thieving nor working, but always living—and all this mass, as it swelled in numbers, fermented and increased in wrath.

It was night. Darkness had fallen insensibly on the face of the great city, and the church-clocks boomed in the night-air the hour of eight. Several had improvised torches, while others had armed themselves with sticks; some few had old swords and guns, relics of the days of the Fronde. In a short time the crowd had gained enormous accessions; it numbered more than a thousand, some coming to know what was the matter, while at the heels of the men came yelping, crying, bawling, many dogs, and more children.

"Down with the *accapareurs!*" cried some.

"Down with the *patrons!*" repeated another.

"Bread at two sous!" shrieked the women.

"Down with the masters!"

"And the *changeurs!*"

"*A bas* Reveillen!"

"*A bas* the famine-mongers!"

"Death to those who lower wages!"

"*Les brigands! les gueux!*"

"Down with the bakers!"

"Down with the butchers!"

"And the grocers!"

"And the meal-men!"

"And the bankers!"

"And the farmers-general!"

"Down with the aristocrats!" shrieked the shrill voice of Jean Torticolis.

The mob paused, as if astounded at this last apostrophe. Brown looked inquiringly at the Abbé, who shook his head; the Doctor's eyes glistened, and though still trying to gain a hearing, he rubbed his hands with an air of intense satisfaction. He began to think there was stuff in the *badauds!*

"*A bas les aristocrates!*" shouted the mob, carried away by their impulse, even to this pitch of audacity.

"*A bas* the priests!" continued Torticolis.

This time the Doctor smiled a grim smile, but shook his head next minute with supreme contempt, for the cry was feebly re-echoed. The Parisians were not yet so far advanced.

The Abbé Roy bounded on his chair, and looked uneasily at the spy.

"These *gaillards* have studied Voltaire," said the policeman, with a sneer.

"Death to all spies—down with the police!"

"And Rousseau!" added the priest, maliciously.

"*Ça iva!*" muttered the Doctor; "but this is folly. These good people will be sliced to pieces by the Royal Allemands, the Crasates, by my countrymen the Swiss. *Peuple Français!*" he began, magniloquently, addressing them from the steps of the door.

Apparently the *Peuple Français*, from want of practice, knew not to whom this was addressed, for they paid no attention to the orator.

"March!" suddenly thundered Duchesne.

"March!" repeated the mob, and the whole assembly moved towards the further end of the street, where was situated the vast factory which Reveillen had erected by his industry, and which supported more than a hundred families in comfort—as this man, himself of the people, in truth was popular; for in hard times, content to be able to work without loss, he kept his manufactory going, when his receipts scarcely covered his expenditure. Many of his artizans were amongst the mob, but ignorant and maddened by drink, they believed the insidious statements of their ruffian associates. The mob is, when utterly uninstructed, the prey of knave and fool; little pity for those who suffer, for they have left them uninstructed.

"It works," said the Abbé; "Reveillen will have a rough *reveil.*"

"He is not at home," replied the spy, without noticing the other's hideous pun, "he attends a meeting of the electors of Paris."

"He will escape," growled Roy, furiously.

"He will be ruined," replied Brown, coldly.

"Ah! 'tis better, perhaps, he lives; he will feel his fall," muttered the priest; "but I should like to know if he has been warned."

The police agent smiled almost imperceptibly, but made no reply.

"Good evening," said Roy, suddenly rising, and then, crossing his hands upon his breast, he walked out of the cabaret.

The Doctor and his companion also, having paid their score, moved towards the door.

"Monsieur," exclaimed the police spy, rising, and addressing the little man politely, "may I request the honour of knowing one who has no nakedly showed the evils under which we suffer?   All good patriots should work together."

"My name is Jean Paul Marat," replied the other, drily, and without raising his eyes.  He was sunk in contemplation of the coming storm.

"He lives with me, Monsieur Brown," said his companion, with an expression of profound contempt.  "Legendre, the butcher, is not unknown to the police."

And the two men walked out, Marat so absorbed as not to have heard the parting words of his friend.

"*Damnés chiens d'aristocrates!*" growled the police spy —for he, too, was a revolutionist—"I think your time is come."

And M. Brown rubbed his hands with an air of the most intense satisfaction, which operation performed, he buttoned up his coat, and went out to see the doings of the mob.

It was, indeed, Marat, that *Mareshal de logis* of his Royal Highness the Soul, as Voltaire, in derision of his arguments in favour of its immortality, called him, who, with Hebert, Rosnin, Clootz, and others, disgraced the revolution from very different motives.  Marat boiled with hatred—he truly wrote with blood and bile—he had been despised, slighted —he, the really able literary man and philosopher, who wrote things not unworthy of preservation, and his soul turned to gall.  All above him were his abhorrence, and he now saw the hope of paying back his sufferings.  Such men are never wanting in revolutions; these are ever— every reader will instinctively point out living examples amid brawling and tempestive politicians—awaiting the rising of the people in a good and sacred cause; these hounds of anarchy, to yell them on to their destruction. More noisy than the sincere friends of freedom, they are the easier heard.

---

## CHAP. VII.

### THE EMEUTE.

THE factory of Reveillen was situated about the centre of the Rue du Faubourg St. Antoine, at the corner of the Rue Traversiere. It was a large sombre building, extending some distance along the two streets. The basement story had no windows on the outside, but there was a vast *porte cochère*, to admit the carts and horses used in the trade. The workshops were along the first floor, the lower being appropriated to store-rooms, offices, and the residence of Reveillen, receiving light from the court and a large garden. Above the workshops were drying-rooms; below the ground story, cellars containing wine, vitriol, turpentine, oils, colours, &c.

About half-past eight, on the evening in question, the factory was perfectly silent. The door had been closed since six, and the neighbours had even noticed that the passage had been previously barricaded. Not a light was to be seen in the house after the departure of Reveillen, who had gone to attend a meeting of electors, at the archbishopric of Paris. It was true, that in the day he had received anonymous warning that there would be riot and noise in Paris, and that ill-intentioned persons might attack his factory. Paying little attention to the warning, he had still acted with precaution.

In the house remained a lad, his only servant, one Antony Brisemiche, so called from having, at an innocent and interesting age, been picked up in the street of that name. To this boy Reveillen had given strict instructions to be on the watch, and, in case of serious alarm, to ascend the garden wall by means of a ladder, and thus communicate with him. This hopeful youth, a thorough-bred Paris *gamin*, though honest and attached to his master, promised strict obedience, with the full intention of first consulting his own pleasure and convenience.

He had, to pass the time, ascended to the summit of the house, and, perching himself at his own garret-window, looked out upon the town, or rather on the mass of tiles and chimney-pots which lay below and about him. The prospect was not enlivening, particularly as the night was dark; but the *gamin* had a pocket-full of peas, which he amused himself by shooting through a blow-pipe upon the worthy *populaire* of the locality, who were strolling by, or were stationed at their doors in refreshing gossip. He had enjoyed this satisfaction for about half an hour, when suddenly, instead of the usual stray passengers which came along at eventide, he heard a strange rumour of voices coming up the street, and tempted by curiosity, he crept out upon the roof and looked down.

About a couple of hundred feet distant, he saw first a glare of light, much smoke and blaze; he heard cries, but distinguished not their import; then he made out men with sticks, and poles, and cutlasses, and guns, and women waving saucepan-handles, and all by the light of hundreds of torches, which were madly waved like banners in the wind.

The boy looked again, this time enviously, for the vagabond was strong in him, and he snuffed the tumult like a young war-horse ready for the charge. There was a sea of heads, of human faces; but what strangely struck the lad was, that he saw myriads of eyes, where he saw nothing else, sparkling in the torch-light. There was waving hair, arms tossed on high, caps upon poles, and a loaf, stuck upon a pike, carried for a banner. A riot would be incomplete which touched not the stomach.

Brisemiche, however, listened, for his ears were assailed with strange sounds, all mixed, and mingled, and yelled forth without connection or order.

"Down with the bakers!"

"Down with the butchers!"

"Down with the corn-dealers!"

"Death to the *accapareurs!*"

"Death to Foulen!"

"*Mort aux aristocrates!*"

"Heu!" muttered the *gamin*, kicking his heels against the edge of the roof, "this is new; it becomes amusing."

Again he looked, and the crowd, now close to the Rue Traversiere, appeared more formidable than in the first instance.

Torticolis and Duchesne were at the head—the former sombre and quiet, his hate of the rich, the titled, speaking on his face; the latter stupidly intent on mischief. Then came the hired ruffians, the night-birds, who had filled the cabaret, with whom were mixed women of a degraded class, in dirty finery, drawn there by the love of excitement. In Paris, wherever there is a mob, there are its Boadiccas. In fights, in street battles, in pillage, in slaughter, there are women — women exciting the combatants, assisting the wounded, removing the slain. When they do not commence an *émeute*, they have their part.

Behind were the masses, the artizans, the labourers; and never more ignorant and soul-darkened materials were brought to light, the children of long ages of despotism, which had stained and murdered, and slain and hanged, and drawn and quartered, and burnt and scarred, and insulted and defaced, and ground, but never taught. To make the rulers of the land discover that the mob have souls, and that education is their due, was alone worth a revolution.

One knowledge they had—they knew that they had endured much misery, much distress, much suffering; bread and fuel had been dear, and there were those who said it was the fault of other men like themselves, and who sat in high places rejoicing, while they munched a morselled portion of a black loaf.

"Revenge!" cried the mob, as this thought came uppermost.

"Death to those who starve our little ones," shrieked the women.

"*Heu!*" said Brisemiche, piteously, "that's but just."

"Halt!" thundered one or two of the foremost, who wished to be methodical in their operations.

"There's a fellow cries halt," muttered Brisemiche— "he! determined I shall have my share. Much obliged."

"*Mort à Reveillen!*" growled the crowd behind, pressing on tumultuously.

"What do the brigands say?" exclaimed Antony, mechanically regaining his window.

"Death to him and his gang," said a voice in the rear, calm and unexcited; "spare not one. Kill that little devil, Brisemiche!"

"*Tieu!*" cried the *gamin*, with a look of more wonder than alarm, "there's the Abbé Roy telling them to settle my account. What's that for? Because I caught him kissing Louise, I suppose, the *scelerat*. But they are knocking."

The lad looked out again, down upon that boiling ocean of faces, half dizzy and stunned by the glare, the light, the noise, the yells, the cries, the smoke and stench of torches which thickened the atmosphere. A band of men, headed by Duchesne and Torticolis had surrounded the gate, and were thundering for admittance.

"Come out, Reveillen! come out!" they cried.

"Hoh! ho there!" said Brisemiche, from above.

There was an instant of silence; the besiegers understood that a parley had been sounded.

"Where is maître Reveillen?" inquired Duchesne, moving back and looking up towards the garret.

"Gone," replied the garrison, laconically.

"Where?" continued Duchesne, the silence still continuing.

"Why wish you to know?" said Brisemiche, in a sneering tone.

"Antoine," cried a number of women, angrily, "you had better answer."

"Heu!" answered the *gamin*, in the most provoking manner.

"Antoine Brisemiche, for such we understand your name to be," said Duchesne, pompously, "you are summoned to surrender."

"To whom?" inquired the imperturbable *gamin*.

"I think the fellow argues with us," continued Duchesne, turning to those behind.

"Enough of parley, in with the door, break it open, down with Reveillen; death to Brisemiche," cried the crowd.

"They are in earnest," muttered the lad, "and I must think of escaping ere they enter. A troop of horse will soon disperse them, but first let me say adieu to the Abbé."

Antony had armed himself as he spoke, with a piece of brick, big enough to have killed a man from that height,

and this in his hand, he once more peered out.  He glanced
not at the mob but behind them, where, secure beneath a
doorway, stood the malignant Abbé gloating over his work.
Quick as thought the reckless *gamin* aimed his missile,
which came heavily on the priest's shoulder, as his arm was
raised in the act of encouraging the rioters.

"Malediction!" yelled the Abbé, whose arm was nearly
dislocated, while a crowd collected round him, attracted by
his shriek and the sound of the falling brick.

"Who threw it?" said the mob.

"Brisemiche," replied Roy, tottering, and speaking at
random.

"Shoot the little devil," cried some, while others pointed
their guns upward; but the boy had disappeared, and the
inside of the house was again silent.

"This door has something behind it," said Duchesne,
after a few vain trials at bursting it open.  "The enemy
were prepared."

"Burn it," replied Torticolis.

"Burn it," answered the mob, thieves and workmen
both, for all were now wild with excitement.

Away flew some ready hands to where a wood-dealer
kept a supply of faggots for general consumption, and,
without waiting even to explain their errand, piled, each
man, two or three upon their shoulders, and running back,
threw them down before the mob, who cheered vociferously.
To heap them against the door to fire them was the work
of an instant, and then the crowd, each instant greater in
numbers, pressed back from the blaze, crushing in its im-
petuosity those behind.

"A famous fire," said Torticolis.

"It wants a roast," replied Duchesne, with a horrible
grin.

"Here, a *reveille matin*," cried one.

"It's a great waste of wood," muttered a woman, thinking of her empty grate at home.

"Bah!" said another, "'twill lower the price."

"Let us dance!" shrieked the woman in gaudy finery,
who had been drinking brandy with the ruffians let loose
by the police.

"After supper," replied the robbers.

Meanwhile, the door was cracking under the blaze, the fire rose higher and higher, the mob yelled, some approached to warm themselves, while others looked round at the wild faces which stood out in that unearthly light, and shuddered. Torticolis gazed on in silence; Duchesne laughed with delight.

"The door will give way now," cried some, as the fire sunk low and but ashes remained.

"Try," thundered Duchesne, retreating.

"Here goes," said a Blacksmith, rushing forward and dealing a blow against the door with a bar of iron.

The planks, hot and carbonised, flew in shivers. The mob, with a shout of triumph, rushed headlong against it, treading out the fire with their wooden shoes; and in another moment, after breaking down the bars and poles which supported the door inside, the whole of the infuriated gang rushed in. Loud and furious shrieks ensued, as dozens were almost squeezed to death; but some entering the dwelling, others the cellars, others the court, others the garden, while still more rushed upwards—there was soon space—until soon the factory swallowed within it the whole of the vast mob. Those who struck for the dwelling were principally thieves, who ransacked and destroyed every article of furniture, in their furious hunt for money; the rest, actuated by less sordid, though not less destructive tendencies, rushed upon everything—machinery, tools, stock—and reduced the whole to rags and sticks. Through every room, through the workshops, in the garden, hunting every hole and corner, went the mob, yelling for Reveillen. But not a living creature was found, and then their blind rage expended itself on the inanimate things around.

Torticolis and Duchesne suddenly met; the former with wild and raving eye, smashing, breaking, shrieking; the latter stealing away with a roll of valuable paper under his arm.

"Duchesne," said Torticolis fiercely, "leave that."

"Why?" replied the hangman, with much surprise.

"We come to do justice—not to steal," continued the crick-neck.

"True," exclaimed Duchesne, and down went the pacquet at his feet.

"What is that?" cried Torticolis, listening. They were beneath the *porte cochère*.

"And that?" said the *bourreau*, pointing upwards.

"Only the fire gaining the workshop," answered the crick-neck, coldly; "but without I hear the tramp of soldiers."

"*La troupe!*" thundered Duchesne, rushing towards the street.

"This way," said Torticolis, dragging him back to the garden by main force.

"*La troupe! la troupe!*" was shouted through the factory with the speed of lightning; and then a panic striking the whole mob, they came leaping, jumping, pushing, driving, all towards the street. The instant the first dark mass issued from the door-way, glared upon by the flames of the house, which was burning in its upper part, a volley of musketry was heard, followed by shrieks, and groans, and imprecations.

"Did I not well?" said Torticolis, still dragging the *bourreau*.

"Yes! yes! which way?" asked the other, who was dreadfully alarmed.

"Let us first see if they will attack the soldiers," cried Torticolis. "But no, they are dashing over the dead and dying to escape by the Rue Traversiere."

Another murderous volley stopped his voice, and then the tramp of the military was heard coming up the street.

"Climb this ladder," whispered Torticolis, pointing out that by which Brisemiche had escaped.

"Yes, my friend," and the *bourreau* clambered up in the utmost haste. No sooner, however, was he at the top than he glided down again, terror on his countenance.

"What is the matter?" said his companion.

"The lane is full of soldiers," replied Duchesne, shaking like a leaf.

"We are caught then," cried Torticolis, coldly; and he moved towards the door, followed by the *bourreau*.

The house was empty; on its threshold lay thirty or forty bodies of men, women, lads, some dead, some maimed, some dying. Outside were the white and green coats of the infantry; above, the flames devouring the workshops;

below, drunkards revelling in the cellars, and some half-dozen wretches in the last agony, who had swallowed vitriol in mistake for spirits.

"Give yourselves up," cried an officer, who, behind the detachment of foot, headed one of cavalry.

Torticolis paused, and shuddered—for he knew that tone which everywhere haunted him—while Duchesne advanced in a trembling attitude to surrender. The crick-neck was listening for the echo of that voice, and gazing in alarm at the figure of his master, Charles Clement, who sat beside the soldiers, peering over as if in search for somebody. The ladies and servants had just galloped away, for he could see them in the distance.

"Bind the knaves," said the officer. "You lads," speaking to the foot, "in quick, and search the factory, ere it be all on fire." "You, my hearties," to the cavalry, "take that *canaille* in the rear."

The foot obeyed, entering the house, the cavalry charging hurriedly down the Rue Traversiere, in search of the fugitives. Four men alone remained, who surrounded Duchesne and Torticolis. Duchesne suffered himself to be bound without a struggle; but Torticolis, who had caught his master's eye, suddenly picked up a stick, knocked down the two soldiers who were about to tie his hands, when they thought him utterly helpless, struck the officer a blow which dismounted and stunned him, and then flew, rather than leaped, behind his master, who, without a word, gave spur, and in five minutes more was far away, beneath the walls of the Bastile.

"Get you home," said Charles Clement, severely, as soon as he saw that they were alone beneath the gloomy fortress. "I have just saved you from a halter; mind you stir not out again until I speak with you."

Torticolis, with a look of profound gratitude and humility, glided from the horse and took his way towards the Rue Grenelle. Charles Clement then put spurs to his steed in the direction of the river, on his return to the Duke's mansion.

# CHAPTER VIII

## THE REVELATION.

As soon as Charles Clement was free from his burthen, his horse, although somewhat fatigued, took its road more swiftly. The Pont Neuf was rapidly gained, and then, aware that his cousin would be alarmed and anxious, he put spurs to his steed, and, without a moment's pause, galloped until he arrived before the door of the Duke's hotel. The *porte cochère* was thrown wide back awaiting his arrival, which was scarcely made known by the rattling of his horse's hoofs, ere the gate closed behind him, and the Duke and Adela rushed forth, regardless of all assertion of dignity, to greet him.

"Nephew! nephew!" said the nobleman, with feigned severity, "what means this folly?"

"Cousin! cousin!" cried Adela, "were you hurt? But that the Countess dragged me home with furious speed, I should have waited."

"The Countess acted wisely," replied Charles Clement, with a swelling bosom. "I am not hurt. The rogue did all that was necessary himself. But where is the Lady Miranda, that I may thank her?"

"In the supper-room," said the Duke. "The ride has fatigued and excited her; she waits us there. Let us join my lovely ward, and there receive explanations of this mad-brained folly."

The young man pressed the withered hand of his uncle kindly and respectfully, and then offering his arm to the young girl, followed to the apartment where supper was laid out for them.

Charles Clement, slightly piqued that the Countess Miranda had not as much sympathy and anxiety about him as his relatives, and recollecting her general coldness, had prepared a frigid reception for the haughty beauty. When, however, within a few steps of the door, his eye, raised suddenly, caught sight of her. She was standing beside a marble pillar that supported the splendid and vast fire-place, paler than the white spray of ocean 'neath the moon. It was not, however, her pallor which struck him, but the strangely-fixed expression of her face. She was buried in another world—that of thought. But her reflections were painful, for her whole face was expressive of extreme suffering.

Charles, scarcely able to comprehend the feeling which prompted him, dropped the arm of Adela, who was close beside her father, and darted towards the Countess, who seemed scarcely able to support herself.

"You are ill, madam," he said, in a voice as gentle as that of a mother to her child, and at the same time taking her hand.

"A slight spasm," replied Miranda, quickly; and as she spoke, her eye rested for a second on him, with a glance which was almost imperceptible, but which satisfied her he was not wounded; her hand trembled, and the pallor of her cheek was quickly replaced by roses as bright as those of Le Notre's gardens.

"It is nothing," she then added, withdrawing her hand, and resuming her usual stately and even protective tone, "I rode so quickly lest the mob should follow us, that I am scarce recovered. But come, my Lord Duke, let me not keep you standing; I shall not disdain my supper; and we learn the clue to this new windmill freak. Since when, M. de Ravilliere, do you have nephews who interfere with the military in the execution of their duty?"

All this was spoken with extreme volubility, while the company seated themselves. Charles Clement, annoyed and hurt, took his place silently beside Adela, who examined her friend curiously.

"Such strange things have passed of late, Countess," replied the Duke, solemnly, "that I am surprised at nothing. A body called together, as *Etats-Generaux*, seems about to take upon itself functions perfectly new, and Heaven knows where their encroachments will end."

"Ah! my Lord Duke," said Charles Clement anxiously —all the fire of his nature at once roused when politics were discussed—"has anything new occurred? Have the orders united?"

"No, Charles," continued the old man, "they are as far from it as ever; though, truly, a minority of the nobles, headed by the Duke of Orleans, have proposed to join the

Third Estate, the *Communes*, as they now call themselves;
but the clergy are giving way."

" Thank Heaven for that?" cried Clement—" the people
and the ministers of God! fit union!"

" Ay! ay! there speaks the revolutionist. But what
startled me to-day, nephew, is to see that the Third Estate
will, if us nobles stand out much longer, arrogate all power
to themselves."

Charles replied not; but a gratified smile, or rather ex-
pansion of the heart upon his face, spoke plainly for him.

" I heard new words to-day," continued the Duke; " for,
guided, I knew not why, by you, nephew, I too have
yielded, and joined the Tiers, who were discussing what
name we should be called by. ' Representatives of the
French People,' said one. ' Yes, it is because this word,
People, is not sufficiently repected in France; because it is
obscured, covered with the rust of prejudice; because it
presents to us an idea which alarms our pride, and against
which vanity is in plain revolt; because it is pronounced
with contempt in aristocratic chambers—it is for this very
reason that we should impose it upon ourselves as a duty,
to raise it up, to ennoble it, to render it henceforth respect-
able to ministers, and dear to all hearts.' "

" And who," said Charles, with enthusiasm, " spoke
thus?"

" The Viscount Mirabeau," replied the old man, shaking
his head.

" I could have wished a better advocate for the people,"
answered the enthusiast, sadly; " genius perverted. I was
reading but yesterday some admirable words, mine uncle,
which apply to him well, as to all great writers who deal in
vice and debauchery. The words were addressed to Voltaire; but they are equally applicable to Mirabeau and
Louvet, both to their writings and their lives. I read them
in an eloge of Gresset in the *Mercury*. I have it in my
vest, with yours and the ladies' permission—"

" Read! read! nephew," said the Duke, thoughtfully.

" ' Are not genius and virtue destined to be united in an
immortal alliance? Have not both a common source in
the elevation, the pride, and the sensibility of the soul?
By what fatality, then, have we so often seen genius declar-

ing war to the knife against virtue? Writers more celebrated for your follies even than for your talents, you were born to soften the evils of your fellow-creatures—to shed some flowers on the path of human life; and you have, on the contrary, empoisoned its flow; to you it has been a cruel sport to let loose all the terrible passions which cause our miseries and our crimes! Dearly have we paid for your vaunted masterpieces; for they have cost us our morals, our repose, our happiness, and that of posterity, to whom they transmit from age to age the license and corruption of our times.'"

"Admirable words, nephew, and such as in calmer hours I would have delighted to comment on, so true are they, and applicable to all those writers who shower depraved features of life upon society. But whose are they?"

"The writing of an obscure country lawyer, whom nobody ever heard of, or ever will, perhaps—one Maximilien de Robespierre."

"It will not be for want of trying, then," said the Duke, almost smiling; "for that very man, deputy of Artois, rose to support Mirabeau, but his shrill voice, or the subject, not being to the taste of the audience, he was put down ere a word of his speech could be gathered."

"But still, my uncle, you think the deputies firm?" inquired Charles, anxiously.

"Yes! and they would be firmer did they understand, as we do, through the reports of the police, how Paris is devoted to them."

"What fear you, then, my Lord?" continued Clement.

"Not their firmness, but the obstinacy of the *noblesse*, nephew. I am not in the secret of the Cabinet, but I have every reason to believe it is contemplated to overawe the *Tiers-Etats* by force, and restrict them to merely voting money."

"And does Louis XVI. allow such plots around the throne?"

"Nephew," said the Duke, sinking his voice, and looking round as if he thought the walls might listen, "Louis XVI., his most sacred Majesty, for whose authority I am prepared to die, and whose just prerogatives—the nation duly thought for—I will sustain while I have breath, is governed by less good-natured hearts than himself; the Queen—this is rank treason, but truth loves not the least restraint—she understands no royal authority which is not absolute; and Monsieur and the Count D'Artois, with Condè, are exactly of her opinion. The *noblesse*, with few exceptions, stand by this great party, for their privileges and power are at stake; they are ready to draw the sword, if necessary, and sheath it in the bosom of France."

"Father," said Adela, little aristocrat as she was, "you treat your class roughly."

"My class, child," replied the Duke, gravely, "is no longer part of the nation. It is an enemy within the State, and will soon cease to exist. Three months of this boy's society has taught me strange things."

"Cease to exist!" cried Adela, with astonishment—"shall I no longer, then, be a Countess?"

"No, girl," said the Duke, fondly smoothing her hair, while Miranda looked on calmly and coldly; "and I shall be plain Monsieur de Ravilliere, even if they leave me the *de*. I know the temper of this Third Estate."

"And you say, my Lord Duke," inquired Charles Clement, all his republican fire roused, and utterly unconscious of the few last sentences, "that you suspect the *noblesse* of meditating a *coup d'état*, and of intending to use the sword?"

"I fear they will be so ill-advised, though some talk of basely deserting their king and country, and flying to foreign parts," replied the old Duke, with indignation.

"Then, my Lord, by the sword will they be answered; and this great moral movement for regeneration, reform, and human happiness, for the application of justice and equity to government, will become a revolution. Misfortune on the head of those who first shed blood!"

"It is because I believe what you say to be true, that I would speak to you of ourselves. I am old, boy, and a few months will probably see my end; but these girls—"

"Monsieur le Duc," said Miranda, rising in some confusion, her face suffused with a burning blush, while a look of apprehension and alarm might be clearly distinguished, "allow me to to interrupt you. I think my head is scarcely well, my spasm—that is, 'tis late, and I and Adela will—"

"Nay, countess," replied the Duke, rising gallantly, and handing her to the door, near which a servant stood with a candle, "you are, I see, unwell; go rest you, my dear ward. Adela shall join you presently; I would say a few words to her."

Adela and Charles remained sitting at the table, their eyes cast down, neither daring to venture to look at the other. Both felt that a most interesting event was about to occur; but no confession, no explanation, having passed between them, each feared to gaze upon the other, lest his or her hope might be too clearly read. There is a luxurious joy in hope, so full, so rich, so swelling, that it comes in strong current to the heart, sweeping out fear and doubt, or leaving them in such obscure corners, that their presence is with difficulty detected. The young Countess and the republican commoner loved; each lived in a world of fancy of their own, awaiting the kind hand which was to open the gates of felicity.

"Children," said the Duke, advancing, and taking their two hands in his, holding both of which he seated himself, "I am not sorry Miranda is gone, for I would say what she might have blushed to hear. I am, with one exception, save ye and her, alone in the world. You two girls provided for, and I can die happy."

"Say, rather, live, dear father," replied Adela, tenderly.

"Nay, though a Frenchman, I make to myself no illusions. Children, this crisis will kill me; not yet, perhaps. I may have a year or so to live; but I wish to be prepared for the worst. My first thought is for your marriage, dear girl."

How beat that little heart—how perseveringly down were kept those gentle eyes; and he, how pale and anxious did he look, he who loved so well.

"I could have wished," the old man continued, "to have seen you two united; but that is impossible."

"Father!" said Adela, with an involuntary cry of anguish.

"Impossible! oh, sir, unsay that word," cried Charles, in a despairing accent; and their love, thus unwillingly told, they tremblingly lowered their eyes.

"And is it so?" exclaimed the Duke, in a tone of astonishment, half sorrow, half anger—"is it so? Have I been so blind, so foolish, so cruel, I may say, so unjust? My poor children, if indeed I understand you rightly, curse the old man who brought you together, who gave you opportunity, who lured you to your destruction! for your union is, as I have said, impossible. Charles, tell me, I pray you, son of my injured sister, do you not love my child?"

"My Lord Duke," replied Charles Clement, "presumptuous as is my declaration, I dare not hesitate to speak the truth. I love your daughter more than my life."

"And you, girl?" said the Duke, almost wildly.

"Blame me not, dear father; he saved my life!" and the young Countess fell on her knees.

"Rise, rise, girl; I have no anger for you," exclaimed the nobleman, clenching his thin and withered hands; "but against myself for not foreseeing this falling out; and I, too, who would so gladly have blessed you!"

"Then do so, sir," cried Charles, seizing the unresisting hand of his young cousin.

"Ask me no such thing," said the Duke, gravely; "the word of a Ravilliere is sacred, and I have said it is impossible. Adela, have you quite forgotten your cousin, Count Leopold?"

"No, dear father; but what of him?" inquired the girl, her charming face all tears.

"When you were a baby-thing, a little laughing blue-eyed child, all ringlets and laughter, I did, for my sins, give you, on my honour as a gentleman, as wife to your cousin, Count Leopold; his father, my only brother, the better to assure the consummation of my promise, took written pledge of my undertaking, of which copy is in yonder desk. Three months back, your cousin, who is poor, and, I believe, in difficulties, claimed your hand. I loved him not, and offered half my estates, all I could alienate; he refuses, and will hold me to my bond. I told you 'twas impossible."

The lovers remained as if struck to stone, for reality was worse than any barrier their imaginations could have suggested. They were without hope.

"Go, my child," said the father, tenderly, "rejoin the

Countess Miranda, who, I hope, will one day win your cousin's heart; for you are another's. I have set my hope on this union."

"Never," replied Charles Clement, firmly; "your daughter denied me—I know no other love. I devote myself the more unto the people."

Adela heard, and an ineffable sensation of delight warmed her bosom, as she moved away to weep her grief upon the bosom of the lovely Italian.

Meanwhile, the Countess Miranda had sought her chamber. She had guessed that the Duke was about to decide the fate of Adela; but, ignorant of the pledge which gave the young girl to the Count Leopold, she expected to hear the old man, whose attachment for the young lawyer was seen by every one, give her hand to his nephew. She felt that it was but right the lovers should have no one present more than was absolutely necessary; and, besides, she was, as she had said, unwell.

Yes! for else, why so pale? why are her hands, so soft and rosy, thus clasped, and why are her cheeks all white, while tears force themselves through her eye-lids? Her look is wild; and she paces the bed-chamber, her maid long since dismissed, with agitated step. Suddenly she stops, this time before a mirror.

"Miranda, Countess of Castelmonte, heiress of the wide lands of Sartiges and Pontois, is it you," she said, with a hard and bitter smile—"you who let thy spirit be thus chafed by a silly boy, whom, a few years back, you would have scorned to speak to? And is it thou, Duke of Ravilliere, who art about to give thy only child to one of the *petite noblesse* of the robe, a revolutionist, one who is a declared enemy of thy order? Hush! hush!" she added, more gently, "can I thus blind myself? It is in vain. I seek to scorn this man, with his impetuous thoughts, his love of liberty, of greatness; his noble ambition, and his true and gallant soul. No! no! I appreciate him but too well, and he—loves Adela, my dear, my sweet, my gentle cousin, the mating of the lion with the lamb. But down, down, my heart," she continued in a calmer voice. "I must tame this unwomanly folly. It was that day, in the forest, when first we met him, when he as yet knew not which to love, that came this idle thought. 'Twas morn when we came upon him fishing; he had near him a book, the *Contrat Social of Voltaire;* he recognised Adela, and we joined him. We conversed, wandering through the mazes of the wood. His language, so different from that of courtiers, and those we used to hear, then interested us. Adela saw his beauty, I his genius; but both admired. All day we wandered, listening to his eloquent words, his new ideas, his fresh and verdant pictures of nature, his criticisms on poetry, on politics—his native and unsought flattery of ourselves, until night drew on, and we were forced to return to the Castle, charmed, seduced, conquered, subdued. Adela was beside me. Led away by some idle words of his, in admiration of my person, and of my ideas, which were his own, I was about to throw myself on her bosom, and confess my sudden and guileless passion, when the artless child, all blushes and confusion, told me that she had lost her heart. My brain seemed to stop its action—my heart ceased beating. My head whirled, and I was struck dumb. Good heavens! I thank thee, for next day 'twas clear which had won his affection. And now the Duke is uniting their hands—"

"Miranda! Miranda!" cried a voice without, "open, love, to your friend."

"Here she comes," said the Countess, with a deep sigh, "to tell her joy, her happiness. But be silent, my weak heart. I come."

Next moment Adela entered, having dismissed her maid at the door.

"All tears and trembling!" cried Miranda, with a smile, and drawing her friend to a seat; "come! come! what ails this little lovelorne thing?"

"He is lost to me for ever," replied Adela, weeping.

"What say you?" said the Countess, with a look of terror; for she dreaded, above all, a futile gleam of hope for herself.

"My father, who never was kinder, has shown us that our union, we so fondly hoped he approved of, is impossible."

"Impossible!" was all Miranda could reply, so tumultuous were the thoughts which crowded upon her.

Adela, as well as she was able, explained the impediment which existed.

"You pledged to another? but this is most unjust, most cruel!" said Miranda, generously; "this comes of rash vows, registered when those they concerned were unconscious children. It can never be."

"So earnest is my father," replied Adela, "that he spoke of Charles paying his court to you."

Miranda shuddered; but by one of those violent efforts of dissimulation, of which we are capable on emergency, she let not the slightest trace of her agitation be seen upon her face, and spoke with a calmness which was astounding, when the state of her mind is considered.

"And Master Charles turned up his scornful lip," she said, with a smile—"the little insolent. Pride, child, will have a fall; 'tis time, when the Clements disdain the Castelmontes."

"But Charles is almost a Ravilliere," said Adela, pouting.

. "I know it," continued the Italian, laughing with all her full rich tones, "and will be quite one yet. Believe me, Dame Fortune will not be so unjust to true love as to give you to the dragoon of a cousin, in preference to the civilian. This is a time when wonders are to be expected, and since the soldier knows you not, and still will have you willy-nilly, we must wage war upon him."

"Cradle me not with hope, dear friend," exclaimed Adela; who, however, could not, despite herself, resist the lively tones of the Countess.

"Have a good heart, sweet cousin," cried Miranda, taking her hands, "we are two women, with one man to stand by us, if not two. Strange changes have come upon things, if we cannot conquer one. I have a head, Adela, which will not tire to do you service, even to the wedding of this bearded cousin myself, for which purpose I shall to-morrow remove to my hotel by the Louvre, and commence the campaign."

"Dear Miranda!" said Adela, more gravely than was her wont, "nothing of all this would be needful, had not my father passed his word. I love Charles—ay, you know, dear friend, that I do, most dearly; but I am not one of those children who will reward eighteen years of kindness by thwarting his will now. I will wed this man, whom I have never seen, if my father bids me—for he has promised by word of mouth and in writing, and the promise holds good for me, his child—and then I will die, and fade away from the earth, leaving behind me the hope that you and he I love so well may together bless my memory."

"Child!" exclaimed Miranda, almost choked by her sensations, "that can never be. Charles loves you, and love in such men as him is no idle thing. Besides, there is no need to be so down-hearted. You are not married yet. Things may not be so serious as they look, and then your father will delay this union. Come now, go to rest; you need it."

"First let me breathe the fresh air," said Adela, approaching the window which overlooked the court.

The Countess followed her friend, in time to catch a glimpse of one who, wrapped in a cloak, and his hat drawn over his eyes, passed beneath the *porte cochère*, and departed along the Rue St. Dominique.

It was Charles Clements, who, after a brief conversation with the Duke, departed to give vent, alone, to his grief.

Adela moved from the window immediately, for he was gone.

---

## CHAPTER IX.

### GRACCHUS ANTIBOUL.

WHEN Charles Clement left the Duke's house, and hurried in the direction of his own home, he was at first overwhelmed with grief and despair. The shock he had received was a violent one, coming as it did after those happy hours spent in her company, when under the influence of gentle and frank affection, he had forgotten all save love. Soon after, however, he gained the street, the morning air—for it was past one—playing upon his heated brow, and his powerful intellect coming to his aid, he became more calm. Reflection showed him that nothing was yet lost. The Count had not appeared; that of itself was something. Then the times were troublous, and the nobleman might be averse to taking upon himself the burden of a wife, when, perhaps, the next day he would have to fly. If, however, he failed, still Charles Clement vowed unto himself not to lose heart. There was his country to love and strive for.

But love is egotistical. Despite his utmost philosophy, the young republican felt that this was an event—the total loss of Adela—which would leave for France but the strenuous determination to do his duty, with but little of the power. At all events, he thought so, for he knew not that time heals up the very wounds we fain would seek to keep open. Luxuriate we in our grief as we may, it passes; and the sorrow of the autumn fades before that of the spring, like one picture after another in a diorama—the deeper the more transient. All things have exceptions, but such is the rule of humanity.

Even death, which wrings from us those joys that curl round our hearts—our little ones, angels flitting upon earth—strikes but for a time. We forget not the sacred dead, but we weep not, we wail not, for grief has commenced the work of time, and our feelings become hardened. The waters, not of oblivion, but of hope and resignation, sweep over the heaving sea of our souls, and we pursue our way, no longer rejoicing, no longer light and merry, but chastened and calm.

Presently, the recollection of the *émeute* in the Faubourg St. Antoine recurring to his memory, Charles Clement bethought himself of his servant; and somewhat anxious to know what chance had placed Torticolis in that position, hurried still more rapidly home. Suddenly raising his eyes, he found himself at the foot of the Pont Neuf.

It was a dark night; not a soul appeared in the streets. Charles pushed on, and had gained the statue of Henry the Fourth, not yet pulled down, when his attention was roused by the voice of a man singing. The tones were rich and full, and the subject such as to at once call forth all the listening faculties of our hero :—

> "Vive le Tiers-Etat de la France !
> Il aura la prépondérance
> Sur le prince, sur le prélat ;
> Ahi ! povera nobilita."

At this stage of the singer's patriotic verse, he had neared Charles Clement.

"Monsieur le Songster," said the young republican, politely, "might I trouble you for the hour?"

"Half-past one, time for bed," replied the musical youth —for he, too, was young. And then, without further remark, he continued :—

> "Je vois s'agiter la bannière
> J'entends partout sa cris de guerre,
> Vive l'ordre du Tiers-Etat ;
> Ahi ! povera nobilita."

"Your song is somewhat rough," remarked Charles, who was striving hard to gain a glimpse of the other's face —the voice not appearing strange.

"Like the subject," said the young man, laconically—

> "Le plébéien, puits de science,
> En lumière, en expérience
> Surpasse et prêtres et magistrats ;
> Ahi ! povera nobilita."

"We will suppose I were a noble," remarked Charles Clement, endeavouring to lead the other into conversation.

"But you are not," replied the other ; and then he continued—

> "Je vois parles dans nos tribunes,
> Six cents orateurs des communes,
> Comme Fox ou Gracque au sénat ;
> Ahi ! povera nobilita."

"I knew you by that *trait*," said Charles, warmly ; "Jacques Antiboul, your hand."

"Charles Clement, my boy," cried the other, seizing hold of the young man's two shoulders, "why, are you, too, in Paris?"

"Yes; and by what chance do I meet you? In what capacity are you here?"

"Waiting on providence," said the songster. "I expect great things will be done, and perhaps may do my *mite*."

"Jacques," exclaimed Charles, "this is a pleasure, indeed. You, my college chum, my aider and abetter in all plans of revolution and democracy; if I have lost a wife, I have found a friend."

"Lost a what?" said Antiboul, with an expression of the most rich tragic comedy.

"My dear friend," replied Charles, gravely, "this is no

matter for joking. We will speak of it presently; perhaps you will serve me in the matter. But the hour is late, where live you?"

"Rue St. Denis."

"At no great distance from me. Are you disposed to give me an hour?"

"Two, or at a pinch, six," replied Jacques, with a laugh, "so you exact payment at once. I accept the more willingly that I live in a garret, have no attendance, and am for the nonce, as free of superabundant cash as Joseph when he went to Egypt."

"Jacques—"

"Excuse me," interposed Antiboul, "but I have just left a re-union of patriots, who meet in the Antre Bouche-feu, and we have agreed to drop all names which reminds us of our ' ancient antique notions.' I, myself, have an objection to Jacques, it reminds me of Haute-pas and la Boucherie, both named after my saint. It rises in my gorge."

"Still the same," said Charles, shaking his head, " still the same. Will you never learn, my friend, that religion and liberty are inseparable?"

"They have been divorced a long time then," rejoined Antiboul, who was incorrigible on this point.

"Because superstition and trading in religion have introduced abuses—because, flying the mysteries and mummeries, the follies and errors of Popery, you surrender your reason to a grinning philosopher, instead of seeking a purer, simpler, and more truthful faith."

"You persevere in your Protestantism," laughed Antiboul, "and in your enmity to Voltaire, who was a great man."

"Not so great but that he assumed the quackish cloak of irreligion to be remarked, as men of small stature wear high-heeled boots; but let us not dispute. Your name is now—"

"Gracchus Antiboul," replied the other, with intense gravity.

"And who gave it you?" inquired Charles, laughing.

"A certain dirty high-priest of liberty, a Monsieur Marat, who does not want for ideas," continued Gracchus.

"Well, brother Gracchus, will you to my lodging? I

have a man sitting up, who will doubtless have a warm fire,
an excellent supper, a supply of wine, several choice pipes,
and some Lafayette tobacco—true republican leaf."

" And, pray, whence fished you all this?" exclaimed the
ex-medical student—for such was Antiboul—pausing in his
walk.

" My dear Jac—Gracchus, I mean—I have inherited a
fortune."

" Is there another to be picked up? if so, send it my
way.  But spoke you not of a wife?  You have not sold
yourself for vile lucre?" ejaculated the other, with ludi-
crous fervour.

" *Mon ami*," said Charles, gravely, " it is to relate to you
my sorrows—to pour open my heart to my early friend—
that I invite you now.  I am still under the shock of an
announcement which I can scarce believe true.  I seek to
hold up, to hope, to be courageous; but when the excitement is over, I shall, I fear, go mad."

" Old story, I suppose," exclaimed Antiboul, carelessly—
" the fair prefers another."

" No!" replied Charles, boldly, this very word giving him
a secret joy.  " I have every reason to think myself by no
means disagreeable to her I love."

" Still older story then; ogre of a papa—tyranny, forced
union with another—and you are suffering from this antique
failing?"

" Again are you wrong," replied Charles, with a slight
feeling of pride.

" *Baste!*" cried Gracchus, " I cease my guesses, for to
suppose Charles Clement in love with another man's wife—"

" I thank you, Antiboul," said Charles, shaking him by
the hand, " you do me justice.  I am neither a thief nor a
knave.  But I will explain all.  In the mean time, I must
tell you that I am reconciled with my noble relatives."

" Sorry for it—no good—*aristocrané!*"

" Gracchus, you are wrong; the Duke—"

" *Aristocroc!*" said Antiboul, using the words already in
circulation, as derisive epithets of nobility—

" Is an excellent old man, while the Countess Adela—"

" *Aristocruche!*"

" And the Lady Miranda!"

"*Aristocrosse!*"

"My dear Gracchus," said Charles, somewhat impatiently, "do you want me to quarrel with you?"

"I never quarrel with my bread and butter," replied Gracchus.

"What *do* you mean?"

"Have you not asked me to supper? besides, I have gained my object.   Which of the two is the fair one?"

"The Lady Adela," said Charles, with a sigh.

"Serious?" inquired Gracchus, tapping his friend's side.

"Antiboul," exclaimed Clement, gravely, "I never before asked you to view a question gravely; it is not your nature. But are you for once disposed to listen to my case seriously, and give me your advice and assistance?"

"My advice is at any man's service, my assistance I rarely offer.   You shall have all I am capable of giving, but it it must be after my own fashion.   By the way, is the Countess Miranda engaged?"

"Why?" said Charles, startled.

"Because, perhaps, the lovely aristocrat might suit my taste, and I am sufficiently a republican to sacrifice on the altar of my country to the public weal."

"The Countess Miranda is not engaged," replied Charles, dryly; "but as far as I can judge, she will be difficult to please—that is, I know not——"

"Charles," said Gracchus, as dryly, "are you in love with both, or are you ready to fall in love with Miranda, if Adela should be torn from you?"

"No," exclaimed the young man, warmly;   "I adore Adela, and if you can win her fair friend's affections, shall be most happy."

"Agreed, then," replied Gracchus, "and to-morrow you will introduce me.   After supper, you shall put me in possession of all the circumstances—that is, all you know; the rest I will find out for myself at an early opportunity."

"Agreed, and here is my door," said Charles; "my servant has kept up—I see a light burning.   The *restaurateurs* of the Palais Royal are open all night now, so supper can be improvised."

"Thanks to liberty," exclaimed Gracchus; "patriots watch night and day, and patriots must live."

The door here opened, Jean Torticolis having been on the watch. The two young men entered, and in a few words Charles, having given his instructions, the crick-neck hastened with wondrous alacrity to obey them. The friends then took the light and went up stairs.

The apartments occupied by Charles Clement was composed of a dining-room, sitting-room, a double-bedded bed-room, and *cabinet*, which Torticolis slept in. The whole was neatly furnished, as far as all bachelors' residences, who have not half a-dozen servants, can be.

"Pretty well for a republican," said Gracchus, with a slight frown. He was thinking of his garret, his fireless chimney, his cold nights that winter past, and other of those sufferings which poverty engenders, and which are doubly felt by those who have known better things.

"Pretty well," replied Charles, who had been watching his countenance; "and such as it is, I offer you half. In that room you will find a bed; there is a second arm-chair, while Torty, who is a republican *enragé*, will do double duty."

"Charles," said Gracchus, gravely, "I cannot accept. I am poor, but I am proud."

"*Au diable* with your pride! are we not brother students, friends, republicans? and must we not aid and assist one another? Besides, I shall henceforth be much at home, and your company will be necessary to keep me from desponding."

"If Charles—" began Gracchus, seriously; but he could not help it—he sank into a chair, and sobbed like a child.

"My dear fellow!" cried Charles—

"Clement," exclaimed Antiboul, after a short pause, "I accept, and never shall I forget, or you have cause to repent your generosity. Away with scruples; poverty is no crime. If I have been brought up to a profession—if I have no means to perfect my studies—to find patients—it is not my fault, but that of society, which looks not to my talents, my fitness, but to my father's name, or who has already employed me. I am the victim of aristocracy, Charles; every place is taken up by the vermin, because they have friends, names, and are of the grand union of knaves who play upon the credulity of mankind, persuading them that they have ancestors older than Adam ; that their blood is purer than that of low-bred merchants, greasy traders, impertinent shopkeepers, sweating artizans, whom they do too much honour to when they kiss their wives, eat their bacon, run in their debt, and break their backs by labour."

" Gracchus addressing the Antre Bouche-feu !" exclaimed Charles, laughing.

" Ah, laugh, thou monster-vampire, representative of society," said Antiboul, rising, " look at these shoes, sole-less, and guiltless of buckles, which have gone the way of all silver ; these darned and used stockings ; this once brown, now russet pair of *culottes*, which promise shortly to make me a *sans-culotte ;* this dirty linen, aged coat, and older *veste ;* this *chapeau* of three seasons since, and this antique cloak which once warmed the shoulders of some Spanish vagabond.  Look at all this and weep, Brutus, for in me you see France !"  And Gracchus Antiboul danced a pirouette to make more visible the penury of his garb.

Ere he had done speaking, Charles had flown to a ward-robe, had taken out, from a numerous collection of new clothes, bought upon the strength of his heritage, a com-plete suit, and laid it before the astounded orator, with the most charming little sword too, that would have delighted the heart of a Marquis.

" Now Charles, just be frank," said Gracchus ; "are these for me ?"

" Decidedly."

" Then bolt your door on the inside.  Since I am to dwell with you, there is no occasion for your man perceiv-ing my tattered garb.  Be you quick, or the knave will be back, and judge me by these tapers, which he could not do in the obscurity of your hall."

Charles laughingly complied ; while Gracchus, with a rapidity which did infinite credit to his education, stripped off his rags, and began assuming the elegant costume which his friend had provided for him.  When Clement returned, he was tying the knot of his cravat, after combing down his exuberant locks.

" Perfect," said Charles ; " they fit you to a nicety."

" They suit me, at all events," replied Gracchus ; and,

picking up the whole of his former garb, shoes, stockings, shirt, cloak, coat, breeches, he unceremoniously piled them on the blazing logs of the fire, and began thrusting them towards the back with the shovel.

"I must not spare your beech trees," he continued, hiding them with fresh pieces of wood.

" But you will put the fire out," said Charles, who was choking with laughter.

" Not a bit of it ; it will damp it a bit at first, but it will burn up directly.  Hush, here's your *officieux*, for servant is not republican.

" ' Vive le Tiers Etat de la France,' " &c.

Charles, stifling his laughter, opened, and Torticolis appeared, followed by two waiters, one carrying the supper, the second the desert, while the crick-neck bore the wine. In five minutes after, the attendants had vanished, and the two friends were seated before their meal, with Jean ready to serve them.

" Do you sup this way every night ? " said Gracchus, moving somewhat uneasily, for he was slightly stouter than Charles.

" Somewhat better of late," replied the young republican; "for this month past, I have stayed every evening at the Duke's.  In fact, I have already eaten myself, but when one meets an old friend, one cannot refuse to do double duty."

" *Peste !* " cried Gracchus, winking behind the back of Jean, " I rather fancy I have an appetite.  That cold fowl looks tempting, while this tongue is delicious ; as for these cutlets—but wait awhile, I will do justice to all.  Besides, I have a long story to hear."

" First let me question you.  If the grief you spoke of "—a wink at Jean also from Charles—" be so strong upon you, how came you to sing so merrily when I met you ? "

" My grief was none of my own making," said Gracchus, between two mouthfuls; " if my aunt—those barbarians of England, say my uncle—has perished, it was no fault of mine.  I gave her all I had—but what are you laughing at ? "

' Nothing," replied Clement, who was, however, sniffing an odour of burnt cloth and rags.

"Jean," exclaimed Gracchus, just as that worthy was about to turn towards the fire, " the burgundy."

" Monsieur has it in his hand," answered Jean.

" The deuce take it ! "

"So I have," cried Antiboul; and then, as if able to restrain himself no longer ; " but harken, Jean, I am a poor devil of an old friend, whom your master found starving, ragged, almost homeless, and whom he has clothed, fed, and given lodging to ; there is the long and the short of it. Now, if you think any the worse of me, you are welcome."

" You are not an aristocrat ? " inquired Jean, his little eye twinkling.

"Heaven forbid !" exclaimed Gracchus, stopping Clement's mouth, who, recovered from his first surprise, was about to speak.

" Then I can love you next to my master," replied Jean, radiant.

" So you love your master?" said Antiboul, still imposing silence on his friend.

" I do," replied Torticolis, with a fervour which was not feigned.

" Why ? "

" Because first he fed, and clothed, and sheltered me, as he did you, Monsieur."

"Jean," said Clement, severely, for he feared Antiboul might be offended.

" Go on, Jean ; mind what I say, we are all republicans here," smiled Gracchus.

" Secondly, because at the peril of his liberty, perhaps of his life, he saved me this night from a prison and an ignominious death."

"What !" exclaimed Gracchus, jumping up and seizing Torticolis by the two hands, "you are one of the *emeutiers* whom Marat spoke of at the meeting. Jean, I am your friend for ever."

"Antiboul," said Clement, gravely, " you do not mean to encourage this man in pillaging and rioting, by which the sacred cause of liberty will be brought into disgrace now and for ever."

"You do not mean to assert that the people have no right to use force!" exclaimed Gracchus, reseating himself, while Jean remained standing, his head bowed, and showing signs of the utmost compunction.

"Certainly not," continued Clement; "and if needed, I will give my last drop of blood in the cause of freedom; but these anarchical attacks on individuals are crimes, and crimes which merit condign punishment. But take you some supper, Jean, and eat; when we have done, you can tell us how this came about."

"Meanwhile, stir up my friperie—*nom d'un diable!*" he thundered, rising, as two slight reports were heard, and a dense cloud of smoke filled the room.

"Why, in heaven's name!" cried Clement, "what is that?"

"Oh! oh! oh!" screamed Gracchus, rolling in his chair, in an agony of laughter; "I forgot the two ball-cartridges in my coat-pocket."

"And may I ask what my friend Gracchus wanted with ball-cartridges?" said Charles, demurely.

"We make a distribution at the *Antre Bouche-jéu*, in case of accidents," replied Antiboul; "but let us finish supper, and take to our pipes, when your *officieux* can relate his adventures."

This was agreed upon, and for a few moments the friends were silent; but no sooner were their appetites sufficiently satisfied, than they drew near the fire, lit their long pipes, of English manufacture, made Jean draw their table near the hearth, and then disposed themselves to listen.

The crick-neck, concealing only his own private affairs, and what he had heard concerning the robbery, related the whole of what passed in the spies' den, as well as what occurred in the Faubourg St. Antoine. Both Charles and Gracchus, though fully aware of the importance of the revelations they heard, were silent until he had concluded.

"Jean," said Clement, when he ceased, "not a word of this. I shall denounce all in due form to the Assembly."

"And I to the Palais-Royal!" exclaimed Gracchus; "but now is your turn. Jean, put on another log, and retire; we can dispense with your services."

"The more so, that you must be tired," added Clement;

"but mind you, be no more led away into such projects. You were serving the cause of aristocracy and reaction."

"I see so now, Monsieur," replied Torticolis, humbly.

"That will do, go to bed and sleep," continued Charles; and as soon as they were alone, turning to Gracchus, he said, "Now then, Antiboul, for my confession."

"My pipe is full, my ears open, my understanding awake," responded Gracchus; and our hero, without farther preface, related all the matters of which the reader is already aware. His friend gave his undivided attention, without interrupting by a single remark.

"Difficult position decidedly," he exclaimed, as soon as the narrative had ended; "but as you love the girl, and she appears worthy of it, something must be done. Thank your stars for sending me to your assistance; for if in these troublous times I do not circumvent your noble rival, my name is not Gracchus Antiboul. I have fourteen ways of getting rid of a rival. Leave me to my reflections—go to bed and dream. I will reflect beside your hearth. A warm blaze, a genial bottle, a cosy pipe, are things so strange to me, I cannot quit them for my couch. As for you, you have to appear before a lady to-morrow, and must drive that heavy look out of your eyes."

"I own I am weary," replied Charles, yawning, "but I cannot leave you alone."

"I want to commence operations at once," insisted Gracchus, "so to bed. Your late supper and wine will make you sleep like Simon Pierre Malisset, Jacques Donatieu le Ray de Chaumont, Pierre Rousseau, and Bernard Perruchot, after they had drawn up the *pacte de famine*, by which they starve France, and fatten individually;—go to bed."

Charles Clement did not require much pressing. His long day, his ride to Vincennes, his ramble in the forest, his agitations of the evening, had completely exhausted him; so that on Gracchus insisting, he retired, after seeing that his friend was amply provided with all he required.

No sooner was our hero gone, and Antibould conceived that he was safely under cover of his alcove, than he rose and entered the cabinet of Torticolis, who awoke with a start.

Gracchus laid his finger on his lips.

"Rise," he whispered gravely, "I have much to say to you. I perceive you love your master. So do I. We must then work together."

Torticolis obeyed, and in a few minutes stood by Antiboul in the dining-room.

"Sit down, take a pipe, fill a glass—I am a republican *sans-façons*, and intend we shall be called *sans-culottes*—and then answer me a few questions."

"I am ready," said Jean, upon whom the other's commanding manners imposed much.

"What was it you concealed from us in your narrative?" asked Gracchus, fixing his eye steadily on the other.

"But, Monsieur, how know you I hid anything?" stammered Torticolis.

"Because I had my eye upon you while you spoke," said Gracchus, quietly; "and mark me, Jean, your master is in a painful position, one from which I wish to extricate him. The more I know, the easier my task. You must aid me. To know and trust you, I must know your history, your secrets."

"I will tell you all," exclaimed Torticolis, after a long pause; and then, without hesitation, he poured forth the history of his life, up to that night. He had not gone far before Gracchus's eye kindled, then he rubbed his hands, refilled his pipe, and inhaled its vapour with vast unction; then he bit his nails, ground his teeth, to keep himself from interruption; but when Jean had concluded, his delight knew no bounds.

"There are fourteen ways of getting rid of a rival, I said," he cried clapping his hands, while the astounded crick-neck looked on in astonishment; "*foi de Brutus!* I have found one."

"May I know it?" said Jean anxiously.

"Not now; go to bed, take a good sleep, and to-morrow we will commence operations."

---

# CHAPTER X.

## THE BREAKFAST

WHEN Charles Clement and his friend Gracchus Antiboul

met on the following morning, and were about to order their morning meal, the former received a note which had been left soon after dawn.

" It smells of aristocracy a yard off," said Gracchus, laughing, and pointing to the missive.

" It is from my uncle," replied Charles, turning pale and red by turns; " doubtless a hint to keep away."

" Read, man—read; faith of Brutus, you seem more afraid of this *poulet* than you would be of a cannon-ball," laughed Gracchus. " Babouc at a dinner-party in Persepolis had not a more puzzled countenance."

" It is a most pressing invitation," said Charles, blushing, " for me to breakfast with them this morning. The Duke is most affectionate, most kind."

" Pity the old mummy, he is such a stickler for promises, especially made twenty years ago."

" His word is his life," said Charles, reproachfully ; " but this invitation——"

" Let us accept it, of course," replied Gracchus, with the most perfect assumption of innocence.

" Us ? "

" My dear boy, are we not henceforth Pylades and Orestes? am I not your jackal, too, in this affair?—Who knows ? Besides, I am not in love ; and I may see things which you do not, and help to get rid of this rival."

" Let us go, then, at once," said Charles ; who, though his position was so much changed towards Adela, still longed to be with her.

Those who love, hope on—hope ever. Nothing but death or actual union with one another removes the halo of illusion from the mind of man, when his affections are sincerely engaged. Charles, shocked as we have described him, yet felt none of the despondency of the previous night. His conversation with Antiboul had rekindled hope, for his wishes were on the same side with the snug goddess of Pandora's box.

Having made a hurried addition to their toilet, and sent Jean for a vehicle, the friends entered therein, and drove hurriedly towards the Rue Dominique.

" My first entrance into the den of oligarchy," said Gracchus, as they arrived before the hotel of the Duke.

"Now, my dear friend," replied Charles, deprecatingly, "recollect that the Duke is my uncle,— that you are about to be introduced to two charming women of the highest rank—"

"Ta! ta! ta! ta!" cried Antiboul, "am I not, first of all, a Frenchman?"

"And no bad specimen of one," said Charles, surveying with pleasure the powerful but handsome figure of his friend.

"But let us enter," cried Gracchus, gravely. "I saw at yonder window a peeping face; I warrant me it was the young Countess Adela."

Charles made no reply, but entered the spacious court-yard, ascended the steps, passed through the door which opened before them, and was ushered with Antiboul into the saloon where his friends and breakfast awaited Clement.

"My dear uncle," said the latter, after bowing to the ladies, and exchanging a half tender glance with Adela, "when I received your note, I had with me a friend who was about to share with me my morning repast. As I could neither dismiss my friend, nor refuse your invitation, I have taken the liberty——"

"My dear nephew, every friend of yours is doubly welcome, for yours and for his own sake," replied the Duke, whom the presence of a stranger seemed considerably to relieve, as likely to avoid a painful topic of conversation.

"I must introduce, then, to you, Gracchus Antiboul; like myself, I am afraid, a terrible revolutionist, but——"

"Like yourself, I hope, not wholly impracticable," put in the Countess Miranda, who saw the necessity of taking up the conversation, which neither the Duke nor Adela were as yet capable of sustaining.

"I am afraid I am very far gone," said Antiboul, accepting a seat which was offered him by the side of the lively Italian.

"Not more so than your friend is in reality," continued Miranda.

"I do not know that," added Gracchus: "a divided mind is scarce fit for political service. I doubt me, but the *denos* will lose my friend, bound in the chains of fascinating oligarchy.

"You are Clement's confidant I see," said Miranda, in a low tone, while her eyes fell upon the Sèvres plate before her.

"Hum," replied Gracchus, sinking his voice also, "we are old schoolfellows."

"You know him well, then?" said Miranda, raising her eyes suddenly to the other's face.

"And love him more than a brother," exclaimed Antiboul. "But none can do any other. Clement is generous, noble, exalted in mind, humble in heart, warm in his sympathies, and knows not what self means."

"You are a flatterer," said Miranda, merrily.

"No," said Antiboul, gravely; "I leave that vice for courtiers—I am a grateful friend."

The Countess took the young man's hand, and shook it heartily, with all the Italian fervour of her soul.

"Clement is fortunate," she said, and continued her breakfast.

Meanwhile the Duke, Charles, and Adela, had been receiving some account of the early days of friendship when they, as students, lived together in Paris. Clement remembering those happy days, forgot for a moment his private sorrows, and grew eloquent in his descriptions of the strange life he led then, as now, by the aspirants for legal, medical, and other honours.

Not that the students were, as now, all smokers, half-idlers, with incredible hats, polished boots, frilled fronts, no shirts, with gold-headed canes, and empty stomachs; but they were then, as now, a jovial race, full of the fire of classic lore, hating restraint, looking on authority as tyranny, and republicans to a man.

"If there be movement," said the Duke, "the *etudiants* will be troublesome."

"Very," put in Antiboul, drily.

"Not more so than any other class," added Charles.

At this moment a carriage drove into the court-yard. The Duke glanced his eye at the vehicle, and turned very pale.

"Count Leopold," he said, hesitating, while his eyes rested with pain on the grave countenance of Charles, and the fluttering half-pale, half-crimson of Adela.

Miranda neither moved nor showed sign of emotion, continuing her conversation with Antiboul, who appeared charmed with her grace and kindness of manner.

In another moment the Count Leopold was announced. The whole company rose. Adela moved involuntarily nearer to Charles, and their eyes met. A world of tenderness and hope against the worst was in the glance. Antiboul surveyed the enemy with an impassive examination, that concealed not some little of contempt. Miranda appeared utterly indifferent. The Duke alone was embarrassed in his mien.

"Good morrow to you," said the Count, a handsome man, but of sinister and fatigued aspect, though young; "to you, my uncle, I need scarce apologise; but hearing of your arrival in Paris, I have come to ask you for a bed and board. You will excuse the rudeness of a soldier, but I have come with bag and baggage."

"You have not mistaken me, nephew," replied the Duke, in a tone which was nearly frigid; "but allow me to introduce to you your cousin Charles Clement, and his friend, Gracchus Antiboul."

"My cousin!" said the Count, seating himself unceremoniously, while his eyes were fixed impertinently on one whom, at a glance, he recognised as a rival.

"Your father's sister's son," replied the Duke.

"I never had the pleasure of meeting you, cousin," exclaimed the Count, with something of soldierly frankness; "but I am very happy."

Charles Clement bowed, and there followed one of those painful pauses, which occur so often in society when there is one too many present.

"A soldier, and of the Royal Allemand," said the Countess Miranda, anxious to keep up the conversation, "you must be able to give us some good news?"

"None, Countess, none; save that measures are nearly ready for crushing the *canaille* of the *Tiers-Etat*, who are playing the part of little kings in Versailles."

"You said *canaille*, I think?" said Gracchus, very quietly.

"I did, monsieur," repeated the soldier, somewhat insolently.

"Ah!" said Antiboul, and he turned away to continue his breakfast.

"But what measures?" inquired the Duke.

"I cannot exactly explain," said Count Leopold, "as I am not in the secret; but you don't suppose the fomentors of such disorders as occurred last night, and which I assisted in repressing, are to be allowed to go on insulting the monarch and the nobles."

"And so the *Tiers-Etat* fomented the troubles of last night?" asked Antiboul.

"Of course," said the Count, positively.

"It is very odd," continued Antiboul.

"Why, monsieur, if you please?"

"Because the police were the leaders, and I scarcely think M. Ducrosne in the service of the *Tiers-Etat*."

"Nonsense!" said the Count, drily, while the rest listened.

"No nonsense, *Monsieur le Comte*," added Gracchus; "for a certain secret agent, a certain priest, a certain prince, and a certain officer, were at the bottom of it all."

"*Ma foi!*" said the Count, who looked angry and excited, "this is rank treason."

"The truth generally is," replied Gracchus Antiboul, with a gravity which he seemed to have assumed for the day.

"But let these riots be police-schemes or not," said the soldier, "the *Tiers-Etats* are on their last legs."

"*Monsieur le Comte*," exclaimed Gracchus, quietly, "the monarchy is far more nearly in the same predicament; but let us not discuss politics before the ladies."

"Bravo!" said Miranda, rising; "and, as the morning is fine, Adela will allow me to propose a walk in the garden of the hotel."

"Go, go!" exclaimed the old Duke; "here is Germain coming with a packet of letters."

Adela kissed her father; and then, in a few moments, the whole party were in the garden.

Antiboul, by an adroit movement, had forced Count Leopold to precede him, so that Charles Clement remained with Miranda and Adela in the rear.

The garden was lovely in the extreme. Though narrow, it was of considerable length, like many others in the Faubourg St. Germain. Lofty trees shaded a long alley that led, from the steps of the hotel, to the high wall separating it from another of similar character.

"An excellent shooting gallery," said Gracchus Antiboul, surveying it with the eye of a connoisseur.

"Do you shoot?" replied the Count, with somewhat of a sneer, while his glance was wholly given to the ladies who hung on the young lawyer's arm.

"Would you like to shoot against me, Captain?" was Antiboul's answer.

"I have several pistols up-stairs," cried the Count, piqued at his tone.

"If these ladies will allow us," said Gracchus, with the bow and smile of a courtier.

"We shall have great pleasure in playing the part of umpires, and in awarding the prize."

"André," cried the Count to a servant, of dull but cunning mien, who stood beneath a side portico, "go to the chamber which has been assigned to me as mine, and bring me down my box of arms."

"You are amply provided," said Gracchus, who was measuring the distance with his eye.

"I am a soldier," answered the Count, haughtily.

"Civilization has made of it a noble profession," put in Charles, mildly, "while it is the least glorious. To defend one's country is great—is good, but the hired combatter is but one reduced to a sad and brutal necessity to get his living."

"Sir," said the Count, contemptuously, "what profession or trade do you reckon nobler?"

"I mean no offence," continued Charles, mildly, "as I speak but settled convictions; but any is nobler—more glorious. The merchant-sailor, ploughing the sea in search of employment and sustenance for the poor; the physician, healing the sufferings of the sick; the man of God, preaching and teaching good; the penman, spreading light and knowledge where was darkness and death; the legislator, making laws, not for the wants of a class, but for his country—are sublime beside the soldier, who takes life, and whose trade it is to make widows and orphans."

"You are against war, of course," said the Count.

"My reason and heart both are, but I know it is a sad

necessity.  I am sufficient of a politician to know that universal peace is the Utopia of a dreamer.  Still, let not those who sell their blood, as lawyers do their brains, for money, be held in too high honour."

"Monsieur is not a soldier," said the Count, with eye kindling.

"Here is the arsenal," put in Gracchus, who feared an explosion of a premature character between the rivals.

As he spoke, André laid at their feet a small box containing a large assortment of pistols.

"May I choose? " said Gracchus, with a bow.

"With pleasure," replied the soldier.

"You are well supplied," observed Gracchus, laying the whole stock upon a rustic bench, and showing a boyish alacrity and curiosity which puzzled Charles Clement; "here are seven pair and an odd one."

"Make your choice," said the Count, taking up a pair which, though handsome enough in that day, would now be looked on as gothic.

"But the prize?" put in Antiboul.

"Whatever you please."

"Choose the odd pistol," whispered Gracchus to Miranda, while Count Leopold loaded his arms.

"A strange choice for a lady," said the Countess, subjugated by the tone and expression of the young man; "but if I be umpire, I will select the odd pistol as the prize of the victor."

"I accept," said Gracchus Antiboul, quietly.

The Count saw that the priming of his pistol was right, and then bowed acquiescence in the desires of those around him.  Gracchus then advanced to the end of the avenue and placed a board upright against it, on which he chalked several circles.

"How many shots?" said he, after measuring twenty paces on the avenue.

"Twelve," replied the Count.

The soldier and the young man took up their position— the former having the first fire.

"A good shot," said Antiboul, with a half-patronising air, "but not a perfect one."

He then fired, and his ball struck the very centre of the mark.

"A good shot," said Charles, much surprised ; "but how is this, Gracchus? students are not generally such good marksmen."

"I shoot for a great purpose," replied Antiboul, gravely ; while the soldier, visibly piqued, took again a steady and assured aim.

But it was in vain, and at the end of the trial agreed on, Gracchus was unanimously declared the victor.

"Had I known," said the Count, quietly, though within a very tempest was raging, "I would not have contended against one so perfect in the art. Where have you served. monsieur?"

"The master I am to serve has not yet appeared upon the scene," replied Antiboul.

"And that master?"

"Is the people."

"The people!" said the Count, much surprised.

"The people, a body very little heard of as yet, but one of which history will, by and by, have also its tale.

"But the prize," said Miranda, holding up the odd pistol——

"Is mine," exclaimed Gracchus, who took the weapon with visible delight ; "I have fairly won it."

"You value it?" smiled the Count.

"More than can be imagined," said the student, with a laugh ; "it is a trophy of a great victory."

"You have, it appears, been used to small contests," sneered the nobleman.

"I have, but this is a great one," said Gracchus.

"Explain yourself," said Charles Clement, who viewed his friend uneasily, for he really thought him mad.

"Not now. My meaning would as yet be indistinct ; but let us walk."

The ladies readily acquiesced. Clement took Adela's arm. Miranda advanced between Antiboul and the Count ; and for more than an hour the party wandered through the charming garden of the hotel, talking of those ordinary trifles which make up the sum and substance of common conversation—conversation often more interesting than more pretentious and serious communion between man and man, and woman and woman.

## CHAPTER XI.

### THE CAFE FOY.

THE *café* Foy was one of the principal centres of the talk of the day. Here crowded the enthusiastic, the hopeful, the lovers of liberty—the men whose voices and pens were engaged in pushing onward the coming struggle. Some came to read the *gazettes*, the "Journal des États Generaux"—the "Moniteur" was not yet in existence—but most to talk, to propose plans, to discuss the actions at Versailles. In those days the press was such an infant, that its records were old, when not incomplete and bare, and men could gather news only from word of mouth. This explains the eagerness with which groups gathered round those who had any details from Versailles—any personal narrative to tell—any letter to read.

It was seven in the evening. The *café* was full. Conversation was hot and loud. Rumours were afloat of the most varied and contradictory character, when Charles Clement and Gracchus Antiboul entered, after dining at the Duke's, and promising to return at a later hour.

"Give me the 'Journal des Etats Generaux,'" said Clement.

A silence followed this demand.

"It is suspended by order of the police," replied the *garçon*.

"Yes, *monsieur*," cried one in powdered wig, lace ruffles, red-heeled shoes, with sword, and silver buckler, "suspended, as our hopes are likely to be."

"How so?" cried Charles, while Antiboul's face became sombre.

"The court has stopped the action of the assembly," replied the Marquis de Saint Hurage, "and announced a *seance royale*."

"We are betrayed," said Gracchus, in a thrilling voice.

"Yes, young man; but this is not all. Troops pour down upon Paris and Versailles——"

"Let us be calm," interposed Charles Clement, gravely; "the position is difficult, and we must reason upon it. It is evident the counsellors of the crown are evil; his majesty is deceived, and our intentions are misrepresented.

Let us draw up a calm and firm remonstrance against those who are falsifying the true state of things, and persuading the king that our just demands are to be answered by the bayonets of foreign mercenaries."

"Bravo!" cried several.

"Yes! let us draw up a petition," cried Gracchus, "and let a hundred thousand armed men bear it to the foot of the throne; let us at once see the Austrian and her crew driven from the king's counsels, and the monarch and his only true advisers, the *mandataires* of the nation, be placed in friendly contact."

"Bravo!" exclaimed several others.

"My friend," continued Charles Clement, quietly, "is supposing an extreme case. If a great demonstration of the people be necessary to show the court that Paris has but one mind, it may be thought of; but a more pacific course had best first be tried."

At this moment a man hastily entered the *café*. He was heated, excited, and splashed with mud as after a long ride. As he was known, everybody crowded round him.

"What news from Versailles?" cried the Marquis de St. Hurage.

"We are betrayed—deceived," replied the other.

"Speak, man—explain. Who are the traitors?"

"This morning the assembly went as usual to their hall of meeting. They found it closed, and occupied by troops, and carpenters preparing for the royal *séance*."

"We are lost, if we act not," thundered Gracchus, in his student voice.

"But the members came pouring down. There was a tumult. Some, among whom were M. de Robespierre and other unknown deputies, proposed coming on foot to Paris."

"Glorious fellows!" cried Gracchus.

"Be still, my friends," said Charles, quite as excited, though with more command over himself.

"Others again proposed deliberating in the *Place d'Armes*, beneath the roof of the heavens."

"The only roof left for the people," muttered Antiboul.

"The people of Versailles crowded round; it was necessary to decide, when Bailly, and Guillotin, a doctor, proposed the *Jeu de Pansee*, which was accepted, and, amid the applause of multitudes who escorted them, they went thither."

"And then?"

"They went to that bare and naked hall—the sky lowering, the clouds pouring torrents, the thunder rolling—and swore with unanimity, save one, to live and die by the National Assembly, vowing never to separate until a constitution should have been obtained for France."

A roar of applause succeeded. The frequenters of the *café* crowded round the new arrival. Details were requested and given, and all saw that a struggle had begun between the ancient and the new *regime*.

"Let us deliberate," said the Marquis de St. Hurage, warmly.

"Let us act," replied Gracchus.

"There is wisdom in both counsels," exclaimed Charles Clement. "To act without deliberation would be madness, as deliberation unfollowed by action would be folly. My idea is to persevere in getting up, no longer a petition—that I scout, after what has passed—but a remonstrance. Let us give the evil advisers of the Crown warning. Let them see that if they have the army, we have Paris; that is, the wealth, intelligence, might, and centre, of the nation. The Assembly abandoned by us is powerless, and will fall; but backed by Paris, the very shade of feudalism will fly."

"Let us deliberate, then," continued Gracchus, bowing to his friend's will.

"Fly," said one, hastily entering the *café;* "a detachment of the *guet*, aided by a body of infantry, is coming to arrest what they call the conspirators of the *café Foy.*"

"Never," cried Gracchus, drawing, "let us defend ourselves."

The whole assemblage hesitated, though alarmed and astounded.

"Folly, worse than folly, guilty madness," said Charles Clement, dragging his friend back; "we shall be massacred without gain to our cause. What can a few swords do against the firearms of the *marechaussee* and soldiers? Every life lost here would be a head lost for liberty."

"But it would be perhaps the signal for the rising of Paris," insisted Gracchus.

"It would be the signal for filling Paris with troops, and dismissing the *Etats-Generaux*," replied Charles.

"True," cried the Marquis, also sheathing his sword, for he had drawn as well as Gracchus.

At this moment the tramp of the soldiers was heard in the gallery without, then a halt, and an officer entered.

But the occupants of the celebrated coffee-room were rapidly escaping by the issue leading into the neighbouring street, and not one was captured.

Charles Clement and Gracchus found themselves, after a few moments, alone in the Rue de Richelieu.

"A narrow escape of the Bastille," said Gracchus, with much of his usual gaiety.

"Very," replied Charles, kindly, "but more so of a useless death."

"True," said Antiboul; "my dear fellow, you are always right."

"Not always, but sometimes," continued our hero; "but our lives are too valuable to be lost in a row. If liberty needs a battle, let us be ready; but there was neither glory nor use in being massacred by an overwhelming force of mercenaries."

"Where go you?" inquired Antiboul, turning the subject."

"I return to the Rue Dominique, according to promise," said Charles Clement, in some surprise.

"Ah, yes, I recollect."

"I have double reasons," said Charles, with a deep and heartfelt sigh. "I promised the Duke, on my honour as a man, to warn him when the hour of danger was come, and it has arrived."

"You are right, Charles, the time of danger and the time of action. But will this not hasten this marriage?"

"It will," continued Clement, with a resigned quietness, which hurt his friend more than any passionate outburst of grief would have done; "but my duty is not changed; I love my sweet cousin, but she is another's."

"Not quite," said Gracchus, laconically.

"The Duke has given his word," answered Charles, calmly, "and she will marry a man she hates, while I endure the torture of losing her I adore, and of seeing her in

unworthy hands.   Still, I have but one course to pursue—
to stand by my good uncle; to show him that I feel to him
no ill-will for an act of involuntary cruelty to me and her;
and, they once united, to give my sorrow free course, or
bury it, and have no mistress, save my country."

"Let us go," said Gracchus, musingly; "the sooner this
marriage is decided on the better."

"What mean you?"

"My friend, ask no explanation of my meaning; but this
I know, the fair Adela shall never marry this ogre of a
cousin."

"Gracchus!" cried Charles, shaking his head, "raise no
hand against this man."

"I will slay him with his own pistol," replied Antiboul,
with a laugh.

"My dear friend," said Charles Clement, pausing in the
street, "I know you—your old love for me—your devotion—
your wish to see me happy; but, mark me, I would not
accept the free hand of my beloved Adela, if her freedom
be the result of a crime."

"And yet will her freedom be the result of a crime,"
said Antiboul drily.

"You speak in riddles."

"I do, but let us hasten to the Rue Dominique; I trow
there are those there who wish you well arrived."

Charles Clement, who knew his friend too well to press
him for an explanation of what he felt convinced was some
wild, and even mad scheme for his success in the dearest
object of his ambition, shook his head disapprovingly, and
then pressing the other's hand, turned towards the quartier
St. Germain.

It was with one of those bitter pangs, which can neither
be supposed nor explained, one of those emotions of void
and misery man sometimes feels here below, that on entering the Duke's salon, Charles Clement saw the Count
Leopold lazily reclining on a couch near Adela and Miranda,
and entertaining them with that idle small-talk, which it is
the want of courtiers and drawing-room soldiers to dispense
in large doses to the unfortunates into whose society they
are thrown.   If, however, under circumstances, there could
be comfort for our devoted lover, there was much in the

animated smile which crossed the face, before cold and indifferent, of Adela, and much too in the gentle, almost pitying welcome of Miranda, whose grief at the young man's sufferings was beyond all he could have imagined.

To love—to have fixed the warm affections of her passionate Italian soul upon Charles Clement—to know that he adored another, and that other her friend, her sister, her cherished companion—to wish, above all the world's joy, their union and happiness—to see her pining, and him crushing, in his manly heart, his hopes, his feelings, his aspirations—to know no means of bringing about their union, was to Miranda a complication of agony. Never did woman love man more than did the Countess the young republican; but never did one selfish thought, one faint idea of what the marriage of Adela with Count Leopold might bring about, tarnish the pure, noble, and earnest desire of her mind, to frustrate the marriage of the affianced pair, and bring about that of Adela and Clement. Miranda was no common being. She had let loose upon the young aspirant for political fame and honour all her womanly affections; her very life seemed bound up in his, but she loved him, not herself, and hoped still to see him happy with her rival.

Mirandas are rare, but they exist.

"What news?" said the Duke to Clement, who came and seated himself in a corner by his side.

"Bad, my uncle," replied Charles; and, without further preface, he related in low tone all he had heard.

"Then you would advise me—" faltered the Duke.

"To see all your cherished plans carried out at once, and to be fully prepared for the worst," said Charles, with eyes brim-full of scalding tears, and with a bosom swelling to bursting.

"Noble boy!" replied the Duke; "noble boy! But I see there can be no delay. Adela may be left alone in a day. Dark hours are coming, and she must have a protector."

"She must," said the young man, mechanically.

"To-day is Saturday," mused the old Duke, with a painful expression of face. "Ah me! this day week I must resign myself to part with my child."

"One week," faltered Charles.

"Could I justly delay longer?" said the nobleman, hesitatingly.

"You could not," replied Charles; and rising, he pleaded severe indisposition, wished the ladies a gentle "Good night," and went out leaning on his friend's arm.

"One week," he murmured, as he threw himself on Gracchus's breast.

"So much!" said Antiboul.

Charles Clement raised his head, and saw a gratified smile on the face of his friend.

---

## CHAPTER XII.

### M. BROWN.

IT was the very next evening after the marriage had been decided on between Adela and Count Leopold, when M. Brown left his interior boudoir, escorting a female companion, who had done the dirty police-agent the honour to sup with him. Despite, however, the coarseness of his garb, his manner was extremely polite, for M. Brown was a man who had seen the world, and derived benefit from his travels. He was a strange mixture. By trade a spy, he had become selfish, sensual, and avaricious; but though he served those who paid him well—though he did his strict duty to the State, and was the ablest of all the several agents in the service of the monarchy, M. Brown hated those whose lacquey and servant he was. Misfortune had made him what he was. Fond of luxury, used to comfort, to the ease and power procured by wealth, he had accepted the tenebrous part of a spy, because it gave him easily what he once had legitimately possessed.

"*Bon soir, Madame la Comtesse,*" said the spy, with a laugh.

"Good night, my dear lord," replied the supposed Countess—a lively, handsome *brunette,* thrust with a title into society by the police to serve their purposes, a practice always common in France.

"To-morrow, according to promise," added M. Brown,

"and mind bring me word what part this Marquis de St. Hurage really played last night."

"He comes to the *soiree* where I am going this evening. Rely upon it, I will make him talk."

And the female agent went out.

M. Brown now advanced to his old chair, and once more took up his ancient pipe and loaded it. Before him lay numerous letters and reports, which it was his usual evening amusement to examine. They were now interesting enough, for all contained true or false accounts of conspiracies, of coming *emeutes*, of the anger of the people, of the suffering among the masses—topics which M. Brown forgot not to insist upon, in his report drawn up for the lieutenant's own eye, as well as that of the ministers, from the notes before him.

Scarcely, however, had the agent settled himself comfortably, put on his spectacles, trimmed his lamp, and opened various documents, than a tinkle of the bell below showed him that he was again troubled with visitors, and one who would take no denial.

As usual, M. Brown moved not, habit having given him the faculty of never being startled at anything.

The next minute the door opened, and the trooper of the *Dernier Sou*, the aristocratic companion of the Prince de Lambese, the friend of the Abbé Roy, entered rather hurriedly.

"Good evening, Monsieur le Comte," said the spy.

"Good evening," replied the trooper, cavalierly, seating himself.

"You have business with me?" continued the imperturbable Brown.

"I want money, and I can stand your delays no longer I asked 100,000 livres for the jewels and papers; you offered 60,000; I will make a sacrifice and take 80,000."

"I am instructed," said Brown, quietly, after examining a note which lay before him, "to offer you at present 50,000 livres."

"What means this insolence?" cried the trooper, angrily.

"It is our rule, if our offers are not accepted at once, we always offer less, especially when we need offer nothing."

"That is to be seen," said the other, striking his gloved

fist upon the table, "M. Brown—tell M. Ducrosne from me, that unless to-morrow he counts me out 80,000 livres, I will make an offer to the parties concerned myself."

"In person?" sneered the spy, raising his spectacles off his nose, and looking provokingly at the speaker.

"Take care!" replied the other, angrily; "I have borne, Maitre Brown, with your insolence long enough. Let me have no more of this."

"Count," said M. Brown, calmly; "let me give you advice for your own good; do not force me to report you dangerous."

"Why?"

"Because your liberty would not be worth an hour's purchase."

"*Tonnere!*" cried the trooper, "this is too bad. What can you allege against me?"

"That you are a thief," replied M. Brown.

"We are all so, more or less," said the other, to all appearance, quietly.

"But in open day—not at night, like a felon," added the spy.

"Your proofs?" laughed the other, hiding thus the remnant of shame which lingered in a once noble breast.

"That is our secret," said M. Brown.

"You refuse me, then, 80,000 livres?"

"I have offered you 50,000. As our time is valuable, and a second interview will cost time, I shall, to-morrow, offer you but 40,000."

"Come! come!" said the trooper, after a moment of reflection, and speaking in a more coaxing tone, "cannot we come to some understanding?"

"What do you propose?" replied the spy, with that equanimity which was so insolent.

"I ask 80,000 livres. They offer 100,000."

"Well?"

"Get me the 80,000, and ten of them are yours."

"I prefer twenty," said the spy, coolly, "and that is what M. Ducrosne gives me. It is my interest to be honest to my employers."

"*Mort dieux!*" cried the other, in a tone of great exasperation, "am I to be cheated, robbed! I, who risked everything, am offered one-half the prize, while you, who run no chance of punishment, share the plunder."

"We have power in our hands to have all. Admire our magnanimity in taking only half," said M. Brown, with a laugh.

" Neither half nor any shall you have, or my name is not the Count de la Tour," thundered the other.

At this moment the door opened, and, unannounced, Jean Torticolis entered the den of the police spy.

" Good morning, Jean," said Brown, coolly.

Jean did not reply, his eyes being fixed with chained power on the Count, whose last words he had heard.

The Count took no notice of him, but hurried past, and went out.

" Count de la Tour," muttered Jean—" I knew him as the Viscount de Montbar."

" During his father's life," said the spy; " but what seek you ?"

" What I have found—the present name and occupation of my enemy."

" You came in very *à propos*," laughed M. Brown; " he was threatening me, and I should have shot him, if he had moved a foot towards me. You saved his life."

The crick-neck shuddered; for, that man dead, the one hope of his life was gone.

" Is he under your protection ?" continued Torticolis.

" Not at all," cried M. Brown. " Do you intend anything against him ?"

" I do."

" What ?"

" He is my marked enemy—the man who robbed me of my wife, home, and fortune; who, by his perjured voice, had me condemned to death, and who took from me legal existence."

" But this does not enable you to be revenged on him."

" No !" cried Jean Torticolis, with a long breath, as if he drew in the sweet savour of vengeance; " but he is a thief, and I can denounce him."

" How a thief ?" said M. Brown, eyeing Jean suspiciously.

" He robbed the Duke de Ravilliere at the inn of the *Dernier Sou*."

"Ah!"

"He came in disguise to the *auberge*, and in the night forced open the Duke's carriage, stole the money it contained, and the Countess Miranda's jewellery——"

"Jean," said M. Brown, opening his eyes widely, "how knew you all this?"

"I saw him do it," answered the crick-neck, sombrely.

"I recollect," said the spy, somewhat relieved, "you there met with Charles Clement."

"I did."

"And," continued M. Brown, "you now wish to be revenged on your enemy. On one condition you shall have every facility."

"And that is——"

"Jean Torticolis," replied the spy, "This man is a noble, and an aristocrat. Do you know his history?"

"Only in part."

"Born of one of the noblest families in France, he at an early age lost his father. Left to interested guardians, he was badly brought up, and scarcely gained possession of his heritage when he spent it. Having now neither money nor credit, he looked around him. A noble relative obtained for him a lieutenancy in the Royal Allemands; but women, wine, and cards required more money than his modest pay, and the Viscount de Montbar, otherwise Count de la Tour, otherwise——"

"Well?"

"But the name which is really his is a secret I must conceal as yet. All the names are his, but he assumes one or the other, according to the circumstances in which he is placed. When he met with and sought to seduce your wife, he was the Viscount de Montbar; among his lower associates he is the Count de la Tour; among his friends he is the Count de la Tour-Neville."

"He is then——" cried Jean, clasping his hands.

"Exactly," replied the spy.

Torticolis, petrified at this lucid explanation, stood trembling like a leaf with anxiety.

"You have now the game in your hands. He is an ungrateful scoundrel. The police have protected him hitherto, because he paid well, and served our purpose; but, convinced that his real character is a secret from us, he grows insolent, and we give him up."

"Wholly?"

"Wholly."

"Then, what am I to do?" said the crick-neck, radiant with the joy of the poor and ignorant, that of trampling on the rich and proud.

"Wait," replied M. Brown, "another is in the secret, who will track him better than us. But be ready; have all your traps set; bide your time, and when it comes, let him have no loop-hole for escape."

"Fear not," said Torticolis, rubbling his hands joyfully; "but think you he knows where *she* is?"

"He does, and so do I," replied the spy, coolly. "If you act wisely, that secret will be your reward."

Jean, who stood about two yards from the police-agent, looked at him, as if to measure the probabilities of a struggle, in which victory would gain for him the intelligence he so coveted. But he saw the butt-end of a pair of pistols peering from among the papers on the table.

"It would be no use," said the other, laughing.

"What?" answered Jean, in the utmost confusion.

"To knock me on the head," said the strange individual, whom M. Ducrosne himself could never put out of temper.

"M. Brown," said Torticolis, almost wildly, "you have my secret. I am dying, because that secret is still one for me. If I could wring it from you by force, I would; I cannot, and I submit to your will."

"I admire your frankness," put in Brown, "and now, recollect my advice."

"I will. I will bide my time, and leave to this other the task which is forbidden to me."

"Rely upon it, Maitre Torticolis, you will play your part, and no mean one."

The bell here tinkled again, and M. Brown waved his hand as a signal to Jean to retire.

On the stairs he ran against a man in a slouched hat and cloak, who no sooner caught sight of the countenance of Charles Clement's servant than he bowed his head, and passed him, without Jean's being able to get the least glimpse of his face.

"I should know that individual, too," muttered Torticolis, vainly, however, striving to tax his recollections.

With this sage reflection, he left the house, and returned towards home, nursing in his bosom the hope of revenge against one who had so direly injured him.

When Jean, after an hour's walk, to calm his agitation of mind, entered, he found his master and Gracchus Antiboul discussing the propriety of an armed struggle against oppression.

Gracchus was for an immediate cry to arms; to which Charles Clement replied—

" There will be a struggle, Antiboul; but how it will end no man can say.   But this is no question, when liberty and the cause of truth are at stake.   The blood of the innocent may be shed thickly, but it will, like the teeth of the dragon, raise up new men to contend against oppression.   *We* may be crushed—our principle never."

" Then why," cried Gracchus, petulantly, " did you force me to run away before the bayonets of the *Chevaliers du Guet?*"

" Because the time was not come," said Charles, calmly. " There *is* a time when more is gained by retiring than resisting."

---

## CHAPTER XIII.

### THE PLOT.

THE *sceance royale* took place on the 23rd June; and the king, pushed forward by a selfish nobility, and a haughty and imperious queen, committed the extreme *folly* of reminding the people of the despotism under which France had so long suffered.   The commons were treated with haughty disrespect: the king's speech was severe, and tyrannic—he broke all their decrees, and ended by commanding them to separate.   The tone was mighty, the means petty.

The commons listened, and disobeyed.

From that moment, royalty became discredited in France.

The consequences in Paris were varied.   The rich, always timid, began to hide their money, to escape from Paris, to carry their money abroad, and commit all those other follies, of which gold is alone capable.

Money had run away. It was exported with women and bonnet-boxes to Great Britain, or Germany, and elsewhere, and the stagnation which ensued produced, with an awful famine, much misery. The people were half-starved, and when they got something to eat, it was wretched black bread—earthy, mouldy, bitter. The court, pampered, fattened on the subsistence of the poor—who alone in those days paid taxes—instead of seeking to allay this suffering, sent troops, and cannon, and ammunition, to slaughter the starving populace, whose hunger made them ready to rise at a word. A breath of insurrection ruffled the agitated sea more and more every hour. The army, on which the court counted, was disaffected, and no regiments were sure, save the Swiss and German, and these were encamped on the Champs de Mars.

Thirty-five thousand troops were placed between Paris and Versailles, to overawe the people and their representatives. Twenty thousand more were hourly expected.

It was under the influence of these ideas that, after walking through the streets, hearing the discussion in the Palais Royal, and dining at home, on the evening which was to precede the marriage of Count Leopold and the Lady Adela, Charles Clement and his friend Gracchus Antiboul, were seated near their fire-place, in earnest conversation. It was a late hour, and for a long time they were engaged in discussing the events of the hour, and in preparing various plans of resistance to the schemes and machinations of power.

"That young man whom we spoke with will go far," said Gracchus.

"Camille Desmoulins," replied Clement: "he will. But I have no great faith in either him or your dirty friend, the doctor. The one is a patriot from temperament, the other from disappointed literary ambition—both bad recommendations. Patriotism, to be great, must be the result of settled conviction."

"Then you and I are great enough," said Gracchus, laughing.

"No man is little who is true," continued Clement;

" we may not be great in the eyes of the world; this greatness is as often the result of accident as of worth, but we shall do perhaps a great part unknown."

" Greatness is truly the result of caprice, not of desert," answered Gracchus, emphatically : " here is this dragoon of a Count Leopold will marry a charming wench to-morrow, whom he does not deserve; while you, who love her truly, and deserve her, will be left alone and hopeless."

" Gracchus," said Clement, turning pale and speaking in a reproachful tone, " why remind me of a misery I would fain forget for ever ?"

" Charles," replied his friend, warmly, " because, on my word and honour as a man and a republican, this marriage will not take place."

" Antiboul! Antiboul !" said Clement, in a tone nearly of anger.

" My dear friend," continued the student, taking the two hands of his companion, " had I not been sure of defeating the schemes of this cousin, think you I would have been so still?   Not only will the marriage not take place, but this rival of yours will have to give up all claims now and for ever."

" But explain," said the lover, shaking his mournful head.

" My dear fellow, he is married already," continued Gracchus, calmly.

" Married !" thundered Charles Clement, rising, and looking wildly at the quiet physiognomy of Antiboul.

" Married !" repeated Gracchus; " yes, married; and so fastly that nothing can untie the union.   All we want now is to secure the proof."

" And how is that to be done ?" said Clement, almost convinced, despite himself, by the calm manner of his old school-fellow.

" Put on your hat and cloak; order Jean to fetch a *voiture;* and let us drive to the Countess Miranda's, near the Louvre, where you know she sleeps to-night."

" But why the Countess Miranda?" said Charles, more pale than ever.

" Summon Jean," said Antiboul, in reply: " we shall want a woman's wit in this affair, and I know no one so fit as the Countess Miranda de Castelmonte."

"Is it necessary to disturb her?" said Charles, hesitating, he knew not why.

"It is," continued Gracchus.

Jean entered on the instant with their cloaks and hats, besides which, considering the times, he brought two pair of pistols.

"Let us walk," preferred the lover; "we shall arrive more quickly than with a coach."

"I agree," said the student.

And they went out, followed by Jean Torticolis, who had not spoken a word.

It was past eleven, and the streets were in that quarter nearly empty. A minute brought them to the Rue St. Honoré, and following this, they soon entered the narrow street in which stood the splendid hotel of Miranda, and to which she had retired in consequence of the changes rendered necessary by the new suites of apartments needed for the young couple. Another reason, that Adela had been so unwell all day as to need a narcotic to make her sleep, and total stillness had been stated by the family physician as the only chance of her rising in a fit state to go through the fatal ceremony of the next day.

The Countess Miranda sat alone in a magnificent saloon. It was all hung with tapestry and adorned by rare old furniture, consoles, and carved buffets, and pictures. She was near a table, in a huge arm-chair that nearly hid her form. By her side was a lamp, on which rested a book, but her eyes were fixed on an empty arm-chair opposite. Her gaze was fixed and vacant. Her eyes were humid, as if tears were forcing their way through, and yet the aspect of her features was stern and rigid.

She was thinking; and the lone splendour around her had cast her thoughts into a peculiar channel. With youth, beauty, all the delights which wealth and luxury could procure, she wanted the one charm of *all*, sweet companionship—the eye to admire her beauty, the love to welcome her youth, the society which would have made her proud of her possessions, were all wanting; and the next day the only friend she had would pass away to the arms of a husband, and become almost a stranger.

Then a vision arose of one with whom, perhaps, Adela

would not have been a stranger; and the Countess blushed crimson as her fluttering heart sent to her a hope which she wished even to think vain.

At this moment a slight noise in the apartment made her raise her eyes, and Charles Clement stood before her, hat in hand, pale and mournful.

"Monsieur Clement!" said the Countess, rising, while consciousness made the blood come crimson to her cheek.

" And my friend, Gracchus Antiboul," replied the lover. " I have very much to apologize for disturbing you at this late hour, but we have believed you would excuse us in a good cause."

" Be seated, gentlemen," replied Miranda, warmly, while she waved her attendants to retire. " I am too happy if I can be of the slightest use either to you or to your friend."

" At present," said Gracchus, gaily, " being heart-whole I have no need of your kindness; but I bring you here a poor lover, in whose case you can do much."

" I !" cried Miranda, blushing more crimson than before, and much astonished.

" Much," repeated Gracchus, quietly; " for with me you can prevent, to-morrow morning, the marriage of the Lady Adela and Count Leopold her cousin."

" Impossible!" cried Miranda, full of conflicting emotions.

" It appears to me also," said Charles Clement, sadly ; " but my friend Gracchus insists that—"

" I told you before, my dear fellow, that you must, for the present, remain in the dark," interrupted Gracchus; " if the Countess Miranda will favour me with ten minutes' interview, I will explain all to her."

" I will retire," said Clement, shaking his head.

" No !" cried the young Countess, " remain seated, I pray you; your friend and I can speak in yonder embrasure, as doubtless your ears will not be too indiscreet."

Gracchus rose gallantly, and casting a triumphant glance at his pale and anxious friend, led the Italian beauty to the further end of the room, where an open window led into a balcony.

Antiboul lost not a moment. In a few words, his plea and ideas were explained. When he concluded, Miranda breathed an involuntary sigh.

"Shall I have your co-operation?" said Antiboul, looking at her, almost coldly.

"Monsieur Antiboul," replied Miranda, firmly, while her eyes were meekly raised to heaven, which she called to her aid, to consummate the sacrifice, "you shall have all you ask."

"Thanks! thanks!" cried Gracchus, triumphantly.

"But why not explain to Charles?—he must suffer martyrdom, poor fellow," said Miranda, anxiously.

"Because I know him well, and know, too, that he would, in his own case, refuse to accept the plot, which he would not object to practise himself for another."

"We must send him away, then."

"Decidedly," replied Gracchus.

"And you?"

"Must remain here," said the student, quietly.

"You are irresistible, Monsieur Antiboul," replied the Countess, with a faint laugh.

"A general complaint of the ladies in my quarter," said Gracchus, complacently.

With these words, the student and the Countess re-entered the apartment. Miranda was very pale; as she turned away from Antiboul, her expression was ghastly, but she had no instant of hesitation—no selfish thought for one moment tarnished the victory over self which she had just achieved.

"Monsieur Charles," said she, kindly advancing at the same time, and placing her hand gently on his arm, "your friend has right on his side. Be hopeful for to-morrow."

"Madam," exclaimed Clement, rising, and looking radiant with hope, "your words are rich manna in the wilderness, and I place myself wholly in your hands."

"Of course, said Gracchus, laughing, "all my promises brought but doubt; the Countess speaks but a word, and you are as happy as a school-boy."

"But you do so love me?" exclaimed Charles.

"And I—" said Miranda, involuntarily.

"Cannot, as does my old friend," replied Clement, without noticing the confusion of the young Italian.

"Nay, I contend not with a schoolfellow," she faintly answered. "But now, Monsieur Gracchus."

"Bid him go home and go to bed," replied Antiboul.

"You hear," said Miranda, smiling.

"And obey."

"In the morning," continued Antiboul, "rise early, and go to the Rue Dominique, according to promise. Never mind how far the preparations have gone ; have faith and hope, and trust in our devotion to your interests."

"I thank you both, and if your good offices fail, I shall never have but one sentiment concerning your wishes. You are my friends ; in you, after heaven, I put my trust."

And Charles Clement, absorbed in his one idea, went out without noticing that both Antiboul and his servant Torticolis remained behind at the hotel of the Countess Miranda. For the while our lover had but one idea.

In about ten minutes after his departure, Gracchus Antiboul, conducting the young Italian, and Jean, escorting her maid Rose, left the house in a direction very similar to that followed by the hero of this eventful narrative.

---

## CHAPTER XIV

### THE WEDDING DAY.

NEVER did brighter morning dawn upon the marriage union of man. The month of June, always charming in Paris, was unusually so. The sun rose in the horizon of a sky wholly free from clouds, and all promised a lovely day. At an early hour all the servants of the hotel in the Rue Dominique were astir, as the wedding was to take place in the mansion itself. Monseigneur, the Archbishop of Paris, was to come in full canonicals, he being a relative ; and such was the importance of the family, that, despite the few nobility in Paris, nearly a hundred guests were invited, who would have been offended if they had not been asked to the ceremony.

By ten o'clock a magnificent breakfast was laid out, the chapel was prepared, and every minutiæ attended to.

Alone in the *salon* was the Duke de Ravilliere. He was pale and thoughtful. To a father, the resigning of a daughter must always be matter, at least, for serious thought, but to the old nobleman it was far more. Adela was the child of his old age—his one, fond, only offspring—and to part with her was a sorrow, however necessary, none the less real. Besides, a whisper he would have fain not heard, came to his heart, which told him that this young girl was not being led to happiness—but prejudice, the killer of more noble things than any other moral scourge of humanity, stifled this sensation, and a word, unwisely given, weighed more than the happiness of a life.

And Adela! She was in her chamber, being decked already for the bridal. Never did fairer victim, or more pale and wan, prepare for the sacrifice. She had slept, but unsoundly; her eyes were hot and weary, her cheek pale, while a fictive and hectic flush marked its centre. Her gaze was fixed. To think of what was to come was nothing; her truant thoughts dwelt on the happy dreams of the past, and on another bridal which would have caused emotions so different. But her maids went on decking her for the hour, when in falsehood and heart-rending sorrow she should stand up to unite love, honour, life to one who should, by rights, have been the very Polar-star of her existence. Brave society, which is so perfect, that those who dare even to suggest amelioration, are treated as knaves and fools.

Vainly her maids asked counsel of her taste. Did this flower suit her hair, or that ribbon her complexion, or did this style of hair please her? To all she answered, Yes. What cared she? He, for whom she was decked, she would gladly have appeared before utterly hateful and hideous.

But the hours come: they go and pass, and Miranda, that promised to be there, tarries yet. A message from her father bids her hurry; and several young and lovely friends, who were to grace her bridal, come to assist and chatter, and be merry and joyous on such merry and joyous an occasion.

Merry and joyous it should be never, this solemn and serious thing, but still less on occasion such as this, when indifference is to wed with hate.

It is mid-day, and nearly all the company is collected. A servant announced that Monseigneur had arrived.

"My Lord Duke," he added, "will be glad of your pre-sence, madam, if your ladyship be ready."

Adela bowed, and then, supported by her young friends, she hastened to the *salon*.

Near the huge fire-place stood her father, conversing with the jovial-faced head of the metropolitan church; and Adela shuddered, for he was but one link in the chain of her misery. Behind, in mincing talk with two celebrated court beauties of the last reign, was the Count Leopold; and Adela shuddered again, for here was another link in the chain. Behind him was the notary with the contract, and Adela grew dizzy as she gained sight of the fatal parchment.

At that instant her eye fell upon a figure which roused all her energies, and made her strive, as far as possible, to conceal her emotions. It was Charles Clement, more pale and cold than the marble near which he leaned.

The Duke no sooner caught a glimpse of his child, than he hurried to meet her, and imprinted on her white soft forehead a tender and affectionate kiss—more tender, more affectionate, if it could be, than usual. It was a father's last unfettered caress.

"Monseigneur," he said, addressing the Archbishop of Paris, "allow me to present to you your niece and child, the Countess Adela de la Ravilliere."

"My child," exclaimed the worthy old man, somewhat pompously, "this is a happy occasion for me. I always looked forward with pleasure to the hope of uniting you in the bands of marriage."

The excellent and reverend personage who spoke omitted to add, that he had resigned himself to this contingency, after a vain attempt at winning his niece and her fortune to the arms of a holier and more fitting spouse—in his opinion.

Adela, however, meekly bowed, and went round to receive the felicitations of the whole assembled company.

"She is lovely," muttered some of the men.

"Charming, though pale," said others.

"Leopold is a lucky fellow," observed several.

"She is very thin," put in a fair one of a certain age, whose charms had received the advantage of gradual development.

"That but adds to her beauty," said a young and lovely girl, by the side of the speaker.

Meanwhile the notary mended his pen, and looked perfectly delighted at having prepared the contract for so charming a bride. In this troublous time, too, bridals were rare occurrences.

But in her round, Adela had reached the spot were stood Charles Clement. The Duke would have hurried by him without speaking, but his daughter, instead of doing so, made a halt before the young man She could not, in that solemn hour, refuse him the consolation of a word.

Count Leopold, before in anxious converse, but whose eyes never were off his intended wife, paused in his conversation, and put on such an air of triumphant and insulting pity, that all near him at once guessed the true position of affairs.

" A rival," said an old Marquis, with the air of having made a profound discovery.

" And a favoured one," replied a lady, sufficiently loud for the future husband to hear—for in all the sex there is an *esprit de corps*, which arms them against those who marry them against their will.

Count Leopold bit his lip, and looked scornful, but the *trait* went home.

" Monsieur Clement," said Adela, with an angelic smile, but with a more gay air than she had yet assumed—for she knew her sufferings would be more poignant to her generous lover than his own—" you have then done me the honour to be present at my bridal ? "

" I always intended to be," replied Charles, with an accent, the anguish of which he could not conceal.

Adela seemed stung with grief at the tone.

" Charles," said she, in a low and trembling voice, " in a few minutes I shall be separated from you for ever ; I am now free, and may say, that I give my hand ; but, until the tie be formed, my heart is yours. Once married, I am his, aud shall learn to forget."

And she moved away, leaving Charles Clement overwhelmed at her generous avowal, her mingled modesty, and firmness of will.

The little Adela was now a woman.

" But the Countess Miranda," said she, looking anxiously

round, by way of diverting her own thoughts from the memory of him to whom she had just spoken.

"This is very strange," replied the Duke.

"I am ready, my Lord Duke," said the notary, with a bow.

"Yes, Monsieur Tirson, but my daughter expects her bosom friend and bridesmaid."

"The Countess Miranda de Castelmonte, and Monsieur Gracchus Antiboul," exclaimed the valet at the door.

Miranda, more majestic even than usual, entered quietly, led by Gracchus, whose air of studied coolness and politeness was somewhat comic. He, however, became grave, as his eye rested on the face of Charles Clement; and leaving our heroine to join Adela, he hurried over to his friend.

"Your promise," said he, faintly, without daring to express hope, even in the tone——

"Is kept, my dear boy," replied Antiboul, gravely; "this marriage cannot take place."

"Monsieur Tirson," said Count Leopold, advancing gallantly, "I think Monsieur le Duc only waits for you."

"Pardon," exclaimed a voice from the doorway, "but I have a duty to perform."

Every one started at this strange interruption, and looked whence it came for an explanation.

At the door was M. Brown, the secret agent of his Majesty's police; behind him, Jean; and, behind him again, a detachment of the *archers* of the police.

"What means this?" cried the Duke, angrily.

"My Lord Duke," replied M. Brown, advancing politely into the middle of the room, and bowing low, "I am grieved to interrupt you, but my orders are imperative. I have a *mandat d'arret* against the Viscount Montbar, commonly called Count Leopold de la Tour Neville."

Adela started, turned pale, and sank on the bosom of Miranda, who, as pale as her, and trembling, could scarce support her.

Charles Clement looked wildly at Gracchus for an explanation of this, to him, astounding event.

The Duke remained as if struck suddenly to stone.

"A trick of some rival," cried some of the women.

"A paltry fellow," responded the Marquis.

"Come, Monsieur the exempt; this is a joke," said another.

"For what do you arrest him?" inquired the Duke, gasping for breath; for the preparations were to him too serious for him to believe it a pleasantry.

"As a thief," replied the spy, coolly, and giving a sign to his men to cut off the retreat of the Count.

"Liar!" thundered the Count Leopold, who, except a slight quiver on the entrance of the spy, had not flinched.

"My Lord Duke," continued the police agent, coolly, "will recollect his misadventure of the first of March."

"I do," said the Duke, mechanically, and looking around him for support in this trying moment. Charles was by his side.

"The thief was Monsieur and your black servant, Fournier."

"A thief," muttered the fashionable crowd, falling back.

"A thief," repeated the Duke.

"A thief," said Charles Clement, astounded.

"Insolent scoundrel!" continued the Count, "your proof of this foul calumny."

"In the first place, here are the jewels of the Countess Miranda de Castelmonte, and all the deeds of her Italian estates, found in your luggage, up stairs."

"Falsehood," said the Count, still calmly.

"But here is the damning proof," continued the immoveable spy.

And he held up the odd pistol, which Gracchus Antiboul had so handily won in the shooting-match in the garden.

"Let none else speak," said the spy, in a commanding voice, advancing towards Miranda; "will madam do me the favour to identify this pistol?"

"It is that won by Monsieur Gracchus Antiboul of the Count Leopold, a few days since."

"Do you know it by any mark, madam?"

"By this notch, cut at the request of Monsieur."

"And this," said the spy, holding up its exact counterpart.

"Is that," said Jean, "found by me on the steps of my Lord Duke's carriage, on the night of the first of March, and laid there by Monsieur le Comte, while bursting open the vehicle."

The whole company, to whom the anecdote was well known, remained silent with astonishment.

"But, why concealed you this?" said Charles Clement, gravely.

"Because, if I had then denounced the Count, none would have credited me, and I should have been considered the thief."

"Nephew!" exclaimed the Duke, recovering his composure, and advancing towards the Count, who stood unblushing and audacious between two officers of the *guet,* "is all this true?"

"Ask your daughter, your other nephew, and his friend," sneered the Count, "who, with the Countess Miranda, have got up this comedy to suit their views."

"Monsieur," replied the old Duke, gravely, "before I condemn you, you shall have a hearing. Adela, child, you have heard what the Count Leopold has said. Knew you of this coming obstacle?"

"Nay, my dear father," said she, *naively,* having recovered herself some little, "or I should have been somewhat more gay and cheerful."

Without noticing this unwitting blow aimed at his paternal authority, the Duke continued.

"And you, my worthy nephew?" he asked Clement.

"My Lord Duke," replied Charles Clement, readily, "I had been told some days back that the Count Leopold would never marry your daughter; but I placed no credence in the promise. It came from my best friend, but I believed it not. So much was I ignorant, that I believed the obstacle to be a former marriage."

"And you, Monsieur Gracchus Antiboul?" said the Duke.

"On me," answered the student, bowing, "rests all the responsibility of this scene. Some days back I became aware, from an unwitting revelation of Jean Torticolis, that the robber of the first of March and the Count Leopold were one. For certain reasons, which you, my Lord Duke, may guess, I was most anxious that this accusation should be brought home. With a man who had robbed his uncle in the night, stolen your ward's jewellery and title-deeds, and offered to sell them back for

100,000 livres, I could have no delicacy. I took my measures accordingly. In a shooting-match, I secured the one proof of the charge, and last night, and this morning I induced the Countess Miranda to identify her property, which the police found in the Count's *valise*, in her presence."

"I thank you, Monsieur Antiboul, for your frankness," said the Duke, warmly, "and still more for having saved my child from wedding a felon and an outcast. Monsieur the exempt, do your duty."

"Silly old man!" cried the Count Leopold, bitterly, "may you never repent this ready credence of those who have planned my ruin—a supposititious cousin, a beggarly student, and an Italian adventuress, with, by way of *pendant,* an unhung bandit."

"Unhung! yes, unhung!" thundered Jean Torticolis, losing patience, "but, no thanks to you, who once strove to hang me, after robbing me of all."

"You, fellow," said the Count, insolently—"I never saw you before."

And waving his hand, the Count Leopold signed to the police to do their duty, and he went out, escorted by the spy, whose politeness of manner and sneering look were greater punishment than all.

"You should have accepted the 50,000," he whispered.

"*Scelerat,*" said the Count; and he spoke no more.

The Duke, after a moment's pause to recover himself, called around him the whole company, who scarce knew what to do after so *brusque* a termination of the wedding party.

"My friends and relatives," said the old man, solemnly, "you came here to witness an act of injustice and tyranny, which the hand of Providence has mercifully prevented. Nay, child, let thy father speak. Many years ago, when that unhappy boy was a bold lad, I and his noble father affianced our children—mine was a smiling infant babe— without knowing or caring if community of taste or fitness would make them happy. My brother died; and I the more held to my promise, that after a while my nephew, an orphan and poor, seemed to remind me of my dear brother, whose word given would have been sacred to him, as I held mine to me. At length the Count claimed his bride, and I, while adjourning their union, confirmed my promise. Meanwhile another nephew, the child of my sister, came to me, wound himself round my heart, and, ignorant of the compact, dared love my only child, who—let this be a day of frankness—returned his affection. Fatal love! for I came between and severed all hope. My promise explained to them, they submitted unmurmuringly. He, noble boy, warned me we were in troublous times, and hurried me to wed my child as I had engaged, though then crushing the warmest hope of his heart. Acting according to this advice, and because, old and infirm, I wished to see my daughter protected before I died, I fixed for this day the marriage. You have come, my friends, all to the wedding. It has been fatally interrupted; but I invite you all to stay; for, casting from me as none of mine the felon and thief, I here publicly affiance my only child, Adela de Ravilliere, to Charles Clement de Ravilliere, her cousin, and my most noble nephew."

Loud was the applause of the astonished party at this second dramatic *denouement*.

Adela held down her blushing head, all tears, and smiles and roses.

Charles seized the hand of his uncle with a look of inexpressible delight, and sprang, Athena-like, all armed with joy and happiness from the very slough of despond.

Gracchus Antiboul rupped his hands, clapped them, and gave way to a series of antics so uproarious, that many present doubted his sanity.

And Miranda? A deadly pallor moved across her noble and expressive features; her hands were pressed half a second on her heart, ready to burst with anguish and joy; and then, crushing her own sorrow and hopelessness as selfish and ungenerous, she moved beside Charles, and, conquering every trace of emotion, spoke.

"Said we not rightly," she said kindly, "and that you had friends who would work well and steadily?"

"I am too happy!" exclaimed Charles Clement, pressing her hand quite fondly, and quite ignorant of the anguish he was causing.

"Come, come," said the Duke, still trembling with emotion, but striving to hide it, "let us forget all save our present happiness."

"*Monsieur le Duc est servie*," cried Germain, pompously, on a sign from his master.

"Now, my friends, to breakfast. Monsieur Antiboul, you deserve it, lead up my daughter;" and the Duke took that of the noble lady near him, and led the way.

Antiboul, with a provokingly triumphant glance at Charles Clement, took the arm of the lovely and half-bewildered Adela, while his friend, whose pallor had given way to a cheerful and sunny glow, offered to escort Miranda, who freely accepted his courtesy. Nor did she lean lightly on him. She needed support; for she trembled like a spring leaf on the rude March breeze.

Monseigneur said grace in the least possible time in which grace could reverently be said; the Duke took the upper seat, Adela the lower, with near her Charles, Antiboul, and Miranda. The guests arranged themselves down the side of the long table, more contented and happy than they had been for a long time. Come to be present at a marriage, they had witnessed a drama, and had experienced almost real emotion, a thing which, amid the rich and idle, is a novelty especially when, by character, education, and habit, they are little prepared for its reception.

Though a tinge of sadness at the painful cause of the disrupted marriage—and none pitied Count Leopold so much as his affianced bride—pervaded the *reunion* at first, the tendency of human nature to accept the present, and to look to the future without caring for the past, soon prevailed, and by degrees the party grew gay. The lovely *fiancee*, the happy husband in expectancy, were freely complimented, in a style which was gallant then, but which would be indecent now; and Charles replied, and Gracchus defended him; while Miranda alone could not shake off her gravity. On the whole, however, the meeting was one of contentment and gaiety, and the old Duke was happy.

But the breakfast is over, and the guests rise, and we with them, for we have arrived at the termination of the first part of this eventful record. Of Clement, and his part in the great struggle, of Adela and her lover, of Count Leopold and his reward, of Antiboul and his republicanism, of Miranda and her fate, of Jean Torticolis and his secret, we have yet to speak.

## CHAPTER XV

### THE CAFE DU CAVEAU.

THE Palais Royal, after it had been turned into the most splendid bazaar in the world, became one of the most celebrated dens of infamy in France. The revolting scenes perpetrated in the dark, in private chambers, under the Regency and during the life of Philippe d'Orleans, afterwards Égalité, were transferred to the hired portions of the same palace. Above, the aristocratic doings of peers and princes, hid from the masses then, but afterwards revealed in memoirs, and reports of police—spies for the information of posterity—below, on a level with the garden, shops, cafés, dining-rooms, &c.; and below again, in the range of spacious vaults, vice in every shape and form which the unhappy fancy of man, in a state of utter depravity, can devise. Two revolutions were required to sweep from this magnificent palace these dens of iniquity. Under the Republic they all disappeared before the unmerciful war made upon every haunt of crime by Maximilian Robespierre and the Convention, which, though filled by many individually bad men, was pure and generous in most of its collective aspirations. Under the Directory, government of show and feebleness, they returned a little; under Napoleon, reign of gorgeous display, riches, and barbaric splendour, they were again alive in all their full viciousness; under the Restoration, reign of hypocrisy and profession (the rulers having religious ceremonials to regulate, had no time for piety and morality), and the horrid dens of the Palais Royal were in their best days. Under Louis Philippe, reign of the middle classes, who respect the family, and who are naturally inimical to debauchery, they fell, it is to be hoped never to rise again. With all the faults of the eighteen years of reign, the public morality of France, in certain things, has, at all events in outward appearance, improved.

It is now our duty to enter one of these resorts; but, lest the just susceptibility of my fair readers be alarmed, I hasten to add that it is one of the least equivocal which we are about now to visit in company.

The Café du Caveau was originally an underground vault

of the Palais Royal. A small door in one of the peristyles opened upon a narrow and dark staircase, following which, you found yourself in a low oblong chamber, about twenty feet wide, and forty long. To the left were a series of square pillars, some sixteen feet in circumference, dividing the main vault from a narrow one, and supporting the weight of the building above—the whole dingy, black, and very ancient in colour. Between each of these pillars were a table and two benches. At the farther end of the larger vault was a rough and temporary stage, on which mounte-banks, singers, and even dancers, of the most impure kind, were in the habit of giving exhibitions to the sound of an orchestra situated in a neighbouring nook.

Beside the stairs by which one descended from the upper regions, was the bar, a wooden counter, behind which sat a rubicund dame, who dispensed wine, and viler liquors, to all comers having wherewith to pay.

No variety of the genus *homo*, male or female, was un-welcome in that den, save one, which is always looked upon with suspicion in every haunt of infamy—the poor. Vice considers poverty a crime; and, to do it justice, it hates both the criminal and his fault with rare intensity. If an honest poor man, by accident or ignorance, entered the locality, to rest or warm himself, he was conducted to the door, with an intimation that that was a place for gentle-men, but of what description no minute particulars were given.

The pictures on the walls, could I venture to describe them—pale, inanimate copies of those which adorned, in those days, the chambers and boudoirs of the rich and fair —might have served, in some measure, as an explanation; but I recollect in time that I am writing for a British pub-lic, and that we have, as yet, made slow progress in inde-cency and a taste for prurient imagery.

A few flickering candles and a swinging lamp gave a thin light to the place, by the favour of which the faces of the visitors remained wholly concealed, when such was their desire; as many visited the den who were in the habit of moving in other circles, this was a consideration.

It was six o'clock in the evening, and not a customer was in the place. The public were crowding round the extempore orator, who discussed state affairs, or lectured the assembly beneath the Palais Royal trees. Two waiters, in faded liveries, were dozing on a bench. The beauty of the place, a plump wench who enacted Venus, Hebe, Juno, Minerva, and other classical heroines; who danced eastern dances—so the more impure exhibitions were called—was hastily devouring a mess of beans fried in oil, with odorous cheese and sour wine, and, at the same time, making up a public face before a glass. At the farther extremity, the band—a blind fiddler, a cymbal, and a drum—were producing a squeaking sound out of one instrument, and an imitation of thunder out of another; while Jupiter, who was to enact one of his moral intrigues, as fully related in all modern school-books, was making an experiment in search of the most majestic face for the father of gods and men.

But suddenly the waiters rose with a start, Venus slided demurely to the tiring-room, Jupiter vanished behind a pasteboard cloud, and the drum and fiddle relapsed into a dismal silence.

A foot had trodden heavily on the stairs above. Business was about to begin.

The Café du Caveau was to be silent no more that night.

The man who had stepped on the landing was rather tall and slight. A very large cloak wrapped him closely round, while a flat three-cornered hat was drawn over his eyes. His legs and boots seemed to denote one in somewhat penurious circumstances, as neither his boots nor his breeches, as far as they could be seen, were very valuable. A sword —not a holiday rapier, but an earnest article intended for use—hung by his side, for the end peered under the cloak.

The man paused on the landing, and looked down. Then he looked back, as if to make sure that he was not followed; and, apparently satisfied, he descended the stairs with the ease of a man who is accustomed to be respected wherever he thinks proper to enter.

" Brandy!" said he, with a wave of the head to the waiter, without throwing back his cloak.

" Brandy!" repeated the attendant, getting up his business voice, and, next minute, a mug and bottle were placed before the stranger, with that rapidity and dexterity which appertains to Parisian waiters of every class.

The man filled a bumper and drank. As he raised his mug to his lips, the waiter noticed that he was very pale and worn, as if with long fatigue and excitement.

"Have you to eat?" he said, in a sharp voice.

"Yes, Captain," replied the waiter.

"What?"

"Bread, cold meat"—the waiter was about to continue.

"A cold fowl, a smoked tongue, bread, and a bottle of champagne," interrupted the other, almost angrily.

At these words the landlady awoke from a semi-doze, the two waiters rushed to obey, Venus peeped out from behind a curtain, Jupiter stroked his beard, and the drummer involuntarily gave a roll of his drum.

In five minutes the required articles were laid before the pale man, and he at once began to eat, with an appetite which was perfectly ravenous.

The whole of the inmates of the Café du Caveau looked at one another. During the previous night a secret club of revolutionists had been dispersed by the police, and its members having effected their escape, had been hunted all day through Paris in vain by the satellites of M. Ducrosne.

"Exactly," said the pale man.

"What, sir?" inquired the waiter, stammering.

"I am one of the Club de l'Egalité," replied the other, who had seen their idea in their eyes, "does that make my money any the worse?"

"No, Monsieur," said the landlady.

"Ah," answered the pale man, with a sneer, "that's lucky."

"I never inquire any person's business," said the rubicund dame, simpering and endeavouring to look more than usually gracious.

"Very good plan," continued the other, who had, while talking, concluded his meal, drunk his wine, and gained both a little colour and a less faint voice. "And now, you, sir, clear this away, put the brandy in that alcove, and send Venus to play a game of piquet with me."

"Monsieur?" said the waiter, hesitating.

The stranger, with the most perfect nonchalance and dexterity, had flung two gold pieces on the counter in front of the landlady, whose eyes glistened with delight, while Venus, without waiting any further summons, came out and took up her seat on one side of the table which the stranger had selected.

The personage who had caused such a sensation in the Café du Caveau was now between two of the pillars of the vault in the furthest end, and hid from the entrance, nor could he see any one coming in from above. With this precaution he seemed perfectly satisfied; and having ordered the most costly refreshment the place afforded for the dulcina of the locality, he began to be most attentive to his game, which he played with all the air of a gambler.

His ease would, however, have been perhaps seriously disturbed, could he have seen the whole of the circumstances which were occurring behind his back.

Scarcely had he entered the subterraneous café, when a head cautiously protruded itself through the aperture of the door-way, and thence surveyed the interior of the vault. The man thus occupied did not cease from his examination until the stranger had ordered something to eat. This seemed to satisfy him, for he then moved away. He was a small man, poorly dressed also like the stranger, and equally cautious, for his head was continually bowed on the shoulder, as if in the act of listening. His eyes were continually thrown about him.

After about a quarter of an hour's pause he moved towards the door of the café, and looked down again. The stranger was just moving to have his game of piquet.

The little man rubbed his hands with an air of singular satisfaction.

" Now is the time," he muttered, as his eye fell upon two officers of the maréchaussée, who were sauntering about the Palais Royal.

" My masters," said the little man, in a humble tone, " is it safe to enter yon underground café ?"

The officers of the maréchaussée looked with all the usual superciliousness of servants of the Prevôt on a poor man, who asked them a question, and laughed.

" Quite safe, poltroon," said one, " so you have the white money to pay your score."

" I have an écu of five livres," replied the little man

humbly, "and would willingly spend it with any one who would accompany me down yonder."

"A good-tempered gaillard enough," laughed one of the two archers, considerably mollified; "what do you say, Pierre, to protecting him?"

"I have no objection to earn a glass so honestly," said the other, with a sly look at his companion.

"Will you precede me, my messieurs?" said the little man.

"By no means," insisted the men of the maréchaussée, politely, "you are our host. Take the lead."

The little man made no great hesitation; and next minute the whole party were at a table in the vault near the entrance, and as far removed as possible from the alcove, occupied by the stranger and Venus, by whose mirth it would appear that she was winning her game of piquet.

"Wine," said the little man, after hearing that his companions were not hungry.

Wine was brought, and the officers of the maréchaussée began to drink right readily, while their companion refreshed himself with extreme moderation. Not a moment were his eyes off the alcove, in which sat the strange couple, the fugitive and dame Venus playing piquet.

Several persons began to drop in, and before long there was an audience present, who began to call for some amusement.

"I must retire," said Venus, at a sign from the mistress.

"Go," said the stranger, without the slightest trace of emotion.

Venus finished her glass, and glided away to the narrow corridor behind the stage, there to arrange herself for the exhibition.

The little man called for more wine, of which the two archers partook with great freedom.

The stranger leant back against the pillar, and seemed about to witness the exhibition. Scarcely had he settled himself when he suffered an unexpected interruption.

"Count," said a voice, close by him, in a low whisper, a hissing voice like that of triumph and hate combined.

The stranger started, and then remained motionless. He, however, replied in a whisper, conquering his emotion—

"Who calls me Count?"

"Listen," replied the other, "I am about to sit opposite to you, to play, or feign to play, piquet with you.  Do not move, do not show the slightest outward dislike of my company, or I denounce you.  At yon table are two of the archers of the Police, who will seize you at a word."

"Take your hand," said the stranger, dealing the cards with considerable equanimity.

And next minute, Jean Torticolis and the Count Leopold de la Tour Neville were in presence.

"Do you know me?"  said Jean, fixing his eyes on his adversary.

"The servant of cousin Charles," replied the soldier, with much of his old swagger.

"Exactly," continued Jean, calmly; "but as I knew you not but as Viscount Montbar, so will you know me better as Paul Ledru."

"Paul Ledru!" said the soldier, as if inquiring of his old recollections, and not able at once to recall the association.

"You forget!" exclaimed the crick-neck with bitter astonishment.

"Ah! I recollect now," said the Count, with a smile of self-satisfaction, "and a monstrous pretty wife you had."

"I had," replied the other, ghastly pale, and fixing a pair of eyes, perfectly glassy with rage and hate, on the soldier.

The Count shuddered, for he found himself for once in the power of an injured husband, who had nursed his rage for years.

"You are not Paul Ledru?" he said, hesitatingly.

"I was," said the other, speaking low; "but play, Count, or we shall be noticed."

"You were saying—" faltered the Count.

"That I was Paul Ledru once, until you by falsehood and  calumny deprived me of home, wife, life itself; for you had me condemned to death.  That I escaped is no thanks to you, or to any man.  It was the will of God that I should live. "Count," said the crick-neck, in a low hissing voice, "you failed to seduce my wife, but she was an awkward witness against you, and you had her shut up for life in a prison."

"I!" said the Count, whose whole manner was changed before that of Torticolis.

The crick-neck replied by a stroke of genius which showed the intense nature of the poor man's feelings. He reasoned thus: "He can tell me what he pleases, but he will be sure to tell me wrong, because she is better a prisoner than free in his eyes."

"Count," said the poor man, in an agony of anxiety, which he, however, succeeded in repressing, "I always vowed to have one revenge. That was, to force you to tell me with your own lips where you had placed my wife. This morning, M. Brown, who knows your secret, told me, at the same time that he told me of your escape. Now, mark me. Repeat the place to me yourself, truly and rightly, as he did, or I denounce you to yonder men, who think you a friend of mine I have accidentally met. Let your words be a lie, and I shall not hesitate a second."

The Count looked the husband, whose whole life in reality was hanging on his words, full in the face, but read nothing there but revenge and determination. He resolved to speak.

"She is in the Bastile," he muttered savagely, as if he bitterly regretted the necessity of telling the truth.

"The Bastile!" cried Jean Torticolis, falling back with horror on his seat, while at the same time he could not but feel delighted that he had wrung the secret of his life from his enemy.

The Count ground his teeth with rage; for the man's manner showed how he had taken his adversary in.

And thus, for a moment, they sat facing one another—the one sullen, bitter, revengeful—the other far away in the land of dreams.

That poor creature, ragged, rough, a while since an outcast on the face of the earth, and now the faithful and attached servant of Charles Clement, had once been a quiet, gentle, unassuming little man; happy, as men only can be when in the enjoyment of the fond affections of God's fair creation, woman, who, wayward though she be, and wilful though she be, is at all events, the poor man's paradise on earth. The affections of the poor, who shall tell? The rich, the gay, the proud, the beings whose lives are a whirl of pleasure, may have warm and lasting affections, may love and cherish those whom they have united to them. But the poor man has nothing else: take from him his wife and his child, and what is he? And let not what is unhappy in marriage afford arguments to scoffers. The good far outbalances the evil, if any; but evil there is none, save of our own making.

Jean Torticolis sat with his eyes closed, quite closed, lost in a reverie. He was thinking of the hours when, a lad of twenty, he had seen first the young girl that had won his heart; he was thinking of the joyous minute when, in answer to his fond protestations, she breathed a soft consent, and vowed to be his, and his only, for this world, and, if it pleased God, for the next; he was thinking of the great day of his life, when she vowed before man, but at God's altar, to be his wife; and of the joyous, contented, happy life they had fled. There the picture sombred. Unholy affection, attempted seduction, his anger, his violence, prison, separation, death for him, perpetual confinement for her, and the Bastile, the hideous Bastile, were before him. Rage at this thought took possession of his heart, and, opening his eyes, he sought for the man whose selfish lust had caused all this misery.

The seat occupied by the Count de la Tour Neville was empty.

Jean Torticolis closed his eyes, and then opened them again, to make sure that he dreamed not. His eyes had not deceived him—his enemy had escaped.

"Malediction," he muttered to himself, but then, with that peculiar command over himself which rarely quitted him, he at once recovered, and moved towards the two officers of the maréchaussée, now semi-inebriated.

"Did you see my friend go out?" he inquired of the less intoxicated of the two archers.

"Yes, mon gaillard," replied the policeman.

"Will you drink?" said Jean, paying at the same time for what had been consumed.

"Ah, that we will," replied the one who was almost too drunk to see.

"No!" said the other, becoming generous in his cup,

"does our friend take us for an *écornifleur*.* We have drunk at his expense, let him now at ours."

"But we have had sufficient," suggested Torticolis.

"Not at all, my fine fellow," said the archer; "what is man but a *botte*? Drink, man! drink! and drown sorrow."

Jean Torticolis, though generally sober, after a moment's pause, sat down between the two soldiers of the maréchaussée, and began to drink. His brain was in a whirl, and he feared for his own reason if he were able to continue thinking.

A drunken man is perhaps the most lamentable of all exhibitions, because we then lose every superior sense of the mind, and appear in all the naked will of the animal; but there are moments in the existence of human beings when the utter stupefaction of intoxication is not to be resisted.

The crick-neck was in one of these critical positions.

But it was in vain he drank, the mind still kept the upperhand, and after a futile attempt at drowning thought, he escaped from his companions, and sallied forth into the open air.

---

## CHAPTER XVI.

### THE 12TH JULY, 1789.

It was Sunday morning, the 12th July, 1789. At four in the morning, the quiet of the huge city had been disturbed by the shrill voice of the criers, who called out the impôt d'honneur proposed by the Duke of Orleans, for the relief of the poor. "The Prince placed himself at the head," says the Marquis de Luchet, "for three hundred thousand livres;" fifty years ago an enormous, at any time a munificent, sum. Despite, however, the interest of this proposition, which was a deadly insult for the minions of the court, all Paris was engaged in discussing another proposition.

"Has Necker been dismissed?"

* Spunger.

Such was the question which was asked by peasant and student, artisan and shop-keeper, soldier and beggar, old and young, rich and poor, male and female, indiscriminately. At an early hour, the *Courrier de Versailles à Paris*, No. 8, was passed from hand to hand, announcing the probable departure of the minister, now in the zenith of his popularity.

The Duke, Miranda, Adela, and Charles Clement, were at breakfast together, at the hotel of the first-named. Since the day of the disruption of the marriage, this had been a regular habit every morning. Generally, Gracchus Antiboul accompanied his friend, but on this occasion he had risen at dawn, and, when Charles started, had not yet reappeared.

The Duke, on whose aged frame the day of the marriage had not passed without giving him a severe shock, though evidently enfeebled, looked far more happy than before; for his child smiled upon him with a free and full joy, which was balm and delight to his fond father's heart. The sacred chord of an old man's affection for an only child, pure as the strings of angel harp, had been touched by a master hand, and harmony itself had started forth, sweet in sound and form. The hour had come for him, when he lived only in another, a sad but happy time; sad, because we know the end of all his coming—happy, because it has pleased God to make the affections of the old even more earnest than those of the young.

But Adela and Charles Clement, they, too, were happy indeed, for they were in the hopeful and halcyon time when all things are of one colour—when the rosy tint fills air, and sky, and waters—and when the sun shines in nooks and corners, where never sun shone before; and when there come, from unknown receptacles of the mind, thoughts and feelings which we with difficulty render an account of unto ourselves.

Miranda alone was grave; for she, amid that group of four, was alone. She loved Adela, she looked with reverential respect on the Duke, she felt avowedly a gentle friendship for Charles Clement, she rejoiced at his happiness; but who shall tell the torture endured by that proud heart, swelling with womanly pride, and crushing every hour the wilful tide of unasked, unreturned, uncomprehended love.

Those who blame woman for loving where their love is not sought are squarers and rulers of human nature. They know not its intricacies, its transports. Love, real love—the rarest thing on earth—is a sudden emotion, coming we know neither why, nor how, nor when, nor where. As well might one ask the cloud why it resembles a ship rather than a castle, as ask love why it fixes in preference on a certain being! If Miranda, then, loved the accepted bridegroom of her friend—if she fixed her affections on him on the self-same day, and had never yet been able to chase the phantom from her bosom—let us not be hard upon the noble heroine of this my narrative. Perhaps with some women love is impossible, until man, by seeking their affection, has removed the timidity of their natures, which makes them fear to confess, even to their own little hearts, that passion and affection have taken possession of the citadel. But the Countess de Castelmonte was not one of these. Above the common multitudes of minds, she even loved originally.

"Nephew," said the old man, after a long reverie, during which his eyes were dwelling fondly on the forehead of his child, "I have been thinking of your wedding-day."

Charles Clement started from his conversation with Adela, while both looked as confused as two lovers could possibly look.

"My uncle!" said Charles, in reply.

"The reasons which caused me to hurry the union of my dear girl with her late cousin—for he is no relation of mine now—became each day more forcible. Do you recollect, Charles, a promise you once made me?"

"Which, my Lord Duke," replied the young man, with beaming eye, while the lovely Adela turned to seek the countenance and approbation of the Countess Miranda.

"That you would always warn me when a day of danger had really arrived, and when it was wise I should provide my child with a permanent protector. Be as honest for yourself as you were for your rival."

At this moment Gracchus Antiboul rushed into the room wholly unannounced. In his hand was a newspaper and a letter.

"Good morning, ladies, and M. le Duc.   Charles, my friend, bad news; M. Necker is dismissed, and all Paris is in motion."

"There is my answer, uncle," said Charles, gravely, while Adela turned slightly pale.

"It shall be taken as such.   This is Sunday.   On Wednesday the marriage."

"Perhaps," said Gracchus, drily, "if we be not in full civil war by then."

"Is the position so serious?" asked Clement.

"My friend, come with me to the Palais Royal.   The voice of every patriot is now needed.   No man knows what twenty-four hours may bring forth.   The die is cast. On Paris depends the triumph or destruction of liberty in France."

Charles Clement rose, his eye kindling.

"My friend," said the Duke, gently, "remember you bear two lives, if not three, about you.   But go; you will do your duty."

"Go," said Adela, deadly pale, and throwing herself on Miranda's bosom; "go, my cousin, but be careful of yourself."

"I shall go," replied Charles Clement, kindly, "because France may need me; but I shall not forget what I leave behind."

He bent low and kissed the forehead of his bride, who, frightened as she was, blushed rosy red.   It was her first kiss.

"I trust them both to you," whispered Charles, rapidly, in Miranda's ear, and embracing in his glance the feeble old man, and the feeble child, for such nearly was Adela.

The Countess Miranda raised her eloquent eyes gratefully to his face, and her whole look was a promise of being true to the faith of the young man.

He was right to leave them in her care, for hers was a bold and firm heart, in whom any, however feeble, would have found a protector.

"Come," said Gracchus Antiboul, almost impatiently. "Come, my friend."

Charles Clement put his arm in his, and they went out.

"Charles," said the enthusiastic Republican, with an in-

tensity and earnestness which was startling, " the hour is
come."

" Think you so, Gracchus ?" replied Charles.

" Now or never. The people are exasperated, and half-
starved ; they have faith in Necker, and he is to be dismissed."

" He is not, then, already ?"

" I know not if he be, or be about to be, but a few hours
will decide. But a great coup d'état is intended. Judge
for yourself."

They were at this moment crossing the bridge leading to
the Place Louis XV., now De la Concorde. It was occupied by a strong detachment of gardes suisses, of the hussars
of Berchiny, the dragoons of Choisseul, and the regiment of
Salis Samade. At their head was Besenval, whose air
was that of ferocious determination.

The place was covered with groups, who spoke in low
and anxious tones. Their aspect was that of utter consternation. Not a word of their conversation could be gathered,
so mysterious and cautious were their words. Paris was
breathing the air of emeute and insurrection.

As they went along, patrols of cavalry, troops of infantry,
cannons heavily guarded, showed that the authorities thought
some measure of precaution necessary. The Maréchal de
Broglie had answered for Paris ; and this, as usual, was the
way in which they propose to make good the promise of
tranquillity.

An equal excitement prevailed in the masses who everywhere congregated, while a large portion moved towards
the Palais Royal.

The gardens of this celebrated locality are sufficiently
familiar to very many of my readers, but in these days they
were very different from what they now are.

In the midst of the garden the Duke of Orleans had
formed an enclosure, covered with trellis-work, and crowned
by a terrace, one mass of flowers, and sprouting waters.
For the convenience of those in the palace, it was reached
by an open passage, and also by a vaulted and secret one,
of which some remains exist to this day. Afar off, this
inclosure offered the aspect of a verdant grove, while, in
reality, it was built as a theatre for feats of horsemanship,

and hence was called the circus. It was now a ball and concert room. At one of its extremities was a basin, flanked by four pavilions. All around were alleys of trees, running along the galleries of the palace. Such was the delightful and voluptuous spot chosen as the centre of insurrection and revolution. It was an open-air club, a forum, a rostrum, the very head and front of the popular movement.

It was about ten o'clock Charles Clement and Antiboul entered the garden of the palace.

"Look," said Gracchus, in an animated whisper, "the tempest is on the waters."

"More in our bosoms than elsewhere," replied Clement.

The whole garden was filled with a dense crowd. So numerous were the arrivals that many had climbed the trees and seated themselves in the branches, while every window above afforded its complement of heads. The multitude were waiting for events. There were no cries, no exclamations, no speeches; but a busy hum, a dull murmur, rose to the heavens, precursor of the terrible hours which were coming.

It was the first death-agony of the monarchy. The spirit of God was moving on the face of the waters, and shaking the once strong man, called Kingship, in its Gallic stronghold. The great change took place by violent means, by means terrible and bloody; but Paris, the capital of the monarchy, was more accursed than Sodom and Gomorrah; and who knows but all that befel it was the just measure of its sins? Has He not said, "I, the Lord, thy God, am a jealous God, visiting the iniquity of the fathers upon the children, unto the third and fourth generations of them that hate me"?

And if vice, crime, and iniquity, constitute hate of God, never was it more rife than in the great city under the last days of the monarchy.

"Salut et fraternité," said Gracchus, pressing a man's hand in the crowd of strange and wild appearances.

"A vous salut et fraternité," replied the man, moving on, without other sign of recognition.

"What mean you?" inquired Charles Clement, curiously: "that was a signal."

"He is of the Ami du Peuple, our club, and that is the password of the day," replied Gracchus Antiboul, carelessly.

As he spoke, a man dashed from one of the galleries of the Palais Royal into the garden, making hurriedly through the crowd towards the centre. He was in a horseman's garb, and seemed as if he had ridden far and fast.

"News from Versailles," shouted those around them.

In an instant all conversation ceased. The crowd stood still. The men in the trees held their breath. The thousands and tens of thousands who filled the Palais Royal garden were silent. Their instinct told them that something decisive was at hand.

"Get up on a chair," cried Antiboul.

The nouvelliste obeyed the request. He was a slight young man, of gentle manners, almost out of breath with eagerness.

"People of Paris," said he, in a voice which thrilled the auditory, "Necker is dismissed. He is on his road to Brussels."

The crowd, though half prepared, remained stupified at a piece of news which proved the counter-revolution to be in one of its moments of triumph. Then a savage impulse of incredulity took possession of the mass. It was a sublime aspiration of hope.

"It is a false piece of news! He is a spy! To the water with him," cried one.

"To the water with him," repeated the crowd, and fifty arms were raised to dash him into the basin.

"Hold!" cried Gracchus, leaping with a tremendous bound towards the young man, while Charles drew his sword, and seconded him, "are you mad, *citoyens?* Hear him."

The crowd, recalled to their senses, paused; and the bearer of the fatal news, who had remained calm, proceeded to give full details. When he had concluded, and no doubt remained, the whole assembly, amongst whom the facts flew from mouth to mouth, remained for a few minutes in a state of torpor. Each man looked at his neighbour as if to ask what would come next.

In the centre of the Palais Royal was and is a cannon,

which goes off on sunny days, precisely as the sun reaches its meridian.

On this morning, there appeared no chance of this event occurring, for the sky was covered by black and heavy clouds.

But just then, while yet the crowd was still—while all men thought within themselves, or spoke in low whispers—out burst the sun, warm, hot, glorious with all the radiance of July, and removing by its influence much of the gloom which prevailed.

A minute after it was twelve o'clock.

The sun's rays were collected in the focus of the burning glass, and the cannon fired its volley.

A half-second of hesitation followed, and then a loud, a tremendous cry, burst from the assembled masses. It was a roar of delight; for the cannon had filled all minds with one thought—that of insurrection.

At this instant a young man dashed forth from the Café de Foy, leaped upon a chair—a sword in one hand, a pistol in the other—and cried aloud.

"To arms," were his words.

"To arms," responded the people.

Next minute he had seized a leaf from one of the trees, and placed it in his hat as a cockade. Every one followed his example.

It was Camille Desmoulins.

"Charles," said Gracchus, in a low whisper, to his friend. "Paris is now in motion. Let us home and seek our arms."

Clement pressed his hand, and they moved away in the direction of the Rue Grenelle St. Honoré.

Everywhere they saw signs of the agitation of Paris, Crowds of people moved along the streets, which next minute were still, for groups had collected to talk; the shops were being hurriedly closed, proof that insurrection and emeute were expected. At the windows above, anxious faces of women, old men, and children, looked down with vague curiosity; while guns fired here and there gave terrible forewarning. Men suddenly appeared with muskets and pikes in their hands.

"The hour is come!" exclaimed Gracchus; "liberty

perisheth or is victorious this day. My friend, let us act together."

"Gracchus," replied Clement, firmly, "you have always heard me oppose untimely violence; but, as you say, the hour is at length come. You will see if the pacific are less active than the brawlers."

"For what fight we?" asked Antiboul, looking curiously at his friend.

"For the Republic," replied Clement, taking his companion's hand and pressing it convulsively.

"For the republic?" repeated Antiboul, radiant with delight.

"Yes," said the young man, leaning on his friend's arm; "enough has France groaned in the chains of feudalism and monarchy. The time has come for freedom; and, scoff as ye will, lawyers and slaves, the Republic alone can assure the happiness and freedom of the people."

"Vive la Republique!" replied Antiboul, though not without making sure none were at hand.

"Yes," exclaimed Charles Clement, gravely, casting up his eyes hopefully to heaven, "and it will live. Opposed by the selfish, the slavish, the timid, the base, the ignorant, the grovelling and vulgar, it will struggle into existence through many a throe and many an agony. The serfs of a monarchy, unused to liberty, will abuse it; much evil will be seen, and many bad days—perhaps, for us, all bad; but our children, and our children's children, will reap what we have sowed; and the day will come when, truly and seriously, the Republic shall live."

"In the meantime let us have a struggle for it," added Gracchus Antiboul, for a moment subdued by his friend's earnest manner.

"Nothing worth having is had without a struggle; and, if need be, I devote myself for my country."

With these words Clement followed his friend up stairs into his apartment, where they remained some time in earnest converse. About three o'clock in the afternoon, with each a brace of pistols, and ample ammunition, they sallied forth in the direction of the Boulevards.

Scarcely had they reached them when they met a vast procession, which was heralding everywhere the coming events.

No sooner had the news spread over all Paris that Necker was dismissed, and that the Duke of Orleans had headed a subscription for the poor by the sum of 300,000 francs, than a dense crowd collected, and, rushing to the *atelier* of the sculptor Curtius, demanded and obtained the busts both of the minister and the prince.

At the head of the procession were two men—one a black-capped Savoyard, who bore the statue of the Duke; the other a young man, fashionably dressed, who carried that of Necker. Both were veiled with crape, while flags waved over them, in sign of the triumph of the people.

There were of all classes in the procession—workmen, artizans, shopkeepers, gentlemen, nobles of the popular party, children, women—some armed, some unarmed, but all animated by enthusiasm, and the most anxious and tumultuous feelings. And the flags waved, and the people cried as they went, " No more joy! no more pleasure! close the theatres! " and the theatres closed at their bidding.

The head of the procession had reached the neighbourhood of the Place Vendome. A body of soldiers were posted on it. By one of those fatalities which often lead to such terrible misfortunes, they thought the column was about to attack them, and one or two of the men fired. The young man bearing the bust of Necker fell dead.

A scene of indescribable confusion ensued. Some cried, " To arms! " Some strove to explain the fatal accident. Others took up the body, and bore it to the post. After some quarter of an hour of intense excitement, the officer in command succeeded in persuading the people that the dreadful event was not wilful; and the bust being raised by another volunteer, the column advanced again, headed by the troops who had fraternized with the people.

Gracchus, holding Clement firmly by the arm, was near the head of the procession.

But Besenval was not in a humour to be trifled with, and no sooner was the column on the place than he charged at the head of his men. A few shots were fired, and the Savoyard fell severely wounded.

" Vengeance! " thundered Gracchus, raising the bleeding and half-senseless body, " Vengeance on the murderers of our brothers! "

"Vengeance!" cried the people.

"Yonder plank!" said Antiboul, pointing to a scaffolding.

A dozen men rushed in the direction indicated. Two planks were procured, and a hand-barrow extemporised. On this the wounded man was placed, with Gracchus Antiboul at one corner, and five others assisting him. The now lugubrious procession returned towards the Palais Royal. Everywhere on its way, it roused the indignation of the multitude, who muttered threats against Besenval. A brutal act of violence on the part of the Prince de Lambesc in the Tuileries, a few minutes after, added to the general exasperation.

This seemed the signal.

In every quarter of the town, the people flew with one accord to arms. The armourers' shops were stripped of all guns, swords, and pistols. Pikes, sticks, stones, were taken in default of anything better.

It was nine o'clock in the evening when Charles Clement and Gracchus, after a brief visit to the Duke's, where they caught some slight refreshment, arrived in the neighbourhood of the Hotel Montmorency. At the same minute, a body of fusiliers of the company of Vaugirard, headed by a corporal named Garde, and a drum beating, came up, followed by a mass of people. The Hotel was guarded by a detachment of the Royal-Allemands, whom the soldiers were coming to attack, but their officers drew them off.

The whole body then moved away in the direction of the Place Louis XV., to attack Besenval. On their way, they were joined by the Gardes Française of the Rue Verte. At their head was a ragged, ugly, tanned, enthusiastic denizen of the faubourgs.

This was Gonchon, a demagogue whose words were electric with the masses.

"Vive Gonchon!" cried the crowd, and the demagogue proudly returned their salutations.

"Now is the time, tonnerre!" cried he; "Gonchon is at your head, do you see? Here are the brave French soldiers with us, ready to drive the foreign butchers back to their own land. On! on! Gonchon leads you to victory!"

The crowd applauded again.

"Do you know him?" inquired Gracchus.

"No!" said Clement.

"A friend of Marat's, and a man who will bring ten thousand men into the field when needed."

"And who is Marat?"

"Our president," said Gracchus.

"Ours!"

"Yes! But, I forgot, you are not one of the initiated."

At this moment, a horseman arrived from the direction of the Place Louis XV

"The foreign soldiers have left Paris!" he said aloud.

"Vive Paris!" cried the masses.

"To the Hotel de Ville," replied one.

"Yes! to the Hotel de Ville."

"Arms!" cried others.

"To the Hotel de Ville!" repeated a shrill voice; "the electors are betraying us."

"Let the tiers-état look to it. The bourgeoisie will get all the profit," said another.

"To the Hotel de Ville!" and away once more the wild column went in the direction of the Municipal Palace.

Charles Clement and Gracchus Antiboul remained a little behind, in order to allow the mass to rush by.

As they went along, they were continually stopped by groups of men who asked for money to buy powder.

They gave all they had.

It was eleven o'clock when they arrived in a narrow, dirty, little street, in the neighbourhood of the Hotel de Ville. Before them was a vast mass of people, behind them a few scattered men.

"The barriers are burning!" shouted one.

"The Allemands are on Paris!" said another.

"A bas l'Autrichienne!"

"A bas Artois!"

"A bas Monsieur!"

"Vive Necker!"

"Vive D'Orleans!"

"Des Armes! Il nous faut des Armes."

Such were the cries of the multitude.

"We shall be out all night," said Gracchus, "and here is a wine-shop, let us drink and eat."

The two friends entered. The lower room was filled with drinkers, but a lad rushed with a low flat candle to show the way to an upper room. The friends ascended the dark, greasy stairs, which creaked under their footsteps, and presently stood upon a small landing. Before them was a small room, with a heavy door. It had in it a rough table and two chairs.

"Bring us two bottles of wine, and whatever you have to eat," said the student.

The lad returned, and laid the provisions ordered on the table.

"Anything else?" said the waiter, with a wooden look.

"Nothing," replied Gracchus, after eyeing the boy suspiciously.

The waiter went out and drew the door after him.

Next minute the turning of the key and a loud laugh resounded outside.

"Locked in!" said Gracchus, rising.

"A joke of that ill-looking little ruffian," replied Charles.

"Not at all," said his friend, examining the door, and rushing against it, "we are fairly prisoners."

"Fairly," sounded without the laughing voice of Leopold Count de la Tour Neville.

Charles Clement rose, pale with anger, and laid his hand on his pistols.

Gracchus seized him by the arm, forced him into his seat, and uncorked the first bottle.

"Trapped," he whispered, calmly, "but not lost. We are armed. We have plenty of ammunition. Let us refresh ourselves, and then act."

"But this villain is free," said Charles; "can Adela be safe?"

"Her father is there to guard her; and, take my word for it, Jean Torticolis is not far off," continued Gracchus, speaking low.

Charles Clement allowed himself to be persuaded, and they both ate and drank.

Suddenly, the whole of Paris resounded with the ringing of bells.

It was midnight, and the tocsin was sounding from the

Hotel de Ville, from Notre Dame, and from every church in the town.   None slept that night but unconscious babes. There they were swinging slow, with sullen roar; their brasen tongues of alarm speaking the sentiments of the myriad people.  They summoned to arms and watchfulness.

"It is time to get out of here," said Gracchus, rising, and making a rush at the door.

The door remained immovable, while a low laugh showed that there was a sentry without.   And still the tocsin sounded, booming from every church top, and waking the great city to insurrection.

---

## CHAPTER XVII.

### THE NIGHT.

WHEN Gracchus Antiboul and Charles Clement found themselves completely caught in the trap, they seated themselves at the table, and, leaning each upon his elbows, held a council of war.

"We are in the power of a scoundrel, that is clear," said Gracchus in a low whisper; "but for how long, is wholly another question.  If I only knew Torty was on our track, I shouldn't care."

"Gracchus," replied Charles Clement, sombrely, for he was thinking of his mistress, "this man is free, and I am not able to guard and watch her I love.  Besides, hark to the tocsin, how it sounds, and we are idle."

"I hear it," replied Antiboul, drily; "but it is only calling the warriors together; the fighting will not be yet. We shall come in for our share.  Let us examine our quarters."

And he raised the flickering tallow candle.

"The door is impregnable; besides, I don't know how many cut-throat scoundrels may be outside."

"The window is hopeless," added Charles, "for the bars are like those of a state prison."

"Last resource—the chimney," continued Gracchus, examining that orifice with assiduity; "too narrow for a man's arm. *Foi de Brutus*, we are in a strange position. Let us look at the ceiling."

Gracchus, with these words, climbed the table, and scrutinized with keen eye the roof.

"Black, dirty, but wooden! Oh, here is the chink! By the head of Necker, it is the flooring of the upper room. All right. Hand me the knife."

The roof was, in fact, formed by two huge beams, across which fell a number of planks, black, and apparently rotten with age. Gracchus, once in possession of the knife, which was coarse but strong, went to work, and, in a few minutes, had cleared away the dirt that filled the chink. A light at once fell through from the room above.

"Whisht!" said Gracchus, alongside whom now stood Charles Clement; "be very cautious, for some one sleeps above us. Use your knife here, the opposite side to me, and slowly, and we shall soon see what is what."

"Make less noise," whispered Charles, "or else those above and those below will equally trouble us."

"Trust me," said Gracchus; "it is not the first escape I have made out of jail."

Ten minutes of hard work sufficed completely to clear the interstices, and Gracchus looked through.

"A bed, a chair, a lamp, several varied articles of furniture, a dozen sacks of flour, and, as I live, a woman. We're done. *Foi de Brutus*, she'll scream like a cat"

"Hush," said Charles Clement, "that is to be seen. Let us get the plank out first."

"There are two ways of doing that," replied Gracchus, with a shake of the head—"to make saws of our knives, or to crack the plank. But here goes."

And seizing the chair from below, he stood upon it, on the table, leaned his back against the plank, and then paused.

"Are you ready?" he asked.

"Quite," said Charles Clement, drawing a pistol.

"Be ready to fire if they enter the room," added Gracchus, in a low whisper.

"Ready," answered Charles, laconically.

"Now for freedom," cried Antiboul, and with a sudden jerk he sent the plank shivering into the middle of the room.

"Follow," he cried, leaping upwards, and kneeling to assist Charles Clement.

"*Aux voleurs!*" shrieked a young and pretty woman, sitting up in a state of indescribable alarm in her bed.

"Shriek away," cried Gracchus, as soon as Charles was by him.  "Do as I do, Clement."

He dashed open the door, and, using his utmost strength, rolled a sack of flour down the narrow stairs, which caught at the turning, and the dozen others rapidly following, the stairs were completely barricaded.

"But," cried the girl, who, after an examination of the intruders, felt no longer so very much alarmed, "why are you in my bed-room?"

"We are very sorry to intrude," said Gracchus Antiboul, with excessive politeness, taking an opportunity at the same time to examine the person whose sanctuary they had so suddenly invaded; "but we were prisoners below, and every means is fair in captivity, as in love and war."

"Prisoners!" said the damsel; "but explain, messires, or rather retire an instant, and I will rise."

The two friends discreetly moved to the landing, whence they had the satisfaction of assuring themselves that their *extempore* fortress of flour-bags was for the nonce impregnable.

In a few minutes the girl opened the door, and hospitably bade them enter, when Gracchus at once, without circumlocution, explained their adventure.  The girl listened with attentive ears, continually interrupting him, however, with exclamations of surprise.

"*Mon dieu*, the holy virgin protect you," said she, clasping her hands, when she had concluded, "for you are in a strangely-bad house.  It is a famous resort of cut-throats and *coupe-jarrets!*"

"How came you here?" inquired Gracchus, drily.

The girl bent down her head, shamefully, as she replied, "I am a poor girl, but honest.  I live near at hand with an old woman, who has adopted me.  About a month since, a fine handsome gentleman saw me, and spoke to me kindly.  He said he wished my good—that I was not in my right position; and he gave me clothes; and "—here the girl blushed more deeply still—" there was a talk of making me a *grande dame*, by giving me his hand. Last night, late, he came to our house in disguise. He had on him a large hat and cloak, while he was stoutly armed. He said that he, as a noble, was flying; for that awful days were come, when a gentleman was to be persecuted, and his life taken. He said he must fly from Paris, and I must go with him."

" Well," said Gracchus, still drily, " your story interests me."

" He told me I must fly with him now, or lose him for ever; and as he was hunted to the death, I must meet him here, where none would suspect him."

" Our man," whispered Gracchus to Charles; " I suspected so from the first. Is your friend tall ? " he added.

" He is; do you know him ? " inquired the girl, anxiously, while her eyes grew more animated and bright than usual.

" Is he slight ? " continued Antiboul.

" He is."

" Describe him to me."

The girl did so with all the minuteness and observation of love, and, though highly coloured, the portrait was too distinct not to be recognized.

" The scoundrel ! " exclaimed Charles Clement, bitterly.

" Monsieur ! " said the girl, reproachfully, raising her blue eyes to his.

" Rather," said Charles Clement, seizing her arm—" rather listen to the fiend himself than to that monster. It is he who waits below to murder us; it is he who, having robbed his uncle, would have made his cousin a felon's wife. He is a profligate, who wished to ruin and abandon you, and from whom God has sent us to save you."

" Leopold a traitor ! " exclaimed the girl, wildly.

" Said we not so ? " continued Gracchus; " the dastard knave Leopold, that is the name."

" Monsieur ! " said the girl, clasping her hands, " I am a poor child, save me from this man."

" And you have really escaped ? " mused Gracchus.

He knew not why, but he waited the answer with intense anxiety.

" I was to be his wife," said the girl, bending down her eyes; " and he respected me, he said, for that reason."

"Double traitor! but let us not tarry longer.  We must to the roof—first, let us cast these mattresses above the sacks "—

And Gracchus raised the whole of the bedding in his arms, and, casting it on the floor, trampled it down, so as to make the impediment as great as possible.  The addition of a few chairs and an old table made it probable that they could not be removed under nearly half-an-hour.  Furniture was then so piled over the aperture in the flooring as to be immovable.

"Now then, away," he continued, taking the lead; " you Charles, assist this girl; I will reconnoitre with this lamp."

With these words, Gracchus Antiboul, who had taken the wretched lamp off the table, ascended the dirty, greasy, narrow staircase, with a slow and measured step.  The house was lofty, and at each landing they listened for inmates in the room.  They were all empty, their usual occupants being too disturbed this busy night to be in bed.  The tocsin still sounded.

They had ascended to the sixth story, and were making for the seventh and last, when Gracchus halted, and bade his companions do so likewise, showing the utmost caution.  Charles Clement moved to his side.  Before them was an open window; and out upon the roof sat a solitary man.  His back was to them, and he was leaning forward, as if looking into the street below.  Gracchus handed the lamp to Charles Clement, cocked his pistol, and crept stealthily up to examine who was this man who stood thus inopportunely in their way.  He held his breath; and, though the old stairs creaked slightly under his weight, reached the landing undiscovered.

Once at the window, he leaned cautiously out, advanced his pistol to the man's ear, and then, as he caught him by the throat, pressed the cold tube to his temples.  The man gave a convulsive shudder, and then turned round calmly.  It was Jean Torticolis.

"Torty!" exclaimed Gracchus, petrified with astonishment, " what do you here?"

"I am watching to shoot Count Leopold," replied the crick-neck, savagely.

" To shoot him!" muttered the girl.

"Jean," said his master, advancing nearer, and speaking in a severe, and at the same time gentle tone, "why would you murder this man ?"

"Because he robbed me," replied Torty, who was evidently still semi-drunk with frenzy.

"Robbed you!" said Clement, with an accent of much surprise.

"Of his wife," answered Gracchus, in a whisper.

At this instant a heavy explosion was heard, and, in a moment, the whole party were wrapped in a dense cloud of smoke.

Those below had endeavoured to blow away the barrier by a small quantity of gunpowder. The very house shook, but the quantity was not sufficiently great to shatter the walls, even within; and the sound of shovels at work a minute after showed that all was not free below.

The landing opened into a garret used as a lumber room. The three men rushed therein, seized old pieces of furniture, planks of beds, chairs, an antiquated wardrobe falling to pieces—anything on which their hands fell; and, in five minutes, had formed a barrier even more formidable than the one below ; a few cords rendered the removal a work of difficulty and time.

"Now," said Charles Clement, "we shall have leisure to escape by the roof. Can it be done easily ?" he added, turning to Torticolis.

"Very easily," replied the crick-neck, "except there will be men below guarding the issue. We must make a long *detour*."

"Here, Torty," said Gracchus, seizing a coil of old rope, "take this, it may be useful."

With this understanding, Torty led the way. Gracchus Antiboul followed, holding the girl's hand; while Charles Clement brought up the rear, having quietly but peremptorily taken the post of honour. Antiboul, whose eyes should have been before him, was constantly looking behind, for fear his friend should be attacked. The road they had taken was difficult and dangerous. A narrow, flat portion of the roof near the gutter enabled them to walk along about twenty yards, passing several garret windows, and then they reached the edge of a terraced roof much below them.

In an instant, Torty had fastened the cord over to the terrace below, and had slid down; both his master and Gracchus then assisted the young girl to descend.

"God be thanked," said she, "this is my house."

"So much the worse," exclaimed Antiboul, "for that will surely be guarded."

He raised the trap leading below, and descended the stair a few steps.

"Are there many persons in the house?" asked Charles.

"Many," replied the young girl.

At this instant the face of the boy-waiter peered over the edge of the roof, and Gracchus saw him turn back and signal to others, disappearing instantly.

The group were standing round the trap, as if about to descend. By their side, in the wall of the lofty house, was an open window. Gracchus drew the girl, by a convulsive jerk, towards it. In an instant the whole party had entered, closed the window, and concealed the lamp. Scarcely had they done so, when a heavy body alighted near the window. In another instant six men were on the terrace, among whom Gracchus recognized the Count.

"Down this trap?" said the Count interrogatively.

"Yes," replied the voice of the boy.

Away went the pursuers, one after another, in hot haste down the staircase.

"Escaped!" cried Gracchus, in a low voice of triumph.

"Lost!" repeated the girl, recovering her breath, "we are in the house we have just left."

Gracchus and the whole party stood an instant, overwhelmed with astonishment. But all three were men of action. They passed through the bed-room they were in, and through another and then entered a narrow, dark passage, into which ten or twelve similar apartments opened, as in so many old houses in Paris. Away they went down the stairs, using caution, though moving quickly, until they had passed by the dirty scene of confusion made by the blowing up of the flour-bags. Before them was an open door, that of a narrow passage along the wine-shop, which was still crowded with visitors. The whole party paused not, but slipping down under cover of the clamorous discussion relative to themselves, gained the street without difficulty. It was a narrow, dirty lane. The girl took the lead, and in an instant more they were out of it. Two or three turns, a rapid motion along, and a hum of voices is heard before them. Another minute, and they are lost in a dense crowd.

It is the Place de Grêve, in front of the Hotel de Ville, and the clock is striking four, and still the tocsin is sounding, and a dull red glare in the sky shows that the barriers are still burning.

"The fight will not take place without us," said Gracchus.

"Adela will rejoice," thought Charles Clement.

"What will *he* say?" mused the girl.

"Not yet! not yet!" muttered Jean Torticolis, as he savagely caressed a pistol in his bosom.

---

## CHAPTER XVIII.

### THE THIRTEENTH OF JULY.

In a few moments the party formed a little knot, apart from the rest of the dense crowd. The girl leaned heavily on the arm of Gracchus.

"What must we do with you?" said Antiboul, addressing her kindly.

"I must not go home; *he* will find me," she answered with instinctive terror, though not without a feeling of regret.

"Hum," replied Gracchus; "she must go to your place, Charles, until our return."

"It is free for you," said Charles Clement, turning to her; "there you will be perfectly safe."

"'Tis best to go while there is a chance," interrupted Antiboul. "Torty, take you this young girl to the Rue Grenelle; show her how to find rest and food, and then rejoin us."

"Where will you be?" said Jean Torticolis.

"You see yon dirty café—there will we breakfast, anon; for the night-work has made me hungry."

"I shall find you there?"

"Wait for us, if you do not find us; and now go, and mind you take care of this girl."

"How shall I thank you?" said the young creature, gratefully.

"We will talk of that at a future time," replied Gracchus, motioning to Jean to lead her away, and watching her until quite out of sight.

Left alone, the two young men fell back to gaze on the crowd. The whole place was one dense mass of men, of all ages and almost every station. There were the bone and rag-pickers, the water-carriers, the market-men and market-women, the errand-lads, the workmen, the inhabitants of the faubourgs and outskirts, the small and great shopkeepers, and nearly all armed with pistol or sword, gun or pike. They stood in dense groups, talking violently, and loudly. They complained of famine and want of work, of the dearness of provisions, of the forestallers and storers up of food. Their rage against hoarders was great. They spoke against Besenval, against Monsieur, against the Count d'Artois, against Marie Antoinette; while the Duke of Orleans, Necker, and the Assembly, received all their praises.

It was now broad daylight; indeed, it had been so for nearly two hours. Along the Quays, around the Communal Palace, in all the adjacent streets, was the busy hum of men.

At this hour, all Paris was in commotion. Many were already armed, but more were looking for arms. It was chiefly for this purpose that the masses were congregated round the Hotel de Ville. They demanded organization and arms. It was announced that the electors were convoked for eight o'clock in the morning, when the wishes of the people should be attended to. This gave them something to expect, and hence kept them quiet.

Every moment, however, the agitation increased. The news came that the Bastile had pointed its cannon on the town; that the forces of the king were concentrating round Paris; that the people were about to be attacked.

"To arms! give us arms," replied the people.

The scene was vivid in the extreme; a sea of heads, hats, caps, of bare, rude hair, of upturned faces, gazing chiefly at the clock. Pikes, guns, sticks, bars of iron, and every instrument which ingenuity could devise, were in their hands. Some had gun-barrels, others, rusty swords; some flails; some, scythes—these were workmen from the out-skirts, who had come in during the night.

"Where are the echevins?" they cried.

"Where are the electors?"

"Where is the provost of the merchants?"

"They laugh at us."

"Go ask Marie Longchamps where is Monsieur de Flesselles," said another, sarcastically.

"But, *messires* the electors must breakfast," exclaimed another.

"And our wives, who are hungry."

"And our children, who are starving."

"Down with the electors!"

"To the Bastile!"

"To the Invalides!"

But all these cries led to nothing. The people contented themselves with bawling, screaming, and hallooing; but they waited. The hour was not yet come.

The clock of the Hotel de Ville struck seven.

The multitude seemed to take a long breath, for they had only another to wait.

In the upper room, the two friends found a number of men congregated, to whom Gracchus Antiboul gave a familiar nod of the head as he entered.

"The hour has struck," said a small, dirty man, with strong emphasis, but in a whisper.

"It has," replied Gracchus, seating himself.

"Man has found out the problem," continued the speaker, "that life is freedom, and that slavery is death. Let him fix it in his memory."

"You speak rightly; but will he fix it?" continued Antiboul.

"When he has done justice on his enemies. To con-struct, you must destroy. To save the body, you must lop off a limb. Cut down, exterminate your enemies, root and branch; there will then be hope for humanity."

"Surely, you would not slay them?" observed Charles Clement, coldly.

The other looked at him with the tenacity and fixedness of a wild cat, ere he replied, which he did in a proverb—*Mort la bête, mort le venin.*" *

"That is a hard doctrine," continued Charles. "Destroy the weapons of our adversaries, but spare their persons."

"Spare not at all," said the little dirty man, hotly; "have they not killed? have they not slayed? have they not murdered us? Have they ever spared us?"

"They have not; but our object is not to copy their crimes, but to replace them by something better," answered Charles Clement; and leaving Gracchus Antiboul in conversation with Marat, he moved to the window, and looked out upon the Hotel de Ville.

The scene of the most wonderful events in French history, this building, by its massive and majestic appearance, would seem to have been erected to hold out against the tempest, and the ruder attacks of popular commotions.

It struck eight o'clock.

The electors of the City of Paris were announced as sitting.

"Breakfast is ready," said the shrill voice of Jean Torticolis, at his master's elbow.

"Have you taken the girl home safely?" replied Charles Clement.

"Quite," answered Torticolis.

Charles Clement glanced at the table, where breakfast awaited him, and saw that Marat was about to join them in their repast.

"A fourth plate," said he, turning to the waiter.

"For whom?" cried Gracchus.

"For Jean," replied Charles, with an imperceptible glance at Marat.

Gracchus Antiboul bit his lip, but made no remark, though he fully felt the reproach of his friend's manner.

The four sat down to breakfast in view of the Place de Grêve. The multitude was more compact, thick, and menacing than it had been even all night. The electors were already sitting, and none seemed inclined to give them long time for deliberation.

But the crowd were silent and noisy by turns. There

* When a serpent is dead, it stings not.

seemed fuglemen among the mass, who gave the word of command. Suddenly, the eye of Charles Clement fell upon a window on the end of the Place, they being on the *palier* directly facing the Hotel de Ville.

The window was situated on the second floor, and a man leaned over the sill, with a broad-brimmed hat upon his head. Every five minutes he moved his hat, and then the shouting arose. The window was that of the room in which were met several of the unknown persons who instigated and guided the insurrection.

Presently a man entered the breakfast-room, and approached Marat.

"The electors are betraying us," he said.

"How?" replied Marat, wiping his mouth leisurely.

"They are discussing the urgency of forming a civic guard, and are ordering the crowds to disperse quietly."

"Let them disperse," continued Marat.

"Where?" said Legendre, the butcher.

"There are arms concealed in St. Lazare."

"They shall go to St. Lazare."

"The Invalides," added the dirty doctor, "are a perfect arsenal."

"To the Invalides," responded Legendre.

"And the Bastile?" inquired Marat, drinking with Gracchus.

"Has drawn up its *pont-levis*, and pointed its guns on the town and faubourg."

"And the foreign troops?"

"No man knows where they are."

"Be sure they are near at hand; be sure the bloodhounds of tyranny and aristocracy are not far off. Be ready."

Legendre made a significant sign, and rushed out, followed by about a dozen men, who had closed round the speakers, and kept their conversation private.

Charles Clement, Gracchus, Marat, and Jean, moved anxiously to the window.

The inert and inactive crowd were still. They were, as usual, waiting for events. Rumours were circulating that the electors were playing the game of power, and discussing the armament of a city guard, as much to repress the people, as to defeud themselves from the aggressions of the Court.

Presently a faint cry rose at a given signal from one quarter.

"*Aux Invalides !*" cried a shrill voice.

A perfect roar succeeded, and, with one accord, a mass of seven thousand men and more made for the Quai.

" Aux Invalides !" repeated they, in a thousand voices.

"*Des Armes !*"

" We are being betrayed!  To arms! to arms!"
Another cry then arose.

"*Au convent de St. Lazare !*"

" To St. Lazare," repeated the crowd.

In a quarter of an hour the Place de Grêve was completely empty.

" They are at work," said Marat.

" Yes," replied Gracchus Antiboul, " and we must go aid them."

" Rather let us go to temper their violence," answered Charles Clement.

" Stay," said Marat, looking suspiciously at them, " they will soon be back ; and here it is men of head are wanted."

" Nay," answered Charles, " I cannot stay.  The Invalides will be attacked.  I must be near at hand."

Gracchus Antiboul knew that his friend referred to the proximity of the Rue Dominique, to the scene of action, and he nodded assent.

" Wait you us here," said he, addressing Torticolis ; " we shall rejoin you anon."

The two friends went down into the Place, which was again beginning to fill, in time to see Flesselles, Provost of the Merchants, go in to the electors at their bidding.

" See," said Gracchus, in a whisper, and pointing with his finger.

" Count Leopold," replied Charles Clement.

The Count was, indeed, standing in the middle of the Place, in conversation with M. Brown, the police spy, dressed in his holiday suit.

The friends, though strangely puzzled, made no delay; but, turning the corner of the Place, entered a stray *voiture de place,* and drove to the Rue Dominique.

# CHAPTER XIX.

### THE EVE.

WHEN Charles Clement and Gracchus Antiboul entered the hotel of the Duc de Ravilliere, they found the whole of the domestics of the establishment congregated in one terror-stricken group in the corridor. They were pale, anxious, and trembling.

"Where is the Duke?" said Charles Clement, entering hurriedly.

"Oh, Monsieur!" cried the servants, "what is the matter?"

"Nothing!" exclaimed Gracchus Antiboul, gruffly; "but answer."

"They are in the *salon,*" said the pretty Rose, with a reverence.

The two friends pushed by, and, hurrying down a small passage, paused on the edge of the threshold.

"Hush," whispered Gracchus, "and look at that superb creature."

Charles Clement turned pale and red, but made no reply.

The Duke was seated in an arm chair, awake, but dreaming. He seemed utterly stunned; his aspect was that of annihilation. His eyes were fixed on vacant space, for he was in deep thought. Every now and then he would look hurriedly round, as if in search of an enemy, and then he would again sink into stillness. Adela, pale, weeping, frantic, was cast back, half fainting, in her chair. Her lovely face was surcharged with anxious grief—grief that utterly overcame her.

Standing upright between them, her brow unclouded, her whole form majestic and grand, was the Countess Miranda. A hand of hers rested affectionately on Adela's head, while to both she gave honied words of comfort and hope. All a woman's devotion and courage seemed hers, and both appeared subjugated to belief and confidence by the force of her earnest will. Her power over them was only subordinate to her power of ruling.

"Thanks, Countess, thanks!" said Charles Clement, advancing warmly across the room; "you redeem your promise most generously."

"You gave them to my care," whispered Miranda, lowly, and now far less firm and energetic in manner; "you see they are still safe."

"Oh, Charles! dear Charles!" cried Adela, rising and falling on his breast; they will not murder us?"

"Murder us! murder us!" muttered the Duke, who was momentarily dreaming.

"Who?" said Gracchus, drily.

"The mob! the populace!" replied Adela.

"The people will fight, not assassinate," answered Gracchus, with a painful contraction of the muscles of his face. He was hurt at the suspicion, but he could not harshly answer the bride of his friend.

"Oh, I know not!" cried Adela, trembling, and clinging to Charles Clement. "I fancy I hear them coming."

"Be not alarmed," replied her lover, tenderly, "we are here to guard you."

"Is there really anything to fear?" inquired Miranda, drawing Adela back to her seat.

"Nothing," answered Charles. "The Court has committed follies, irritated the people, and made them seek for sure means of defence; but there is nothing more. Should the insensate advisers of the King further madden the people, the consequences will be terrible for them; but you—what can you have to fear?"

"I fear nothing," replied Miranda, gently; "but, you see, my Lord Duke has been much shocked, and so has this dear girl. I would have them reassured; that is all I ask."

"Nothing to fear, Charles?" said the Duke, as if waking from a dream, and gazing with confidence and affection on his nephew.

"Nay, my Lord, not for you," replied Charles, moving beside him. "Paris has risen to defend itself. It is said that Necker is dismissed, that a ministry the enemy of all liberty has been chosen, that the National Assembly is to be annihilated, and the Revolution be crushed."

And thus for some time the two young men remained, calming and consoling the two weaker inmates of the hotel, while they added strength to the resolution of her who had become their guardian and protector.

Once a little recovered, Gracchus adroitly turned the

conversation, and, in his dry and humorous way, began to recount their adventures of the past night. The three friends became immediately interested. The Duke listened indignantly at the recital of the action of his nephew Leopold, Adela in semi-alarm, Miranda with admiration of the cool strategetic talent exhibited by the young men during their night's siege in the Cabaret.

"And where have you concealed the young lady from our good cousin?" continued Miranda.

Clement blushed.

"In Charles's lodgings," replied Gracchus, coolly, almost innocently.

The two young ladies, unable to restrain themselves, threw themselves on one another's necks in a paroxyism of inextinguishable laughter.

Gracchus looked puzzled.

"Clever young men," said Miranda, recovering herself; "our worthy cousin will never seek her in Charles's apartments. May I ask if you intend keeping her there?"

This was said with a woman's ineffable slyness, while Adela checked her laughter, and listened carefully.

"Until I find her a home," answered Gracchus, stoutly.

"Well said, young man," exclaimed the Duke; "gallantry always. Never forget you are a Frenchman."

At this moment a friend, or rather retainer of the house, entered. He had just come from the Hotel de Ville. The municipal palace was the scene of the utmost confusion.

"What do the electors?" asked Charles.

"They are forming a city guard," replied the other, who was the man of affairs of the Duke; meanwhile Paris is in awful commotion. I have been embraced by fifty strangers on my way here; everywhere green cockades are being distributed; the women throw them out of windows. The *rappèl* is being beat by the people."

"And the electors?" insisted Gracchus.

"Have ordered the formation of the *Malice Parisienne*, which armed, all other persons are to give up their arms and retire home."

"The insolent usurpers!" exclaimed Antiboul, striking his hand upon his chair; "they want to disarm the people."

" Who is to command this city guard?" said Charles.

" The Duke d'Aumont," replied the man of affairs.

" Has he accepted?" exclaimed Charles.

" He has taken twenty-four hours to consider," was the answer.

" He is a traitor."

" The second in command is the Marquis de la Salle."

" And he?"

" Has accepted without conditions," replied the intendant.

" Vive the citoyen La Salle," said Gracchus.·

" It is time to go see what is doing," observed Charles, on receiving a signal from Antiboul.

" Already?" said Adela.

" Already," repeated the Duke.

The friends hesitated.  The worn and anxious face of the old man seemed to lose all hope, as he was left by Charles Clement; Adela sighed, turned pale, and looked reproachfully at both; but Miranda whispered a few thoughts of duty, which made the wilful, gentle, lovely girl bow her head and acquiesce.  Miranda bade them go, but to be careful of their lives.

The young men replied by comforting words, and then once more sallied into the streets, and made their way to the Hotel de Ville.  The Place de Grêve was filled by another angry crowd.

A dense mass was congregated in front of the principal entrance.  There was a general cry for arms.  Flesselles promised to send for some to Charleville.  The word treachery was whispered from man to man.

" Powder," cried some of the crowd.

" There is none here," said the door-keepers, duly instructed.

" It is false!" exclaimed several voices behind; "some barrels were taken in, in the night."

" Treachery!" bawled the indignant crowd, and a desperate rush was made forward.  Two or three led the way, and in a few minutes the whole body succeeded in gaining the office of the *payeurs des rentes*.  The door was dashed open—a dense and motley crowd rushed in. A dozen barrels of powder stood piled one upon another before them

" The traitors!" exclaimed Gracchus, who, with Charles Clement, had forced his way in.

" *Vive la Liberté!*" cried a *faubourien*, brandishing a loaded pistol.

" Do you wish to blow us all up?" asked Antiboul.

"*Mille noms d'un bombe, non!*" answered the *faubourien*, alarmed.

" Then put up your pistol, and stand back.  Who will head the distribution?"

" I," said a meek voice.

Gracchus Antiboul turned round in some surprise.

It was a priest who spoke—his name was Lefebvre; and without another word he began his dangerous duty. For sixteen hours did this undaunted man of God, surrounded by armed men, by boys, by women, continue intrepidly his tremendous task.

Had similar acts been committed by many priests, the Revolution would have gone on differently.  But these pretended men of God looked to their church and themselves, and not to the people, and the people rejected them.

Gracchus and Clement went elsewhere.  The night was coming on, and they advanced to within near the Bastile. Hundreds of armed men were roaming about in knots and groups, or alone; while now and then a crowd would collect in low and earnest debate.  The friends paused several times to listen.  On the first occasion, they had scarcely stopped, when the shrill voice of a man gliding by threw a sentence to the crowd:—

" To-morrow, the Bastile!"

They moved away, for the group became silent for an instant, and then resumed.

All the houses were illuminated, giving light to the knots of men who waited for the morrow.

They stopped at several, and at each they heard the same shrill voice say the same words:—

" To-morrow, the Bastile!"

" I know that tone," observed Charles.

" It is Jean Paul Marat, the President of our Club," replied Gracchus.

Here and there were voluntary sentries doing duty for the nation, while every now and then they would notice a red glare and the noise of a blacksmith's shop.

It was the people forging pikes.

The sound of the sledge-hammer, however, soon alone broke the stillness of the night, except when the slow and sullen step of a *bourgeoise* patrol was heard coming down a street in the distance.

It was the night of the 13–14th July, the eve of the capture of the Bastile.

Paris was never more glorious than on this occasion. The whole night was passed in preparations for the inevitable struggle, and on the morning the great city was ready.

* * *

## CHAPTER XX.

### THE BASTILE.

AT the extremity of the Rue St. Antoine and of the Boulevard rose the dungeon-tomb, known as the Bastile. Eight heavy and massive towers, linked together by huge walls, and surrounded by a fœtid ditch : such was the aspect presented by the building. In the year 1369, Charles V., when erecting the gate of St. Antoine, had several towers added to it, and in 1370, Hugues Aubriot, provost of Paris, laid the first stone of the prison fortress, to be shortly afterwards one of the earliest victims who sighed and despaired within its walls.

The general aspect of the locality was frightful, and the sombre genius of a Dante amid jailors appeared to have presided over its erection. Everything around savoured of the luxurious and careful cruelty of despotism. An air-hole in a wall a dozen feet thick, with three intervening gratings, was all the means of light which the majority of the cells possessed. There were even rooms with iron cages in the centre, while the horror of the dungeons of the caves below was beyond all conception. The hideous lair of toads and lizards, enormous rats and spiders, their furniture consisted in a stone covered with straw, while the only air came foul and thick through vent-holes from the ditch into which fell the sewer of the Faubourg St. Antoine. Such were the refinements of the French monarchy, of which sentimental philosophers still deplore the fall.

Still it was not the prison of the poor. It was the dungeon of aristocracy, of wealth, of talent, of the Rhoans, the La Bourdonnaies, the Birons, the " Lallys," the Richelieus, and others. It rarely opened its gates to the poor, except poor literary men, who had dared to speak their mind and tell the truth. But the people knew only that it was a prison; of whom they asked not, nor did they care.

It was the dawn of day, or, rather, the light was beginning to break in the sky, when Charles Clement and Gracchus Antiboul arrived in the direction of the Bastille by the Boulevard. Both were armed, and on the face of both, too, appeared that determination and courage which makes the countenance sternly beautiful. A small wine-shop was open. They entered it, and seated themselves at an open window, and there in earnest converse passed the time scarcely conscious of the lapse of the hours.

When it was quite morning, many men, some well dressed, others in working costume, entered the cabaret.

" The Hotel de Ville has been gutted of powder," said one.

" And the Abbé Lefebvre nearly shot," replied another.

" The Royal Allemands are at the Barriere du Trone ! "

" Royal Cravate are massacring the people of the Faubourg St. Antoine."

" The Rue Charonne is running with blood."

" The regiments of St. Denis are advancing ; they have gained la Chapelle."

Such were the rumours brought by men who spoke, and then glided away unnoticed.

They were the conspirators of the day rousing the people to action.

Soon the tocsin sounded everywhere, by order of the *comité* of the Hotel de Ville ; and at once the streets were unpaved, barricades were erected as if by magic, and ditches dug to impede the advance of the troops. The insurrection was general. All Paris was in arms.

" The Invalides are captured," cried a new comer, suddenly.

" The arms are in the people's hands," added the same shrill voice as before.

" La Bastille ! La Bastille ! " shouted without a thousand voices.

The young men rushed into the streets, to join in the struggle.

From the Rue St. Antoine, coming from the Hotel de Ville, a dense column of men poured forth under the walls of the fortress. Pikes and muskets, blunderbusses and poles, sticks, swords, pistols, the rough workmen, gentlemen in bag-wigs and rapiers, women—all in solemn and terrible mood, coming to lay siege to the tyrannic stronghold that for so many years had insulted the majority of the people.

At the head was a little man, who screamed as he went, until his very throat was hoarse—

"To the Bastille! To the Bastille!"

"Torty!" cried Gracchus, astounded.

"My man!" exclaimed Charles; "always in trouble."

"This time let him alone," said Antiboul; "he is wiser than when he played the old royalist game in the Faubourg St. Antoine."

"Let him alone," repeated Charles Clement, after an instant of reflection.

In an instant more another mass came pouring along the same street. It was the column from the Invalides.

"The second army of the people," said Charles.

"See the third," cried Gracchus, pointing to the Boulevard.

There was in the Rue des Boucheries, in the Faubourg St. Germain, a certain *restaurateur* or eating-house, where the demagogues, conspirators, and agitators of these days took their repasts, as they do now in equally aristocratic localities. Here they planned and plotted, discussed and debated the events of the day; and hence departed the mysterious emissaries who spread abroad the signal-word, and lit the signal-fire. A large number of guests were, on the morning of the 14th, assembled at breakfast. Suddenly the door burst open; a man entered, perspiration pouring from his brow, his clothes in rags, his hat cocked insolently on his head. In his hand was a musket, the butt-end of which he struck violently on the ground.

"We are free," he cried; and in a few words, he narrated the capture of the Invalides, the distribution of arms, the emotion and enthusiasm of the people, the state of Paris on the other side of the water ; and all in a biting, sarcastic, incisive way, which added tenfold force to his words.

It was Camille Desmoulins stirring up the Parisians, and risking his person, unlike Marat, who pushed others on, but never acted himself.

" What next ? " cried the guests.

" *Vive la Liberté !* " replied Camille, the *Vieux Cordelier* that was to be ; " to the Bastille ! "

" To the Bastille," responded the company with one accord, and Desmoulins leading the way, they rushed into the street. Their first impulse was to gain the Palais Royal, where they found thousands of uncertain men waiting for leaders. They were received with enthusiastic shouts.

" *A la Bastille !* " responded Camille Desmoulins ; and placing himself at their head, they made for the Boulevard, and gained this way, swelling as they went, the frowning fortress of the Bastille.

This was the third army pointed out by Gracchus Antiboul to his friend.

The whole dense mass of the people, in the utmost excitement, surrounded the Bastille. The principal force was directed against the entrance, but no hostile signal had as yet been given on either side.

M. de Launay, governor of the Bastille, was not taken unawares. For some days he had seen the disposition of the people, especially in the Faubourg St. Antoine, which he overlooked, and on which he cast the heavy and gloomy shadow of terror and despotism. He was well aware that the prison of which he had charge would be one of the first places attacked, and accordingly he had fully prepared himself. Whole cart-loads of paving-stones had been taken up to the summit of the towers, to be cast down upon the heads of the assailants ; while pinchers had been contrived with which to loosen chimneys and abutments. He had opened embrasures, loopholes, closed windows with oaken staves, *assemblés a rainures et languettes,* and taken out of the arsenal twelve of these rampart guns called the *amusettes du comte de Saxe !*

Besides, he had placed fifteen pieces of cannon on the

edge of the towers, three field-pieces in the interior court, fronting the grating of the entrance; these, with four hundred *biscaïens*, fourteen coffers of *boulets sabotés*, three thousand cartridges, were the governor's materials of defence.

To work all the deadly articles, the Bastille contained thirty-two Swiss mercenaries of the regiment of Salis-Samade, and eighty-two Invalids, in all, a hundred and fourteen men, but with courage and determination behind those hideous walls, they were equal to an army.

But mistakes had been made. De Launay, from selfish grasping at money, had weakened himself terribly. To reach the first drawbridge, to which we have already alluded, and which was called the *pont-levis de l'avancé*, it was necessary to follow a winding passage, with barracks on the right, and a row of shops on the left. These latter were so situated as to serve as a covered road to the besiegers, and De Launay had not removed them, because the rent derived from them was his perquisites.

Thus were placed in presence the two parties—the besiegers and the besieged.

About two thousand assailants were as yet only collected round. Their manner was as yet not hostile. They were armed, but they lounged about in knots, waiting the final signal of the attack.

Charles Clement and Gracchus Antiboul were leaning against the wall of the tavern in which they had passed the morning. Both were examining the solemn and silent fortress, and the flood of its enemies every moment became more numerous. All faces were radiant with hope and enthusiasm. They were about to attack the infernal monster, hitherto untouchable, and near which men had long passed without daring to look up.

One group close to them particularly attracted their attention. About a dozen well-dressed men, among whom Gracchus recognised Legendre, the butcher, were collected round a speaker, who addressed them with animation and vigour. The two friends approached. The orator was young, delicate in appearance, and elegant and fantastic in costume. A red cap confined a mass of exuberant and rich auburn hair; a close-fitting frock or tunic showed a full and peculiar shape; while, instead of breeches, she wore long and loose pantaloons. A red sash supported a brace of pistols and a sword, while a musket served her to lean upon.

"No compromise, *mes amis!* Death to the enemies of liberty. Too long an insolent aristocracy—corrupt, rotten, selfish, debauched, reckless—has lorded it over us. Down with them to the dust. It is they who have ruined France; they who bred famine; they who starve the people—·to the ground with them."

"Who is that?" said Charles.

"Theroigne de Mericourt, the Aspasio of the rich demagogue society of the Faubourg St. Antoine."

"Why hates she so the nobles?"

"One of them ruined her."

"How still the Bastille is!" rejoined Charles Clement, turning towards the fortress.

"And how still the multitude is!" answered Antiboul.

The passage leading to the entrance of the prison, the open space around, the streets, the tops of the houses, the windows, were all being calmly filled with armed men, but not a shot was fired. The ramparts of the Bastille were naked. Not a sentry was to be seen. The huge donjon watched but in silence.

At this moment a man appeared at the extremity of the Rue St. Antoine, bearing a white flag. The crowd made way. It was Belon, an officer of the arquibusiers; Billefond, sergeant-major of artillery; and Chatoc, ex-sergeant of the French Guards, coming as a deputation from the Hotel de Ville.

The Parliamentaries forced their way easily through the crowd, which yielded before them. They reached the entrance of the Bastille. M. de Launay presented himself, and, on the populace retiring to a distance, allowed the deputation to enter, and received them even with courtesy. Like most *bourgeoisie* schemes, their demand amounted to a nullity. They promised, if Launay would draw in his guns, and pledge himself to commit no act of hostility, that the Faubourg St. Antoine should desist from their intended attack.

De Launay very politely promised to conceal his cannon, which he did, and the deputation retired.

At this instant, an advocate of the Parliament of Paris presented himself, and demanded an interview with the governor in the name of the district of St. Louis de la Culture.   It was Thuriot de la Rosière.   He turned for an escort to the crowd.   Charles and Gracchus sprang forward.

"Courage, but discretion," whispered a voice gently in the ear of Charles Clement.   He turned round sharply.   A man in a slouched hat and heavy cloak was moving away. He had no time to see farther, for the future president of the Convention, "president of assassins," as Robespierre was one day to call him, waited for his escort.

"Who was that?" said Gracchus Antiboul, in a low whisper.

"Did you hear the voice too?"

"Aye, but I knew it not at all."

"Strange!" mused Charles, "I knew it, and I knew it not."

"'Twas soft for a man, and yet it was a man," said Gracchus, trying in vain to rouse his mind to recollection.

"Gentlemen," said Thuriot, mildly, "we are at the gate of the dungeon."

The two friends raised their heads.   The drawbridge, still down, received them, and everywhere they were received without difficulty.

At length the grating was passed, they were in the interior of the Bastille.

----

## CHAPTER XXI.

INSIDE.

When Charles and Antiboul entered the Bastille, they found three large pieces of cannon posted at the mouth of the avenue leading to the Place, and by which De Launay expected every moment to be attacked.   The Swiss stood to their arms around the court.   The Invalides, in whom he had less confidence, were behind.

"Monsieur," said Thuriot de la Rosière, "I come in the name of the nation to represent to you that the cannon on your towers are filling Paris with alarm. I beg you will remove them."

"These pieces have always been on the towers, and I can only take them down on an order from the King."

Such was the loyal reply of the Governor of the Bastille, under the delusion that the royal personage he alluded to was all-powerful, and inviolable in all time.

"But Paris is infuriated," said Thuriot de la Rosière.

"Her blood is hot," added Antiboul.

"Monsieur de Launay," said Charles Clement, politely, "nephew of Monsieur the Duke de Ravilliere, I am in some sort your relative: hearken to me, and give way to the will of the people."

"I am proud to call you my relative," replied the Governor, "but my answer is given. Having been informed that the sight of the cannon has given alarm, I have drawn them in."

"I am to have no other reply?" said Thuriot.

"None."

"Gentlemen," exclaimed Thuriot, aloud, addressing the officer and men, "since your chief, from a mistaken view of honour, is about to bring misfortune on his head and ours, save him. I summon you, in the name of the nation, to surrender!"

A whisper of hesitation ran round the ranks of the Invalides, but the Swiss giving a decided and dogged negative, the question was settled.

"Monsieur Thuriot," said the Governor, "you see we are of one mind—determined to do our duty to our King."

"And the nation?" asked the *avocat au Parlement de Paris.*"

"Is a personage of whom I have heard too little to bow to his authority," said De Launay.

Charles Clement and Gracchus Antiboul exchanged meaning glances.

"Monsieur de Launay," said La Rosière, severely, "I fear your obstinacy will make you and the nation better acquainted before long. It waits without."

"The mob of Paris the nation!" exclaimed the soldier, with a sneer.

"Its heart, soul, and expression," replied Thuriot; "the

*Parisien* represents the whole people, and mob, as you call him, will say and do wonders."

"This discussion is useless," interrupted the Governor; "can I serve you in any way?"

"I would fain report, from eyesight, that the cannon are drawn back," answered the *avocat*.

"I am sorry to refuse to show you my fortress," continued De Launay, coldly.

"If all that you have said has been done," insisted Thuriot, "this request is but reasonable."

"Monsieur de Launay!" exclaimed several of his officers, drawing him on one side. Some efforts seemed to be made to induce him to yield.

A brief conference took place.

"I am ready to show you, gentlemen, to the top of my tower," said De Launay, after a moment of debate.

The delegate of the district of St. Louis de la Culture, followed by Antiboul and Clement, hastened to ascend the tower stairs, where De Launay preceded them. Strangers to the horrors of the Bastille, they shuddered, ascending the dark and gloomy stairs, with its doors opening upon vaulted and prison cells.

"Haunt of despotism and tyranny," said Antiboul, in a whisper to Clement; "this is thy last hour."

"It is a strong fortress, too," replied Charles Clement, shaking his head.

Conversing thus, they reached the very summit of the tower.

"*Qui vive?*" cried the sentry.

"Antoinette," said the Governor, giving the pass-word of the hour.

The whole party stepped out on the platform of the old tower.

"You see, messieurs," said De Launay, pointing with extreme politeness to the cannon which garnished the summit of the tower called Bazinière, that which they had ascended, and the arms were withdrawn from their embrasures.

"They are drawn back, but not removed," replied Thuriot.

"They may be needed to defend ourselves," answered De Launay.

"Against yon people!" cried Thuriot, angrily. "Look!"

And he stepped to the edge, leaning on the parapet. De Launay followed him ; the rest looked also down.

The view was tremendous.

Up every street came armed men. The whole Faubourg St. Antoine was in motion. Lane and *impasse*, street and place, courts and gardens, were all filled with insurgents. All came in one direction. An irresistible attraction seemed to lead them to the Bastille. Thousands and tens of thousands of combatants were now on their way to surround the frowning fortress. The threatening rumour of voices reached upward to the very summit, and many guns were angrily pointed from the Place, from windows, and from the summits of houses, against those who stood on the summit of La Bazinière.

De Launay turned pale.

"Monsieur," said he, catching Thuriot by the arm, "what means all this? You play me false; recollect you are a hostage."

"If you say another word," replied Thuriot de la Rosière, "one of us will lie in the ditch in half a moment!"

"Take warning!" exclaimed Antiboul, warmly; "yon thousands and tens of thousands will soon attack you, and thousands others are ready to join them."

"Gentlemen," replied the Governor, assuming a stiff, formal, and pompous air, "you do your duty—I will do mine."

"Let us descend," said Thuriot, who, while acting with all his characteristic resolution, did not fully share the sentiments of his companions. "I will see if the people can be reasoned with."

"Nothing will calm them but the surrender of the Bastille," put in Antiboul.

"*Y pensez vous?*" said De Launay, "an impregnable fortress, well garrisoned, and well provisioned."

"Nothing is impregnable in Paris," replied Gracchus.

"We shall see," said De Launay, with a satisfied smile.

The lower court was gained during this conversation.

"Gentlemen," exclaimed Thuriot, turning to the Governor and the garrison, "I am satisfied of your good intentions. I will convey them to the people, who will doubtless consent to place a garrison within, to guard the Place conjointly with the troops."

"I will receive a *garde bourgeoise* of fifty men with pleasure," replied De Launay, catching at an offer which gave a chance of avoiding hostilities.

Gracchus looked at Clement with a meaning look.

"Monsieur de la Rosière is one of the Hotel de Ville clique," whispered Antiboul. "Anything rather than the people should get the upper hand."

"They fear the people," replied Charles Clement, in the same tone, "because conscious of injustice; they know how long they have wronged them, and they dread retaliation."

On their way out, Thuriot de la Rosière entered the Governor's house, and appearing at a balcony, motioned for silence.

The crowd below were silent in an instant.

Thuriot de la Rosière began, and his first words betrayed his views. He proposed that fifty chosen men should enter the fortress, and keep watch and ward with the garrison, in the name of the nation.

"To the lantern with him!" thundered Camille Desmoulins. "The Bastille must surrender at discretion."

Thuriot waved his hand for silence.

"A court spy!"

"A city traitor!"

Such were the cries which now assailed the legal delegate of the district of St. Louis de la Culture. In revolutions, half measures are always impossible. Before all Paris in arms, it was needful that the Bastille should fall. The first day of the tremendous hurricane that was to sweep monarchy, aristocracy, feudalism, prelacy, and despotism, into the abyss of the past, to reappear only at the last gasp in vain efforts at again deluding mankind, would have been less sublime had the Bastille not been first laid violent hands on.

Thuriot de la Rosière went out, guarded by Charles Clement and Gracchus Antiboul. A thousand imprecations greeted him.

"To the lantern with the *bourgeoisie* traitor!"

"Drown him in the *fosse!*"

"Knock him on the head!"

Thuriot moved undauntedly between the double row of his assailants.

"Some one guard him to the district," said Charles Clement, calmly.

Four men started forward, with muskets on their shoulders, and, surrounding the *avocat*, escorted him through the dense crowd.

Charles Clement and Gracchus Antiboul turned towards the wine shop to get their guns, left there in charge of the landlord.

"Brave but prudent," whispered once more a voice in the ear of Charles Clement.

The young man turned round, his blood tingling and his heart leaping, but no form or face could he see which could appertain to the speaker of these words.

Flan! flan! flan!

Three musket shots.

The siege of the Bastille had commenced.

---

## CHAPTER XXII.

### THE SIEGE OF THE BASTILLE.

THE battle between the flags of despotism and liberty had now, in fact, begun in earnest. Ten thousand armed men surrounded the hideous Bastille, and a scattered but utterly useless fire was directed against its walls. The avenue leading to the first bridge, the Place, the adjacent streets, were choked up with *extempore* soldiers. Volleys of musketry excited them to a pitch of mental intoxication perfectly contagious; but all the enthusiasm, valour, and determination of the mass appeared utterly futile.

The proud old Bastille was silent; not a man was seen on its walls; not a volley answered the vain discharges of the multitude, pouring forth upon the stones the rage, hate, fear, dread, and pent-up wrath of ages. A traditional horror hung over the spot hundreds longed to see to the earth, they knew not why.

It was clear that nothing could be done unless the first bridge were passed.

This bridge crossed a ditch that protected an outer court, in which was situated the Governor's house, a *corps de garde*, and other buildings. From want of garrison, this court remained undefended, particularly as it could be swept from the inner court.

The side of the ditch towards the Place was covered with shops. Near the spot where the bridge, when lowered, rested, was a perfumer's shop, the roof of which shelved over the ditch.

While the tumultuous and useless volleys of the people continued, Antiboul and Clement were surveying the out-works.

" 'Tis useless wasting good powder after this fashion," said Antiboul; "this bridge must be lowered."

Looking round among the crowd, Clement saw several men armed with axes. Two were procured in an instant, in exchange for their muskets.

"Come!" exclaimed Charles Clement.

The two young men entered the perfumer's shop, un-perceived by the wild multitude firing at every cranny and loop-hole, and shouting, "We must have the Bastille! We must have the Bastille!"

Wild beat the hearts of the prisoned victims within. Dead to life, ignorant of some of the events of twenty years, their thoughts must have lent wonders to the noise without. A foreign enemy, a civil war, a siege of Paris, a mere popular tumult—these could strike their minds; but that the savage monarchy was going—that the hated system was near the block, was incredible. The imagination of a Dante or a Homer, who for twenty years had been in the Bastille, sent there by a Louis XV., a Dubarry, a Pompadour, a Choiseul, could scarcely have feigned to credit, for the re-presentative of these creatures, prisons, Bastilles, axes, scaffolds. But the hour was come, and the blockhead king and worthless queen were to wind up the history of real kingship in France.

When Clement and Antiboul entered the perfumer's, they saw before them a narrow stair.

"Close the door, that none may follow us," said Charles.

"We have our glory shared already," replied Gracchus.

Two old soldiers, Aubin Bonnemer and Louis Tournay, stood within the shop, each an axe in hand.

Aubin closed the door.

"More would embarrass us," he said, "but four are needed. Monsieur," he continued, addressing Clement, "do you command—we obey."

Charles Clement rushed up, and, followed by his three coadjutors, found himself in a garret.

He looked out.

A deep ditch was below, full of dark, thick, fœtid water; for the drains of the Faubourg St. Antoine oozed into it. Though the roof of the perfumer's house leant considerably over the ditch, still from thence to the wall opposite was good seven feet.

"A beam from the roof," said Antiboul, "would reach across."

In an instant a transverse beam, which aided the support of the roof, was seized, and the axes of four men soon brought it down.

The noise continued unceasingly without; discharges of musketry were heard every minute; but not a volley from the Bastille, which was menacingly quiet. The sentries on the summit of the towers were invisible; this enabled the four men to act in considerable security.

The beam was laid across. Antiboul moved, as if to cross.

"It is my place," said Charles Clement, quietly.

Gracchus at once assisted the other two to hold the beam steady.

Charles Clement then climbed through the window, his axe upon his back, seated himself across the beam, and slided down the inclined plane which it formed. Next moment he was seated on the wall.

The others crossed cautiously, and in a brief space of time the four were over. The last man let the plank fall in the ditch.

Not a word of comment was made upon this dreadful accident, which, in case of evil turning, left them wholly at the mercy of the besieged.

The wall connected the *corps de garde* with another

building.  It was high, but beneath was the court which
they sought to gain.  They slipped down one after another,
axe in hand.  Clement cast a glance at his forlorn hope;
enthusiasm and hope were in every eye.

"We must cut the chains of the *pont-levis*," he exclaimed,
"since the wheel is well secured."

"I go across—you stay here," said Gracchus.

"Obedience to orders," replied Clement.  "I and one
of these, our excellent friends, will cross to the other side
of the *pont-levis*; you cut at these chains."

With these words, Charles Clement, followed by Aubin
Bonnemer, dashed across the court, and in another minute
the crashing sound of four axes could have been heard
hewing away at the chains of the *pont-levis*.

Meanwhile, the furious crowd without pressed to the very
edge of the ditch, as if about to leap it, in their eager desire
to attack.  Volley after volley was poured upon the insensible walls; cries of vengeance and hate rose from the
myriads around; new armies pressed behind to the assault.

Crash! crash! went the axes.  The chains, cracked and
strained, began to yield.  Several links were broken; the
very last were about to give way.  On the side of Charles
Clement, the chain had broken, and hung downwards.

Charles Clement raised his head to lean on his axe, and
gain breath.

On the very edge of the ditch, where the bridge would,
in its fall, strike heavily, were dozens of people, all standing
within range of certain death.  Among the very foremost
was the man in slouched hat and cloak, whom Charles suspected to be his friendly whisperer, his face bent eagerly
towards the *pont-levis*.

"Stay, on your life!" cried Charles, turning to Antiboul.

It was too late!  The bridge was yielding.  Another
instant and it would fall.

"Back! back!" thundered Charles, standing up, and
waving his axe.

"Back! back!" cried Antiboul.

"The *pont-levis!* the *pont-levis!*" shouted the crowd
behind.

Those in front pressed back, while those in the rear,
ignorant of the danger, pressed forward eagerly.

The bridge yielded, gave way, and, with a tremendous crash, fell, rebounding upwards several times. One man lay killed, another had his arm broken. The stranger in the hat had disappeared.

The crowd paused an instant in horror at the sight of the man crushed to death, and then giving way to an impulse of delight and triumph, dashed across the bridge, to fill the exterior court, and thence attack the Bastille. The second bridge leading to the inner court was also up.

"*Feu!*" resounded from within.

A murderous discharge of musketry greeted the dense mass as they filled the court. Twenty of the assailants fell dead and wounded. The crowd pressed back; some took shelter in the *corps de garde*, near walls, behind stones, while others turned back across the bridge, to relate how De Launay, after entrapping them across the *pont-levis*, had treacherously massacred them. This false statement, receiving at the time full credit and belief, added to the fury of Paris, which was still further roused by one of the dying being borne about on a plank through the whole town.

"This fortress is impregnable save by cannon," said Antiboul, "there are two on the Place de Grêve; let us go fetch them."

"Willingly," replied Charles.

Tournay and Bonnemer were at hand. They called them; and they again summoning some friends, the whole party, well armed, rushed towards the Hotel de Ville.

At the corner of the Rue St. Antoine, they were startled to find themselves in front of a detachment of the grenadiers of the company of Ruffeville. They were two hundred. The party commanded by Charles was but fifty. He ordered a halt.

"Present arms!" cried the officer commanding the grenadiers.

"Present arms!" replied Charles, enthusiastically.

The two armed companies saluted one another. They were marching in the same cause.

"*Vive les grenadiers!*" cried the people.

"*Vive les Parisiens!*" replied the soldiers.

And the two bodies of insurgents separated with mutual marks of affection.

"Who goes there ?" cried Charles Clement the next instant, again meeting soldiers.

"The fusiliers of the company of Lubersac," said Serjeant Labarthe, who commanded.

"Where go you ?"

"To the siege of the Bastille," answered the soldiers.

"Present arms!" cried Charles, ranging his men to let the others pass.

The fusiliers marched by amid cheers, and the party hurried on. Every moment they met beleaguers marching to the attack, and, just as they reached the Grêve, were passed by a body of about two thousand, headed by Pierre Auguste Hulin, director of the *buanderie** of the queen, a perfect giant in dimensions.

On the Place de Grêve they found the two pieces of cannon guarded by four sentries. Without waiting for questions, the crowd, seizing ropes from an adjacent shop, tied them to the cannon, which, with their *caissons*, they at once dragged away in the direction of the Bastille. Clement leaped on one, Antiboul on the other, and, in an instant, were rattling furiously down the Tixanderie and into the Rue St. Antoine, amid the uproarious applause of those who, gathered round lanes and in doorways, were awaiting the issue of the fight.

A tremendous shout greeted their arrival on the scene of action. The people were in ecstacies at the possession of cannon.

Events had progressed. Dense clouds of smoke rose on high, curling up the walls, and wrapping the old fortress round in a vaporous veil. Flames burst on high with a roar and a crash that added to the horror of the scene. The *corps de garde* of the outer court, the hotel of the governor, the barracks, were all in flames, while Santerre, the celebrated brewer of the Faubourg St. Antoine, had fired some carts of manure, and packed them on the edge of the ditch. All this impeded, instead of serving the besiegers.

Charles and Antiboul placed their cannon in front of the *pont-levis.*

"These carts must be removed," said our hero, quietly.

"It is impossible," replied Santerre.

* *Buanderie,* washhouse.

The two friends looked.  The besieged had made two loop-holes in the *pont-levis*, and through these, two *amusettes du Comte de Saxe* protruded, loaded, as the crowd said, with grape.

"Let us draw these carts away," cried Charles, motioning to Antiboul.  Four men followed them; two fell dead; the other two with them reached the carts, the poles of which they seized.  One they tumbled into the ditch, the other they drew away.

"The cannon! the cannon!" shouted the friends.

They were brought down; twenty old soldiers rushed to serve them.  The grenadiers and the fusiliers poured volley after volley against the fortress.  The cannon were ready in an instant.  They were fired.  The cracking of the wood of the *pont-levis* showed that the discharges took effect.  Rapidly they were reloaded, and, served by enthusiasm and love of liberty, they poured their shot unremittingly on the old Bastille.

All around, too, the besiegers poured their volleys.  Every house was a battery, every house-top a tower of attack.  Not a sentry could be seen on the walls, the fire of the people forcing them to hide.

Suddenly, however, there appeared on the summit a body of men, who dragged the cannon forward, and pointed them on the Place.  Volley upon volley was poured at them, but they paused not.  Next moment they had them in the embrasures, and the contents of three heavy cannon were belched forth upon the people.

A yell, a screech of despair, rose from the Place; a heap of wounded, dead, and dying, lay upon the ground; the whole crowd rent the air with cries of fury and indignation.  While some hurried to remove the victims, others rushed headlong to the combat.  The cannon were loaded, and poured unceasingly on the entrance.  The whole scene was tremendous.  From every loop-hole and window of the castle came shot upon shot; smoke and flashes filled the air.  Beneath the castle walls, the cannon, commanded by Charles Clement and Antiboul, were unremitting in their discharges.  Behind, bourgeois, merchants, traders, physicians, lawyers, workmen, nobles, women, and children, pressed on with eager cries, and armed in every way that accident provided to do combat with the hated castle. Farther in the rear, other men and other women bore away the slain and the wounded to the temporary hospitals erected for them, or rather provided—the houses in the Place having opened their doors.

"A parliamentary! a parliamentary!" cried some behind.

A man of lofty stature, dark and singularly handsome countenance, in the habit of a priest, came on, waving a 'kerchief, in sign that he desired a parley.

"What conditions propose you?" said the crowd.

"That the Governor surrender to the Permanent Committee, and receive a *bourgeoise* guard."

"Back! back!" shouted the besiegers; "let him surrender to the people."

"Down with the Permanent Committee!"

"Down with the *bourgeoisie!*"

"Down with the parliamentary!"

The Abbè Fauchet shook his head, and retired to the corner of the Rue St. Antoine, where he remained during the rest of the fight.

The attack recommenced.

Instantly the attention of the multitude was again caught. Another parliamentary appeared, with a drum beating before him, and a white flag waving in the hand. He was, moreover, escorted by armed men.

It was Ethys de Corny, *procureur* of the city of Paris. The electors, alarmed at the prospect of a popular victory, which promised to take the government of the city out of their hands, were unceasing in their endeavours to effect a compromise. Besides, it was reported that a royalist army was marching on Paris, and these whilome warm patriots were eager to gain time.

"Cease firing!" cried Charles.

"Cease firing!" repeated Camille Desmoulins.

The populace obeyed.

"A parley!" cried Ethys de Corny, addressing the Invalides on the roof.

The Invalides put their hats on the top of their guns, in proof of a wish to fraternise with the people.

Corny advanced to the very edge of the ditch. The

Swiss at the same moment fired a murderous volley. The people fell in dozens around him.

"To the lantern with Corny!" cried the populace, as if they thought he had led them into a trap.

Charles, Desmoulins, Antiboul, with Morin, Maillard, Bonnemer, Hullin, and other memorable names in this day's fight, rushed with drawn swords to the rescue of Corny, who was with difficulty torn from the furious hands of the people.

A loud shriek was heard—that of a woman in distress.

"Away, Charles," whispered the well known voice.

Clement obeyed, without looking round.

While Ethys Corny had gone up as parliamentary, half-a-dozen wild and savage-looking men had brought down to the edge of the ditch a graceful, well-dressed girl, whom rumour said was the Governor's daughter. They bound her hands together, and laid her on a heap of straw.

It was a fearful scene. A young and lovely girl, bound hand and foot, surrounded by men half-naked, their arms and faces blackened with gunpowder, their eyes gleaming with furious excitement, waving around arms and a blazing torch.

"Surrender!" shouted one with stentorian lungs; "surrender, De Launay, or we burn your child before your eyes!"

A man leaned over the parapet of the tower, in the uniform of a Swiss officer. It was Monsigny, the father of the girl. Two musket-shots sent him reeling back, severely but not mortally wounded.

"My father!" screamed the poor girl.

"Burn the whelp of the Bastille!" cried one.

"More straw!" said another.

"Vengeance for the victims of the Bastille!"

"Come, De Launay, and see your turn!" said a fourth.

"Save me! mercy!" cried the poor girl, in vain struggling with the cords which bound her.

A dozen men here leaped amid the ruffian band, striking right and left with the flat of their swords. It was the gallant band of leaders of the day's fight.

"We are not assassins and murderers," cried Charles.

"Women are under the safeguard of St. Denis of France,"

said Camille Desmoulins, "or of Juno, when in the straw."

And the *Vieux Cordelier* laughed aloud.

The mob fell back, ashamed at their own inhumanity, and the attack recommenced.

The siege seemed in vain. The combatants had become half mad with rage and hopelessness. Fire-pumps were brought to bear, in the futile hope of wetting the cannon, on the tower. The water fell in vapour less than half-way up.

The battle had been bloody. Eighty-eight severely wounded lay in the hospital, while eighty-three dead bodies were ranged in three rooms used as the dead-house.

The combat had raged five hours, and not the slightest impression had been made on the old Bastille.

The stronghold of the monarchy appeared impregnable. As with the monarchy itself, there and elsewhere, appearances were deceitful.

* * *

## CHAPTER XXIII.

### WITHIN.

THE Bastille was perhaps physically impregnable to a dis-organized mob, without materials for a siege, and with but few elements of discipline amongst them; but the garrison had no faith, or union, or sense of right. The Governor had plunged headlong into the fight, without knowing if he were right or wrong. He knew not if he should be supported or blamed at Versailles. Besides, he knew that the Place without was spread with the dying and the dead, all victims of his obdurate will.

"Keep good guard," said De Launay, suddenly, to his officers; "I will go rest awhile within."

And with pale face and haggard eye, the Governor moved away to the chamber he usually occupied within the Bastille.

On his way he passed the door of a cell.

The man shuddered.

"'Tis as jailor they hate me and call for my blood without," he muttered.

And for the first time perhaps in his life he began to think over the nature of the office he had to perform. He ruled and governed a prison, not used to punish crime, but to satisfy the base passions of kings, courtiers, and courtesans. There were men cooped up because they had written a few lines displeasing to some haughty beauty, who sold her charms to power—for power and wealth. The Pompadours, Du Barrys, and other women, whose name and station are not to be used in polite ears, were constant feeders of that fearful life-gulf, where men ceased to have a name, and were spoken of as number 10 or number 100 ! An epigram —a pasquinade—a line in which a sentiment of freedom breathed—a poem indignantly lashing the vices of the court —an appeal to the nation in favour of some oppressed victim—a mere fault of etiquette at court—such were the chief crimes which fed the Bastille. But worse still : a faithless wife discovered by a husband, sent him to the Bastille if her paramour were high and mighty ; inconvenient relatives, wives, fathers, uncles, sons—any who troubled the avarice, lust, or selfishness of the rich—could be sent by a *lettre de cachet* to this State prison. Even troublesome creditors were thus despatched out of the way by noble debtors.

Once in, no hope. Communication with the world was hopeless. The horror of the place was its living death. The injured husband could not even appeal to his wife's generosity ; the son to a father's love ; the wife to her husband ! It was a tomb. Kings were born and died, wars came, peace returned, their nearest, dearest friends disappeared from the face of the earth, and none within knew a word. There they lived, rotted, and died ; because such was the system necessary to support a wretched monarchy, a vicious, worthless aristocracy, and a debased church. Violence, death, prison, alone saved the whole fabric from extinction.

And De Launay, as he went to his chamber, thought all this.

"And to defend this yawning tomb," he cried, "this sepulchre of living humanity, I have slain hundreds of my fellow-men. There they be yonder, dead, in heaps, and I, a Frenchman and a soldier, have massacred these Frenchmen."

And this man, never remarkable for much strength of mind, but who was rather of a kindly disposition, leaned his hands upon his knees, as if sunk in deep thought.

"They will kill me," said he, sternly rising, and his brow darkening.   "Never!"

The soldier overcame the man.

"Never!" he repeated under his teeth.   "They would lead me in triumph to their Hotel de Ville, with all the Court laughing at me next day.   Never!"

He walked up and down the room once or twice without speaking.   After a moment he turned to a drawer, which he opened with a key carried about his person.   He drew out the picture of a woman and a bundle of letters.

"And to govern this accursed dungeon, I gave up her love, I trampled on her affection, I bade her forget me, and for this!"

A lamp was burning on the table, the room being low and dark.   He lit one or two of the letters, threw them on the hearth, and the rest after them, with the portrait.

"There ends this life's illusions.   Poor Henriette! she will think of me when she hears of my end."

The soldier took one or two more turns while the papers were consuming.

"And now ends this scene.   It has been a wild and chequered life.   Let us go all whence we came.   *Vive Dieu!* all the world shall ring with the death of De Launay."

The Governor took in his hand the lamp off the table. His face was pale with anxiety and fatigue.   His eye seemed wild and terrible.   He trod the ground firmly.   He left the room.   In one hand was a key.

He began slowly to descend the stairs; in a few minutes he was on a level with the court.

"*Bas les ponts! bas les ponts!* cried the people without.

"Death to De Launay!"

"Ye shall die with him," muttered the Governor.

"Let us open the gates," said the Invalides.

"Let us die first," said the Swiss.

De Launay stroked his moustache; the last hope was gone.

"I will never be less brave than my Swiss.   To surrender is now a vain thought."

He continued his descent.

After going down some twenty steps or so, he arrived at a small, low door.

Over it was a small inscription—

**Sanctus Antoninus.**

*1490.*

It was a little chapel to St. Antoine once, in the early days of the Bastille.

The Governor placed the key in the heavy lock, and, turning it, the door flew back on its hinges heavily.

De Launay entered.

It was the powder magazine; and the wretched Governor was about to blow up both the castle and the quarter, rather than surrender.

"Twenty-six barrels," he muttered; "enough to blow up Paris, if needed."

There he stood, like Milton's Lucifer, hesitating to cross the abyss. His mind had been warped and pained by the bloodshed without, and he was about to commit suicide, at the same time destroying perhaps thousands of his fellow-creatures.

"Here ends this bitter struggle," he repeated; "they thought to capture the Bastille—to catch an old soldier in his own den. They will catch a rough one."

He laid down his lantern on a bench, took from his pocket a cannon match, one end of which he thrust into the last barrel of powder that had been opened.

"*Bas!  Bas les ponts!*" faintly reached his ears.

"Ye are marvellously in a hurry there, good people," he growled; "see you wake not from your dream of victory."

He caught at the lantern.

"Hold! madman," cried a voice, while two men sprang upon him.

"Let me go," bawled the Governor.

"Not here," replied one of the men.

"Unhand me!" said De Launay, grasping towards the lantern.

"Hold fast," cried one.  "Keep the light without."

A fearful struggle took place.  In a few minutes, however, the Governor disarmed and worn out, was at the foot of the steps without, while one of his assailants held the key of the well-locked magazine.

The Governor raised his eyes sulkily.

The men were Captains Bequard and Ferrand, two of his favourite officers.

"Many excuses, Colonel," said Bequard; "but we had no wish to take a flying leap above the old towers. But why this folly?"

"Hush, man," replied De Launay, regaining, when with men, his firmness and composure; "the fit is passed. Not a word above."

"*Foi de militaire*," said they.

And De Launay, after taking back his sword, ascended before his officers in a calm but sulky manner, as if disgusted and disappointed.

He passed into the court.

"*Bas les ponts! Bas les ponts!*" was cried from without in menacing shouts.

The Invalides murmured. They were evidently eager to surrender; but the Swiss were for defending themselves to the last.

"Monsieur," said the Swiss commander, in his rough way, "hundreds of this noisy *canaille* have been killed, and we have yet lost but three men. We cannot think of surrendering. Give but the word, and I will sweep the outer court as clean as my hand."

De Launay turned hesitatingly to Ferrand and Bequard.

They made no sign.

"Give me paper and ink," said the Governor.

It was brought him, and he wrote the last death-warrant of the old Bastille:—

"*Nous avons vingt milliers de poudres; nous ferons sauter le garnison et tout le quartier si vous n'acceptez pas la capitulation.*" *

He handed it to the Swiss officer.

"But, Monsieur the *governeur*, this is a surrender," cried the astounded soldier.

* We have twenty thousand pounds of powder; we will blow up the garrison and the whole quarter, if you do not accept the capitulation.

"I know it."

"But we can hold out a week."

"Go, give the paper."

The trade of the Swiss soldier was obedience. He moved away to the entrance, and thrust the billet, on the point of a sword, through one of the *pont-levis* loopholes. A loud hurrah greeted it.

"Spare us! Kill us not!" cried the Invalides.

The Swiss ranged themselves in a line.

Without, the difficulty was to get at the billet; it but just protruded over the ditch. Suddenly, a dozen men came rushing forward with a plank thirty feet long. Half of this was suspended over the ditch; a dozen men stood upon the other half. It being once thus supported, a man hurried forward. He walked firmly along the plank, leaned forward to catch the billet; a chance shot went off, and he fell dead into the ditch. Nothing daunted, on rushed another. It was Maillard. He boldly stood on the very edge of the plank, and seized the billet, which he handed to Charles Clement, pressing behind.

Our hero read it aloud, with a voice so clear and distinct, it was heard by thousands.

A thundering shout hailed the reading.

"*Bas les ponts! bas les ponts!*" was again lustily cried.

"*La Bastille est pris,*" screamed a shrill voice—that of of Jean Torticolis.

Down slowly came the huge *pont-levis*. The people fell back, utterly annihilated with astonishment, and high into the very heavens went up a shout of joy, of hope, of enthusiastic delight; for the stronghold of despotism, of monarchy, of feudalism, of aristocracy, of bigotry, of oppression, was in the hands of the rough democracy of Paris.

The bridge rested on its abutment, the *grille* swung back, and away dashed Charles Clement, Antiboul, Torticolis, Maillard, Morin, Bonnemer, and all the other heroes of the day, followed by thousands, into the very jaws of the enemy.

The Bastille of the Faubourg St. Antoine was taken.

# CHAPTER XXIV

### JEAN.

AMONG those who burst into the Bastille with most intense eagerness, and in whose heart beat the warmest, and, perhaps, the most noble hopes of all those who had crushed the sting of despotism, was Jean Torticolis. The crick-neck had never for one moment lost memory of the words uttered in his ear by the Count. "She is in the Bastille,' was implanted in his mind, and he every moment repeated them to himself.

When the victorious mob, made up of the great and the little, the good and the bad, the selfish and the generous, reached the inner court, they found the Swiss standing around, headed by De Launay and his officers, while the Invalides kept back, knowing well how deep was the popular hatred against them. All had laid down their arms, and awaited the verdict of the people.

The tumult which ensued was terrible. Some were for putting to instant death the whole of the defenders of the Bastille.

"Death to the murderers of the people!"

"Death to the bombarders of the city of Paris!"

"Death to De Launay!"

"*Mort aux Suisses!*"

Charles Clement, Antiboul, Maillard, and other assailants of the Bastille, at once interposed. Camille Desmoulins stood on one side, a stolid frown upon his face, while a youth with long hair, face chisselled in a Grecian mould, pale, his eyes flashing, brow lofty and stern, muttered bitterly to himself.

"They are our enemies. So much the fewer will remain."

"Your name?" said Camille Desmoulins, turning round with a look of admiration.

"St. Just," said the youth, who recognised the orator of the Palais Royal.

"It is false mercy to spare these valets of the king and the Austrians," said the Vieux Cordelier.

"More enemies to contend with by and bye," replied St. Just.

"Truly this is but the beginning," muttered Camille.

"Ay, of the death of all tyranny, and the sacred advent of liberty."

"Of the Republic!" said Camille, enthusiastically.

"Of the Republic," replied St. Just, coldly.

Meanwhile Jean had disappeared.

On entering the court-yard, he had noticed at the girdle of one of the Swiss a bunch of keys; in an instant he was at his throat, and, none paying attention, dragged him unresistingly out of sight by the first door which presented itself.

"Spare my life!" said the Swiss, piteously.

"I want not thy life," replied Jean, choked with emotion, and holding a pistol to his head, "but where are we?"

"In the goaler's room," replied the trembling Swiss.

Jean turned round and bolted the door.

"Are you the goaler?" asked Jean.

"No; I am his deputy."

"Do you know the way to the cells?"

"To every one."

"Well," said Jean, convulsively, his voice nearly choking him, "have you any women prisoners?"

"One," replied the deputy.

"One!" responded the poor crick-neck, faintly, his heart failing him; "one!"

"But one," answered the other.

"Has she been here long?"

"I know not. We know nothing."

"Is she young?"

"I never saw."

"Take me to her," said Jean Torticolis, rousing himself; "take me to her, and my hopes are crushed or made at once."

"This way," said the deputy, moving inward.

Torticolis followed his guide, tottering rather than walking after him. The intense and devouring hopes of years were about to be gratified, or perhaps to be for ever blasted.

"Take care," exclaimed the deputy, as the other nearly fell upon him, as they ascended a steep and narrow staircase.

"Go on!" said Jean, rousing himself.

The stair was narrow, cold, and winding. The stone steps were worn and used by ages, while the walls, damp and cold, showed that no warmth or sunshine ever penetrated to them. At the first landing the guide halted.

A small door faced them, barred and plated with iron. The lock seemed too rusty for use, as if long abandoned.

"In there?" whispered Jean, in a low, thrilling whisper.

The guide nodded assent.

The poor crick-neck took the key out of his companion's hand, took from him also the light which he bore, and then bade him go.

"But shall I wait without?"

"Go!" repeated the other, hoarsely.

The Swiss turned, and escaped as rapidly as he could down the steps.

Jean placed the key in the bolt and turned it. The door gave way. This done, by an almost superhuman effort he conquered his emotion, and entering, looked around him.

It was a small, gloomy room. At one end was a rude truckle bed. By this was a table and a chair, and on the chair sat a woman, her back turned to the door. She moved not nor gave any signs of life. Jean placed the lamp and pistol on a stone bench, and once more looked around. On the table was a jug of water, a bit of bread, and a rind of cheese, which had been bitten off for want of a knife. The walls were bare stones, covered, however, with charcoal drawings, found in the cells of all prisoners. Here, however, it was the prison of a woman: rude imitations of flowers predominated. Various names were written, some of old date, some fresh.

The crick-neck could scarcely read, but his eye wandered anxiously among these.

"Paul."

Such was the word which everywhere covered the damp and cold stone.

The poor man staggered forward.

"Marie!" he cried.

"I am No. 26," said the woman, without turning; "why insult me with a name I had nigh forgotten?"

"Marie!" repeated the crick-neck.

The woman replied not, but turned sharply round.

"Paul! Paul!" she shrieked, "are you come at last?"

And the unfortunate, but now wildly happy couple, fell senseless in each other's arms.

"Is it you, my love?" said the poor man, gazing on her pale and haggard face, still pretty, however: "is it thee?"

He waited for no answer, but kissed hands, face, eyes, forehead, lips, holding her back to gaze on her, drawing her to him, and all to be sure it was really her, and that he was the victim of no delusion of his senses.

"Hush, Paul," whispered the woman, trembling, and looking to the door; "they will hear you, and drive you away. Not yet! not yet!"

And she clung to him convulsively.

"Never!" cried Paul Ledru, for he feared not to be called so now; "never! You are free, my love! free to follow me. Come! come! let us away from this infernal cell. It chills me, it is so cold."

"I don't feel it, Paul," she said; "I am used to it."

"Come away!" he repeated.

"But, Paul, I cannot walk, my life, my love!" said she, gazing at the man, whose deformity she never noticed, with inexpressible affection; "but is this no vision, as I have had twenty times before?"

"No vision, Marie," he answered, raising his wife in his arms; "but God's reward for our patience and long suffering."

"But I am heavy," she said.

"As light as my heart," he answered; "but stay, I must give you the light."

With these words he deposited her on the bench, gave her the light, put the pistol in his bosom, and, his wife once more in his arms, went out and began to descend the stairs.

"But you totter under me, *enfant!*" she said, gently.

"'Tis with emotion, Marie; hold me tight round the neck and fear not."

In a few minutes more Paul Ledru, whom we shall call no more Jean Torticolis, had reached the goaler's cell with his precious burden.

"A prisoner! a prisoner!" he cried to the crowd without, for fear of hindrance.

"A victim of accursed tyranny!" shouted several voices; "bring her out."

Paul moved into the open air, amid the uproarious and tremendous crowd. As he did so, his burthen became doubly heavy in his arms. She had fainted at the sight which she could not understand, of an armed and furious mob in the court-yard of the Bastille.

"Help! help!" cried Paul, in the utmost terror.

Several rushed forward, but two men succeeded in pushing aside the rest.

It was Charles Clement and Antiboul.

"Give her to me, man," said Charles, taking her from her trembling husband, and bearing her to a fountain that poured its water into a basin in the court-yard.

"Thy wife?" asked Gracchus, slapping him on the shoulder kindly.

"My wife, my Marie!" replied Paul; "but oh, how weak, how worn!"

"What odds, man! Liberty and good air will soon restore her."

Paul made no reply, but hurried beside Charles Clement, who was bathing her face with cold water, while a crowd of curious spectators, silent and anxious—the same men whilome so bitter and so fierce—stood around.

"More air, *tonnerre!*" cried Gracchus. "Go, my friends, there are more prisoners to free."

And away at this intimation hurried the crowd.

"Oh, Paul!" said the wife, reviving, "these horrid men!"

"Are our friends, and thy deliverers," replied Paul, proudly. "The people of Paris have taken the Bastille."

She made no reply. It was too incomprehensible. She did not understand it.

"And now," said Clement, "get her out of here as quickly as possible. Once free, take her to our home, where await us. Stay—hurry rather to the Rue Dominique, and bear news of us."

"In half an hour we will go ourselves," replied Gracchus Antiboul.

"True! hurry home, then, and remain near thy wife."

Paul thanked his master by an eloquent look, and once more, bearing his wife in his arms, hurried out of the Bastille.

The task was one of no small difficulty; for though the old fortress was almost as full as it could hold, crowds still continued to press in, eager to catch a glance at its mysterious interior.

Still, the sight of a pale and fainting woman made hundreds give way, and at last Paul Ledru had gained the place in safety, a confirmed Revolutionist, for its first act had given him back his wife.

---

## CHAPTER XXV

### PARIS AFTER THE BATTLE.

SCARCELY had the news flown over Paris that the Bastille had fallen into the hands of the victorious people, than the whole town became as it were intoxicated with delight. There were, of course, those to whom the circumstance gave far from satisfaction, but these, being of the privileged orders and the middle classes, were so few as not to mar, by their gloom and sullen regret, the general sensation of pleasure. Men who had never met embraced one another, nor did the terrible episodes incident to valourous insurrections serve to chill the enthusiasm. The death of Launay, assassinated by an unknown hand, and the carrying about of his head on a pike, bloody trophy of revenge, was known, but little noticed.

Charles Clement and Gracchus Antiboul, after in vain endeavouring to save the unfortunate governor De Launay, had left the now harmless Bastille for the Hotel de Ville, where the electors sat trembling for their necks. Their attempts to deceive the people weighed heavy on their heads. They knew of the awful fate of the governor, and they imagined the whole of the armed people animated by the same sentiments as the assassin of De Launay.

They were mistaken. But few joined in any such feelings. The general feelings were those of delight at victory.

"To what will lead this day?" said Gracchus, as they moved along.

"To the end of the monarchy of Charlemagne," replied Clement's enthusiasm; "it has seen its last day. Plaster it up as they will, it must fall, it must perish. But we must expect evil days, and many; for the chivalry of France will rally round the King and defend him. We must fight them inch by inch. But of ourselves," continued Charles, after a moment's pause and thought; "my marriage with Adela must take place. The dear girl must have a protector through all the rough times we have to come."

"Marry her," said his friend; "for soon none will be able to think of marrying."

"And the Duke himself," observed Charles, "he begins to need a guide; these terrible times will shake him more than ever."

"And the Countess Miranda," said Gracchus, turning round and looking at his friend.

"What of her?" replied Charles.

"What will be her position, you once married?"

"I don't comprehend you," said the young man.

"Is she to be left alone?"

"She is rich and happy!"

"Rich, yes," said Gracchus, drily; "but happy! can't say. At all events, she has no longer the companion she once had."

"My home and that of my wife will always be hers," exclaimed Clement.

"She will not visit it," said Antiboul.

"You wrong her," replied Clement; "she is not the proud creature you think her."

"I said not she was proud, only that she would lose her old companion."

There was something dry in the tone of the young Republican, which made Charles Clement feel uncomfortable.

"Gracchus," he said, warmly, "explain yourself."

"I have no explanation to give," replied Antiboul, almost impatiently; "by the way, and my little girl?"

"I had quite forgotten her," said the other; "let us return home awhile."

"It were as well," was Antiboul's answer, "for the fight has given me an appetite."

"You are always hungry," laughed Clement; "let us home and dine, and then for the Rue Dominique."

"If you are wise," said Antiboul, "you will take a priest with you, and let the marriage be at once. Heaven only knows what to-morrow may bring forth."

"But the Duke?"

"Will thank you. These are no times for ceremony."

"The advice is good, and shall be acted on. You and Miranda will serve as witnesses; the thing is decided on at once."

"*Vive l'amour!*" cried Antiboul.

At this moment they were stopped by a dense procession. Thousands of men, armed with pikes, guns, sticks, and every kind of offensive weapon, barred their passage. At their head marched one with something on the end of a pole. It was a bunch of keys, those of the Bastille.

"*Vive Paris!*" cried the people.

"*Vive Paris!*" replied Gracchus.

"Ah! ah! brave soldiers of the escalade," cried Bonnemer; it is thus you use modesty. You fight and steal away lest we thank you."

A thousand men at once surrounded the two friends, recognizing them as combatants of the day, and ones, too, who had contributed much to the victory of the people. Despite every resistance, despite the blows of Antiboul, they were both captured, and hoisted on the shoulders of the applauding multitude. "*Vive* the *bourgeois* friends of the people!" they cried.

"But, my good friends!" said Charles.

"Put me down!" bellowed Gracchus.

"Carry them through the town!" cried the people.

"Holla! the *troupe!*" thundered Gracchus.

In an instant the two friends were free; and the people believing a detachment of soldiers after them, began to look around, preparing their arms.

Not a soldier was to be seen.

"Ha! ha! ha!" laughed Gracchus, pulling his friend away.

The people at once saw the trick; and as none love a joke more thoroughly than your true Parisian *faubourien*, the whole party laughed, and let the friends pursue their way.

"Penalties of popularity," said Gracchus Antiboul, still laughing.

They reached the door of their apartment, and entering quietly, caught sight of a scene which made them both pause.

The young girl whom Antiboul had insisted on sending home to the lodging of Charles Clement, after their parlour adventure in the low *cabaret* near the Hotel de Ville, was standing with her back to them, looking out of the window. On a chair near the fire sat Marie Ledru, the wife of him who had been Jean Torticolis. She was eating from a basin, supported by Paul, who knelt at her feet in an attitude and with an expression of indescribable happiness, his eyes greedily devouring every feature of her countenance.

"Six years, how they have passed!" he said, with an involuntary shudder.

"Poor fellow," said Marie, pausing and laying her hand upon his forehead, "and you knew not where I was?"

"Not I. Never was a word breathed of where they had placed you. I thought you dead; and yet I felt that if you had been, you would have come to me in vision to ease my sorrow."

"Dear Paul!"

"Dear Marie!"

"And that man, our enemy?" said she, shuddering.

"Is a murderer, an outcast, made so by my hands," answered Paul; "but I bear him now no enmity; I am rewarded."

"But how are we to live, love?" inquired the wife; "he ruined you, I know."

"I have a good and noble master," answered Paul.

"Bravo!" cried Gracchus, advancing; "well spoken, Torty, my boy; and I'll answer for it he will not let you starve."

As he spoke, the girl turned round with a blush.

"Excuse me," said Paul, stammering, while his wife rose.

"Sit still," exclaimed Charles, addressing the wife, "and

while Jean gives us some dinner, we will talk over your affairs. What would you like to do?"

"We had a small mercer's shop before," said the wife, gently, and looking alternately at her husband and at Charles.

"Like the one down stairs?" inquired Charles.

"The very same," replied Paul Ledru.

"I am not a rich man, but I have ample," said Clement; "and if you wish to establish yourselves as you were before, and can persuade the widow down stairs to sell, I will find the money."

"And you can take this young person as assistant," put in Gracchus, with almost a blush. The student was getting timid.

Paul came near to his master, and took his hand; he said not one one word, but his silence was deeply eloquent. He then turned away to serve the supper.

In a few minutes Gracchus and Charles were at supper; the others had eaten. Neither spoke much. The former cast continued glances at his new friend; while Charles thought, with hope and joy, that Adela was about to become his wife.

Supper ended, and it lasted not long, Charles and Gracchus bade the others a good night, and, taking their arms, went out in the direction of the Rue Dominique St. Germain.

----

## CHAPTER XXVI.

### THE MARRIAGE OF CLEMENT.

It was night, and despite the fatigues of the preceding days, and of the combat, Paris was still under arms. All manner of rumours were afloat. Besenval was at the gates of the city; the Court was marching an army on Paris; the capital was on the point of being bombarded. Such were some of the reports which kept the masses alive.

Every house was illuminated, to assist the patriots in the exercise of their duty.

"Strange night for a wedding," said Charles Clement, with a gravity which made his companion start.

"But the more needful that it be over," replied Gracchus.

"Where shall we find a priest willing to venture through the streets?"

"Leave that to me," observed Antiboul; "there is a certain Father Michel, of the St. Germain l'Auxerrois, a jolly father, truly, but honest, who will come, and gladly."

"He is no vinous priest?" said Charles.

"He can drink his bottle," replied Antiboul, with a laugh; "but it is yet too early for him to have paid many visits to the wine cellar, especially on such a day as this. Be sure he has been at his orisons from sunrise to sunset."

"I trust to you," responded Charles; "so the Duke and Adela be content, I care not."

"An' they be ready to wed, the priest will not matter. On any night but that of an insurrection I would'nt be of your company. I have no desire to be shown the door, as if in my cups."

"She is mine!" said Charles, fervently, "promised to me, whene'er I chose to take her. Events move with fearful rapidity. Even now, perhaps, I am too late."

"Courage, man!" exclaimed Gracchus, pausing; "but here is the street in which dwelleth Pere Michel. 'Tis none of the sweetest in Paris, St. Thomas du Louvre, though it be called, but 'tis near the church. Stay you here, while I go up in search of him."

With these words, Antiboul hurried up the narrow and dirty street which led towards the palace of the Louvre, and in which, it appeared, Father Michel held his habitual residence.

Charles leaned against a *porte cochère*, already impatient, though Gracchus Antiboul was scarce yet out of sight. The young man, though quite convinced that, under the circumstances, the Duke and Adela would excuse his bold initiative in the matter of the marriage, yet could not conceal from himself the boldness of the act. Besides, he felt anxious as to their safety.

"He tarries," muttered Charles Clement, as Gracchus Antiboul stooped for a stone to throw at the priest's window.

The lover was impatient. He was in those halcyon days of life, when love, with rosy fingers, touches all around, and gives a bright and sunny hue to every feature of life.

"Mine! mine!" muttered Charles Clement, forgetting all around—forgetting insurrection, Bastille, Gracchus, priest, everything, in fact. "Can it be true? That gentle, sweet being, mine. I can scarce conceive it possible. But she loves me; oh, she loves me, my own, my dear Adela. She has told me so fifty times; and, if I wanted confirmation, has the dear hope not been as many times repeated to me by the Countess Miranda?"

A slight chill came over Charles as he pronounced these words. Miranda! Why did his heart stay beating, and why did joy fly from his lip, at the very mention of the name of that noble, generous, devoted woman?

"If Antiboul would but love her, and she but love him," he muttered.

Why did he pause?

Instinct, more rapid than thought, brought to his soul some reason, floating in the air, in the chaotic void of sensations yet unknown to Charles, which made him hesitate.

"My God," he whispered to himself, "what ails me? What to me is it that Miranda be another's, that she love another? What is she to me? I do not love her—cannot, will not. Adela has every affection of my soul; every fibre, every thought, every pulsation of my heart is her's. Sweet love, sweet girl, this night thou wilt be mine, and there will be no idea left for another."

"A lover every inch, you see," said Gracchus, at his elbow; "talking to himself by the yard!"

"It is a very general symptom," replied another.

Charles Clement turned round, and Gracchus Antiboul and Father Michel stood before him. As far as he could judge by the dim light of the evening, the *Père* was well enough to look at. He was tall, seemingly solemn in manner, and reverend, though somewhat gaunt. His voice was a little thick, as with good living, but that could be no matter of reproach with those who love the church.

"Here is the only true love doctor," laughed Gracchus Antiboul, who was trying to be very gay, "whose prescription is warranted to affect a cure of the deepest case of passion, love, affection, or other such complaint, in three months."

"How?" said Charles, scarcely knowing what he asked.

" By marriage !" exclaimed Antiboul, with pretended cynicism.

" I've known the most tremendous love cured in twenty-four hours by this remedy," said the priest gravely. " Marriage raises many a mark, not often so quick, but often in too brief a time."

" But you have known love to continue after marriage ?" said Charles Clement, rather drily.

" Well," replied Father Michel, " I have, but not often in Paris society."

" Where then ? "

" Amongst the poor, to whom a wife is a real treasure ; and where, with a little foundation of real affection, there is much happiness."

" I'm half inclined to try," said Antiboul, with affected lightness.

" With whom ? "  inquired Charles Clement, rather quickly.

" With my little girl at home," replied Gracchus, in a careless tone.

" You are joking, Antiboul ? "

" Why ? "

" You don't know her."

" Quite enough."

" But —— "

" Is she not pretty ? ——"

" Yes."

" Young ? "

" Yes ; but— "

" Likely to love me ? "

" Very likely ; but— "

" A woman."

" Yes."

" Is she not evidently simple, and trusting as a child ? "

" I should judge so."

" Would she not make a gentle, confiding, and affection-ate wife ? "

" She might."

" And all you have to say against her is, that she was nearly betrayed by a scoundrel, whose character once known, she turned from him in hate and scorn."

" But second love."

" Second love ! " said Antiboul ; " What of that ? "

" I would have a woman's first thought of love ! "

" Then marry her very young.  But a woman, must she not, too, ask a man's first thought of love ? "

" Unless she think so, she cannot be happy."

" Wait for experience," said Gracchus Antiboul, rather drily; " and now to make a clear breast of it, I give you fair notice that I intend to marry this young girl to-morrow."

" I wish you joy, Gracchus ! " exclaimed Charles, fervently; " for you will have a good, true, little wife, who will make you happy."

Antiboul replied not, but he shook his friend by the hand.

Talking, they had crossed by the Seine, and had reached the Rue Dominique.  They were not more than fifty yards from the Hotel of the Duke de Ravilliere.

" Hasten your steps," said Charles, " they must be waiting for us with anxiety."

They were before the Hotel.  As they expected, the outer door was closed, and not a sound came from within.

" Like all the *quartier*," exclaimed Gracchus, gravely ; " they have barricaded themselves against the people."

Charles Clement made no answer, but rang impatiently.

No answer came at this first summons.

" We have been wrong to delay so long," said Charles, with anxiety ; " they have been fearfully alarmed."

" Ring again," replied Gracchus Antiboul.

" Knock you too," exclaimed Charles.

They rang and knocked violently.  Heavy steps were at once heard crossing the yard.

" Who is there ? " said the voice of the maître-d'hôtel.

" I," replied Charles.

The wicket door opened, and the three entered.  The maître-d'hôtel closed the door after them.

" How is the Duke ? "

The servant hesitated.

" Tell me ! " said Charles, anxiously.

" Monsieur," stammered the servant, " I know not.  He is gone."

"Where?" thundered Charles.

"Monsieur, we know not," answered the domestic, alarmed at the manner of the young man.

"And the lady Adela?" said Clement, with forced composure.

"Gone too, monsieur."

"And the Countess Miranda?"

"Likewise."

Charles Clement leaned convulsively on the arm of his friend.

"But explain," said Gracchus, sternly, for he regretted having allowed Charles to come out; "how went they?"

"When, monsieur, the cannon was heard, my lord Duke started up, and wanted to go out, but the Countess Miranda prevented him."

"Go on."

"Leaving my lord in our charge, she went out alone."

"Ah!" said Gracchus, "how dressed?"

"As usual," replied the servant. "About two hours ago she returned. She wore a cloak and hat, and was very pale."

"My God!" said Charles, recollecting the mysterious friend of the Place de la Bastille.

"My lord Duke and the lady Adela, dressed as poor people, were just going out. The Countess stayed them— they went into my lord's room, and soon after came all out together, and, bidding none follow them, went away."

"And said not where they were going?"

"No, monsieur, but there is a packet."

Without speaking, the two friends rushed into the house, followed by the priest and the servant.

"Here it is, monsieur."

Charles took it. It was a large sealed packet, addressed to him.

He opened it.

It was a deed by which the Duke de Ravilliere made over the whole of his property, real and personal, to Charles Clement, at his death, Duke de Ravilliere, by special permission of the king. It was dated some days before.

"Not a word," said Charles Clement, dropping the deed, and falling senseless on the ground.

" Quick ! assist me ! " exclaimed Gracchus.

They raised Charles Clement up ; he was as if life had departed, and, after long efforts, he but recovered to fall again without sensation.   He was in a raging fever.

Gracchus Antiboul had read the paper.

" Help me to take your master to bed," he said, addressing the servants, " and remember you have none other now."

Antiboul was essentially a man of action.   He took the deed and read it out.   The servants bowed low.

" Now, then, to the best bedroom : that first."

Charles Clement, in ten minutes more, was in a warm bed, by a warm fire.

" Now, then, an arm-chair for me—a mattress for Father Michel."

" Me ?" said the priest.

" Yes," replied Antiboul ; " we will nurse him.   When you sleep, I shall keep watch ; when you watch, I will sleep.   I am the doctor, but not alone."

" The family doctor lives by the Louvre," said one of the maids.

" Tell the valet to go fetch him at once ; and as he is there, tell him to call at Monsieur Clement's, and bid Jean, Marie, and their friend come here at once."

" But if the doctor won't come ?" said the valet, who stood behind.

" Bring him by force !" replied Gracchus, fiercely.   " Tell him your master's nephew is ill, and if he don't come, I will fetch him."

The valet hurried away to obey his behest with alacrity. All the house loved Charles Clement and Adela, and the servants counted them as one.

After the lapse of about an hour, a noise was heard without ; the valet entered, with a face of consternation and alarm.   Marie and the love of Antiboul followed, and then Paul Ledru, who was holding a man by the collar, a pistol to his side.

" A thousand excuses," muttered the valet, alternately to Gracchus and to the strange man ; " but monsieur the doctor would not come."

" So you brought him," replied Gracchus, without allowing

him to tell his story. "You did right, and saved me a journey."

"Sir," said the doctor, a small old man, who was trembling in every limb.

"Let him go, Paul," said Gracchus. "Monsieur the doctor, a thousand excuses! My friend, Charles Clement, nephew to the Duke, is ill, and Paul here loves his master."

"No excuses," said the doctor, shaking himself, and looking round a little reassured; "the fact is, the town is in an uproar. I did not know—in fact, I thought—insurgents—danger—stray ball—and so——"

"Not a word," answered Gracchus; "but this way, doctor; here is your patient."

The doctor, who, since his arrival in the house of the Duke, had been recovering, now stood grave and solemn before the young man.

"Clear the room," he said, "and give me a glass of wine."

The servants went out, but Paul and his two female companions remained, with Gracchus and the priest. The doctor then drank a glass of wine, smacked his lips, wiped his mouth, and methodistically approached the bed.

Gracchus followed him.

"Doctor, the exact truth?"

"I never lie," replied the little doctor, drily.

"Pardon," said Antiboul.

"No cause, sir."

"But how is he?"

"Not the least danger. Fever, hot pulse, dry skin, and so forth; but good constitution. He will be well in a week."

Gracchus embraced him.

"Pens, ink, and paper."

Gracchus brought it, while Paul and Marie looked at one another with intense joy.

The doctor had said there was no danger.

"Now," said the man of medicine, "a servant home, who can fetch the draught, and I will come in the morning."

In an hour more, Charles had taken his medicine; Gracchus and Father Michel were sipping wine by the fireside: Paul and his wife had had a room assigned to them, as well as the young girl; and the whole house was still.

Gracchus said not a word.

He was thinking how to get back Adela to the house before the recovery of his friend.

---

## CHAPTER XXVII.

### THE MINISTER.

It was five o'clock in the evening of the 12th June, 1791, and in the *salon* of the Minister of the Interior. The apartment was arranged with extreme neatness, but without much elegance. Books, papers, journals, copies of the *Moniteur*, of the *Morning Chronicle*, greedily devoured by the minister to learn England's opinion of affairs, were scattered in all corners. The apartment was empty, but, just as the clock struck five, two men entered it, ushered in by a servant in plain clothes.

One of these men—both were young—dressed with scrupulous neatness according to the modern fashion of the day, was pale, haggard, and thoughtful. His glance never rested still one moment; he seemed looking perpetually for something; his mien showed one worn by much long suffering.

His companion was about his own age; and, though calm and sedate enough, yet his exterior showed much more mental and material happiness than was evidently the lot of his companion.

The first was Charles Clement, the second Gracchus Antiboul. Two whole years, fruitful in events, had passed by, and no tale or tidings of the Duke, of Adela, or of Miranda had been heard. Their disappearance had been complete and miraculous. Not an agent of the house could tell whither they had gone, and the two first were rated amongst the emigrants. One or two notes in a feigned hand had come, bidding Charles hope; but six months had now elapsed since he had even had this small comfort. He had devoted himself calmly, solemnly, gravely to his country. He was an influential member of several revolutionary clubs; but his heart seemed dried up, he never smiled, he never laughed ; his tongue was bitingly satirical ; he was a man disappointed, and half broken-hearted.

Gracchus Antiboul had married the young girl whom he had saved from ruin, and the family lived together in the Rue Dominique. Paul Ledru had remained the confidential head-servant of Charles Clement, while his wife was the housekeeper. They had preferred doing this to entering upon business, which took them away from one they loved so much. Antiboul and his wife lived as guests in the hotel. Charles had preserved all the domestics of the Duke. His principal care had, however, been to sell the property of the old Duke, and his own too, which, seizing a good opportunity, he had done to good advantage. The proceeds in hard cash he had remitted to England, in whose funds the whole of the proceeds had been invested, to be gradually, and as occasion offered, resold and remitted to the United States of America.

These duties had formed his occupation during the two years which had elapsed since the taking of the Bastille. In vain the friends tried to explain to themselves the flight of the three persons who bore with them the heart and hopes of Clement.

"We are early," said Charles gravely ; "too early, I am afraid."

"Nay, not so, for here comes our hostess," replied Gracchus.

At this moment a lady entered, and approached the two young men.

It was a woman about the middle height, with a rich full bosom, elegant figure, and an erect walk and rapid step. She seemed about thirty, but was more. Her shoulders sloped gracefully, while her remarkable head stood firmly up from her body, with some little pride of manner. Her skin was singularly fresh and fair ; her mouth, without being pretty, was sweetly soft and seductive, with lips which, with a peculiarly-shaped chin, bespoke a naturally-voluptuous character. Her eye was not very large, of an auburn grey, but in the very *juste-milieu* where it should be, open, frank, lively, soft, crowned by dark-brown eyelids and lashes, and hair ; its expression was most varied, now grave, now proud, now humble, now gentle—it had a most caressing look. The nose was what we should call a pug, or rather, it was larger than it should have been at the extremity. A large open forehead, with thin red veins, which swelled or disappeared in a most rapid manner, added to the noticeable character of her countenance. Her complexion was clear, while her cheek was red and white with wondrous rapidity, according tô the emotions of the mind. A soft skin, round arm, pretty hand, fresh and good teeth, the *embonpoint* of health. Such is a rapid outline of the hostess who received Charles Clement and Gracchus Antiboul with a grave politeness which savoured a little of the pedantry in which she had been brought up.

Such was Madame Roland, the celebrated and unfortunate friend of the Girondins, whose influence over those brilliant but inefficient men, as much as anything else, tended to their ruin.

"I am glad to see you, M. Clement," she said, with a kindly nod to Gracchus; "still grave and solemn."

"Madame," he replied, bowing, "if I had no private sorrows, the troubles of my country would make me sad."

"But we must be hopeful," replied Madame Roland.

"In what? In the King, who plots with the Court to violate the constitution he has sworn to; in the General Lafayette, who intrigues and dallies with the Court; in the Assembly, torn by conflicting factions? We have a dark future before us."

"The Court party is truly too powerful," said the wife of the Minister of the Interior; "but, excuse me, here comes a fresh visitor." And she moved away.

A stout, heavy, ugly man, with thick lips and nose, entered. His head was like a bull's, his hair loose and shaggy, while his whole face and mien showed one torn by wild passions, by ambition, love of power, and of the good things of this world.

"Good evening," he said in his rough way, "I come to ask you for a bason of *soupe*."

"Good evening, M. Danton," replied Madame Roland rather coldly, as she turned to receive several younger men and one older.

The new comers were Brissot de Warville, Barbaroux, Buzot, and others of the Girondins

Roland entered immediately after with an air of fatigue and anxiety, followed by Paché, who had not joined the Commune.

Charles Clement and Gracchus remained alone, but were soon joined by a new comer, whom Madame Roland did not receive much more cordially than she had done Danton, the tribune of the people, the most energetic man of the revolution. Madame Roland liked splendid dreamers and talkers, not men of action.

The new comer was a slight man, with thin, hard face, small eyes, a sallow, bilious complexion, who was dressed with scrupulous nicety. His forehead, compressed lips, and student's pallor, showed one of thought and reflection. His manner was cold and retiring; there was an air of modesty, tempered by conscious power and stoic worth.

This was the soul of the revolution, the rigid, earnest, and incorruptible Maximilian Robespierre.

"Good evening, citizens," he said, after shaking hands with Clement and Antiboul; "what news?"

And he began to gnaw his nails in that nervous feverish way which denoted the never-tiring restlessness of his mind.

"I believe we are near a *coup d'état*," replied Clement, "the Court party is mad, and does not know us."

"It will learn in time," said Robespierre, with a frown, and clenching his fist.

"But will the people resist?" observed Charles.

"The revolution is scarcely begun," interrupted Robespierre.

"Alas! poor France."

"Messieurs, to dinner," said Madame Roland; and the whole party, to which Dumouriez had been added, moved at once to the dining-room.

There were no women. Madame Roland never received any. She desired to reign alone in her little court; besides, her favourite Buzot, the man she loved, without, it is thought, ever going beyond the bounds of practical propriety, was a married man—and had she received women, she must have received his wife, which would have been painful, especially as, she says, as a kind of excuse for her own passionate attachment for him, "he had a wife who appeared not up to his level."

The dinner was plain, but the most mighty affairs were there discussed, affairs that were to change the face of the whole world.

When the dinner was ended, the company dispersed about the room in little knots. Roland, Dumouriez, and the other ministers held council in a corner; Brissot, Buzot, Barbaroux, Louvet the author of *Faublas*, and a bright specimen, formed another group, while Danton, Robespierre, Clement, and Antiboul spoke in whispers in a corner.

"We must act with more vigour," said Danton, addressing them. "I have certain information that the Court means to crush us. These well-meaning men are losing us. The *côte droite* is ruining the cause of the revolution. The King, the Austrian, and the Royal Princes, are only biding their time."

"I will go this very night to the Jacobins," replied Robespierre, "and try and move them to a little more energy."

"I will go," said Charles.

"And I," added Gracchus.

"But what shall we do?" urged Danton, looking them all hard in the face; "action is better than talking."

"I am ready for anything," said Clement, firmly, "even to the overthrow of the monarchy. Nothing else will change affairs. Why pare the claws of our enemy, while we can get rid of him altogether?"

"You are the man," answered Danton.

"But what would you do?" said Robespierre, biting his nails.

"That's to be seen."

"But I enter into no conspiracies," answered the Jacobin, and the greatest amongst Jacobins, too; "my business is to enlighten the people, to watch the march of the revolution, and to do my best to see that the people take advantage of it for their good."

"Each man to his task," replied Danton, with a slight sneer.

"Do you come to the Jacobins?" said Robespierre.

"We all come," answered Danton; and the four revolutionists glided from the apartment of Madame Roland, leaving the ministers to talk, the Girondins to dream, while they went forth to act.

# CHAPTER XXVIII.

### THE JACOBIN CLUB.

Iᴛ was eight o'clock. In the spacious hall of the Jacobins, far too small for the force of the society, sat twelve hundred men. In the chair, that evening, was some unknown liberal. The business before the meeting was formal, the election of members, and the affiliation of branch societies was being made known.

An orator was addressing the club, with all the pedantry of a lawyer—with more learning than talent—when the four friends entered. Robespierre and Danton moved higher up than the entrance, to where they saw friends.

Charles Clement and Gracchus Antiboul kept in the background, behind the shadow of a pillar.

The hall was ill-lighted, and few faces could be distinguished.

Near to Charles Clement and Gracchus Antiboul stood several persons, all visitors to the club, introduced by the privilege of members. There were five on one bench; they wore heavy cloaks and slouched hats, and held back in a retiring manner.

"Look!" said Gracchus, with an imperceptible glance at the other two.

Charles Clement fixed his eyes on them, and turned pale. One was M. Brown, and the other the ex-Count Leopold. A cloud of painful recollections rushed to his mind; and he did not notice, which Gracchus did minutely, that they both wore the most extreme costume as yet adopted to distinguish the patriots from the Feuillans, the Royalists, &c.

"What seek they here?" said Charles, in his most sombre tone; for all his sorrows now rushed upon him, fresh as the first day.

"They are police spies," answered Antiboul, drily, while his eyes wandered upon the cloaked figures with intense curiosity.

Those in the cloaks had noticed this, and they had bowed their heads still lower. Clement suddenly fixed his eyes upon them, at first carelessly, then curiously. Presently some fancy crossed his mind, and he turned eagerly to Antiboul.

"They are women," said Charles Clement.

"They are women," replied Antiboul, drily.

At this instant Danton approached.

"Robespierre is going to speak," he said; "but he will resolve nothing."

At this instant he saw the two cloaked figures.

"Good evening," said he, approaching them with rough politeness, and with undisguised pleasure.

"They are friends of Danton," whispered Charles Clement, with a sigh; and he turned away—his flickering hope had fled.

"Danton knows who they are," replied Gracchus Antiboul, still watching them.

But Charles Clement had lost all interest in them the instant he had discovered that Danton knew them.

Robespierre had begun to speak. His first words, bad as was the manner, had riveted the attention of the assembly. *La patrie est en danger!* he had cried, in his shrill tones. This exordium laid down, he had proceeded to show in what way it was in danger. He painted the King, Court, and aristocracy, leagued with the *côte droite* against the revolution, and consequently against the people. He showed that if the nation was not determined and firm in its support of the patriotic party, that the monarchical, or rather despotic, party would triumph, and all the ground gained by the revolution be lost.

Loud cries interrupted him.

"*A bas Monsieur Veto! A bas Madame Veto!*"

Monsieur and Madame Veto were Louis XVI. and Marie Antoinette.

"No!" cried Robespierre. "I cry not *à bas!* All I ask is, that the King should govern according to the constitution, and that persons who are not covered by ministerial responsibility should not interfere in the affairs of the State. I ask only that the King should act according to his own personal wishes, unguided by a gang of selfish, grasping, and ungrateful courtiers, who would place themselves between the nation and the sovereign to deceive the one and trample on the other"

Murmurs arose.

" I am aware," said the orator, " that many of you would have done once for all with monarchy; that you desire to see the French people govern themselves by laws without a sovereign. I am perfectly of your opinion. It is the perfection of human government. A king is a brute force to coerce and tyrannize; it is a compromise with truth to have a constitution admitting the rights of the people, and keeping a king, an emperor, or by whatever other name you call the tyrant."

Loud applause greeted Robespierre, who continued, however, in his cold way, unmoved.

" But how are we to effect this? France is an ancient monarchy, her people are for the most part brought up in kingly and priestly prejudices. They know not the meaning of the word democracy. They can neither see it, nor feel it, nor touch it, and therefore they know it not. With these elements we should not hope to found a commonwealth. Let us be satisfied if we can drive back the landmarks of despotism, and gain any, even the most moderate portion of freedom. For myself, I am ready to endure persecution. I have endured it; I have been threatened with prosecution, and have hid my resting-place from my enemies; but I have my reward in my conscience and in the approbation of my fellow-citizens."

The club applauded, and Robespiere descended from the tribune, having, as usual, proposed no particular line of conduct, because just then he could see but one, and that one he always disapproved of—and disapproved of once too often—insurrection.

Danton rushed to the tribune.

" Action," he cried with a perfect roar, " will soon be required of you. The Court is about to act itself. It is about to seize all patriotic deputies and thrust them into new bastilles. I ask of you to be ready, and when the signal is given, to rally round the men of the good cause."

The club applauded, and a long discussion commenced relative to the form of a proclamation to the provinces, to enlighten them regarding the events which were passing in Paris.

Danton, however, did not remain, but coming up to where Charles Clement stood, spoke to him.

"*A cette nuit!*" he said significantly, and left the club.

Charles Clement remained, puzzled and surprised; for, having given no rendezvous to Danton, he could not understand where he was again to see him that night.

He sought Antiboul for an explanation, but Antiboul had gone out; the police spy, the Count, and the three mysterious persons in cloaks and slouched hats, had also disappeared.

Clement moved away also. At the door he met Gracchus Antiboul, whose face was radiant with joy.

"Which is the best way to get to Charenton?" said he, taking the other's arm, and drawing him rapidly along.

"Why?" exclaimed Charles Clement.

"We have to meet Danton in that neighbourhood about midnight. The men who are disposed to aid the monarchy hold council there."

"That explains Danton's words. But why out yonder?"

"Because the position is less watched. But let us calculate our time. We have much to say and do this night."

"You are mysterious."

"I will explain presently."

"But why walk so fast?"

"I know not what I am doing. But what o'clock is it?"

"Ten."

"It will take an hour to walk to Charenton. We had best walk, to avoid suspicion."

"We can take horses."

"It will be best not. They will be awkward to leave while at the rendezvous."

"As you please."

"We will start at eleven. We have time to take our pistols."

"Let us turn to the Rue Dominique, then."

"We are coming from it. But I am still puzzled."

"Why?"

"We must be back in Paris by four o'clock."

"But why?"

"Do you see yon palace," replied Gracchus Antiboul—

they were on the Place Louis XV.—"where lies the tyrant and his vile horde?"

"I do."

"At four o'clock to-morrow morning, ere the dawn has scarcely broken, we must at the *guichet* on the river."

"But what means all this?"

"A sentry will be within the *grille*—"

"But you are dreaming."

"To whom we shall say, "*Salut.*'"

"But why?"

"And he will reply, '*Peuple.*'"

"But, my dear Antiboul, what is the bottom of all this?"

"We are just at the top, the bottom has yet to be found."

"Go on your own way, my dear fellow," said Charles, gravely.

"The sentry will open. Inside we shall find a servant in livery, who will ask our names, and, after certain other formalities, we shall find ourselves in the presence of Marie Antoinette, Queen of France and wife of Louis XVI., the celebrated original of Monsieur Veto."

"If I understand a word of this—"

"It isn't fit you should. Suffice that your best friends understand for you."

"Antiboul," said Charles, stopping, "there is something under this. Do not keep me in suspense."

"I have told you nothing," cried Gracchus.

"Then go on, in the name of all that is good and gracious."

"On leaving the Queen's Chamber to return, two of her waiting-women will be there to lead us out."

"Yes."

"And these will be the men in cloaks of the Jacobin Club."

"Who are?"

"Miranda and Adela."

Charles Clement leaned against the parapet of the bridge, which they had reached, for support.

"Courage," said Antiboul, with a joyous laugh, "your troubles are over."

"But why did they hide from me?"

"They feared your joy."

"But their absence?"

"Alas!" said Gracchus, shaking his head, "the poor old Duke received a sad shock on the day of the taking of the Bastille. I fancy his senses must be gone. He curses your name, vows you robbed him of a son-in-law, and vowed upon the head of Adela an eternal malediction if she held the remotest communication with you."

"My God!" cried Charles Clement, "what she must have suffered."

"Less than you," said Antiboul, warmly; "and had she not her devoted and attached friend Miranda?"

"And do you count yourself for nothing?" exclaimed Charles; "you who saved my life, who nursed me through my long and dangerous illness, who were father, mother, brother, everything to me."

"*A bah!*" cried Antiboul, whistling a tune, "talk of them."

"I will," said Charles, taking his friend's hand.

"It appears that they have been to England, to Germany, and have only returned to Paris within a fortnight. The old Duke insisted upon returning to die alongside his King, to whom, in this his dotage, he has become devotedly attached."

"How he must hate me."

"Not at all. The calm of the interior of the palace seems to revive him, and they told me he had become far more himself. He has let drop a hint that he would like to see you. He has not found all he could wish in the palace of his King."

"I have, then, hope."

"Besides, Adela told me how noble Miranda had fought for you all along; how she had taken advantage of everything to support your memory, to instil your ideas, your thoughts, into his mind; and she has, I think, succeeded."

"Noble heart!" cried Charles.

"Noble heart, indeed," replied Gracchus Antiboul, with a shake of his head.

"But Adela, how looks she?"

"A little pale and thin, but lovely, more lovely than ever."

"God bless her."

"She looks not an hour older."

"Thank you; and Miranda?"

"Is the same magnificent creature she ever was, the very beau-ideal of majesty and beauty."

"I wonder you never loved her," said Charles musing.

"I did."

"You?"

"I."

"And how did you never speak?" exclaimed Charles.

"Because I knew it was vain."

"You amaze and astound me. She was no proud dame to refuse you because you are poor."

"I know it."

"But then ——"

"She loved another."

"Another?" cried Charles Clement, almost fiercely; while, he knew not why, his heart leaped wildly to his mouth.

"Another," repeated Gracchus Antiboul.

"And that other is ——" said Charles, gloomily.

"That is her secret—not mine. Some day I will divulge it."

"You are a gentleman and a man of honour," said Charles kindly; "but was it a love not to be told?"

"Not to be told."

"Above her, or below her?"

"Neither."

"Then I can understand nothing. The lady Miranda was wholly devoted to us, went nowhere, received no one ——"

"My dear friend, you would never discover; and I shall not tell you now—perhaps never will."

"Here is the Rue Dominique."

The two young men entered the hotel with very different sentiments to those with which they left it. There was lightness in their steps; and when they entered a small room where the wife of Gracchus sat working, with Paul Ledru and Marie near her, their manner was eloquent.

"News?" said the wife of Gracchus.

"Good news!" replied Antiboul, taking her up in his arms and kissing her.

"They are found?" she said.

"They are," replied Gracchus.

"Found!" repeated Paul and Marie, in one voice.

"Yes!" cried Charles Clement, radiant with joy and hope—another man from him who the same evening entered the salon of Madame Roland—"they are found, and, please God, will soon be restored to us."

"But let me tell the story," said Gracchus, "while Paul will ring the bell, and bid Joseph bring our cloaks, pistols, and swords."

"You are going out?" exclaimed his wife; "there is more fighting?"

"Not yet, love; but there will be soon."

"My God!" cried the good little creature; "and you will expose yourself!"

"My love, it is not from choice, but duty."

A servant entered, Paul having rung.

"Our pistols loaded, with ammunition besides, a sword apiece, thick cloaks, and slouched hats," said Gracchus.

His wife held up her hands in despair.

"Now for my story," he said; and he explained all he knew relative to the re-appearance of the Duke, Miranda, and Adela.

"How happy you must be, Monsieur Charles," exclaimed the wife of Gracchus when he had finished.

"I am happy, and thankful to God, said the young man fervently; "my dearest hope and wish is gratified."

"Duty first, pleasure afterwards," put in Antiboul; "here are our arms, and it is eleven o'clock passed. We have a good hour's walk before us."

"Where are you going?" said his wife.

"A secret, my dear. By the way, Paul, do you not come?"

"I was about to ask permission," said Ledru humbly.

"Come! this night you will learn how men of heart are required, and what is to be done."

"Be careful," said Marie, too proud of their taking him to resist; for hers was that true love which looked not to self, but the object loved.

"Away, then!" cried Antiboul, Paul being ready in an instant.

The women received a few words of comfort and con·solation, and the three men went out.

Paul Ledru walked first, alone. Charles Clement and Gracchus Antiboul walked behind.

"Will you tell me," said Charles Clement, after a short pause, "why, if you loved Miranda, you married your present little wife?"

"To tell you why, would be to tell the whole secret; but still——"

"Don't say a word, if it pains you."

"I needed a woman's affection, sincerity, and truth, to draw me from the thought of her. I found this girl; I married her, and I am happy in the possession of her true and innocent heart,—though, crushed under this love, the old rises victorious sometimes."

"This is inexplicable. Miranda in the end would not have remained insensible to your affection, and you might have won her."

"Precisely what I would not have done."

"But why?"

"Oh, why! My dear friend, that is a mystery which time may and may not elucidate. There is a mystery between me and her you know not of, and perhaps may never know; but still I think you will, without hoping it."

"I lose myself in conjectures," replied Charles Clement.

"Paul," said Gracchus, addressing their companion, who was ahead, "lead the way; we make for Charenton."

---

## CHAPTER XXIX.

### THE CONSPIRATORS.

PARIS was dead, to all appearance. Scarce a soul was in the streets. Few ventured to show themselves out after eleven o'clock, save clubbists returning from their political meetings. Several of these were met by the two friends; and even when they had passed the Hotel de Ville they became numerous. The wine-shops of the Faubourg St. Antoine were even full.

"One would fancy the work was for to-night," said Gracchus Antiboul.

"I fear there is some counterplotting," replied Clement.

"Oh, no! 'tis but the agents of Danton and the Jacobin stirring up the people for the coming day."

"But what mean you to do this time?" said Paul, curiously.

"To end with monarchy altogether," replied Gracchus.

"*Vive la Republique!*" whispered Ledru.

"That's it, man," said Antiboul; "that's the cry which in a few days will wake all France, and rouse amid the dull and heavy partisans of monarchy some life and courage."

"But will there be courage enough in the masses?" inquired Paul.

"Have you forgotten the taking of the Bastille?" said Antiboul.

"Have I forgotten that I live?" said Paul, warmly.

"Remember that day, and the march to Versailles; remember the faubourgs, and then feel no doubt. The day the signal will be given, the monarchy will fall."

Charles Clement was walking alone behind, thinking.

Suddenly, he advanced to the two speakers.

"Do not turn your heads," said he, "but listen. We are followed; every footstep we take is dogged."

"*Peste!*" cried Antiboul; "that will not do at all. What can be done to ascertain the truth?"

"Let us enter this wine-shop," replied Charles.

It was the celebrated *locale* whence had started the attack on Reveillon.

Scarcely had the three friends entered, than two men in cloaks passed the door, taking a hurried glance inside. They then, watched by Gracchus, turned down a lane opposite, and halted in the dark.

"M. Brown and Count Leopold," said Gracchus.

Paul Ledru shuddered.

"Let us straight to them," replied Charles, drinking up the wine they had ordered.

"Not yet," said Antiboul; "wait until we are out on the road. If then we cannot get rid of them, we must retrace our steps."

"But," continued Charles, "if they are going where we are going?"

"*Foi de Brutus!*" cried Antiboul; "it is quite probable."

" Then let them follow us."

" Agreed.   At any rate, we will soon discover their intentions.   *En route.*"

And the three went out, and retook the road to Charenton, without a glance at the place of concealment occupied by M. Brown and Count Leopold.

Scarcely, however, had they proceeded twenty yards further, when they heard them coming up behind with cautious and measured step.

The three walked rapidly, without a word, along the Rue du Faubourg St. Antoine.   Soon they were in sight of the barrier.

" The *grille* is shut," said Charles, in a whisper.

" It will open to us," replied Antiboul ; " and, once outside, follow me like wild goats.   I will see to the bottom of this affair."

Gracchus made for the *guichet*.   A man stood near, with a musket in his hand.

" *Qui vive?*"

" *Patrie!*"

" Where go you?"

" To the good work."

The sentinel lowered his musket, pushed open the small side-door, and, as soon as they had passed, closed it again.

" Now," cried Antiboul, rushing towards a wood-yard which stood outside the barrier, and which was protected but by a low wall.

Next minute the three were ensconced in the middle of a pile of wood, whence they could see without being seen.

Scarcely had they done so than the *grille* opened, and M. Brown and Count Leopold passed.

" *Sacre bleu!*" cried the Count, " where are they."

" They have taken a run for it," replied the spy, drily. " they liked not the look of your mug."

" But what are they up to?"

" To the meeting," said Brown, drily ; " and mind you be cautious there.   That Antiboul has the eye of a fox If he discovers you we are lost."

"He will not discover me," replied the Count; "for I must revenge myself on him, and I hope to see the whole meeting hanged, or guillotined according to the fashion proposed by the excellent Dr. Guillotin."

"Bah! the Court won't have pluck enough for that. It will imprison a few, buy some more, and threaten the rest."

"Not at all. Antoinette will force the King to be rigorous. She and her friends are right. Severity with this *canaille* Assemblée National, or ruin."

"Mildness, concession, and sincerity would be better," said the spy. "Antoinette should not play with edged tools."

With the above words the two men were out of sight.

"Charles," said Antiboul, grasping his friend's hand, "leave these two men to me. Whatever they do or say, leave them. I will settle them in time."

"They are yours, the more that my personal hate of the Count would make me hesitate to act against him."

"Let us proceed. They are far enough ahead to be unaware of our presence. Besides, we can keep beneath the trees which line the road."

The three companions moved on rapidly in silence, and it was not long ere they reached the village of Charenton. They paused not in the hamlet, but turned on one side into the fields.

"We are near the end of this journey," whispered Gracchus Antiboul.

As he spoke, they had entered another lane, in which appeared a small country house.

"That is our destination."

Charles and Paul examined the house curiously. It was close shut. Not a shutter was open, and not a glimpse of light was to be seen. It had all the appearance of an uninhabited dwelling.

"Here, for months past," said Antiboul, "have met the patriots who would deliver France from the yoke of tyrants; here sits the tribunal which is to judge, condemn, and execute the monarchy."

They had reached the house. All was silence. Not a sound came from within.

Gracchus knocked thrice at a shutter beside the door

No answer.

" There is no one here," said Charles Clement.

" Wait!" replied Antiboul.

He knocked again, this time twice; and, when a minute had elapsed, once.

The door opened; and the three companions, rapidly entering, closed it behind them.

They were in a passage obscurely lighted up by one solitary candle.

" This way!" whispered Gracchus; and he led the way to the further extremity, where was a door.

He opened the door, and entered.

They found themselves in a kind of dining-room, also dimly illumined by one candle.  A sentinel, armed with a musket, walked up and down.

" Marseilles and Paris," said Gracchus Antiboul.

The sentinel nodded assent, and, without a word, allowed them to enter an inner apartment.

Here sat the conspirators round a large table, while numerous subordinate agents stood around, wrapped in large cloaks.  Among these were the two spies of the police, keeping as much as possible out of sight.

At the table sat Danton, Santerre, Fabre d'Eglantine, Panis, Huguenin, Gonchon, Marat, Alexandre, Camille Desmoulins, Varlet, Lenfant, Barbaroux, and one or two others.

" Welcome !" cried Danton, addressing Charles and Gracchus; " here are two vacant chairs.  The patriot who accompanies you must stand for want of sitting."

Charles and Gracchus seated themselves, while Paul Ledru took up a post near the door, to watch that the spies did not escape.

" Well," said Danton, " I was saying—no more words— we waste time—why so much ceremony with aristocrats and tyrants?  Do like them—you were under, put yourselves over; that's the whole revolution."

" But how ?" said Marat.

" That's what we have met to decide," exclaimed Danton  " I have a plan.  I would show the King and the National Assembly the power of the people.  I would give them one chance—the King, of giving up his traitorous designs against France, his league with foreign enemies, with the traitor Lafayette; the Assembly, of putting an end to its vacillation and weakness. I want neither to put down the King nor the Parliament, if they honestly observe the constitution, break with the emigration and the enemies of liberty, and stand by the people."

" A dream," said Marat, while Charles and Antiboul applauded.

" What would you then?" cried Danton.

" Proclaim the republic, and have done for ever with the whole race of kings," replied Clement, warmly.

" With the King in the Tuilleries, supported by half Paris?—with an army whose patriotism is doubtful?—with a populace who know not what it means? No! That will come all in good time, if you have patience; but the pear is not yet ripe."

" Then, your proposition?" said Santerre.

" Is this. Let the Faubourgs rise *en masse*, let them go to the Tuilleries and show their force, let them enter the palace of Louis and teach him what he has to expect if he be obstinate—trust the rest to chance. If there be resistance, we must fight; if there be none, we must content ourselves with a moral victory. We shall thus have the mind of Paris. Not that I oppose the extreme act being complete at once; but I doubt if the mind of the masses is sufficiently prepared."

" We shall see," said Santerre. " I answer for my Faubourg; before daylight it shall be in motion."

" And I for the Cordelieu," said Marat.

" And I for the *cité*," cried both Fabre d'Eglantine and Gonchon.

" But let us discuss the details and distribute the *rôles*," said Danton, taking a sheet of paper.

This important part of the business occupied an hour. The insurgent chiefs showed themselves consummate masters in the art of getting up a popular movement. They spoke and arranged details with the precision and correctness of military men. They saw what was wanted at a glance.

It was nearly two o'clock ere the arrangements were all completed. Charles Clement and Gracchus Antiboul had skilfully escaped taking any leading part in the affair.

"Now for action," said Danton.

"Not yet!" cried Gracchus Antiboul, rising, and speaking in a voice of thunder.

The whole company started.

"Not yet," he continued, "for the most important part of our sitting has yet to come.  To succeed in our enterprise against the Court, the Court must remain unaware of our intentions; they must remain lulled in profound security, or we are lost!"

"Yes! yes!" cried the conspirators.

"Now, this is impossible, if we separate as we are now. There are traitors in our midst."

The assembly stood, as it were, stunned; but not a man spoke, awaiting the explanation.

"Police spies! two men, who, I know not how or by what means, have penetrated here to report our proceedings to the King and to the Government."

"Who are they?" thundered Danton.

"I!" said M. Brown, who saw the eye of Antiboul resting on him.

"I!" repeated the Count Leopold, unabashed.

"Kill them!" said Marat, who was trembling like a woman, with his cheeks as pale as ashes.

"No!" cried Danton, who had quivered and lowered his eyes as the two men advanced—Danton, who, while betraying the Court, took its money for his pleasures and debauchery.

"Death to the spies!" said Santerre.

"We have but done our duty," exclaimed M. Brown, calmly; "we have been caught; we are ready to pay the penalty."

"To death with them at once!" repeated Marat.

"Perfectly useless murder," said Danton, quietly and contemptuously.  "These two men can be kept here under guard, disarmed, and bound hand and foot, in a cellar, until their report is too late; then they can go freely about their business."

"I call for death," said Marat.

"Let it be decided by a show of hands," said Danton.

"Agreed! agreed!" rose from all sides.

The two criminals before this strange judgment-bench

were removed to the end of the room while the vote which was to decide their fate took place. Both were a little pale, for their position was so far worse than death that it was undecided.

"Those who are for putting the two spies to death," said Danton, "hold up their hands."

A number of hands were held up. Marat, Fabre, Panis, Huguenin, Gonchon, Varlet, Lenfant, voted for death.

"The contrary," said Danton, with a frown.

Santerre, Charles, Gracchus, Paul, Alexandre, Camille Desmoulins, and Barbaroux, raised their hands."

"The numbers are equal," cried Danton; "it rests with me. *Scelerats; brigands!*" he continued, addressing the spies, "you deserve death, but I spare you. Learn to be better citizens. But who will guard them?"

"I, with the porter," said Paul.

"And who answers for you?"

"We do," said Charles Clement and Gracchus; "one of them is his bitterest enemy."

"Then why did you vote against his death?" inquired Danton, curiously.

"For that very reason," replied Paul.

"Good! You answer for them, then."

In two minutes more the police spies were searched, deprived of their arms, and tied back to back. In this state they were borne to a cellar, and placed upon a heap of straw.

This done, the conspirators dispersed, each gaining Paris as rapidly as possible. Danton and some friends had a vehicle; Santerre was mounted on a horse.

"There is place for two in my cart," said Danton, addressing our two friends.

Charles and Gracchus accepted.

"Roland is dismissed, you are aware?" said Danton.

"No!" exclaimed Charles Clement, much surprised.

"It is true; I have it from Barbaroux. The letter came announcing it soon after we left. The Court is determined, if it can, to end with the revolution."

"Madness," said Charles. "By the way," he added, in a whisper to Danton, "I shall be in the Tuilleries before you."

" How ? " inquired the tribune of the faubourg, looking hard at him.

" I will have an interview with Marie Antoinette."

" What for ? " said Danton, gravely.

" I know not," replied Charles Clement.

" Ah ! " cried Danton, as if taking a sudden resolution ; " stay there then as long as possible ; and when the attack comes, defend the Queen's person if the mob should seek to outrage her. Insults, contumely, she must expect, because she has deserved them ; but I would not have her personally injured."

" I am afraid you have been inveigled by her charms and seductions," said Charles Clement, with a smile.

" Not I," replied Danton, almost brutally ; " but I have promised to protect her as a woman, whatever I do against the Queen."

" I will stop," said Charles, " the more so that I have friends whom I wish to be near."

" Adela de la Ravilliere and the Countess Miranda," whispered Danton, with a laugh. " It's the talk of the palace, how the heiress of the noble house loves the rabid young Jacobin. Look to her, my boy," said Danton, kindly ; " a woman's heart is worth more than all."

In such talk the conspirators whiled away the time, which soon brought them to Paris.

Danton took the two friends as far as the Place de la Bastille. Here they separated as the clock struck half-past three.

" What day of the month is it ? " said Charles to Gracchus, as soon as they were alone.

" The 20th of June," replied Antiboul.

" I shall ever regard it as one of the happiest days of my life."

" And the Monarchy, as one of the worst."

Gracchus was right ; the 20th of June was but the prelude of the 10th of August and the 2nd of September.

" Are you tired ? " said Antiboul, as he felt his friend's arm trembling in his.

" No ! I feel fresh and vigorous ; but the passionate delight I feel at the prospect of seeing her makes me waver like a drunken man."

" You are not happier than I," said Antiboul, gently.

" I know it, my friend, I know it," repeated Charles Clement, " and never shall your noble friendship be forgotten."

" To speak of other things," said Antiboul, gravely, " I have my suspicions of Danton.  He is with us, but he is not incorruptible like Robespierre.  His secret workings with the Court bring him money."

" And yet, to-night ? "

" He will act against them.  But though I feel convinced he will remain with the people, I am sure he takes money under pretence of betraying the popular cause."

"I think he has promised to save the persons of Louis XVI. and Marie Antoinette," said Charles, " without acting for the Monarchy.  I don't blame him.  I hate them both ; the one a fool, an inane driveller, who coquets with people, Austrians, army, demagogues, anybody ; the other a tyrant by blood, race, habit—in fact an Austrian, to say nothing of her notorious faithlessness to her husband.  And yet, what Danton would do for money, I would do for nothing.  I would save them."

" I fear they will not let us.  They are blind, obstinately blind."

" We shall see ; but courage, my heart, here is the trial."

They were at the *guichet* of the Tuileries, in sight of the sentinel.

---

## CHAPTER XXX.

### LOUIS XVI. AND MARIE ANTOINETTE.

As Gracchus Antiboul and Charles Clement passed, the sentry, who stood inside the *grille* of the Tuileries, appeared to examine them attentively.  He was a Swiss, and maintained, even while fixing his eyes curiously on them, all that rigid air of discipline which characterized his corps.

" *Salut,*" said Antiboul, his eyes fixed full on the soldier.

" *Peuple,*" replied the Swiss, in his thick accent.

" Open," continued the Republican.

The soldier called a man who stood in the background, and who, advancing, inserted a key in the lock, and opened the gate. The young men entered, and the *grille* closed quickly behind them. The man said nothing, but moved across the court before them, and soon reached a small door in the body of the palace. Here a man in livery was stationed, who seemed waiting for them. Without asking any questions, he motioned them to follow him, and began ascending the narrow stairs which, until lately, served the kings and princes of France to reach their private apartments.

"Courage," said Gracchus, pressing his friend's arm.

"But why this interview with the King and Queen?" replied Charles. "It can lead to no good."

"It was necessary to reach the others. We are bound to nothing," answered Antiboul.

"But we shall be questioned closely; and, just as the last blow is about to be given to the Monarchy with our connivance, I shall feel in a false position."

"Do you think the King is not as fully aware as you are of the insurrection of to-morrow?"

"Then, why not prevent it?"

"Because Petion, our *Maire*, king Petion connives at it, and will only call out the National Guard to swell our army."

They had reached the very top of the stairs.

"Wait in this *salon*, gentlemen," said the servant, respectfully, "while I announce you."

Antiboul spoke truly. The National Assembly, the Commune of Paris, the *Maire* Petion, the National Guard, all connived at the insurrection, thus preparing the way for their own fall. But as the Court was only striving to gain time, and waiting for foreign armies to crush the Constitution, and restore despotism, they had no choice. There was great fault on both sides; but on the part of the Court, treachery.

The two young men stood silent a moment, and then the servant returned, and threw open the door of the next apartment.

The two young men entered, and found themselves in the presence of two persons.

The first was a man of heavy features, blue, large, and clear eyes, a retreating forehead, an aquiline nose, with large and wide-spread nostrils, with a tolerably-shaped mouth, thick lips, a fresh and even rosy skin, and a clear complexion. In shape he was short, thick, and even unwieldy, while his whole mien was that of one restless, uncertain, and weary; with an undercurrent of spirits and good humour which rarely abandoned him, and made him sometimes appear firm, when he was most undecided and timid.

This was King Louis XVI.

The woman was of tall, slim, and graceful carriage, with light-brown hair, lofty and prominent forehead, blue eyes, a nose which, for a woman, was much like that of the King; large mouth, full, projecting lips, a countenance beaming with all kinds of emotions, and giving a dreamy air of voluptuousness to her whole appearance, while now and then came the haughty, scornful smile of an Austrian Princess.

This was Marie Antoinette.

They were seated side by side, that King and that Queen, doomed already, and with but a slight span of life between them and eternity.

King Louis XVI., a good-natured man, who wanted to be popular, but who had not the firmness to be honest and consistent with the nation, paid for his own folly and treachery and the crimes of his ancestors.

Marie Antoinette—despotism incarnate in her ideas—perished from not understanding that the day of divine right was over, and that if the people wanted a despot, it must be one of their own choosing. But nothing but the terrible intoxication of the time is any excuse—nothing is a palliative for the execution of this woman, who was only dangerous in Paris as a flag of conspiracy; who, sent back to her own country, would have been powerless, and utterly without influence in the affairs of France. I consider the man who sent Marie Antoinette to the scaffold, on the same level with Charlotte Corday, who assassinated in his bath a man who had never injured her, and who, whatever his crimes and errors, was still a man.

But history glorifies Charlotte Corday, and treats the

President of the Revolutionary Tribunal as a monster.  He killed a Queen, and Charlotte Corday murdered a Republican.

But I have left Gracchus Antiboul and Charles Clement in presence of the King and Queen.

The apartment into which the young Republicans had been shown was small, and elegantly furnished, while the obscurity of the night was only dissipated by a dull lamp.

"Advance, gentlemen, and be seated," said Louis XVI., pointing to the chairs placed close to himself and the Queen.

They bowed, placed their hats on a chair, and advanced to the seats offered them; while Marie Antoinette fixed her eyes somewhat kindly on them, especially on Charles. Deeply impressionable herself, and full of the rich affection of a woman, she understood the feelings of the young man. Perhaps, as a woman, none more loveable was ever known than Marie Antoinette.  Her whole soul was love, romance, passion.  But Louis XVI. understood nothing of such sentiments; and his wife had to seek in friendship—her enemies say in other love—the outpourings of her heart.

"Gentlemen," said the King, with some slight hesitation, "I am fully aware that I do not count you among my friends; but, at all events, you are loyal enemies.  I have heard high praise and warm praise of you both.  I have been told that you have ideal theories of government; but that you are of those who, if the Constitution were successful, would not touch the Monarchy.  Am I right?"

"Your Majesty, apart from the partial opinion of friends, has been rightly informed," said Charles Clement respectfully.

"Well then, you are the persons to give me the information I seek.  Rumours reach me of coming insurrection, of an attempt to overthrow the Monarchy.  Personally, I freely offer up my crown; but I have my children to look to—I cannot part with their heritage.  But, Monsieur," continued Louis, "what I ask is this—What do the people want?"

"Your Majesty," replied Charles Clement, "must, if you would satisfy the just demands of the people, take back Roloust, Claviere, and Servan, or any such other ministers who meet with the approval of the majority of the National Assembly."

Marie Antoinette made an impatient motion, but the King staid her.

"I am then a mere tool of the Assembly!" said Louis XVI. reproachfully.

"Your Majesty forgets that the Assembly is the nation. It would be idle to discuss with your Majesty the abstract question of the relative rights of kings and people. The knot is cut. The nation has resolved to govern itself; but as it requires a chief magistrate to execute the laws, and as, guided by a representative assembly, a king is quite compatible with liberty, the nation delegates to your Majesty the execution of the laws."

"Better die than be king at that price," said Marie Antoinette passionately.

"I know not," said Louis XVI., who loved ease and tranquillity above everything; "to be king thus were, perhaps, better than to have the cares and responsibilities of reigning really. But, tell me, young man, are there not those who seek my life?"—and Louis XVI. looked at him with a scrutinizing air.

"There are, but very few; and those will never have power to carry out their will, if your Majesty and the National Assembly go on in harmony together."

"But then the National Assembly will be the real masters of France."

"Sire, they are France; while, excuse me, you are but the representative of a thing gone by—the irresponsible and forcible rule of one over many."

"But," cried the Queen, impetuously, "are not the factious, the agitators, afraid that we may succeed in restoring the royal authority, as it came down to my royal husband, when the fever of rebellion is gone?"

"No, Madam," replied Charles Clement, mildly, "because they know the time is past for that. No reign of the *bon plaisir* can again last in France. The day the Etats Genereux met the Monarchy, it was ended. That which is dead can never be brought to life."

"But why do the populace hate me?—why sing they

atrocious songs under my very windows?" added Marie Antoinette, with tears of grief and rage.

"Because your Majesty is accused of being against the nation, of wishing to restore the *régime* of Louis XIV., even by means of foreign armies; because your Majesty is accused of giving absolute and hasty councils; because the people, who feel rather than reason, accuse you of carrying on secret correspondence with our enemies."

Louis XVI. listened almost wildly; while the Queen buried her face in her hands.

"They want my life," she cried; "let them take it."

"No, Madam," replied Charles Clement, "they wish your Majesty to be the mother of her people, to join with the father of his people, as your royal husband has been often called, in procuring them happiness, tranquillity, good government, and peace; they ask no more."

"Young man," said the King, solemnly, "and I ask honest and good advisers; can I take the Petions, Rolands, Clavieres—who betray me to the mob—and trust them?"

"There are patriots in the National Assembly," answered Clement.

"There are," said the King, mournfully; "but, with few exceptions, they have resolved to have done with royalty. Can I take to my councils those who would make of me another Charles I. ?"

Charles Clement paused, as if seeking a reply.

"I love France, I love my people," continued the King, energetically; "and if I knew the way to make them happy, I would. I cannot undo the faults of my ancestors."

"I know it," said Charles in a low tone; "your Majesty's position is a difficult one. The Revolution is unchained, and to stop is impossible. All we who lead it can do is to direct it to as calm a port as possible."

"Do your duty," answered the King, sadly, "do your duty, gentlemen; and I will seek to do mine. God has given me a terrible task, and, be it what it may, I will not shrink from it."

"And your Majesty will triumph," said the Queen, with that buoyant confidence which so often misled her.

"We shall see, for time alone can say," replied Louis XVI.; "and now, Monsieur Clement, if you will pass through yon door, you will find friends. They are fortunate to have you as such, for you at least are honest and sincere; you do not work against me, and profess to be ready to do anything in my service. Go; and if we never meet again, remember that Louis XVI. bears you no ill-will because you conceive France could be happier without him."

The King turned to his wife; and the two young men, much moved, bowed respectfully, and advanced towards the door indicated to them.

----

# CHAPTER XXXI.

### THE INSURRECTION.

It was four o'clock in the morning, and the insurrection of the day was already making its preparations. Danton, a map of Paris before him, sat in the small room of an obscure cabaret, near where once stood the Bastille, surrounded by his lieutenants. The room was small, and it was therefore as full as it could hold. A solitary lamp, placed so as to illumine the map, alone lighted this cave, whence was to issue sedition and terror.

There were present Santerre, the popular brewer of the Faubourg St. Antoine; Legendre, the semi-butcher, semi-sailor; Panis and Sarjent, two members of the Municipality, who brought the assent of Petion to the deeds of the day; Huguenin, Alexandre, Marat, Dubois, Crancé, Brune, Mormoro, Dubuisson, Fabre d'Eglantine, Chabot, the ex-monk; Laregnie; Gonchon and Duquesnois, who represented Robespierre; and Carra, Rolondo, Henriot, Sillery Louvet, Laclos, and Barbaroux, who represented Roland and Brissot —who, like Robespierre, never compromised their persons in the details of such affairs.

An almost perfect silence prevailed. Danton had been recognized chief, and he issued his orders. Panis and Sarjent were sent to rouse the Faubourg St. Marceau and the neighbourhood of the Jardin des Plantes; Laregnie was detached to the Faubourg St. Jacques, aided by Malard, Isambert, and Gibon, who had been at work all night; while the rest rapidly dispersed to their respective neighbourhoods to awaken the masses, to give them a direction and a password.

Soon Danton remained alone in the little room, looking out upon the place covered with the ruins of the Bastille, upon which the dawn was slowly breaking. And Danton began to think. That wondrous man who, with honesty and principle, might have mastered the Revolution, wanted the austerity and contempt for money which characterized Robespierre. He was purely ambitious. Ambitious of power, fond of pleasure, good living, women, wine, and, above all, of the intense excitement, of the mortal wear and tear of revolutionary times, which is manna to a man of a certain order of genius. Danton scrupled not at means. He worked for the people, whom he despised, because he thought them the best ladder for himself. Robespierre loved the people, was a fanatic, a Luther in his belief in the truth of his principles, and sanctioned crimes from the rigid logic of his mind, which placed before it an end to be reached, no matter how. Danton scorned blood; Robespierre bathed in it. Danton cared not who perished, so he rose triumphant.

Danton had, therefore, now but one thought — deep anxiety for the success of his conspiracy. Neither he nor the Girondins, under whose impulse he acted in a great measure, had any very clear or defined notion of what the day was to lead to. Most of them simply desired to humiliate the King, and force him to abandon all connection with the accursed coalition, at the head of which his brothers were striving to lead foreign armies to the conquest of France. The King had for some time been playing with the Assembly, delaying, gaining time, evidently deluded by the Queen into the belief that an Austrian army would be in a month in the capital.

The Court and the National Assembly were two moral forces in presence. The Court relied on foreign bayonets; the Assembly on the army of the people, and they were invoking the people to show their force. Who, under the circumstances, can blame them?

But on Danton's shoulders rested the responsibility if the insurrection failed: and multitudinous thoughts came to his mind as he stood, gloomy enough some of them, when he was suddenly interrupted.

"Good morrow, Danton!" said a sweet voice behind him.

The Tribune of the people turned. The society of a woman was the very thing to make him forget the thoughts which burned within.

It was Theroigne, or Lambertine de Méricourt. This beautiful young woman wore a riding-habit of the colour of blood, a plumed hat heavy with feathers, a belt with pistols, and a sword.

"It goes bravely," said she, fiercely; "and to-day we will laugh at the Austrian."

"It marches," replied Danton, kissing the lovely but frail and terrible creature; "but until the hour comes for business, let us not talk of it. *Sacre bleu!* I have talked all night. Wine there, of the best; Theroigne, breakfast with me."

And the terrible Tribune, who was waiting there to set his seal on the death-warrant of the Monarchy, at once seated himself with the Aspasia of the Faubourg St. Antoine; had up such refreshments as the house could afford—which, in consideration of the patronage of the rich demagogues, was of the very best character—and forgot for half-an-hour, in the pleasures of the table, and the society of a pretty woman, the whole business in hand.

At the end of about three-quarters of an hour, a knock at the door roused them to remembrance of what was dawning.

"Enter," said Danton, filling his glass.

A tall man, of commanding aspect, with an air of reckless dissipation, entered.

It was the Marquis de St. Huruge.

"Welcome," cried Danton to the agitator of the Palais Royal, scarcely less influential with the masses than himself.

"Welcome, citizen *sans-culottes*," replied the Marquis; "and doubly welcome to thee, my bonny Theroigne. This is a great day—a splendid day. The King will learn what it is to tamper with his people."

"But," cried Danton, a little excited by his libations,

"but will the Assembly know how to act when thus backed by the people?   They are talkers, not actors."

"Don't fear, my friend," said Huruge, with a sinister smile; "they must act.   The whole royal *journée* dispatched, they must do something."

"You don't mean to touch the King?" asked Danton, fiercely.

"What are we rising for but to have an end of the *chateau*," observed the Marquis, sullenly.

"Bah!" said Danton, "you must have a puppet.   As well Louis XVI. as Louis XVII.   All we want to let him see is, that if he has the name of master, we have the reality. He will learn that to-day."

"You may keep *Veto* if you like," cried Theroigne; "but I demand the Austrian."

"What for?" asked Danton, fiercely.

"To march through all Paris, and show her what hovels poor mothers live in, while she conspires against them in her palace."

"But why this hate?"

"Is she not one of us?" said Theroigne, repeating the popular opinion about Marie Antoinette; "and how dares she live, respected and surrounded with luxury, in a palace, while we are pointed at as lost and worthless creatures?"

Thus spake the outcast from among women, a class who have no pity, no mercy for those of their own sex who sin, and yet are not touched with the brand of shame; who are frail with impunity, and who receive all honour and love. The popular opinion is, that such was Marie Antoinette; but with that we have nothing to do; whatever her faults as a woman, as a wife, as a queen, she expiated them.

"Theroigne," replied Danton, "you are a fool.   If one finger be laid upon the person of King, or Queen, or Princess, our plot is ruined."

"If they outlive the day," replied St. Huruge, "our plans are abortive."

"Do as you will," said Danton; "I wash my hands of all connivance in anything like assassination."

"We shall see," was the answer of St. Huruge, who looked expressively at Theroigne; but Theroigne was for

the moment the " friend " of Danton, and she appeared influenced by his words.

A dull murmur on the Place de la Revolution now gave
token that the army of the insurrection was collecting. St.
Huruge and Theroigne went out to reconnoitre, and Danton
once more remained alone.

It was dawn, and several battalions of the National Guard
had taken up positions on the outskirts of the Place de la
Bastille, their arms piled, not to resist the assembling of the
people, but purposely sent by Petion to fraternize with the
masses, and swell the vast mob who were about to fill
Paris with insurrection. They were picked battalions, selected by the Girondin *Maire*, who played a part which,
beside that of Danton and his friends, was infinitely disgraceful. They were free men, free to act as they thought
fit; while he was a magistrate, whose first duty was to
preserve order. Great talkers about peace, law, and order,
the Girondins only disliked turbulence when it served the
purpose of their rivals, the Jacobins. This day they acted
together.

And now groups of workmen began to assemble. Out
they came from their dark and gloomy holes, where always
dwell the sons of poverty and labour—the hand which rears
up fortune for the favoured few; and who had seen the
misery, ignorance, and degradation of that terrible mob,
debased and trampled on by violence and power, had neither
wondered nor blamed their taking their hour of revenge.
They came from the Faubourgs St. Marceau, and the Quartier St. Jacques, from Popincourt, Quinzevingts, De la
Grêve, Port au Blé, the Marché St. Jean, and, most of all,
from the suburb of Antoine, so terribly famous in history.

Soon the crowd became terrific.

Rags and uniforms mixed freely together, and every
minute the crowd became denser. Fresh recruits came up
every instant, and the whole city seemed there ready to
march against the King they despised, and the Queen whom
they hated.

Suddenly Santerre, mounted on a huge horse, and in the
uniform of an officer of the National Guard, appeared on
the Place, and surrounded by a staff of men, the leaders of
the sedition. This revolutionary chief went round haranguing

the people, bidding them be calm and solemn, to march in regular columns, and, above all, to be silent. Then his staff hurried about, forming the columns as well as possible, with an ease which belongs alone to the Parisian mob. Flags were placed at the head of every different body, which, once organized, took its station wherever sent, and waited for the orders.

A terrible sight was this. The marshalling and en-regimenting of the army of sedition proceeded as regularly as would the laying-out on a field of battle of an army of regular troops.

Time passed rapidly, and the numbers swelled prodigiously. Danton came out, and examined the aspect of the scene. A roar of applause greeted him.

It was eleven o'clock.

More than twenty-five thousand were assembled; and Danton signified, by a sign of the head, to Santerre, that it would do, and then hurried away to prepare the fashionable quarters of the town for what was coming.

And now began the march of this wild and hideous army, whose weapons were as diversified as their costume.

First marched the Faubourgs, some in uniforms, with guns, pistols, and bayonets. These were commanded by Santerre. Then came the mixed rabble, of all kinds and shapes, and the head of these was the Marquis de St. Huruge. The rear was brought up by the very refuse of the mob—thin old men, women, children, the pariahs and outcasts of society—armed against it, because it knew them not. Theroigne de Méricourt, a sword in hand, a musket on her shoulder, and seated on a cannon drawn by a number of men, led this forlorn hope of the day.

Some went by the boulevards, some by the quays and the Pont-Neuf, but all tended to one point.

The Tuileries was the castle they were about to storm.

Nothing was wanting to excite the masses. Inferior demagogues, Rossignol, Brierre, Gonar, Jourdan *Coupe-Tete*, Lazouski, flew from rank to rank, inflaming their ardour; while at every step the arrival of reinforcements added to their confidence.

But the flags, most of all, showed the character of the sedition. They were terrible. Some just, some foul.

"Sanction or death," cried the mob, and a flag answered to their words.

"The recall of the patriot ministers" was written on another.

"Tremble, tyrant; thy hour is come," was one of the first hints that the death of the Mona hy was the real object of the movement.

Marie Antoinette was the intense antipathy of the masses; and a man bore her effigy, depending from a gibbet—awful prophecy!

"Beware the lanterne," was written on it.

A band of ferocious women, lost to all sense of shame, human ghouls, bore on high a *guillotine*, on which was written "National Justice on Tyrants—Death to Veto and his wife."

Dire were the crimes and the wickedness, terrible the responsibilities of the Monarchy, which had bred all this; for no just man can find a word of excuse. The errors and vices of royalty and aristocracy made this population. It was but meet it should reap what it sowed. I pity the high who perished. I pity more the people who could be what the Paris people were in 1792 and 1793. It was not their fault.

It was now nearly mid-day, and the insurrection had reached the neighbourhood of the Palace of the Tuileries.

---

## CHAPTER XXXII.

### ADELA AND MIRANDA.

WHILE these terrible events are preparing one of the scenes in which our hero was destined to play a conspicuous part, Charles Clement and Gracchus Antiboul were actors in a different drama.

When the door closed upon the King and Queen, and the two young men turned round, they could scarcely speak from the emotions which filled their bosoms.

On a canopy sofa, in a large and splendidly-furnished apartment of the palace, reclined Adela des Ravilliere, her hands pressed upon her beating heart. Beside her sat the

Countess Miranda. Miranda was thinner and paler than she was used to be; but still the beautiful, magnificent being she had always been. Adela, more womanly than in times gone by, had gained in loveliness.

"Charles," half shrieked Adela, leaping from her seat, and darting towards him.

"My own, my long-lost Adela!" said the young man.

The lovers were clasped in one another's arms in silent rapture; while Miranda and Gracchus Antiboul embraced cordially. Miranda looked on them as if in triumph.

"There she is!" she exclaimed, as Charles Clement, his eyes beaming with rapture and delight, seated himself beside Adela on the sofa, "the same frank, pure heart you knew her."

"How can I show my thanks," said the young man, taking the Countess's hand, "to you, to whom I owe so much?"

"By making the best of husbands to dear Adela," replied the Countess, in her soft rich tone, tinged, despite herself, with a shade of melancholy regret.

"Can I still hope for that happiness?" said Charles.

"I am your wife already," answered Adela, tenderly; and laying her hands in his, "whenever you like, I am ready to go through the ceremony."

"Then, be my own beloved—and my Lord Duke?—"

"The Duke," said Miranda, while Adela became saddened with the word, "has never recovered, until within a few days, the shock of the taking of the Bastille. Since he has been here, however, he has been gradually recovering. He sleeps above in the very roof of the palace, and as we heard there might be disturbances, we wish to keep him there. To-morrow you shall see him."

"You must leave the palace," replied Charles, solemnly.

"Why?"

"All in it are doomed," answered the young man; "to-day—to-morrow, they may escape, but they will not long. To-morrow, the Duke and you should return to the Rue Dominique. You shall not be included in the common ruin of the Monarchy."

"But the Duke will never desert the King," said Miranda.

"He will leave this," replied Charles, "if I have a voice to be heard. Desert the King!—the King has no need of any guards but his people, if he be true. If false, a feeble old man and two innocent women can avail him nothing."

"We came here against our wishes," said Adela, and would most gladly leave."

"We are wholly at your orders, Charles," said Miranda, with a smile.

"Both?" asked Charles, with a laugh.

"Both!" cried Miranda, not without colouring violently.

"I shall be jealous!" said Adela, with a pout.

"Of me?" said Miranda, shaking her head.

"Of you," answered Adela, with mock solemnity.

"But come," cried Miranda, rising, as if a sudden remembrance struck her, but in reality to change the conversation; "let us to our own apartments, where breakfast awaits you. Over this we can talk; and all of you have much, I doubt not, to say."

With these words she moved towards a small side door, opening on a staircase leading to the vast number of apartments which existed in this immense palace, and one of which the Duke and the two ladies occupied.

Clement took the Arm of Adela, Gracchus that of Miranda, and they moved upward.

The stairs were narrow and lofty, for the palace was so crammed that they, late comers, had been ill-provided. They lived in the garrets of the Tuileries.

At length the chamber of the ladies was reached, and a waiting-maid opened the door. It was Rose, the faithful attendant on the Countess Miranda.

"Welcome, Messieurs," said the girl, heartily.

Clement and Gracchus thanked her warmly. They were happy.

"Does your master still sleep?" asked Miranda, who had placed the girl at the service of all.

"He sleeps soundly; he has never moved," replied Rose.

"Close the door between us and him," continued Miranda, "and then we will breakfast."

The apartment was small and plainly furnished, but it

was extremely comfortable; and the whole party drew round the table with feelings which none of them had known for two long years.

Happiness is charming to look at; but to the human beings who follow the fortunes of their fellow-creatures for amusement, a picture of poor, unadulterated felicity soon palls. The four friends now presented this picture. They had much to tell, and much to hear; and when, as the clock marked eleven, Rose announced the waking of the old Duke, they all started in astonishment.

Charles Clement and Gracchus Antiboul looked at one another. They were thinking of the great insurrection of the day.

"Adela," said a voice from the inner room. "Adela, love, I feel better this morning. I shall get up."

It was the Duke.

"Who was that talking?" asked the Duke.

"You shall see directly," cried Adela, rushing in to aid her aged parent to dress.

"He speaks more naturally than ever," whispered Miranda.

"I long to embrace him," replied Charles.

Meanwhile Gracchus Antiboul drew Rose on one side, and, giving her a few directions, sent her down to glean some news of what was going on in Paris.

In a few minutes the Duke appeared, leaning on the arm of his child. He was much changed. Age had weighed heavily on him. He was a feeble, bowed, old man.

"My son!" he cried, prepared somewhat by a hint of Adela.

"My father!" replied Charles Clement, rushing to his side.

"Welcome, boy, welcome!" said the old Duke, sitting down beside him.

The whole party drew at once around them; and it was deeply affecting to see the long greeting of that young and that old man.

They spoke long and warmly. Charles had to narrate rapidly all his adventures, which the Duke listened to with almost childish curiosity; while Adela and Miranda hung on the young man's words with an intense interest, which would have furnished an admirable subject for a picture.

Suddenly, in the very midst of his narration, a loud knocking was heard at the door, Gracchus ran to open it, and Rose rushed in.

Miranda had risen and faced her with an air of menace which made Charles Clement stand transfixed with surprise; but, as he noticed an almost imperceptible sign towards the Duke, he understood the meaning of her act.

"Speak, girl. Some bad news?" said Miranda; and she added, in a low tone, "be cautious."

The girl, who was more excited than frightened, remembered her instructions never to relate any alarming news before the Duke.

"There is a great crowd of people round the National Assembly, and they talk of coming under the window of the palace."

"We will go see what it is," said Charles Clement, rising with Gracchus Antiboul; "remain ye all here until we return."

They then promised to return rapidly, and moved to the door.

Miranda followed them.

"What is it?" she whispered.

"Perhaps the death of the Monarchy," replied Charles Clement in a low tone; "but, happen what may, you must not stir out."

"I will not."

"Are you afraid to remain locked in?" asked Charles.

"Afraid of nothing you propose," replied Miranda, with unusual fire.

"Then, God bless you, and watch over them. I shall lock you in, and take the key. Remain still, and fear nothing."

The two young men hurried out, locked the door behind them, noticed that it was thick and heavy, and rushed down stairs.

It was a quarter past twelve o'clock.

# CHAPTER XXXIII.

### THE INVASION OF THE PALACE.

CHARLES CLEMENT and Gracchus Antiboul soon reached the bottom of the stairs, and from the passage, on which they paused an instant, looked out upon the Tuileries garden. It was filling with a portion of the vast column which had defiled before the National Assembly, after presenting the petition which had been the excuse for the congregation of the masses.

" The day has begun," said Charles Clement.

" And what part do you mean to take ? " asked Antiboul.

" A passive one. I shall look on. If necessary, I will protect the persons of Louis and Marie Antoinette," replied the other.

A valet stood at the entrance of the chamber where the young men had that morning met their friends.

" Where is the King ? " asked Charles.

" In here, Monsieur," replied the domestic, who looked fearfully alarmed.

" Admit us," said Antiboul.

The valet opened the door, and they entered.

The King, the Queen, Madame Elizabeth, and the royal children, were congregated in the apartment. The whole party assembled round a small table. The King was pale ; so was the Queen.

" Welcome, gentlemen," said the Monarch. " I may, perhaps, learn from you the meaning of this."

" It means, your Majesty, that fifty thousand armed men have surrounded your palace ; and that if any resistance be made, the consequences may be fearful."

" And if not ? "

" The tumult will end in words. The leaders will present their address to your Majesty ; and if their wishes be in future complied with, they will be satisfied."

" But my wife—my children ? "

" Should the palace be invaded, and the populace enter, I have but one advice to give to your Majesty : Go forth to meet them alone, and leave the rest of your family here."

" But they will be abandoned," answered the King.

" My friend will remain with them ; I will accompany your Majesty."

" I accept," said the King : " and now go you forth, and examine what is taking place."

" But I have no free pass," replied Charles Clement.

The King took pen, ink, and paper.

" Let pass the bearer, Charles Clement ; and obey his orders in all things."

Charles Clement coloured violently as Louis read the paper. The Republiean, despite his knowledge of how just were the complaints of his party against the Monarch, felt a momentary pang at being the enemy of one who showed in him, in a moment of danger, so much confidence.

He went out ; and his pass giving him unlimited obedienee and information, he soon found what was the actual state of affairs.

A force, perfectly sufficient to have defended the palace, was drawn up in the great court of the Tuileries, and in the garden. Three regiments of regular troops, two squadrons of gendarmes, and several battalions of the National Guard, with very many cannon, could have held the palace with ease, unless the sedition had turned into an insurrection prepared for a siege. But Clement at once saw that no defence was intended. The people, the women, the children, called loudly to the soldiers, who promised not to fire ; while the officers of the Commune, creatures of Petion, displayed the utmost sympathy with the movement. Three persons only tried to influence the troops to energetic action. These were Rœderer, Aclocque, and De Romainvilliers. Charles Clement sided with no party. With sympathies in both camps, his province was strict neutrality. His mission was only to try and save the lives of the Royal Family. To him they were but men and women, and the violation of their dwelling but the right of other men and women whom, in his opinion, they had injured, betrayed, and outraged.

The garden of the Tuileries and the Place de Carrousel were both in possession of the insurgents.

Charles Clement was standing in conversation with the

commander of the artillery, St. Prix, when the gates of the court were forced, and in came the mob rushing furiously on the palace of the King they hated.

"Draw back the cannon to the door," shouted St. Prix.

The artillerymen replied by turning the cannon on the windows of the palace.

"The chateau is taken," cried Charles Clement; and he rushed in to inform the King.

"What is the matter, Monsieur?" asked the King.

"The chateau is in the hands of the populace; the troops have unloaded their arms, and nothing can save your Majesty but facing the mob, and thus disappointing the obscure agitators, who hope to find you hiding, and who would murder you in a corner."

"You cannot—must not go," cried Madame Elizabeth, passionately.

"There are two parties in this insurrection," said Charles Clement, firmly; "the heads of one party want only to let your Majesty see that the people are ine arnest; and that, if deceived and disappointed, they can be terrible. Of these are myself and my friend. Another party wants your head."

The King rose firmly.

"I confide in you!" he exclaimed; "you are a candid and loyal enemy. I trust my children, and my wife, and sister to you."

This was addressed to Charles Clement.

"They are women and children," replied the young Republican; "not a finger shall be laid on them."

"You will be murdered," said Marie Antoinette; "at least, let us go with you."

"Your presence would do the King more harm than good," observed Charles, gently.

Louis XVI. walked firmly towards the door. Charles moved beside him.

In a few minutes they reached the *Salle du Conseil*.

It contained six men.

These were Marshal de Monchy, M. D'Hervilly, Aclocque, and three grenadiers, Lacrosnier, Bridau, and Gosse.

It was all that remained faithful at that moment to the Monarchy, which paid the penalty now of its crimes.

"Gentlemen," said the King, "I come to meet the people."

"And we are here to defend you with our bodies," replied the Marshal de Monchy.

"I shall want no defence, I hope," answered the King, gently.

Two *valets de chambre* here took their station, one on each side of the closed door by which the insurgents were coming. They were named Hue and De Marchais.

The next apartment was called the *Salle des Nobles*, and a terrific clamour was now heard within it. Hundreds of men were rushing into it with shouts.

Next minute a terrific blow was struck against one of the panels, and it fell at the King's feet; while through the opening were thrust sticks, pikes, guns, and swords, while all the abuse which hate and suffering could imagine were showered on the head of Louis XVI.

"Open the door," said the King, calmly; for in all cases of danger his character seemed to rise far above its ordinary level; so much so, that had he been left to himself, with popular Ministers, he might have saved the Monarchy.

The door opened, and the ringleaders of the column burst headlong in. The insurrection stood face to face with the King.

Louis XVI. stood in the act, as it were, of advancing, his visage calm and serene; and the populace hesitated. The long ages of Monarchy under which the people had lived had made them look hitherto on the person of the Monarch as something sacred, and a few years of revolution could not at once wipe out this feeling which had been the origin and cause of so much misery and crime; for between proper respect for a chief magistrate and their feelings, there is the difference of slavish submission and manly obedience.

The small party who occupied the chamber took advantage of this moment of suspense to place themselves between the King and the crowd; and then, at the suggestion of Charles Clement, Louis XVI. moved, surrounded by his body-guard, to the Salon of the *Œil de Bœuf*, which, being large, admitted of more persons seeing and speaking with the King.

The terrible crowd followed, and, just as they gained the apartment, a young and beautiful woman rushed, with dishevelled hair and tearful eyes, to place herself near the King.

"The Queen! the Queen!" cried some of the women of the Faubourgs.

"Madame Veto!" said another.

"Death to the Austrian!" shrieked a third.

It was an awful moment. Two or three of the mob, infuriated at the name of the woman they so much hated, raised their arms, and rushed forward to strike. The King drew her towards him. Both were in peril of their lives.

"It is Madame Elizabeth!" thundered Charles Clement, striking the axe of a *faubourien* with his sword.

The arms fell down, and the crowd retreated respectfully. The King's sister was as much respected and loved as the Queen was hated.

Charles took advantage of this movement to remove the Princess to an embrasure of a window in a corner.

The King stood in the centre recess of the salon on a bench, the grenadiers at his feet warding off the pikes, scythes and sticks which were waved about by the crowd.

"Down with the Veto!" cried one.

"The camp of Paris!" repeated others.

"The Patriot Ministers!" cried others.

"Where is the Austrian woman?" yelled some women of the Faubourgs.

Several individual attempts were made to reach the King, and to kill him; but these were repelled with ease by the King's Guard, augmented now by several National Guard, the more readily that the mass had no other object than to show their force, and strike the enemies of the nation with terror and alarm.

And now new crowds poured in. From doors and windows, in they rushed, while others ran round the palace, viewing its secrets, and still hunting for the Queen, who was, however, even under more perilous circumstances, enduring precisely the same as the King. A crowd had found her out.

"The King's head!" cried people from below.

"Pitch him out to us!" repeated the ringleaders from

without, too cowardly to come in and kill the King, but striving to incite the mob to assassination. But the people, as usual, were infinitely more moderate than their leaders.

Suddenly it was said that the King was dead; and Charles Clement, hearing a great shouting, looked out from the window. Marat, Gorras, Garat, and others, even members of the National Assembly, were applauding and making jokes upon the supposed end of the Monarch.

The young Republican turned away in disgust at these men, who made assassination a part of their principles.

But not one of the mob seemed inclined to obey the hints which were profusely given them, and a murmur of disappointment spread among the chiefs.

"Kill him," whispered a man in the ear of a huge *faubourien*, who bore the *bonnet rouge* of the ultra-democratic party.

"Bast!" replied the man, "not I. But I will offer him my cap," and whisking off his *bonnet rouge*, he handed it, on the end of his pike, to the King.

"There, Monsieur," said he, "put on that. 'Tis more honourable than your crown."

Louis XVI. looked puzzled more at the word *Monsieur* than anything else; but, recovering himself on the instant, took the cap with a smile, and placed it on his head.

"*Vive le Roi!*" thundered the crowd, laughing and clapping their hands.

A dead silence, and a look of consternation, pervaded the group of ringleaders below.

"What say they?" shrieked Marat, addressing our hero.

"They say, 'Long live the King,'" answered Charles Clement gravely.

"They'll turn on us in five minutes!" roared Marat.

"What is that?" asked Garat, as another cry arose.

"This time," said Clement, "it is *Vive le Roi sans-culotte*."

A grim smile went round the Girondins below, who chiefly desired the humiliation of the King, for expelling them from office, and who were the most rank in exciting to his murder. At this moment a beggar stood forward with a bottle in his hand, and held it up.

"If you love the people, Monsieur the King, drink their health," said he.

The guard pushed the man back.

"Give me the bottle," said the King.

"But, Sire, it may be poisoned," cried D'Herville.

"Give it me," replied the King, mildly.

"Let Monsieur drink without fear," said the beggar, with considerable indignation; "it's not so good as he's used to, but it's what his people drink."

The King raised the bottle to his lips.

"To the nation," said he.

Rapturous applause followed.

"*Vive le Roi!*" repeated those in the next room, and at the same moment Clement saw Marat dive through the crowd, and make off.

The day was a failure.

It was drawing towards evening; and as the whole affair was lost, as far as the wishes of the Girondins were concerned, they grew alarmed lest the devil they had raised might be turned against themselves, and resolved to stop the scene. They had no inclination to see the insurrection made use of by anybody but their own party.

A loud cry in the court-yard soon showed that they thought events had gone far enough.

"*Vive Petion!*" cried the mob.

The King frowned; and Charles Clement saw at once that he saw through the prolonged absence of the *Maire* of Paris. Petion soon appeared, borne on the shoulders of the populace, who set him down near the King.

"I have only just learned the situation of your Majesty," said the *Maire*, in a tone of haughty respect.

"That is very astonishing," replied Louis XVI., very sad and very indignant, "for I have been here long enough."

Petion made no reply, but, addressing the crowd, told them that their right of petition both to the King and the Assembly had been amply exercised, and begged them to retire. He then moved about, and soon succeeded in his object. In a few moments the King was alone with his friends; and taking Charles Clement, Aclocque, De Monchy, and D'Aubier with him, hurried at once with Madame Elizabeth to join his wife and children.

They were safe in the chamber in which he had left them, but which during five hours had been invaded even more violently than that of the King.

Louis XVI. found Marie Antoinette weeping. On seeing him, she threw herself into his arms.

"Leave us, gentlemen!" said the King, dashing the red cap at his feet.

The whole crowd hurried to obey, and the Royal Family were left alone, the servants rushing to light their fires, and prepare dinner.

Charles Clement and Gracchus Antiboul at once availed themselves of the permission, and hastened up-stairs to relieve the anxiety of Adela and Miranda.

---

## CHAPTER XXXIV

The twentieth of June was but the prelude of the tenth of August. The party of the Revolution now knew well that they had no choice between a Republic and between despotism. The struggle had assumed a character which made a conference impossible. Lafayette, weak and fickle, alarmed at the movement he had himself aided in impelling forward, had joined the party of the Court. Without energy or decision, his aid was rather injurious than beneficial. He lost himself, and did the King not one atom of good.

The persons of this narrative were variously affected by the events which rapidly occurred. From the twentieth of June to the tenth of August, various efforts were made to remove the Duke, Miranda, and Adela from the Tuileries. It was in vain, however. So many more-important affairs occupied both the Commune and the authorities of the palace, that neither Charles Clement on the one side, nor Miranda on the other, could in any way effect the object they had in view. Few interviews could be had, and the lovers were almost as much parted as they had been before.

But the tenth day of August came, and the movement of the twentieth June was renewed. This time the leaders of the insurrection were determined not to be baulked in their intentions.

At ten o'clock at night, on the ninth, the sections were insurrectionally convoked.

At twelve, the tocsin sounded.

An insurrectionary municipality sat at the Hotel de Ville. It called the Commander of the Tuileries before it. He was assassinated as he left.

At three in the morning, a hundred thousand men were around the Tuileries.

At four, the Council sat with the King.

At five, the Royal Family were all up and dressed.

At six, the National Guard showed signs of wavering. Some battalions were removed from the palace.

At seven, the tocsin was still sounding.

A short time after, the army of the people commenced its attack, and the Royal Family sought shelter in the National Assembly.

At ten o'clock the fight really commenced, and for hours continued in the most bloody manner.

In the evening, five thousand dead bodies lay in the palace and gardens of the Tuileries.

At midnight they were burnt; and their ashes were, in the morning, cast into the Seine.

The Monarchy had perished in oceans of blood. Louis XVI. had paid for the crimes of his ancestors, and for the folly of his Queen, and his own incapacity and want of good faith.

Bitter anguish at their hearts, but performing what to them was a stern and solemn duty, Charles Clement and Antiboul had fought in the front ranks of the people. They had sought, as much as possible, to restrain the terrible vengeance of the wretched masses of whom the great historian has said, "The men of Marseilles and Brest, the masses of the Faubourgs, fell back into their barracks. They had done their day's work, and paid, with upwards of three thousand six hundred dead bodies, their disinterested tribute to that Revolution whose fruit was only to be reaped by their children. These soldiers and this people had not struggled for power, still less for booty. They returned, with wearied arms, but empty hands, to their workshops. The *bourgeoise* fought for itself; the people for its ideas."

While yet the stairs were strewed with dead bodies,

while the furious and excited populace were everywhere seeking new victims, Charles Clement and Gracchus Antiboul, covered with blood and dust, wounded, and sick at heart, rushed along with the mob into the palace. Up stairs they went—pale, rigid, silent—death at their hearts; so many had perished. Cannon had been directed at every aperture, and stray balls might have reached those whom they loved.

The staircase was rapidly gained by which they had gone up on a memorable occasion. Not a soul was yet near it. They hastened onwards. In a few minutes, exhausted and out of breath, they stood at the door.

Gracchus knocked.

The door flew open, and the whole party appeared terror-stricken on the threshold.

"Take nothing, but come," cried Charles.

"Where?" said the Duke, vacantly.

"From this accursed dwelling-place," answered the young man.

Adela and Miranda gazed painfully at the bloodstained garb of the young Republican.

"You are hurt?" asked the young girl.

"A scratch," replied Charles, almost sternly. "Ten thousand dead bodies strew the court and rooms of this house of death. Those who are only wounded may well thank God."

"But come," cried Gracchus.

"Put on the coarsest cloaks you have," said Charles, "and no hats. Wear caps. To save you will be difficult. We may have to fight our way."

Charles, having hurried the necessary preparations, took the arm of Adela; Miranda and Gracchus assisted the Duke, while Rose came close behind them. They moved as rapidly as possible.

Shouts, screams, oaths, yells, the report of muskets in and around the palace, at once reached their ears, while dense volumes of smoke poured in through the broken windows from bonfires burning below—bonfires of furniture, pictures, books. It was the same scene, minus the deaths—though even then, many Municipal Guards were killed, like the Swiss formerly—which I witnessed on the 24th February, in all it details.

The bottom of the staircase, which brought them on a level with the exasperated populace, was soon gained. The noise was terrific. The whole party paused. A narrow passage runs along a portion of the Tuileries facing the garden. Charles Clement, guided by Miranda, followed this. In a few minutes they had reached a door.

"This is the Queen's bedroom," said Miranda, in a whisper.

"We must enter," said Charles, in a husky voice.

A body lay across the door.

Shrieks were heard from within. A door burst in, just as Clement opened the one at which he stood, after removing the body. He only opened it, however, an inch, and looked through. Miranda did so likewise.

The Princess de Tarente, the Ladies Laroche, Aymon de Ginestous, and the young and lovely Pauline de Tourzel, stood facing a door through which rushed a number of Marseillaise, headed by one who bore the *insignia* of a popular leader. The mob paused, gazing at the women.

"Monsieur," said the Princess de Tarente, taking by the hand the young Pauline de Tourzel, a trust from the young girl's mother, "strike me, but shield the honour and spare the life of this young creature. She is a sacred trust whom I have sworn to give back to her mother. Send her child to her, and take my life."

"Madam," replied the sanguine and excited southerner, "we war not against women. Trust in me all, and not a hair of your heads shall be touched."

"Dabessé," cried Charles, entering the room, followed by his friends, "confide them to me. Here are friends of ours. I will see them all safe together."

"Welcome, my gallant friend," answered the *fédéré* of La Drôme, "the nation owes you much to-day, for you have done your duty. Take a dozen of my men, put these women in a place of safety, and then return to your post."

"What news?" asked Gracchus.

"The King is dethroned!" cried the *fédéré*.

"Vive la Republic!" responded Antiboul.

" A National Assembly is convoked," continued Dabessé; " but of this at the club."

" *Salut!* " answered Charles, taking the command of his small party. "And now, my *braves*, let us save these helpless women, and then you can return to the defence of the nation."

The women crowded all together, with hope in their hearts. The looks of Clement inspired confidence. They were placed in a group, with six *fédérés* before and six behind, and led towards the small wicket opening on the Seine. On that side there had been no attack; and, after some delay, the party succeeded in issuing forth into the street. Charles Clement at once thanked and dismissed the Marseillaise, who rushed back to their work; and then, crossing the bridge, conducted the whole party in safety to the Rue Dominique.

The sensations of the Duke, Adela, and Miranda, on entering this once happy and cherished abode, were most varied and tumultous; they wept from intensity of emotion. The first burst of feeling, however, over, they hastened to perform the duties of hospitality to the fugitives, who, after taking rest and refreshment, departed, under cover of the night, to their respective homes.

The Duke, Clement, Adela, Miranda, Gracchus Antiboul, his wife, Paul Ledru, and his wife, now sat down together to speculate on what was to be done.

There was happiness and hope in this meeting. They were once more united, after many sad and terrible days; but under what circumstances?

The Monarchy was overthrown, Paris was a battle-field, and no man could say what would come on the morrow.

" Where will this end?" asked Adela, fearfully.

" In the happiness, renovation, and prosperity of the nation," replied Charles. "We feel the storm; our children will enjoy the harvest."

" But what plan can we adopt?" said the Duke, slowly rousing himself from the torpor into which the excitement of the day had thrown him.

" If we would avoid an atom of suspicion," replied Charles, addressing the old man, respectfully, " we would avoid the least relic of aristocracy. Paul Ledru and his wife have long taken a shop, which my affection for them has induced them only to occupy by deputy. They will gladly take possession at once. To this, it is my advice, you and Adela, Monsieur the Duke, should repair. Paul Ledru and his wife will be the masters of the house; you, Monsieur, will pass for the father, Adela for a younger sister."

" And you think this necessary?" said the Duke.

"Absolutely necessary for a time; for the attack on France, by foreign foes, and by the children of her own soil, in the name of renewed tyranny and despotism, will cause much misery. This selfish, wretched emigration, has ruined France, ruined the Revolution."

" Your wishes, Charles, my dear boy," said the Duke, speaking as of old, " are orders, are commands. We owe you all. Dispose of us as you will."

This, then, being settled, the whole party again entered upon a consideration of their position, and it was arranged that Charles Clement and Gracchus Antiboul and his wife should remain in the house of the Rue Dominique, their civism being undoubted: that Miranda, protected by her character as an Italian, should reside in her usual home; that the Duke, now *citoyen* Dubois, should, with his daughter, join the Ledrus, as agreed on; that Charles should there pay his court to the *citoyenne* Dubois, and be married without exciting attention, in an humble, quiet way. Paul Ledru and his wife, joyously agreeing to anything which would serve his old master, retired into a corner alone.

" Have you seen anything of M. Brown and the Count Leopold since we caught them at Charenton?" said Charles.

" No; they had a dose that day,—and the three days they spent in the *cave* did not give them any wish to make further acquaintance with us."

" But beware of them. Revenge will make them bold. Watch, Paul, over this precious deposit as you would over the wife of your bosom. Never forget you are my friend."

The crick-neck was moved almost to tears, but he made a solemn promise; and, the conversation becoming general, further details were entered into.

The Duke retired at midnight; but the broad day streamed in before Charles, Gracchus and the two ladies parted.

# CHAPTER XXXV

### PAUL AND DUCHESNE.

A LITTLE after six in the morning, Paul Ledru sallied forth on his journey towards the Rue Grenelle St. Honore, there to prepare his new residence for the arrival of the ex-Duke and his lovely daughter. The hour was far too early for the object; but Paul could not rest. He had already gone out at midnight into the street. He had found the night calm and lovely. At that hour he had seen the gardens of the Tuileries full of promenaders, the National Assembly surrounded by armed hordes, and all Paris alive and excited with the tremendous events of a day which had cost the lives of five thousand of her citizens, who had fallen fighting one against another—one party for the future and for liberty—the other, chiefly, however, Swiss, for despotism.

The streets were still busy and excited. The uniform of the National Guard had almost disappeared. Pikes and ragged clothes had replaced them.

The day before, Marat, on the strength of his raggedness, his dirt, and his sufferings, had been made commander of a battalion. This respect for the signs of beggary was natural. It was the well-dressed who had been hitherto the people's oppressors; the people now, in the first burst of their rage and their hate, looked with hope to those who least resembled the " aristocrats," as they now denominated all the rich.

Paul Ledru had, in his rambles, reached the prison of the Abbaye, and had a moment paused before its gate— gloomy entrance of a gloomy place—which had *cachots* even more terrible than that of Bicêtre. The principal one was dug thirty feet below the ground, with a vault so low that a man could not stand upright in it, while the water floated the straw of the prisoner's bed. Twenty-four hours of existence here was followed by certain death. But when I observe that this dungeon was built by the same persons who instituted the Inquisition, wonder ceases.

He paused, I have said, before it, and looked up. The great door stood before him; and at that very instant its wicket opened, and a man came out, as if pushed headlong forth.

"*Nom d'un pipe!*" said the man; "that is a civil way of treating a man who is, as it were, an official."

Paul Ledru shuddered, and turned away. The voice was far too familiar to him.

"Ah! ah!" cried the man, "is that Torty? How are you, my *garçon*? The devil, you look quite a *bourgeois!*"

"I am not a *bourgeois*, I am a *patriote*, citoyen Duchesne," said Ledru, recovering himself.

"*Citoyen!* what is that?" cried M. Duchesne, familiar to the readers of the early part of this narrative.

"Where have you been?" asked Paul Ledru, with astonishment.

"Where have I been? ahem!" replied Duchesne; "why, in there; on bread and water for two years, in a dungeon."

"Why?"

"Because of the affair of Reveillon," replied Duchesne.

"Of Reveillon?" cried Paul Ledru, in astonishment; "why, you must have been missed."

"Missed?"

"Yes!"

"By whom?"

"By us."

"By you; when?"

"When we searched all the prisons for every patriot we could find."

"I tell you what, Torty—"

"Paul Ledru—"

"Well, Paul Ledru. I've been in that cursed place two years in a solitary *cachot*, never having seen a creature save the jailor, who had a spite against me."

"And who kept you in without authority."

"The scoundrel! But I was saying I have been on hard allowance; I have no money. Will you line my inside with some bread and cheese, and a bottle of good wine?"

"With pleasure. Yonder is a *cabaret*."

"Come, then, and Heaven bless you," said the ex-hangman, with fervour which was heartfelt. The poor fellow looked starved.

Paul Ledru, though his prejudices and his recollections armed him against the man, was too good-natured, and too much of a practical democrat, to allow them to influence him; and they moved at once towards the tavern. Its little, dirty, dark sitting-room was vacant.

"Two bottles of good red wine, bread, cheese, and a half-pound of ham," said Paul.

Duchesne's eyes twinkled, and he rubbed his hands. His gaunt, pale, hollow cheeks were for a moment touched with crimson.

"You are a prince!" he cried.

"The devil!" replied Paul, hurriedly; "do you insult me?"

"What mean you?"

"Prince is the worst affront you could give me."

"But why?"

"They are *à l'index.*"

"Have they offended the King?"

"There is no king, or will be soon none."

"You craze me. Where is he?—is he dead, dying?"

"We upset him yesterday, and the National Assembly will proclaim his *déchéance* to-day."

"*A bah!*—Why, it seems you've been at work since I saw you."

"A little."

"Tell me."

"We've not left a stone of the Bastille!"

"Paul, you're taking advantage of my two years' absence."

"Not a whit! there's not a stone of it standing. Ask Palloy, who calls himself *entrepreneur de la démolition de la Bastille;* he took it in a day. He pulled it down in a year, made medals of the iron chairs, busts of Rousseau and Mirabeau of the stones, and models, too, of the prison."

"Bah!" said Duchesne, as the breakfast was laid before him; "but just tell me all about this."

"The shortest way will be to tell you my life since we parted," replied Paul Ledru.

"The very thing," said Duchesne, his mouth half full.

Paul began and sketched rapidly his existence since the day of the Reveillon riot. The ex-hangman made no remarks, he was too busy eating. At last, however, the narrative stopped.

"And that's where we are now," he exclaimed.

"Exactly."

"And what are you about just now?" asked Duchesne.

"That's a secret, which seek not to violate. I am acting for others. I must leave you now, but will not forget you. Take a bed here, and I will come and see you in a day or two. In the meanwhile live on this."

And he handed him a sheet of paper.

"What is this?"

"An *assignat* of fifty francs."

"But what good is it?"

"Try."

Duchesne called the woman of the house, and handed her, with an air of considerable doubt, the dirty, rumpled piece of paper.

"I will get change, *citoyen*," said the woman; and in a few minutes she brought a bundle of similar rags, worth ten, twenty, a hundred *sous*, and gave change. The hangman looked puzzled.

"But for the *assignats*," said the woman, "I know not what I should do. The rascally aristocrats have exported the *numeraire*."

"If they had only done this?" replied Paul Ledru.

"What else have they done?" asked Duchesne, after calling for brandy.

"*Infame!* Men inimical to the Revolution, and wishing to precipitate the people into misery, imagined a diabolical scheme. They went round into the markets, and bought up all the corn and flour they could get, to hide it away in woods, caves, and barns. With a splendid harvest we have had famine. Then they incited the people to lay the fault on the bakers, and got up riots, notably that of Francois, whom they pushed the people to kill."

"The *gredins!*"

"But the Assembly routed them out; and what then think you they did? They threw bread into rivers, sacks of flour were destroyed by thousands, whole fields of corn were laid low in the night by fire, and all to breed famine and discontent, and bring back the old system."

Paul Ledru spoke not half the truth. Such were but a trifle of the acts which the infamous party of the emigration, the hired agents of the aristocracy, and the foreigners, were guilty of. It was this series of events which, maddening the people, made them turn on their oppressors, and seek to drown in blood the infamies of their enemies. Not a head fell but the enemies of the country were answerable for it.

"But," said Paul, rising, " I must leave you."

" Good-by," replied Duchesne, who was very merry by this time.

" Until to-morrow," said Paul; and then he added, as he went by the mistress of the cabaret, " take care of him; he is not used to drink."

Paul Ledru, who was a little behindhand, moved rapidly onward; but, to avoid the crowd which he could see round the Tuileries and the Louvre, descended to the Pont Neuf.

As he came up, he saw a crowd of *fédérés* marching, banner flying; while one at their head, who wore a crown of laurel, waved a sword in his hand.

It was *l'Ami du Peuple*, the citoyen Marat.

Paul Ledru recognized both his face and his rags.

" Good day, citizen Ledru," exclaimed the fervent Revolutionist.

"Good day," said Marat; " this *is* a day. We have crushed the *infame*. No twentieth of June now. We've got him safe."

" And what dost thou mean to do with him ? " asked Ledru.

" Try him," replied Marat.

" And then ? "

" Judge him."

" And then ? "

" Execute him ! " said the Tribune, fiercely.

At the head of the bridge they parted, after shaking hands and expressing mutual hopes of the triumph of liberty.

It was with difficulty Ledru gained the Rue Grenelle, the confluence of the people in the quarter being immense; but at last he entered the street, and stopped before the house. The shop was open, despite the excitement and alarm.

Ledru occupied but a few minutes in settling his business and giving all the necessary orders. He then came out and turned towards his home again. As he did so, two men paused on the opposite side of the way and took note of the house. They then followed Paul, taking the opposite side of the way, and stopped only when they saw him safe in the Hotel of the Rue Dominique.

They were M. Brown and the Count Leopold.

----

## CHAPTER XXXVI.

### THE REMOVAL.

THE arrangements for the removal of Adela and the Duke from the Rue Dominique were not completed until the Monday about two o'clock in the afternoon, when the whole party, dressed in the simplest manner, issued from the hotel as if about to take a walk. They moved slowly round by the Pont Louis XVI., then Pont de la Revolution, now de la Concorde. There was Adela and the Duke, Charles Clement, Gracchus Antiboul, and the Countess Miranda. Paul Ledru and his wife had gone on before.

Crossing the Place de la Revolution, they gained the Rue St. Honore, but found it, near the Place Vendome, choked up by a dense crowd. They filled both ends of the Rue St. Honore—the rue now called Castiglione, but then I forget what. They were waiting evidently for some spectacle.

" What is all this crowd ?" asked the Duke, trembling.

" I know not," replied Charles Clement.

" It's Louis Capet going to the Temple," said a woman near at hand; " to the prison of the Temple, ah ! ah ! the Assembly wanted to send them to the Luxembourg, in grand style, but the Commune wouldn't have it."

It was a quarter past three o'clock.

At this instant a confused mass of cries hailed the arrival of two carriages. They were open, and surrounded by pikemen and gendarmes. In the first rode Louis XVI., with Pétion and Manuel.

The second carriage contained the Queen, Madame Elizabeth, and the children.

They moved slowly. It was the revenge of the people. In that city where kings and queens had tyrannized and towered—where they had trodden underfoot every sentiment of decency, humanity, and justice—where wretches like Louis XI., Henry III., Charles IX., Louis XIII., Louis XIV., and Louis XV., had gloated over popular suffering and wretchedness—the very mob their vices had created was now assembled to rejoice over the degradation of the Monarchy, which, however, was in a few years again to rule that great city.

"Who is that they are insulting?" said the Duke, in a whisper. He had been kept back.

"The King," whispered Adela.

The old man groaned, but his act passed unnoticed; and next minute the slow mourning cortège had passed, and the way up the Rue St. Honore was free.

"Come away," said Adela, who noticed how her father trembled.

The whole party passed rapidly along the now nearly empty street, and hurried towards the Rue Greselle.

"Woe is me, my friend," said Miranda to Charles, after an interval of painful silence; "but we have fallen on evil days. But now hasten, I pray you, your union with that dear girl; and let us hope for the best."

"Generous Miranda," replied Clement; "always thinking of others. Would, indeed, our union had taken place; for each day, I fear me, times will be more troublous."

"Pause not a day," continued Miranda, "or the death of the Duke will indefinitely delay it."

"This is Monday. On Thursday our union shall take place. Do you know a priest?"

"The King's confessor, M. de Firmont."

"Can you find him?"

"Oh, yes! he often came to the palace, and I took his address down. I will give it you."

"I will find him out to-morrow," said Charles, warmly; "but here we are."

They had reached the shop of Paul and Marie Ledru, who were standing outside waiting their arrival.

"Thank God !" said the Duke, "for my legs were trembling under me."

The whole party passed through the shop, and the back sort of parlour, where dinner awaited them.

The apartments formerly occupied by Charles Clement and Gracchus Antiboul were set apart for the Duke and his daughter; who, however, for the sake of variety and liveliness, and to prevent the necessity of trusting an *officieux*, or servant, were to take their meals in the apartment of the Ledrus.

Miranda, wishing to pass her chief time with them, requested Charles so to arrange that she could return somewhat late at night. Charles undertook to get her a certificate of good patriotism.

This settled, and despite the importance of events occuring without, the friends passed a long evening together, and it was nearly midnight ere they parted. Gracchus Antiboul went to the Jacobins about ten, and Charles undertook to see Miranda home.

The young man wore a sword and a brace of pistols, and he hesitated not a moment to turn through the narrow streets which led to the dwelling-place of Miranda, where Rose had preceded her. They moved along some time in silence. They were thinking; but how different were their thoughts. Charles was dwelling on the dear hopes which lay before him; Miranda was asking of the future its unfathomable secrets.

"It is strange," she suddenly exclaimed, with a short laugh, "to see us walk along thus silent."

"Pardon me, Miranda," said Charles, recovering himself.

"No pardon, Charles; but let me ask you a question. Could I use my position and my fortune in any way to be useful to the Revolution, and at the same time to ourselves ?"

"Indeed you could, dear lady," exclaimed Charles Clement, eagerly; "open your salons to the leaders of the popular party, both Girondin and Mountain; make yourself agreeable to them, and no one can say how much influence you might have on all our destinies."

"I will do it. Give me a list of persons to invite, point out to me how to receive them, come, too, and I will devote my whole energies to the task."

"And great will be the good done. Danton you have already secured, but you must not neglect him for that. It may be of incalculable use to make friends with men whose power will soon be dictatorial."

They had reached the door of Miranda's house.

Charles Clement prepared to bid her farewell.

"Will you not come in?" said Miranda, almost faintly. "I should like to talk over this plan of ours, as well as of your marriage."

Charles Clement gladly assented, and they went in. Rose was waiting with supper laid in the delicious boudoir, which, in days gone past, she had so delighted to adorn.

They sat down, and, Rose waiting on them, supped alone for the first time.

They knew not why, for there are secrets in our hearts we know not of ourselves, but both Charles and Miranda felt a strange restraint. They ate almost in silence, mechanically. The lovely Italian was pale in the extreme, while Charles Clement, with a frown on his face, sought to sound the depths of his heart.

"Well," said Rose, suddenly, "I hope you are like an old married couple, who have said all they have to say, and can't think of anything new."

Both started, and both coloured violently.

"Well, it does look like it," exclaimed Miranda, with a forced laugh, while Charles apologized for his silence.

Conversation now began freely, and both entered into the spirit of the talk with zest and interest. It was the Revolution they spoke of chiefly, and here they agreed. Miranda's warm Italian heart sided with the people, and she had little maudlin and sentimental pity for their oppressors. They were each equally delighted with the other's conversation, and it was with surprise and shame that they heard the clock strike three.

"Heavens! Charles, it is very thoughtless of me to have kept you thus," said Miranda; "the streets may be dangerous."

"Not to a patriot, and an armed one," replied Charles Clement, rising; "but I thank you for a most charming hour. Will you be in the Rue Grenelle at twelve?"

"Without fail," said Miranda, quickly.

18

They shook hands and parted.

Miranda sent her maid to bed, buried her face in her hands, and wept.

Charles felt a kind of strange feeling at the heart he did not understand.

But neither ever spoke of that interview to any one, neither next day nor ever afterwards.

Why?

---

## CHAPTER XXXVII.

### THE SANS-CULOTTE.

THE reign of the *sans-culottes* may now be said to have commenced. The pikemen and the *sans-culottes* were one. When at first citizen soldiers put on uniform and mounted guard, many did their duty in their working clothes and cotton caps. They were the *bisets* of '89, whom, what were called the *habits-bleus* never forgot to insult, and whom they kept at the very bottom of the corps-de-garde, sending them out to mount guard between midnight and four in the morning. They were prohibited from appearing on parade; the *bonnets-de-laine* would have dishonoured the dandy gentlemen in fine uniforms, varnished leather collars, and powdered shoulders. But they were patient, for they had their hope of triumphing in their turn, and they supported with perfect resignation all the sarcasms which these aristocrats of a new kind poured on them. Many public writers defended them; and this alone was hope and encouragement. Some journalists even prophesied the reign of the cotton caps; and they mounted guard in the night gaily, looking to the future. Called *sans-culottes*, they gloried in the name.

Prudhomme wrote, in 1793, " The true *sans-culotte* is a natural man, or a man who has preserved all the energy of one in the bosom of a civil society, regenerated by the Revolution. He is a patriot, robust in head as in body, who has always exposed his person, and made a step in advance, and who, in consequence, never waited for his country to call him. It is this workman and father of a family, who, gifted with right sense, instead of giving to the Republic the leavings of his time, thought himself in permanent requisition in person and faculties, from the 12th July, 1789. A true *sans-culotte* is what was once called the man of the people, frank, cordial, sometimes rude, but always humane, even at those revolutionary moments when one is compelled to cast a veil on the statue of humanity. The true *sans-culotte* willed the death of the despot and of all conspirators; he is seen on the road of all traitors going to punishment; he even presses round the scaffold, because humanity excludes not justice."

After the 10th of August the National Guard disappeared, and the pikemen and *sans-culottes* took their place.

The latter were never more than 5000 in number.

It was about eleven o'clock, and Paul Ledru, now citoyen Regulus Ledru, was at his counter serving a young girl, when a man suddenly entered who seemed to be the very essence of a patriot, or a *sans-culotte*, but one of an aristocratic order. He wore a red felt hat, approaching somewhat the shape of the cap of liberty, while his face was covered with a profusion of hair, which, mixing with that of his head, made a perfect forest. His coat was of rude blue, while his waistcoat was a very tri-coloured flag of itself. His pantaloons were made of three stripes of red, white, and blue, while a bundle of heavy metal seals and keys hung from his waistcoat. In his hand was a huge stick.

"*Salut* and fraternity, citizen," he said, in a rough voice.

"*Salut*," replied Ledru.

"Hast thou a red cap, a true liberty covering?"

"I have," answered Ledru, showing several.

"Citizen," said the energetic visitor, seating himself, "I have to complain of thy civism."

"How so?"

"Thou art never at thy section. Ten thousand cannonballs! but a man must devote himself to his country."

"But, citoyen, I only came in yesterday."

"Ah! that accounts for thy face being unknown to me. Know, then, citoyen Ledru, that I am president of the Club *des Sans-culottes*, true patriots all. Wilt thou be one of us?"

"I will attend one of thy meetings."

"We never meet. Dost thou take us for lawyers? We've something else to do besides talking."

"The work is ——"

"That of aristocrat hunting. We have vowed eternal war to the race; and we spend our days and nights in routing them up."

"Hum!" said Ledru, who had paled somewhat, "it's rude work."

"Rude! I expect it is; but patriotism is its own reward. Thou art a brother; I am thirsty, give me a glass of water. Between true men these things may be asked without ceremony."

Ledru intimated his willingness, and moved inwards. At the same instant a man, followed by half-a-dozen *sans-culottes*, entered the shop.

"In there," said the aristocrat-hunter.

The party burst into the little back parlour of the shop, where sat the Duke, Adela, and the wife of Ledru.

"Arrest those two ex-nobles," cried the man of the red cap; "I denounce them."

"Scoundrel!" cried Ledru, gazing wildly at the party.

"Ah, M. Brown! you will protect us."

"He said *you*," said the aristocrat-hunter.

"Thou wilt protect us?"

"I perform my duty," replied M. Brown doggedly.

"But that is surely not to trouble my quiet home?"

"I am ordered by the citizen at the head of the police department to arrest the ex-Duke de Ravilliere and the Lady Adela his daughter. There they are, are they not?"

"And who touches them?" cried Charles Clement, bounding in, followed by Gracchus Antiboul.

Ledru took courage, and seized a pair of pistols.

M. Brown politely explained the state of affairs.

"And this rascally denouncer?" said Charles Clement, pale with rage and horror.

"I am a true patriot," replied the man, sullenly.

"Then show thyself in thy true colours, ex-thief! ex-aristocrat!" cried Charles, tearing away his beard and hair.

The eye of a rival had been clear. It was Count Leopold.

"My nephew!" shouted the Duke.

"My cousin!" cried Adela.

"Now, am I not revenged?" said the Count Leopold, folding his arms and gazing on them with Satanic fury.

"Oh, oh!" cried one of the *sans-culottes*, "this *quidam* is a *ci-devant*, who uses the sacred cloak of patriotism to seek private revenge. Comrades, we must punish this villainy."

"*A la lanterne* with the spy," said another.

In the instant the Count Leopold was seized by four of the *sans-culottes*, inflexible against aristocrats, but furious at being made the tools of private revenge. The disguised man struggled violently, but in vain. In a few minutes he was out in the street. M. Brown made not an effort to save him.

"But I must take these two persons to the Conciergerie," he observed, coldly.

"Why?" cried Charles, while the whole party looked on in mute despair.

"It is the order of the Commune."

"Bear up, uncle dear, Adela dear," said the young man, bitterly; "go with them. I will to Robespierre—Gracchus to Danton—and your release shall be signed within an hour."

The *sans-culottes* started.

"Thou wilt scarcely be so successful," said Brown, sneeringly.

"It cannot be other. Here are three combatants of the 14th July, of the 20th June, of the 10th August, three well-known Jacobins, ready to bear witness to the utter harmlessness of these persons."

"Thy evidence in civism is great; but in the mean time we must away."

A yell of fury called the men of the party to the door of the shop. At that instant Miranda came up.

"They are hanging a man," said Miranda, wildly.

"Is that all?" cried M. Brown.

"He deserves it," said Charles Clement.

Miranda looked astounded.

"He is my cousin—save him!" shrieked Adela, fainting.

Charles Clement and Antiboul rushed forth.

The four *sans-culottes* had dragged the Count Leopold beneath a lamp supported by a projecting piece of iron, and across this they had thrown a long rope, procured from the first shop. A crowd had collected, who hearing that it was intended to hang an aristocrat for assuming the disguise of a patriot and thus serving private revenge, all joined heartily in the tragedy. The Count struggled violently; but they had succeeded in binding his hands behind him, and placing him on a stool.

The Count, his body covered with rags, his face haggard and pale, cast his eyes round the crowd in search of one look of pity or encouragement. Not one responded to his hope.

"Off with him," cried one.

"*Santé marquis!*" said another.

"*Bis!*" shrieked a third.

"Take him to the *Conciergerie*," put in Charles Clement.

"Let him have a trial," cried Gracchus.

"Dost thou wish to join him?" said one of the *sans-culottes*, menacingly.

"Will no man save me from these devils?" cried the Count, in a faint voice; "I am a true patriot."

"A *ci-devant*," answered one.

"An aristocrat."

"A spy."

"I am a true patriot; ask Danton, ask Robespierre —"

"Silence, liar!" thundered the *sans-culotte* who had threatened Charles and Gracchus, kicking the stool from under him.

The Count whirled round with a convulsive shudder; and, when the rope hung straight and steady, he was a corpse.

Charles Clement and Gracchus returned to the shop, where they found Miranda weeping in the arms of Marie Ledru.

M. Brown had hurried away with the Duke and Adela, while the above tragedy was taking place.

"Close the shop," said Charles, sombrely, "and let us discuss the means of saving our friends."

The shop was rapidly closed, to open no more; and all gathered round a table.

"Not to have let me go with them," said Miranda, sobbing.

"You shall soon be with her," exclaimed Charles, kindly; "there is no evidence against them. Let us lose no time. Ledru, see the Countess home, while I go to Robespierre's."

"And I to Danton," said Gracchus.

And they went out.

---

## CHAPTER XXXVIII.

### THE GRAVE-DIGGER.

THE flight of Lafayette—that weak, vain old man—the capture of Longwi, the surrender of Verdun, the entrance of the army of the coalition into France, the flight of the aristocracy and their traitorous junction with the enemies of the nation, roused Paris to boiling heat. The people had been satisfied with overthrowing the monarchy, and crushing the iniquitous power of aristocracy; but now they became furious, and asked for two things—revenge and the driving out of the enemy.

Danton was omnipotent.

He was minister of war, and governed the Commune, which governed France. Roland, Menge, Lebrun, Servan, were mere tools in his hands.

Robespierre had not sufficiently aided the 10th August to have much power as yet. He bided his time.

Danton showed himself at once what he was, an unscrupulous man of genius. At his bidding armies rose in every corner of France.

But he thought that it was necessary to strike his enemies with terror by an act of unheard-of audacity. He decided on one which was both audacious and atrocious.

Danton, Petion, Marat, Santerre, Maillard, Tallien— the men who pretended to overthrow Robespierre from a spirit of clemency—these were the authors of the September massacre.

Charles Clement and Gracchus Antiboul had in vain sought the freedom of the Duke and Adela. Robespierre himself had asked it of the Commune; but Danton had refused.   The two young men had taken a lodging near the Church of St. Jacques du Haut Pas, and had left the women in the Rue Dominique.

Miranda had opened her saloon, as they had agreed, to the members of the liberal party.

It was the 28th August, at six in the morning, and Charles Clement, with Gracchus, had risen early to wander round the prison of the Abbaye, to which Adela and the Duke had been removed.

They looked out of the window, and their eyes fell on a small house opposite, at which two men in heavy cloaks and slouched hats were knocking.

"One of those men is M. Brown," said Gracchus, in a low whisper.

"Some villany, I doubt not," replied Charles.

"That man has a most intense hatred of his old masters, the nobles."

"But the other?"

"Is Hebert of the Commune."

"Let us watch them."

At this instant a man came to the door.

"It is our landlord, the grave-digger," said Gracchus, with a shudder.

"My God!" cried Charles, "the Republic is about to be stained by some great villany."

"Poor Republic!" said Antiboul, sadly; "and it will be held answerable for the monstrosities of a few villains."

"But we must watch these men, and discover their purpose," replied Charles, solemnly.

The two men spoke to the grave-digger, who went in, brought out his tools, and prepared to follow them.

"Let us go," said Charles.

"Come."

And next minute the two friends were in the street, following the agents of the Commune and the grave-digger of the Church of St. Jacques du Haut Pas.

They were some distance before them, walking quietly. The two friends kept close up against the wall, and hurried on their track.

"Merciful God!" whispered Charles, "what can this mean?"

"I know not, and yet my blood runs cold."

"Danton is at the bottom of this. That man will ruin the Revolution."

"Pity, that with genius that man has so little heart or principle. Power, money, applause, pleasure, is all he cares for."

"But where do they lead us?" asked Charles, in a low, husky whisper.

"To the catacombs!" replied Gracchus Antiboul, and the men halted at the site of the quarries, which, on the removal of the cemeteries of Paris, had been turned into catacombs.

The agents of the commune had turned into the quarries.

Charles and Gracchus concealed themselves close to them, behind a pile of rubbish, after looking to their pistols, resolved, as they were, to put the two men to death if discovered by them.

They looked over.

The grave-digger was leaning on his spade, gazing curiously at the two men, who had unrolled a map.

"Go to yon stone," said M. Brown.

Hebert went.

"Turn due north, and wait," said the spy.

Hebert did as he was directed, while M. Brown advanced to a post at some distance.

"Now make seventeen full steps," cried M. Brown, "and then halt."

M. Brown had placed himself looking due west, and began to step at the same moment as M. Hebert.

M. Hebert walked seventeen full steps, and halted. M. Brown joined him in a minute.

"That is it exactly. Seventeen steps due north from that stone, and nineteen due west from that post. Here is the mouth."

M. Brown took a spade from the grave-digger, and began marking out a hole.

"Citoyen Pleuniche," said he, severely, "here is the mouth of the catacombs. Here is money. Get the necessary labourers, and let the pit leading to the mouth be open in four days."

"Why?" said the grave-digger, sullenly.

"Why!" replied M. Brown, looking at Hebert.

"For thy carcase, along with the aristocrats, if you ask questions or speak a word. Thou sawest, citoyen, the orders of the Commune?"

"I did," replied the grave-digger, sadly. "I am a good citizen, and hate kings and aristocrats as I do the devil; but they are Frenchmen."

"Thy business, friend, is to bury the dead, and not to pity the living."

"Go about thy business now," cried Hebert; "go hire the needful workmen, and if one of them speaks, let him descend into the catacombs."

The grave-digger laid down his tools, wiped his forehead, cold with sweat, with his hand, and walked away.

"This is a mighty stroke," said Hebert, rubbing his hands. "In five days more there will not be an aristocrat in Paris, and we shall be able to drive back the brigands from the frontiers in peace."

"Citoyen Hebert," exclaimed M. Brown, calmly, "I care as little for these aristocrats as doest thou. I know that a general massacre of all would-be-emigrants, aristocrats, sedition-mongers, and royalists, will infuse salutary terror throughout the land, and cause the orders of Paris to be obeyed without a murmur; but this deed will kill the Republic, and bring back accursed despotism."

"Never!" cried the ferocious, bloodthirsty Hebert. "We must strike until we have no enemies left."

"For every one we strike a dozen will arise. I know, with all Europe armed against us, with more enemies in our bosom than without, with enough suspected to fill a city of prisons, we have no resource; but Danton will live to regret this deed."

"What deed?" said Charles, in a low, hasty tone.

"I see it! I see it!" replied Antiboul, laying his hand rudely on the arm of his friend. "Let them go before we speak."

Hebert and M. Brown moved away.

"What deed?" said Charles, mechanically.

"A general massacre of all the prisoners," replied Gracchus Antiboul.

"And the Duke—and Adela?"

"What is to be done?"

"My brain whirls."

"They must be saved.   They must! they shall!"

"How?"

"Let us first to Robespierre!   If he can do nothing, we must try Danton.  If Danton refuses, we must try money."

"Let us to Robespierre."

----

## CHAPTER XXXIX.

### ROBESPIERRE AT HOME

IN the Rue St. Honore, opposite the church of the Assumption, in the house of the carpenter Duplay, in a small and humble apartment, lived François-Maximilien Robespierre.  This man, so diversely judged by the ferocity of hate and partizanship, by the unscrupulous and savage pens devoted to priestcraft and kingcraft, whom Lamartine has cleared of nearly every drop of blood imputed to him—this man, who fell because Tallien, the ferocious accomplice of Danton in the massacres of September, knew of his earnest wish to end the Reign of Terror, by sweeping away the terrorists—lived in peaceful, calm, and humble retirement. Poor, having money in contempt, his pleasures were in the society of the carpenter, his wife, and daughters; of St. Just, Lebas, Couthon, and one or two more republicans of the school of Rousseau, who had no other dream than founding a happy and Arcadian Republic, but who in those awful times were the unwilling accomplices of deeds which the audacity, fury, and monstrosity of their enemies rendered necessary.  The material position of France, the frightful misery at first caused by the emigration of the rich, with their unceasing efforts to replunge France in hourly massacres, were, with the brutal ignorance of the monarchy-educated people of Paris—the mob that had risen beneath the shelter of the Bastille, the Louvre, the Palais-Royal— the parc-aux-cerfs, and which naturally followed such men as Hebert, Marat, and others, the causes which continually compelled the philosophic republicans, in that hour of supreme peril, to use the very weapons of their enemies.

This was, in most cases, intense weakness and cowardice. But Robespierre and his party thought future liberty worth any price, even as he said himself, " The price of my name, my memory, my reputation, which will be held up to universal execration."   Almost every good institution in France is, however, due to the time of the Reign of Terror.   With all their great faults, the Mountain and the Gironde loved France.   The latter, with a visionary love, testified in their idol and inspirer Madame Roland; the former, with a masculine love, which only wanted peace to develope itself in all its greatness.   Robespierre was poor.   The rent of his little farms in Artois was very irregularly paid, and his salary as deputy supported himself and his sister.

He lived, as I have said, in the Rue St Honore, No. 396.

Duplay, his host, had a wife, a son, and four daughters, all equally devoted with himself to the democratic leader.

One of these daughters still lives; and it is to the solemn words culled from her lips that history owes much of the history of this extraordinary man.

Robespierre loved Eléonore, or, as he called her, Cornelia Duplay; and the love was returned by her, and approved of by her family.   Their love was pure and sincere.

" The total want of fortune," said Robespierre, " and the uncertainty of the morrow, prevented him from marrying her until the destiny of France was determined on; but he only awaited the moment when the Revolution should be determined and wholly concluded, in order to retire from the turmoil and strife, and marry her whom he loved, retiring to live in Artois in one of the farms which he had saved from amongst the possessions of his family, there to mingle his obscure happiness in the common lot of his family."

The apartment of Robespierre was a low garret chamber above some cart-sheds, and looking out upon a small court.

It contained a wooden bedstead, covered with blue damask, ornamented with white flowers, a table, and four straw-bottomed chairs.   This was his study and sleeping room.

Some wooden shelves supported his papers, his manuscripts, his reports, while a few books lay beside them.

On a table was the breakfast of Robespierre.   A loaf of

bread and some camomile tea, which he took much of, from his bilious tendency.

At about eight o'clock on the morning of the 28th August, a man sat near this table. He had white powdered hair, turned up in clusters over his temples, a bright blue coat open over the breast to display a white vest, short yellow-coloured breeches, white stockings, and shoes with silver buckles.

This was Robespierre, then thirty-one years of age.

He was reading Racine, when a knock came to his door, and Charles Clement and Gracchus Antiboul entered.

"*Salut*, my friends," said Robespierre, looking a little uneasily into their pallid and terror-stricken faces; "what is the matter?"

Charles Clement sat down, laid his head solemnly and earnestly on Robespierre's shoulder, and narrated all he had heard.

"This is dreadful," cried Maximilien Robespierre; "but what can I do? I have friends, too, in prison."

"Can we not overthrow Danton? You are there to take his place."

"Charles," replied the Deputy for Arras, fixing his eyes firmly on him, "my time will come, because my principles are inevitable. But Danton would crush us like flies if we dared to move against him now. He has arrogated all the merit of the 10th August to himself, and he is omnipotent."

"But he will grant you any lives you ask for."

"Charles," said Robespierre, "did the Lady Adela know anything of Danton's dealings with the court?"

"She did."

"Then ask not her life of Danton. We must strive to save her otherwise. There is one man in the Abbaye whom Danton shall give me up."

"And who is that?"

"The Abbé Béradier, head of the College of Louis-le-Grand, my old schoolmaster."

"But our friends, my wife?" cried Charles.

"My friend," said Robespierre, solemnly, "what I can do, I will do. I cannot prevent this massacre. Danton, Panis, Santerre, Marat, Billaud-Varennes, Tallien, Hebert rule the Commune, where my voice is powerless to restrain; but I will ask for a dozen safe-conducts, of which you shall have two."

"Thanks! thanks!" cried the two young men.

"But screen your friends well afterwards, and take care to give good evidence of your patriotism, or I may not always be able to serve you. Even now, Danton may succeed in having the safe-conducts refused me. So seek to find out the details of this bloody affair, and take your measures accordingly."

"But where will Danton find men to execute his bloody will? the people will have nothing to do with it."

"The people!" cried Robespierre; "they will only know of it after it is over. But Danton will find two hundred butchers in Paris, who will obey his will; and when it is over, he will lay the blood to the spontaneous anger and indignation of the people."

"You are going out?" said Gracchus.

"I am going to the Assembly, and thence to the Commune. Come and see me to-night. You will meet St. Just and Lebas, and we will talk over our plans for the future. *Salut*, my friends, until this evening."

And Robespierre parted from them at his door, whither they had descended while talking.

"He will save them if he can," cried Gracchus; "but another plan strikes me."

"What is that?"

"Let us make friends with some of the assassins, and buy them."

"But to find them out."

"Paul Ledru is our man."

"Let us to him."

"He will set to work that Duchesne, his old acquaintance."

"The very man for us. He is capable of enrolling himself for a good sum."

"A desperate remedy, but the best. With an agent among the murderers, and a lavish expenditure of money, all may be done."

"I know not. The very wretches who will be hired for this butchery will have their point of honour. They will take money, wages, for a day's work to do; but we must be cautious whom we try."

"You are right. But, Charles, we will save these unfortunates, or we will die in the attempt."

"Thank you, my friend. It is not my intention to survive them."

At this moment the drums began to beat, and a proclamation covered the walls in every direction.

The people hurried precipitately along the street.

An order had been issued for every person to be within their doors, which were to be left open. The barriers were closed. Armed boats lay on the river, to prevent escape in that direction.

All Paris was to be searched for Royalists and suspected persons.

Charles and Gracchus hurried to their section instead of going home. They could thus be amongst the searchers, instead of amongst the searched.

In half an hour the streets were entirely empty, save of pikemen, *sans-culottes*, *fédérés*, and agents of the Commune.

Santerre, with forty-eight aides-de-camp, visited all the portes on horseback.

Charles and Gracchus were posted in the neighbourhood of the Rue Dominique, and their hotel was only visited for form's sake; their patriotism was known. Besides, Danton had privately ordered this house amongst many to be excepted from real search.

"Miranda gives a reception to-night. Danton and his friends will be there. We must go when we leave Robespierre."

"But beware, Charles," cried Gracchus, "not a word about what we know. If he knew we possessed his secret, he would immolate us without mercy."

The search commenced: and before night five thousand Royalists, or suspected Royalists, were in the prison of Paris.

Before morning the next day, three thousand of these were set free on producing evidence of their civism.

The rest went to the Abbaye St. Germain, to the Conciergerie, to the Chatelet, to the Force, and to the other atrocious prisons erected by the defunct monarchy to support its decrepid and rotten structure.

Meanwhile, Charles and Gracchus, having performed their duty, and seen Paris restored to its ordinary state, went to the Rue Dominique, where they found Miranda, and the whole party assembled.

"You are safe then?" cried the Countess, gazing anxiously at Charles.

"Safe, but heart-broken," he replied. "Oh! Miranda! Miranda! the worst trial is now on us."

And he narrated all.

"Merciful heaven!" exclaimed Miranda, pale and trembling; "the Duke and my beloved Adela likely to be massacred. This can never be. Your fears make you wild."

"I am too much in earnest."

"Danton shall give me their freedom," said the Countess, with a sickly pallor on her face. "This evening I will drag it from him."

"Oh! blessings on you, beloved friend," exclaimed Charles; "surely Danton will not refuse you?"

"He will not," said Miranda, with a strange expression of wildness in her eyes; "he will not—I am sure he will not."

"But your idea about enlisting Duchesne?" said Paul Ledru.

"Must be carried out, too," said Gracchus. "Each person must try his best. Robespierre, Miranda, us, Paul, all at work—they must—they shall be saved."

And a long conversation of deep and solemn interest followed, in which every plan of salvation for the Duke and Adela was turned over.

In the midst of all this a note came for Charles

He opened it and read :—

"I have procured a safe conduct for the Abbé Bérardier by name, but blank ones have been refused, though Danton has used hundreds. Try him personally. I will use more exertions again to-morrow. *Salut.*

"ROBESPIERRE."

The whole party listened in silence.

There was no hope but in Danton.

# CHAPTER XL.

## AN EVENING AT MIRANDA'S.

EVEN during the greatest convulsions caused by political revolutions, by the struggles of parties, by the civil discord, which tear the bosom of the land, and set father against son and brother against brother—and all because a few selfish aristocrats believe themselves born to govern and oppress—Paris never forgets its gaiety and pleasures. Receptions, soirees are given, even when barricades compel the visitors to go on foot to their friends.

The 10th of August was hardly forgotten, and sullen rumours of something much more terrible were afloat in the air.

Paris was entirely governed by the Commune, and by its devoted army of *sans-culottes*.

The Commune was governed by Danton.

Danton, just now, was governed by Marat.

And yet, at eight o'clock that evening, the *salons* of the citoyenne Miranda were full. Deputies, journalists, demagogues, clubists, crowded to converse in the apartments of a lady who had cast herself headlong into the Revolution, and where they were sure to meet some relaxation from the terrible cares of those days.

Charles Clement and Gracchus Antiboul were the first. They had dined with Miranda.

Miranda was pale and anxious. Her lovely features were haggard and full of suffering. They reflected the misery of Charles Clement, whose mind was racked by the idea of the sufferings of Adela in the prison of the Abbaye.

"Miranda," said he after some moments of silence, "if everything else fails, I am resolved on one thing. I will go to the bar of the National Assembly. I will denounce Danton. I will open the eyes of Paris to his atrocious projects, and call on the patriots to save us from the disgrace of the coming scene."

"You would perish," replied Miranda, hurriedly, her cheek at once suffused with crimson.

"I can but die; and, Adela dead, I have no other wish."

"Hush, Charles," said Miranda, reproachfully; "a man has always his country and his friends."

"My country will have deprived me of her; friends I have none, save you," replied he, taking with one hand the hand of Miranda, with the other that of Gracchus.

"And think you we can spare you?" said Miranda, tenderly.

"Charles!" exclaimed Gracchus, drily, "it is not a man who speaks in you, but a child."

"My friends, reason with me. Adela is to me life, light, the world, all. I live only in her love. She dead, of what avail is existence to me?"

"Charles!" cried Miranda, more pallid even than usual, "Adela must die eventually. If she perishes now, which I feel and know she will not, you have no more cause to die than if she died after ten years of happy marriage. It is violent passion speaks in you now; but the heart is ruder than we think, and breaks not easily."

Too rude! How few have loved unto extinction of life beside the perishing one! And wisely is it so. We are born to live, to suffer, and to die at a time appointed. But one often does despise oneself and human nature when gazing on the smiling faces and smirking lips of those who, perhaps, six months before, were broken-hearted with grief at the loss of a wife, a child, a brother, a parent.

Visitors arrived, and the conversation ceased.

There came Roland and Servan, Robespierre and St. Just, Camille Desmoulins, Fouquier Tinville, the elegant Barrere, Brissot, Louvet, Tallien, Hebert, Vergniaud, Buzot, Barbaroux, and all the republican leaders of the day, meeting in somewhat friendly intercourse on this common ground.

In a few minutes everybody was engaged.

St. Just and Lebas spoke apart; a knot collected round Gaudet and Vergniaud, who carried on a friendly dispute in their silvery tones, alive with eloquence. Roland spoke with Brissot about the war, while Robespierre paced up and down the room, with Charles and Gracchus by his side.

"Danton is admirable to knock down," said Robespierre, "to rouse vigour into the people—he is the man of the

Revolution; but he is unfit to consolidate—he is too ambitious and too reckless."

"I foresee awful scenes," said Charles.

"I see beyond a great and happy France; I see behind a miserable, perishing land of wretched serfs and insolent nobles; and I hesitate not. If the Revolution does nothing but disseminate property, and annihilate an iniquitous priesthood, who make of France a temple of luxury and a shrine of theft, it will have done enough."

"I am prepared for all. Give me but my wife, Robespierre, and I devote my every energy to thee."

"We shall see," said Robespierre, who became suddenly silent.

Danton had just entered, and was paying his respects to the mistress of the house with that air of gallantry which he always assumed, for Danton was passionately attached to the fair sex.

"Look at that smiling face," whispered Charles; "who could believe it covered so much atrocity?"

"The man has no heart," answered Gracchus.

"It is a charming thing," said Danton, bowing and kissing the extended hand of Miranda, "in these days of difficulty and danger, to be able to sun oneself awhile in the smiles of beauty."

"Danton a flatterer," replied the Countess, smiling. She was determined to use profound dissimulation with this man.

"I am no flatterer when I praise your beauty," said Danton, fixing his bold eyes upon her.

"If you are sincere in admiring me, perhaps you might *feel* sufficient good-nature to accord me a great favour."

"And what is that?" said Danton, seating himself, apart a little from the rest of the society, beside Miranda.

"A safe-conduct for Adela and the poor old Duke."

"Why?" said Danton, with an almost imperceptible frown.

"Because none know better than yourself that they are in danger."

"They will be tried in due course by the regular tribunals; and, if there be no evidence against them, they will be acquitted."

" Evidence of what ? " said Miranda.

" Of their having conspired."

" Danton ! you know they are not conspirators. They are my nearest, dearest friends ; set them free at once."

" You conceive them in danger?" asked Danton, curiously.

" I know them to be in danger," replied Miranda, fixing her eyes full upon him.

" They are, perhaps ; but it is not easy to obtain their deliverance," said the demagogue, speaking in a low tone, and fixing on Miranda a peculiar look which made her bow down her eyes; "you are aware, *belle dame*, how much I adore you. Give me some glimpse of hope, and I promise you the *safe-conduct*."

Scorn on her lip, Miranda rose as if to meet a new comer. Tumultuous thoughts filled her head. The insult she had received made her very blood boil with indignation; but the memory of the danger of Adela, the anguish of Charles, and the power of Danton, made her resolve on one more trial.

She returned to her place.

Danton was speaking with Roland, with whom five minutes after he went out arm-in-arm.

Charles approached the Countess.

" What news ? "

" He is inexorable."

" What is to be done ? "

" I know not."

" Miranda ! I shall go mad."

" Have you seen Paul yet ? "

" No."

" Then go at once : I see little hope but in some desperate effort. In the hurry and confusion of this bloody scene, they may be saved."

" They shall be saved, or I will perish ; reason not with me, my dear friend."

" You will return ? "

" I will."

" At what hour? "

" At midnight. Keep Gracchus till then. When your company is gone, we can resume our plans."

Charles went out, and met Paul Ledru at the door.

" Well ?"

" I and Duchesne are engaged by Maillard among the workmen for the 2nd September."

" And what have you to do ? "

" We know not.  On the evening of the 1st September, Maillard will give us all the necessary directions."

" But you may be placed in an awful position, Paul," said Charles.

" I care not.  If I save Adela for you, my benefactor, I am amply repaid."

" Thanks, Paul! thanks; I am fortunate in having such a friend.  But go now about the town and seek some further details of what is coming."

They shook hands and parted, Paul to wander from wine-shop to wine-shop, Charles to hurry beneath the walls of the prison of the Abbaye, there to wander round the spot which contained his mistress.

At midnight only he returned to the residence of Miranda, whom he found alone with Gracchus; but Miranda told him not one word of the insult she had received at the hands of Danton.

---

## CHAPTER XLI.

### THE SECOND OF SEPTEMBER, 1792.

IT was Sunday morning, the 2d of September, 1792, and in the apartment of Miranda.

The three friends sat stupified with horror and astonishment, looking at each other, wholly incapable of speaking.

Paul Ledru had just left them, after detailing the full particulars of the horrible scene which was to be enacted that day in Paris.

Every prison was to be emptied of its occupants, but by death.

Two hundred ruffians had been hired, men of lost character, or wild enthusiasts, to do the work of blood.

Twelve judges had been selected, over whom presided the Huissier Maillard.

But their judgments were all settled beforehand. Danton had examined the prison register, and put a mark against every name.

Maillard had his axe. To some he was to address these words :—"Let this gentleman be set at liberty."

These were free.

To others he was to say, "*A la Force!*"

These were to be massacred piteously.

Paul Ledru had been selected as one of the judges who were to assist Maillard; and it was by his connivance and that of Duchesne that there was hope of setting the father and daughter at liberty.

All was arranged. Charles and Gracchus had obtained leave to mount guard in the neighbourhood of the Abbaye, near a *fiacre stand*. There they were to await Adela and the Duke, if the plans of Paul and Duchesne were successful.

It was as connivers at the escape of the Princess de Lamballe that they had succeeded in obtaining this dangerous post. Maillard himself and all the judges were resolved to save this young and lovely woman; but as a friend of the hated Marie Antoinette, they dared not openly avow their intention.

The house of Miranda was to be the place of refuge for both their own friends and the Princess de Lamballe.

At two o'clock in the afternoon of the day, Charles and Gracchus were to mount guard.

At one o'clock they left her alone; and no sooner were they out of sight than a prodigious change took place in her.

"Rose!" she cried.

Her maid entered.

"A cowl, a cloak, and a *fiacre*, instantly!"

The maid hurried to obey.

There stood that lovely woman, petrified as it were into stone, her eyes fixed on vacancy.

She determined to make one more effort with Danton.

The maid re-entered with the cloak and cowl.

"We will go meet the *fiacre*; I know where it stands."

Rose followed her mistress without speaking, for she saw that something extraordinary was the matter.

At the corner of the street they met the coach coming; and Miranda sprang in.

"Chez Danton," she cried; and the man drove quickly to the residence of the Minister of War.

Miranda threw herself back, almost insensible, in the coach, and wept in silence.

The Countess Miranda left the coach, and stood in the courtyard of the minister's residence.

It was filled by national guards and *sans-culottes*, while mounted *estaffetes* were coming and going in all directions.

" What seekest thou, citoyenne ? " asked a *sans-culotte*, gazing curiously at the pallid and frozen beauty, whose flashing eyes alone betrayed the inward struggle.

" The citoyen Danton."

" Thy name, citoyenne ? "

" Miranda."

" Wait a moment, my pretty aristocrat," said the good-natured *sans-culotte*, laughing.

The republican soldier went in, and gave the name to an official.

Miranda stood underneath the portico, wrapped within herself, and insensible to all around. Her mind was wandering on the past. The future was too black and awful to be considered.

" The citoyen minister waits for thee," exclaimed the voice of the *sans-culotte* at her elbow.

" I come! I thank thee," she continued, as the soldier made a clear passage in the crowd for her.

Several couriers arrived at this moment, and a great bustle ensued ; but Miranda noticed nothing.

In two minutes she was in the cabinet of the minister.

Danton, with a red cap on his head, a sabre by his side, supported by a tricoloured scarf, stood with his back to the fireplace. A table covered with papers, two chairs, and a long *bureau*, comprised the whole furniture of the room.

" *Salut*, madame," said Danton, offering a chair. " What procures me the honour of your visit at this moment ? "

" I come to save my friends," replied Miranda, sinking on the proffered chair, and burying her face in her hands.

" How ? " said Danton.

"How!" said Miranda, raising her head, and looking him full in the face.

"From what; and how?" repeated Danton, coldly.

"Danton, no hypocrisy with me. I know all." And Miranda coldly narrated all that she knew.

"You are well informed," said Danton, sternly. "Did I perform my duty, I should send you under arrest to the Abbaye."

"Why?"

"For conspiracy with prisoners."

"But you will not."

"I will not. But let us understand one another. What ask you of me?"

"The freedom of my friends, the ex-Duke and Adela."

"Miranda," replied the minister, "it is true I love you. Were I free, I would offer you my hand. I am not; but you can still be my adoration, my love. Miranda, listen to me. I adore you. For you I would do anything. I could be guided by you, led by you. For you I would stem the revolutionary torrent and become worthy of you, as you would wish me to be. But to do this, I must have your love, your affection, your esteem. Could you promise me this?"

"The heart cannot give itself."

"It can, madam, if free. A woman who has no prior attachment can bring herself to love one who does much for her, who devotes himself to her, who lives by and for her."

"But my heart is given."

"Where?" said Danton, with an air of bitter disappoint·ment.

"That is my secret. But I offer you my fortune."

"It is too late, madam," said Danton, roughly.

"Why?" cried Miranda, wildly.

"Because the sacrifice is useless——"

"They are, then, dead?"

"They are free, madam. Last night I gave orders for their being treated with leniency, and sent home to their friends as soon as circumstances allowed."

"Danton!" cried Miranda, grasping his hand and pressing it to her lips, "I thank you. May this act of mercy be counted to you."

"Madam, it was my duty," said the minister, coldly; "and now, madam, I must hint that my time is precious."

"And when shall I see my friends?"

"This evening. Go, wait for them at home."

And the Countess and the massacrer of September parted—the one to await her friends in deep anxiety, the other to hurry on his awful and horrible work of blood.

## CHAPTER XLII.

### THE ABBAYE.

It was about half-past two when Charles Clement and Gracchus Antiboul reached the Pont Neuf; and their attention was at once called by the crowd which blocked up its entrance, composed almost wholly of a band of the ruffians paid by Danton and the Commune for the bloody work of this day. They recognized the massacrers of Avignon, some galley-slaves of noted ferocity and rascality, and some ferocious but sincere *fédérés* from Marseilles, whose hot blood made them do with zeal what the others did for money.

"Something is about to be done to-day, which, in after times, shall be thrown in the teeth of every man who dares speak for liberty and the Republic," said Charles, mournfully.

"But men will separate our party and our ideas from the *saturnalia* of a gang of monsters," replied Gracchus.

"They will not. Mankind is struck by sound and noise. This deed is done under the name of liberty, the enemies of which will give it as a necessary concomitant of liberty, and they will be believed."

"By the credulous and silly, too idle to judge for themselves."

"The credulous and silly are the majority."

"Do we stain all monarchy with the Bartholomew massacre?" asked Gracchus.

"Of course not; but the friends of liberty reason, the mass follow old prejudices. They will excuse any villany in monarchy, an antique form; but they will damn liberty eternally with the disgusting deeds of this day."

"See, where come yon carriages? These men are evidently waiting for them."

Five coaches, each containing six priests, came up at this moment, guarded by loose detachments of volunteers. They were taking them to the massacre of the prisons.

This removal in the open day, on Sunday, was a diabolical trick invented by Marat and Danton. They had posted ruffians along the whole line, whose duty it was to rouse the populace to kill them, that the people might be implicated in the bloody deeds of the day. But it was a vain attempt. The people were not assassins. They fought, they did not murder; and the whole direct guilt of that day rested on Danton, Marat, the Commune, Santerre, Maillard, and the hired band of ruffians, who slaughtered, like butchers for forty sous a-day. The people of Paris remained petrified with horror and astonishment; the Assembly crouched in terror; but they were not implicated in the guilt. The 2nd of September is the crime of a knot of brigands.

The escort of the priests was itself of the band, and excited the people by invective and sneers. They pointed to the priests; called them agents of the foreigners, of the Prussians, and poured on them every invective which foulness could suggest.

"*A bas* the priests," cried the mob, which was not in the secret; but this was the whole amount of their attack.

The escort looked at each other with anxiety. The plan did not seem to take.

Charles and Gracchus followed behind the guard.

At the Correfour Bassy, the crowd became so great as to block up the way, and the carriages stopped a moment.

A man at once rushed from among the hired gang, passed through the escort, which did not seek to prevent him, leaped on the step, and thrust his sword wildly into the carriage. It went through the body of a priest, who gave a cry of anguish. The assassin thrust him through again, and then held up his sword, reeking with blood, to the people. The people replied by yells of horror.

"*A bas l'assassin!*"

"Coward!"

"Scoundrel!"

"Away with these royalists," said the escort, driving the mob before them, amongst which were Charles and Gracchus. The mob, unarmed, yielded.

The assassin continued to strike, now into one carriage, now into another; and presently the assassins of Avignon, who formed the escort, their blood warmed at the sight of the streaming gore, thrust their bayonets in likewise. The scene was awful beyond conception. The yelling priests, the blood staining the street, the ferocious assassins striking, the terrified people flying in all directions, made it seem a city taken by storm.

"My God! if these be the ruffians we have to deal with," said Charles, "we shall never save them."

"Courage! courage!" replied Gracchus, who had less hope than Charles himself.

They had reached the Rue de l'Echande, where they met the captain of their section, who at once placed them as sentries under the windows of the Abbaye, and close to the entrance.

Eight dead bodies of priests were taken from the carriages, the rest sprang out; four were murdered on the threshold, some entered, two or three sprang in through a window to where a committee of the section was sitting, where they found a momentary refuge.

* * * * * *

Meanwhile, Adela and the Duke had remained all these days enclosed in a cell, furnished with some regard to comfort. Their apartment was divided into two rooms; and, except their utter isolation from without, their position was not wholly wretched. They had books and the *Moniteur*, and pens, ink, and paper. Adela showed a resignation above her age, but which is a great attribute of her sex, often greater in hours of suffering and danger. She talked to her poor old father, she cheered him, she gave him hope, she read to him; and only when he slept did she think of herself. Then she wrote, now to Charles, now to Miranda, letters which reached them only at a time when these letters were scorching irons that burned to the very hearts of both receivers.

On the morning of the 2nd, Adela had, as usual, joined her father in simple and earnest worship, never before so deep, so sublime, so devoted. She knew nothing of her danger, but she had prayed even more fervently than ever on that Sabbath Morn.

Until half-past three, the father and daughter had sat talking of the absent, when suddenly the shrieks of the priests, the yells of the ruffians around them, and a general movement in the prison, attracted their attention.

"My God!" cried the now feeble old man, "what is this?"

"Holy Virgin, I know not!" and Adela rushed to a window which overlooked the outer court. The scene which lay before chilled her very soul to stone; and until a strange voice disturbed her, she looked on in silence, almost without seeing.

A large table was placed near the last wicket of the outer court, on which lay papers, pens, ink, the registers of the prison, bottles, glasses, pistols, swords, pipes, and tobacco.

Round the table sat twelve men, chiefly of athletic proportions, in the centre of whom was one who wore a grey coat, a sabre, who had a pen in his hand, and whose features seemed carved out of marble. This was Maillard, a bailiff once, an executioner now.

The judges wore woollen caps, vests, coarse shoes, and butchers' aprons. Some had tucked up their sleeves, but others kept their arms covered. These were superior agents, sent to push on the bloody work, and guide Maillard in his work of selection.

At the moment when Adela looked out, the court was surrounded by the gang which had escorted the priests, armed with sabres, knives, and pikes.

"Silence!" thundered Maillard, looking at the register, "and bring out the Swiss."

The gang howled with eager rage, while two or three infuriated enthusiasts cried "*Vive la Nation!*"

The Swiss, a hundred and fifty in number, were brought out. They were the officers and soldiers saved on the 10th August. They entered the court in trembling horror.

"You assassinated the people on the 10th August. This

people demand vengeance. You are to be removed to the Force."

"Mercy!" cried the Swiss, falling nearly all upon their knees, and satisfied that they were about to be murdered; "mercy!"

"It is idle to ask for mercy," said Maillard grinning. "You are going to *La Force;* thence you will go for trial. If innocent, you will be acquitted."

"Death to the Swiss!" cried the mob outside.

"Mercy! mercy! we know we are about to be murdered!"

"*A la Force!*" said Maillard, waving his hand.

A door was opened by a butcher.

"Come! come! are you going?" said he; "the people are impatient."

But the Swiss huddled up together with shrieks and yells of despair. Hired mercenaries, they lost all self-possession when without arms.

"Are you all cowards?" said one of the judges; "will not one go?"

"I will!" said a young and handsome officer, waving his hand to his comrades; and he plunged headlong through the open door upon a hundred bayonets. This was a signal for a general slaughter; and in a quarter of an hour two awful heaps of dead bodies, one on each side of the court, were all that remained of the Swiss.

The scene grew more awful. The king's guards, the officers of the *gendarmerie* followed the Swiss, and then the assassins paused to drink and smoke, while the carts of the Commune removed the dead bodies. During the process, women and children danced the Carmagnole.

"Water could no longer wash away the blood," says the great narrator of this scene, "in which the foot slipped; and the assassins, previous to resuming their bloody work, spread straw thickly over the court, on which they laid the clothes of their victims. They then resolved to kill on this litter, in order that the blood might be absorbed by it before it reached the stones."

They drank again, and lay down to sleep, as did the judges, after a supper in the lodge.

Adela lay down also, and exhausted nature fortunately let her sleep.

At dawn of day, she was summoned, with her father, to appear before their judges.

---

## CHAPTER XLIII.

### THE PRINCESS DE LAMBALLE.

WHEN the Duke de Ravilliere and the Lady Adela stood before their judges in the court of the Abbaye, the scene, though still fearful in the extreme, had somewhat changed. No dead bodies were visible. The court, it is true, was saturated with blood, but this was in part concealed by the litter of straw which lay upon the ground. Maillard sat rigid at his table. The Duke and Adela gazed with wondering horror at him and the rest of the judges.

Adela quivered with alarm, and then with surprise, for she had recognized Paul Ledru among the twelve judges who surrounded Maillard.

There was a sentry at the entrance of the outer court, while only some two dozen of the assassins surrounded the prisoners.

Adela and the Duke were not alone.

A beautiful and lovely woman stood beside them.

The Princess de Lamballe, ex-Savoy-Carignan, was the widow of the youthful son of the Duke de Penthievre. She belonged to a royal house; and her extreme beauty, amiability, and mental charms had created in Maria Antoinette a passionate attachment for her. This circumstance caused her confinement in prison at the period of the September massacres. The popular hatred of the Austrian Queen, *l'Autrichienne*, made them equally hate all around her. Louis XVI. would have been far less loathed had he had a French princess for his wife; and the Princess de Lamballe would probably never have seen the inside of a French prison but for her devotion to the ill-advised but unfortunate Queen.

She had at first followed Marie Antoinette to the Temple; but the Commune of Paris allowed none but the royal family to remain in this locale. The Princess de Lamballe was speedily transferred to another prison.

When the September massacres were bruited abroad, the old Duke de Penthievre became alarmed. The old man loved his daughter-in-law, the widow of his dead son, as if she had been his only child. Living in retirement at the Château de Bizy, in Normandy, he watched over her from afar. A secret agent was despatched to Paris, with 300,000 francs to purchase the safety of the princess. This money, well spent, had had its effect. In the Commune, amongst the judges, and amongst the executioners, the Princess de Lamballe had friends.

As Adela and the Duke came down, the princess arrived from another door. A single *femme-de-chambre* accompanied her.

"I am to be murdered," she whispered, and fainted in the arms of her servant.

The assassins murmured; but Hebert and Lhuilier, who stood by, and who were in her interest, interposed, and held them back.

The princess soon recovered to clasp Adela to her breast, and then to answer the questions of the judges.

It was now broad day. A bright autumn sun was streaming through a cloudless sky over the old roof of the ex-convent. Nature seemed sleeping in calm repose, looking in upon that blood-stained speck upon the earth. Hideous indeed was the scene. The judges, bloated with drink and excitement, were, however, calm beside the assassins. These men, their naked arms and feet saturated with human blood, stood glaring with eager impatience at every new victim. A yell of delight greeted all condemnations; a yell of fury met acquittals.

But these very men washed their feet and hands to lead home prisoners whom Maillard had declared innocent, and the judge seemed to take a wild delight in absolving all those against whose name no black mark was appended. It was a fearful struggle between a feeling of justice and a horrible thirst for human blood.

"Your name?" said Maillard, sternly.

"De Lamballe, ex-Savoy-Carignan."

"Thy age?"

" Twenty-five."

A few other indifferent questions were put and answered readily. Adela, who expected the same ordeal, studied carefully the questions, in order to reply.

" Thy answers to my questions are satisfactory," said Maillard. " Swear the love of equality and liberty, and hatred of kings and queens."

" I will willingly swear the first," replied the princess, " but as to hatred of the king and queen, I cannot swear— it is not in my heart."

" Swear everything," said Paul Ledru, leaning towards her, " or thou art lost; we cannot save thee if the people become angry."

The Princess de Lamballe, a little alarmed, did not seem to understand, and remained silent.

Adela touched her gently.

" Say anything," said she, " what matter, so we escape from here ? "

" What am I to answer ? " asked the Princess.

" Thy answers have satisfied us. Thou hast doubtless been a victim, not an accomplice, of the Austrian woman. Go out; and when thou art in the street, cry *Vive la Nation*."

" May I wait for my friends ? "

" If thou wilt ; but perhaps they are not so innocent as thou," said Maillard, rather uneasy at saving three victims, one after another.

" I am sure Adela is as innocent as a babe," replied the princess.

" We shall see," said Maillard, sternly,

" Thy name ? " asked another judge.

" What ? " replied the old man, whose mind was wandering.

" Thy name ? " thundered a judge.

" What does that *monsieur* say ? " said the Duke mechanically.

" I am not a *monsieur*, but a *citoyen*," replied the judge, fiercely.

" The old fool is mad," said Paul Ledru, stoically, " let us question the daughter."

" Luckily for him, he appears to be so," observed the

judge, whose indignation had been roused at being called *monsieur.*

" Thy name, *citoyenne ?* " said Maillard.

" Adela Ravilliere," replied the young girl firmly.

The judges smiled at the way in which she dropped the *de,* and thus plebeianised her name.

" Not de ? " observed Maillard.

" I want no distinction from my fellow-citizens," said Adela, who, though she had never joined in the political discussions of Miranda and Charles, now remembered their lessons in the time of need.

A murmur of applause showed her how rightly she had judged.

" But thou art an aristocrat," said a judge.

" I am not," replied Adela firmly, " I am a *citoyenne.*"

" But," put in Paul Ledru, " what proof have you ? "

" The name of my affianced husband, and his bosom friend."

" Ah ! ah ! the *citoyenne* seeks to do her duty to the Republic," observed a judge.

" What is the name of *thy man ?* " said Maillard.

" Charles Clement, the friend of Robespierre."

" *Vive la nation ! Vive Robespierre !* " cried the crowd.

" And the name of his friend ? "

" Gracchus Antiboul, one of the conspirators of Charenton," said Adela, looking at Maillard.

" Thy proofs of civism are good," said the judge ; " but what part didst thou play in the Tuileries, on the 10th August ? "

" We remained there because Charles Clement told us to do so."

" Thou wert not, then, afraid of the people ? "

" Why should I ? " said Adela, naïvely, " Charles Clement had taught me to love them and pity them."

" Thou art an excellent *citoyenne,*" cried Maillard, " and thou art free to go with thy father where thou pleasest."

" But the father is an old aristocrat," murmured the crowd.

" Citizens," cried Adela, with a sublime effort, her nerves still strong, her heart still calm, " my father is a child. Give him to his only child."

"Go! go!" answered the assassins.

"But," said one—it was Fournier, the American, the ex-coachman of the Duke—stooping down, glass in hand, and raising it filled with human blood, "drink to the annihilation of all aristocracy, in this."

The Princess de Lamballe raised her hand, as if to strike down the glass.

"Hand it to her, or you are dead," whispered Truchon, the man who had engaged to save her.

The princess handed the disgusting portion to the young girl.

She looked to the heavens — at her father — and she thought of Charles.

"Drink," said Fournier, doggedly.

"To the annihilation of aristocracy," cried Adela; and she raised the glass to her lips.

When she took it away, it was empty.

This horribly sublime act of devotion had saved her father.

"*Vive Adela! Vive la nation!*" cried the assassins; and they were permitted to depart.

The Princess de Lamballe could scarcely walk: Truchon, *alias Grand Nicolas,* and another man, supported her.

The whole party then moved towards the outer court. On reaching this, the Princess de Lamballe, who was first, caught sight of the dead bodies.

"My God! how horrible," cried she, recoiling.

"Silence," said Nicholas, putting his hand upon her mouth.

Adela held her father by the hand, and looked neither to the right nor to the left.

The street was reached. In the distance were two coaches waiting; one for her, one for the Princess de Lamballe.

Outside the gate of the Abbaye was a crowd of the assassins reposing an instant from their work. They were armed with pikes, swords, and knives; and as the three respited victims passed, they murmured.

"The people are betrayed," said one.

"They are good citizens," said Nicholas.

They passed on.

"*Vive la nation!*" said a drunken hair-dresser, named Charlot, coming out of a wine-shop.

The Princess de Lamballe was close to him.

"*Tien?*" cried the intoxicated brute; "a pretty aristocrat, and a pretty cap she wears."

And with his pike he, by way of brutal and drunken bravado, tried to strike off the cap she wore.

The pike, ill-directed, struck the beautiful princess on the forehead, and blood spurted forth from but a small wound.

The assassins of the gate rushed forward, as if this had been a signal.

"Off! off!" cried Nicolas, at the peril of his life; "the *citoyenne* has been declared innocent."

"She is a friend of the Austrian woman's," said one Grizon, who—brutal and infamous wretch—felled her to the ground with a log of wood.

"*A bas l' Autrichienne,*" said the drunken Charlot, seizing the stunned princess by the hair.

In an instant she was dead, an axe severing her head from her body; and one of the awful crimes of history was consummated.

Adela, who held her father's hand, stood petrified with horror. Her very eyes seemed starting from her head. Her brain whirled. She could not see.

Charlot had the head of the wretched princess in his hand. He held it up to the face of her unfortunate friend.

Adela gave a wild shriek, and fell senseless in the arms of Charles Clement, who had seen her afar off, and who, with Gracchus Antiboul, had left his post, just in time to save Adela from the fury of the assassins of Madame de Lamballe.

"Bear her to the carriage," whispered Truchon, who was now joined by Paul Ledru and Duchesne.

Charles raised the insensible girl in his arms.

Gracchus took the hand of the Duke.

Truchon, Paul Ledru, and Duchesne, armed to the teeth, brought up the rear.

"Stop the aristocrat," bellowed Charlot.

"Hold thy tongue, *mouchard,*" responded Truchon, felling him like an ox to the ground.

At this moment, the *fiacre* was reached. The Duke was assisted in, Charles bore Adela on his knees, and Ledru, Truchon, and Duchesne, following on foot, with Gracchus on the roof, they drove to the residence of the Countess Miranda.

They went slowly; and scarcely had they entered the court, when a horrid procession passed.

Charlot, Rodi, Grizon, Hamin, four infamous names, "eternally pilloried in history," as Lamartine says, after placing the head of the princess on a tavern table, while they drank, had now stuck it on a pike.

The procession was on its way to the prison of the Temple, to show the head to Marie Antoinette.

Charles Clement ordered the coach door to be closed; and, leaving Ledru to attend to their other friends, bore Adela to the room where Miranda waited for them in an agony of suspense.

"Saved!" cried Charles, wildly, as he deposited his lovely burden on a sofa.

"Welcome, Duke," said Miranda, as she helped the old man to an arm-chair.

The Duke made no reply. This time, his reason was irrevocably gone.

Adela was in a raging fever.

"A doctor," said Charles, bending over her with frenzied mien.

"I will go," replied Gracchus.

"Be quick, my friend," cried Miranda.

When the doctor came, Adela was ill of a brain fever. He ordered her to be put to bed, gave prescriptions, and, after leaving numerous directions as to their conduct, went away.

As he retired from the room, Miranda caught his eye.

There was so much of earnest imploring in her mien, that the doctor involuntarily shook his head and shrugged his shoulders.

"Poor Charles," muttered Miranda, as she sank insensible in her chair.

# CHAPTER XLIV

### ADELA.

By night the position of the fugitives from the massacre of the prisons—still continuing with even more hideous details than those which we have given—had become painful in the extreme. The Duke and Adela lay in contiguous rooms. The old man was insensible in his bed. Adela was under the influence of the awful fever which had been brought on her, more, it is probable, by the sight of the death of the Princess de Lamballe than from any of the scenes through which she had passed so heroically.

Miranda sat by the bedside of the lovely sufferer, having herself not long been able to support herself after the severe shock she had received. Her eyes were fixed mechanically on the bed ; but, though she looked, she saw not.

Charles Clement stood upright by the fire-place. His brow was stern, while his haggard face showed marks of the intense suffering he had now endured for days. He looked sometimes at the bed, but oftener his thoughts gained the upper hand.

He was thinking of the Revolution. He was calling to mind all that it had made him suffer.

"You hate the Revolution," said Gracchus Antiboul, gently; "I don't wonder at it. You have cause."

"No," replied Charles, in a low whisper ; "I am not so blind. The Revolution was necessary ; but I hate the men whom the depravity of our manners and the ignorance of our population have allowed to gain the upper hand."

"And I," said Gracchus ; "these men are our greatest enemies. But do not look so desponding—so hopeless. Adela has a good constitution. She will suffer severely; but a week will see her your wife at last."

"Hush !" said Charles Clement ; "talk not of her being my wife. Let Heaven spare her life—that is all I ask."

"Did you speak, Charles ?" asked Miranda.

"To Gracchus," replied Clement, moving over to her.

"She sleeps," whispered the Countess ; "see, she is still."

"But she is too still," said Charles, trembling.

"Hear you not her soft breathing, like that of a child?"

Charles Clement bent hurriedly over her, and the faint heaving of her pure bosom was at once visible.

"She is less feverish."

"The illness is gone," said Miranda, hopefully.

"Thank our God."

"Speak not so loud, my friend," continued Miranda, gently. "Let her sleep, it is all she wants."

At this moment the physician entered.

"Welcome! welcome!" cried all, advancing to meet the old man who had always been in the habit of attending Miranda.

"Well, how go our patients?" said he.

"Better," answered Miranda; "at least, it appears so to us."

"Yes! yes!" muttered M. de Semonville, after examining the Lady Adela with a scrutinizing glance; "much better. The fever is reduced. When she wakes she will be sensible. We must be careful, and there is great hope."

"Merciful God, I thank thee!" cried Miranda.

Charles Clement pressed her hand convulsively; his heart was too full to say a word.

"Now for the Duke."

"Ten minutes since, he slept composedly," replied Miranda, moving with the doctor to the Duke's room.

The apartment was one of state. The vast and magnificent bed, in a rich alcove, was surrounded by heavy curtains, that threw a deep shadow within. A lamp burned in the centre of the room.

The Duke lay with his head on a pillow, his face turned towards the party as they entered.

His eyes were open; and, as they met those of Miranda, he gave one long, inquiring look, and seemed to try to speak, but failed.

He then closed his eyes.

"Well, my lord Duke," said the physician, who had seen this mute and solemn appeal, and knew it to apply to his daughter, "the Lady Adela is doing better; I hope you are?"

A slight trembling of the closed eyes was the only reply.

"Let me feel your pulse," said the doctor.

The Duke made no reply, either in words or by motion.

"I am sorry to disturb you," continued the physician; "but I must try your pulse." He passed his hand beneath the bedclothes, and found the Duke's hand.

"My God!" cried the doctor, letting fall the hand.

"What?" said Charles.

"The Duke is dead."

"No! no!" half screamed Miranda; "he looked at me this instant."

It was the last effort of nature. Sense and consciousness returned for an instant, and he died without a pang.

The Duke was indeed dead. The painful scenes which were soon to follow were spared him.

The grief of the whole party was immoderate. Charles and Miranda threw themselves on the bed, to embrace the lifeless form.

"And he died alone!" sobbed Miranda.

"Come! come! my dear Lady Miranda," said the doctor, "recollect our poor patient in the next room."

And, assisted by Gracchus and Charles, the physician removed the Countess Miranda to the bedside of her young friend.

The Duke's body was then left alone with the servants, whom M. de Semonville had at once summoned.

At this instant, a knock was heard at the door, and a man entered hurriedly. It was Maximilien Robespierre.

"Citoyen Robespierre!" cried Gracchus.

"My friends," said the deputy, in a low voice—his haggard form trembling with emotion—"do you know what is going on?"

"There is one dying victim—in the next room is one dead," replied Gracchus, in a low voice.

"But cannot this infernal massacre be stopped? Danton! Danton!"

"It is too late. The Commune has it all its own way. The National Assembly is terrified; the people are lost between horror and fear. What are we to do?"

"Three hundred resolute men would stop it all," cried Robespierre.

"But these men, where are you to find them?" replied Gracchus Antiboul.

"I thought you and Charles Clement might have roused two or three thousand."

"Not now. Again, I say, it is too late."

"Then we must stand by, and be called accomplices of this fearful crime," said Robespierre, recovering his calmness.

"Charles Clement will not quit, I fear, his dying bride. I am useless without him."

"Pardon me for intruding at such a time; but I could not help it. I have not shut my eyes the whole night. *Salut.*"

And Robespierre went out.

Charles had remained by the bedside, attending to Miranda.

"Charles—Miranda," said a faint voice.

The weeping friends sprang to the bedside.

Adela was awake. Her face was lividly pale; but there was a smile of joy on her lips. She was surrounded by her friends.

"Weep not," whispered she; "I am better. I have had a fearful dream. It is past. Let us never speak of it. How is my father?"

"He is in the next room. We placed him on the bed," replied Miranda, veiling her face in a fond embrace.

"Beloved girl," said Charles Clement, in a tone of supreme anguish, "you must, you shall recover."

"But you must not tease her with questions," said the doctor, gravely. "The Lady Adela is better, but very weak. I will send her a potion to procure further sleep; and then to-morrow we may allow you to talk."

The doctor then, after some few observations, went out.

The four attached friends remained alone.

Adela cast a long, fond glance at her affianced husband, who, pale as a marble statue, with watching, with want of sleep, and with anguish, stood by the bedside.

"Go rest you, my love," said she: "you will be ill next. Miranda—Gracchus, I pray you force him to go."

"Never, child," cried Charles Clement; "until you are out of danger, there can be no rest for me."

"But, if you will lie down an hour or two with Gracchus,"

said Adela, " I can rest also; and then we can talk more freshly. In the morning I shall be better still."

There was something so imploring, so beseeching, so humbly impressive in the look and in the tone, that Charles Clement pressed her hand to his lips, and left the room with Gracchus Antiboul.

Miranda and Adela were alone.

The room was vast, and lighted up by two swinging lamps. The alcove was sombre : and the contrast between the two women was marked, in the dull light of their position.

Adela, thin, pallid, with a slight hectic flush upon her cheek, was angelic in her beauty. Her eyes were radiant with love. Purity and holiness sat upon her lips, upon her whole mien ; and, as she closed her eyes a moment to reflect, she looked a sleeping seraph, whom some other angel was watching.

Miranda, in the full richness of womanly form, resplendent with health, though pale from fatigue and anxiety, formed a marked contrast with the young girl, over whom she watched with an anxiety deeper than even that felt by Charles Clement. There was a sombre expression in her eyes, a wildness in her look, a nervous twitching in the muscles of her face, which showed how intense was her emotion.

The death of the Duke, whom Miranda loved as a father, had stunned her very mind, which was slowly recovering its equilibrium after the shock.

When the door was closed, and five minutes had elapsed, Adela broke the dead silence which had hitherto prevailed.

" Listen," said she, softly ; " come hither."

Miranda pressed close unto her.

" What is it, child ?" asked the Countess.

" I must talk with thee."

" But fatigue —"

" Miranda, do not deceive yourself," said Adela, with angelic sweetness ; " waste not the precious minutes. I am dying."

Miranda started back, looked wildly at her friend ; and one cry told her anguish—her inexpressible anguish—and her sublime devotion and love for the affianced husband of Adela.

"And Charles! oh, my God! what will Charles do?" and, in perfect agony of spirit, she clasped her hands together.

Adela looked at her gently, but with a slightly-scrutinizing look, and then spoke.

"It is better than I wished," said she. "Miranda, sister, calm yourself, and listen. I feel that I am dying—that a few hours only are left me. The shock of the prison was too much for me. I know that my father is dead: you cannot hide anything from me; but I grieve not, for I shall join him in a few hours. It is for the living that I feel. Miranda, you know all. My existence has been, until lately, a happy one indeed. I loved, and was beloved; and never man merited better the affections of woman than Charles Clement. I am dying. He must resign himself to lose me. This is my pang—that my death will wound this heart so dear unto me. Miranda! oh, Miranda! calm my dying hours by one promise, and I shall die calmly, happily, and go unto the bosom of my God with humility, and hope, and joy."

"Adela, child, I am thy sister, thy slave; thy will is law," said Miranda, choking with sobs.

"You love Charles Clement, Miranda; you have always done so. I see it all now. Your noble devotion to him and me—your sacrifice of self to make us happy—you, who could have permitted my marriage with my cousin—all is now clear to me. I love you more than ever, sister; and this knowledge gives me sweet and earnest hope."

"Hope!" said Miranda wildly; "there is no hope, if you die."

"Miranda, you will replace me. Charles will learn to love you. You must make him love you. His heart will be full to bursting when I am gone; he will be ill, he will suffer much, and he will never forget. But time will calm his grief, will blunt the acuteness of his sorrow; and thou be his comforter, his angel, his wife."

Miranda sobbed aloud; her anguish was choking her.

"Speak, dearest—speak, love," said Adela.

"It is more than I can promise —"

"Miranda," said Adela, almost rising in the bed by a strong effort, and bending a deep and anxious glance on the Countess, "do you wish him to wed some one else?"

"No," replied Miranda, speaking from sudden influence.

"That is enough," said Adela, allowing herself to be again placed upon her pillow. "Charles would perhaps never think of another; but grief might make him feel lonely, and he might marry, simply to chase away sorrow, and not to be alone with memory. But none will cherish and love him as you will."

Miranda made no reply, but buried her face in the bosom of her dying friend, and sobbed herself to sleep.

At dawn the weeping and the dying were both in deep slumber, and the chamber of death had all the silence of a tomb.

---

## CHAPTER XLV

### MISERIMUS.

It was about eight o'clock when Charles and Gracchus returned to the sick room. So great had been the fatigues of the few previous days, that sleep had overpowered them. They found Miranda preparing a potion, while Adela, refreshed by some hours of quiet, seemed a shade better.

"I was talking of you, Charles," said Adela, as the young man entered, with anxious look.

"While I was sleeping in stupid forgetfulness," replied Charles Clement, bitterly.

"Hush!" answered Adela; "talk not thus. Had you not rested, you had been ill, like me; and now you are ready to talk with me."

"But not if it fatigue you," said Charles, taking the place which Miranda made for him at the bedside.

"It fatigues me not," replied Adela; "besides, I want to talk to you very much."

Charles took her hand in his, kissed it fervently, and prepared himself to listen. Miranda, at the same moment, drew Gracchus on one side; and, after a word, they left the room, and closed the door behind them.

"Gracchus," said Miranda, no longer hiding her bitter and heartfelt anguish, "advise me, guide me. I shall go mad. She is about to bid *him* an eternal farewell, and he knows not she is dying."

"She is dying!" exclaimed Gracchus, with a convulsive tremor.

"She is—beloved angel! Oh, she is right! God is taking her to him. She is too pure for this earth. Too pure—too good! The dreadful scenes of the prisons have killed her."

"My God!" cried Gracchus Antiboul, greatly shocked, "Charles Clement will die with grief. I shall go distracted."

"It is of him I wish to speak. You, Gracchus, are his friend, his brother, his confidant—the master of his thoughts. Let us devise how, when the first burst of anguish is over, his mind may be so occupied, that not a still moment may be given him."

"There is but one course open : to plunge him headlong into the Revolution, to occupy him night and day in clubs, in demonstrations, in the Assembly—in all the scenes of the drama which is about to be enacted in all the public places of Paris."

"You will then assist me," said Miranda, thankfully.

"With my heart and with my soul," replied Gracchus. "He is my all in all—more than wife, more than all the world—my friend, my brother."

"But he will suffer horribly. Our task will be painful and difficult. I look at it with fear and trembling."

"Miranda!" cried a shrill, piercing voice, full of a world of anguish.

"That is Charles," said Miranda, shuddering and looking fearfully at Gracchus Antiboul, "he calls me."

"She has told him," whispered Antiboul, turning pale.

"We must go in," added Miranda, leaning tremblingly on his arm.

We must, however, before we accompany them, explain the cry of Charles Clement.

When they were alone, Charles, who was full of hope and joy, who saw in a speedy recovery the reward of all his sufferings, took the hand of Adela, and pressed it to his lips.

"You love me very much," said the sick girl, with a smile.

"I cannot answer that question. It would be wrong to say how much I love you."

"But why do you love me?" continued the gentle girl, looking thankfully and gratefully into his sparkling eyes.

"Because you are good, gentle, and beautiful; and because my heart could not resist your fascinations."

"But with what view do you love me?" insisted Adela.

"With the hope of calling you my wife, and of devoting my life to making you happy."

"But, then, these feelings last not, dear Charles."

"Not in their first intensity; but where affection, passion, and respect are combined, they last for ever."

"Your chief wish, then, is to see me happy?" asked Adela.

"My chief object of existence."

"And if you have me happy, you would be happy?"

"Undoubtedly, beloved."

"But if I were happy in another world, in the bosom of my God?" said Adela, with some little of terror, as she watched the features of Charles.

"But I am selfish," replied Charles Clement, with a smile. "I wish to share and see your happiness; to call you by the dear name of wife."

Adela shook her head. It was clear the security and hope of Charles Clement was complete.

"Beloved husband!" said Adela, drawing him near unto her; "come near me: kiss not my hand, but my lips. Call me your wife once."

Charles, somewhat astonished, pressed her lips passionately to his, and remained in a tremor and ecstacy of delight for some minutes.

"Charles," continued Adela, first interrupting the silence, "you have called me your wife. I am your wife. Are you not satisfied?"

"I am happy, not satisfied. I wish to continue the dear delight of calling you my wife."

"Oh, Charles!" said Adela, with a supreme effort, "must I open your eyes, must I tell you that you will be a widower in a few hours!"

Charles started back, looked wildly at her, and stood to his feet.

The heavenly, and sad, and mournful smile of Adela smote to his heart.

"Reproach me not," said she, involuntarily; "I cannot help it."

She seemed to think, in her grief, that he might reproach her with dying.

"Miranda!" cried Charles, faintly, in a tone of bitter anguish.

The Countess and the Republican entered.

"Miranda!" repeated he, wildly, "is this true? Is she dying?"

"Pardon me, Charles, for hiding it!" said Miranda, falling passionately on her knees. "I dared not tell you."

Charles sat down without saying a word, leaving Gracchus to raise the prostrate Countess.

"Charles," said Adela, gently, "what is the matter?"

He made no reply. He neither heard nor saw.

"Charles!" repeated Adela; "Charles, my beloved! my husband! my adored! speak to me!"

A copious flood of tears, and a spasmodic sobbing, here seized the young man.

"He will speak in a moment, dearest," said Miranda, taking his hand.

"I am better," murmured Charles; "but oh, my God! my God! can this be true? Adela! Adela! are you leaving us?"

"I must!" she cried in bitter anguish of soul, as she saw his bitter grief; "a wise and inscrutable Providence calls me. Let us not murmur."

Charles Clement took her hand once more; and, the pallor of death upon his face, tried to speak in a less heart-broken tone.

The four conversed some little time. They spoke of the past, of their futile dreams of happiness, of their once bright hopes, and of the fearful Revolution which had crossed their path.

"But," said Adela, faintly, "when I am gone, Charles, let not your private feelings change your public ones. You have hitherto followed the path of duty. You belong not to the monsters of the Revolution; you are one of its noble apostles. Continue; serve your fellow-creatures when you can, and let not the memory of Adela ever restrain a noble or patriotic aspiration."

"Noble child!" murmured Charles.

"But I will rest awhile," said Adela, "or else I shall be able to talk no more."

And she turned away and slept.

Several hours passed, and the evening drew in, before the lovely girl again awoke.

"Charles," said she, "I have been in Paradise with you. But I cannot see you now. Charles—Miranda, where are you?"

"Here," cried both, in a tone of inexpressible anguish.

"Take each a hand—let me feel you. Oh, my brother— oh, my sister, I am going. Pray for me."

And Miranda and Charles Clement burst into a passionate prayer.

"I see pikes and swords—men waving bloody banners— I hear shrieks. But I feel your hands. Beloved Charles, beloved Miranda, adieu, adieu; my voice is going. Hold my hand until I die."

She spoke no more. Her eyes closed. Her hands pressing those of her attached friends, and, every now and then, giving a gentle pressure, she lay for half an hour. But her breathing grew quicker, then fainter; and, suddenly, her hands were convulsively shaken. By a sudden effort, she clasped them together, and placed the hands of the two—of Miranda and Charles—one within the other.

Next minute she was dead.

Gracchus threw a veil over her face, and drew Charles and Miranda, who stood hand in hand, like statues, away from the inanimate clay, whose pure spirit had flown to those regions of everlasting felicity which God has, doubtless, prepared for the good.

"Miranda!"

"Charles!"

And the anguished pair clasped each other in a wild embrace, and wept convulsively on each other's bosoms. Suddenly Charles started away, as if for the first time conscious that he was pressing a woman to his breast, and went back to the bedside. The Countess threw herself on a sofa. It was only sleep, after some hours of wild sorrow, that enabled Gracchus to have them removed.

The next day Charles rose without speaking, dressed himself, and went to place himself beside the two biers which contained the mortal remains of the Duke and his child. The calm of the young man was fearful. It was useless to speak to him, he answered not a word.

Miranda rose to attend the funeral, which took place next day, in a quiet and unassuming manner.

They then returned to the house. Charles shut himself in a room, which Miranda had set apart for him. Miranda did the same; and Gracchus Antiboul went home, to find, in the society of his wife, some relief from the oppressing emotions of the last few days.

My tragic narrative draws to an end.

---

## CHAPTER XLVI.

### THE REPUBLIC.

CHARLES CLEMENT, during the time which intervened, between the death of Adela and the meeting of the Convention of the 21st September, had remained wholly secluded from the world, and even from his friends. He had shut himself up in his room, and abandoned himself to that unavailing and bitter grief which wears the body and mind, reducing the one to emaciation, the other to incapacity. All efforts to wean him, even from solitude, had proved unavailing. Both Miranda and Gracchus Antiboul had tried every means which friendship and affection could suggest to induce him to join them in the *salon*, in the hope that conversation might, in some measure, draw him from the contemplation of his bitter grief. But in vain. All efforts had been useless. He scarcely deigned an answer, but sat, his eyes fixed on vacancy, or moving about the room with all the fury of a madman.

Miranda had ceased her parties. The death of Adela was a sufficient excuse, but she was too heart-broken to have held them if it had been ever so necessary.

Danton was no longer minister. The jealousy of others, his own weariness, and the fact that his wife was dying, had removed him from office. This stern and terrible tribune wept by the bedside of the dying mother of his two children, whom, despite all his debaucheries, he respected and loved.

The Convention had been elected. The Girondins were powerful in numbers—the Mountain, in energy and talent.

The Girondins, friends of an aristocratic republic, as oppressive and exclusive as the worst monarchy, were anxious that this new form of government should not be proclaimed until they were sure of the executive power, and could mould it at their will and pleasure.

The Mountain, as Lamartine expresses it, wanting "that Christian and fraternal democracy of which Robespierre was the apostle," desired the immediate proclamation of the republic, relying on their own energy to mould it afterwards at their will.

The brilliant affair of Valmy, where Kellermann, Dumouriez, and Louis-Philippe, forty years after King of France, distinguished themselves, had rendered the fear of the coalition less lively.

Paris belonged to the Mountain, to the party of Robespierre ; it had sent to the Convention, Robespierre, Marat, Danton, St. Just, and others, prepared to go any lengths.

Such was the position of affairs.

Gracchus Antiboul, who had completely identified himself with the extreme Republican party, had, on the previous night, dined in the Palais-Royal with St. Just, Sergent, Panis, Billaud-Varennes, Collot D'Herbois, and others, when the duties of the next day were discussed.

Gracchus Antiboul was one of the members for Paris ; and his deep regret was, that the utter seclusion of Charles Clement had prevented his also being a member of the great Convention.

After dinner, the word Republic was discussed. St. Just urged that it should be thrown in the teeth of the Girondins, the *reaction* of the present day.

"If they accept it," said St. Just, "they are lost, for it was imposed by our party; if they reject it, they are doubly lost; for, by opposing the will of the people, they will be crushed by the unpopularity we have heaped upon them."

The whole party agreed; and Gracchus had reported the news to Charles Clement, on his calling at the house of Miranda, on his way home.

Charles Clement seemed to rouse himself slightly at this piece of intelligence.

" And now, my friend," cried Miranda, seizing the opportunity, " do not remain here any longer. Come out of this room a little. You are killing yourself. Dine with me, at all events, to-morrow."

And Charles Clement bowed assent.

Rejoiced at this unexpected victory, the two friends left him immediately.

Next day, Miranda took much trouble in preparing the dinner. Everything which could tempt the appetite of an invalid was provided, with good wines, in the hope that he might thus, in a slight degree, be revived from his lethargy.

Miranda received Charles Clement at the dinner hour alone, Gracchus being at the Convention, while Paul Ledru and his wife, with the wife of Antiboul, were in the Rue Dominique.

Clement, out of respect to Miranda, had taken some slight trouble with his *toilette*.

Miranda was pleased at this. It showed that his mind was not so utterly prostrate with grief as she had feared. For herself, her deep affection for Adela had caused her grief enough; but her attention to Charles Clement had fortunately occupied her mind. The image of the dead was, in part, chased away by that of the living.

" I am glad, indeed, to see you, Charles," said Miranda, gently, as she offered him a chair opposite her at the table.

Charles took her hand, and kissed it, but said nothing. A glance round the room had raised memories which filled his eyes, and raised a choking sensation at his heart.

" Where is Gracchus? " inquired he, after a short pause.

" At the Convention. It met at twelve o'clock, and its adjournment will probably be very late."

" Oh," said Charles, sinking into silence.

Miranda saw at once how difficult was her self-imposed task, but she shrank not from it. She assailed Clement with questions which he was compelled to answer; she made him, despite himself, eat of everything at the table; she made him taste of the excellent wine; and, gradually, without his being conscious how it came about, drew him into a grave and earnest conversation on the position of France.

Without alluding to the massacre of September, Miranda narrated all that had occurred during his seclusion, dwelling with affectation on political events disagreeable to Clement, recounting the vile and disgraceful conduct of the gang of royalist invaders, called the emigrants, without exception the most despicable political party which ever existed, until she began to rouse the indignation of our hero, who could not forbear from exclaiming against them.

"But our revolution," said Miranda, "will need the support and aid of every true man. Not one of its friends must desert it. All must labour with courage and assiduity in the cause."

Charles Clement was silent. He gently shook his head, and looked down upon his plate.

"You know what I mean," said Miranda, perseveringly, "and I cannot take silence for an answer."

"What would you have me do?" answered Charles, all the agony of his recent loss rushing fully to his mind.

"You should have been in the Convention. But that is now impossible until a vacancy. But there are clubs and patriotic societies without number; join one, and use your talents and genius to guide the ignorant but willing instruments of parties."

"But I am incapable of thought or action."

"Shame, Charles! shame! Deep and everlasting must be, and should be, your grief, at the loss you have incurred. No term of life could efface from my mind the memory of her who is gone; but you cannot, dare not, say that your career in this world is stopped wholly, because of this tragic termination to your dearest happiness."

"But my hope, my future, my existence," replied Charles Clement, moodily, "was bound up in her——."

Miranda turned very pale, and restrained with difficulty the gushing tears.

"She gone, hope, future, existence—all seem to have

ceased to be.   Why should I care to live, to be useful, to gain fame, or even forgetfulness, now that she is gone ? ”

“ My God ! ” cried Miranda, in an accent of despairing anguish which she could not restrain, “ have you no other friends—have you lost all with her ? ”

Charles Clement looked searchingly at Miranda, who, her first impulse over, sat confused and alarmed, and moved not his eyes for some minutes off her downcast face.

To the utter and inexpressible astonishment of the young man, a gush of tenderness, of unseen and unfelt joy, rushed to his heart—he knew not why or wherefore.   Something ineffable, something mysterious, seemed to be radiant around him.

But, up rose on the instant the figure, dear and adored, which a few days before had been their common bond of union ; and, without asking himself or her any further questions, Charles Clement sternly fell back upon himself, and sought not even to explain the hidden cause of the exclamation of Miranda, and of its effect upon himself.

Miranda, frightened at her own energy, and indignant with herself for allowing, for one moment, a sentiment she wished eternally concealed to get the upper hand, spoke not a word ; and Charles Clement, the dinner concluded, was about once more to retire to his own apartment, when Gracchus Antiboul entered hastily, his face flushed and animated.

“ *Vive la Republique !* ” cried he, throwing his hat up to the roof.

“ What news ? ” exclaimed Miranda.

“ Royalty is dead, the Republic is proclaimed, the reign of despotism and iniquity is over.”

“ This is indeed great news,” cried Charles Clement ; “ but of the war ? ”

“ Dumouriez is inexplicable,” said Gracchus ; “ the coalition is powerful in numbers, but I have great faith in our generals.”

“ Their armies are strong, and ours are weak.”

“ But we are freemen, fighting for liberty ; they are slaves, fighting for a king.   We are defending our country.”

“ And the Republic is proclaimed at last ! ” cried Charles Clement.   “ Thank God, I have lived to see this day.”

"But already the Republic has powerful enemies in its bosom," replied Gracchus. "Madame Roland and the Girondins are already striving to put down Robespierre and the people, to inaugurate the reign of the middle classes."

"Dream!" said Clement; "either the Republic will be popular or it will perish. And Louis XVI.?"

"Will be tried!" replied Gracchus.

"The King tried!" exclaimed Miranda, unable to control the surprise which the unity of the two words, "king" and "tried" caused in her mind.

"Charles I. of England was tried by his people; and since that day England dates her prosperity."

"But Charles I. was executed," said Miranda, with some alarm.

"It is probable Louis XVI. will follow in his footsteps," replied Gracchus Antiboul severely.

"Your republican zeal urges you too far," said Charles Clement; "the political scaffold is always a crime. I would neither guillotine a king nor a peasant. Besides, it is doubtful if this man is not more to be pitied than hated. He is more fool than tyrant."

"But we have paid the penalty of his folly."

"But is there any chance of his being executed?" said Miranda, quietly, but with restrained excitement.

"Every chance, unless we have peace without and tranquillity within," answered Gracchus.

"And when will his trial take place?"

"I know not."

"Shall you vote, Gracchus, for his death?"

"That depends on circumstances. I cannot say."

"Are you of the convention?" cried Charles Clement.

"I am. And now, adieu! I must to Robespierre's. We meet to-night in council."

And Gracchus Antiboul, now an important man, went out, after shaking his friend affectionately by the hand.

"Charles," said Miranda, kindly, "you know that I am as democratic as you are—that I acquiesce in most of the patriotic schemes of your friend Robespierre—but blood must not stain the white robe of the republic. Louis XVI. and Marie Antoinette must not die."

"I fear they will. For myself, I hate them heartily; but I would do much to save their lives."

"Let us save the Republic from itself, Charles; and, despite the dangers of the task, if the royal family be condemned to perish, let us save them."

"Miranda, you know my principles. I am a republican in every thought; but I hold, as I have said before, political scaffolds to be crimes. Count, therefore, on me to aid any plan to save the ex-king, if condemned to death. If their punishment be imprisonment or exile, I shall approve and support it."

"And I also. The nation has every right to retaliate on their tyrants; but to kill this man and woman would be awful!"

And the two republicans drew near the fire, and began to plot how they should save the life of a king and queen they both despised, while one very nearly hated.

---

## CHAPTER XLVII.

### THE REGICIDES.

"Empires are sometimes saved by a drop of blood—never with tears." Such were the words of the Girondins, and on this ground they prepared to place Louis XVI. on the scaffold.

Maximilien Robespierre—or *de* Robespierre, as he was at first called—attached, above all things, to liberty, was not originally bigotedly devoted to a republican form of government. He would have preferred passing through genuine constitutional monarchy, honestly administered, and to arrive at democracy and a republic by the force of events. He had, therefore, no desire to see Louis XVI. perish on the scaffold. He became a rigid republican and a regicide from the force of events.

Danton, who was merely an ambitious man, loving power above all, and too unprincipled himself to believe in honesty in others, cared neither for monarchy nor a republic. All he wanted was to be the head of whatever existed. To him the life of Louis XVI. was more useful than his death.

He had, moreover, been paid to save the royal family, and he liked the idea of being their saviour. It flattered his enormous vanity.

Marat, whose politics consisted in a savage hate of the rich and happy, and in a blind love for the poor and miserable, saw no advantage to be gained from the death of the King, and was therefore, as yet, wholly indifferent to it.

Vergniaud, Brissot, and the heads of the Girondin party —too much party men, and too ambitious to be sincerely republican—wanted the King as a hostage against the coalition and against the French party out of France, ready as was the Abbé Sieyes to replace him on the throne if circumstances rendered this act useful.

But the young and fiery Girondins, Fonfrede, Guadet, Buzot, whose whole policy was summed up in a dreamy love of liberty and an intense hatred of despots and despotism, thought the King's death right and necessary.

Still no party was prepared to take the initiative, and Louis XVI. would never have been executed by any faction, had they been wholly independent and free from external influences. Had any of them been sufficiently powerful to be independent, he would never have perished.

But the people were knocking at the door. Children of the reign of Louis XIV., Louis XV., the Regency, and the commencement of the reign of Louis XVI., they had derived nothing but misery from monarchy and its correlative institution, aristocracy. Totally deprived of property— serfs, slaves, with whose lives a noble could sport with impunity—subjected to factitious famines to fill the coffers of king, ministers, and tax-farmers—bearing, with the middle classes, the whole burden of taxation, which the aristocracy, supported by the king, refused to share—the French people were, before the revolution of 1793, one of the most miserable, half-starved, and oppressed people on the face of God's earth, as since they have become the most generally prosperous, happy, and well-fed.

This being the case, the mass of the people were as ignorant, brutalised, and savage, as a people well can be. Living under a despotism, it could not be otherwise. Partial liberty has almost wholly altered their character, though the coercion of Napoleon, the Restoration, and the reign of

Louis Philippe, have kept up much of the evil passions inevitable in slaves and those who approach serfdom, even in the mildest form, as do and have done the people of every monarchy, however mild, save only that of Great Britain.

Revenge was the great and yearning desire of the French people—revenge against the persons and fortunes of their oppressors.   This was but natural in newly-freed slaves.

The two names which represented most forcibly to the popular mind the body and shape of despotism were those of their king Louis XVI. and Marie Antoinette his queen.

Louis XVI., because he was a Bourbon, and, more than all, because he was a king, and therefore the embodiment of tyranny.

Marie Antoinette, because she was a queen, the well-known head and heart of the reaction, and, more than all, an Austrian, a thing which a Frenchman hates above almost everything.

Thus it was that the death of the King and Queen was the hope of the mob, and of a large party of subordinate agitators.

It became, therefore, an instrument of popularity to be favourable to the execution of the tyrant, as the King was called.

What the Girondins dreaded above all was the ascendancy and popularity of Robespierre.  Rigid, grave, devoted, sincere, never losing sight of the end, always advocating everything favourable to the mental or physical happiness of the people, Robespierre's power with the masses increased every hour, especially since the Girondins had committed the blunder of accusing him each day in the Convention and in the journals.

The Girondins saw this, and looked round for some means of struggling for popularity with Robespierre and the Jacobins.

They saw nothing better than to give up the head of Louis XVI. to the blind cries of popular vengeance.  It was their bidding for immediate popularity.

Roland and Madame Roland, whom it is the fashion of some sentimental politicians to cry up, with Charlotte Corday, the assassin, as the great names of the Revolution, were the first instigators of the accusation. These charming specimens of antique republicanism, whom certain historians have held up to admiration above the bloody Marat and Danton, planned the accusation of the King and Queen to serve a party purpose.

Roland and Madame Roland, sending Louis XVI. and Marie Antoinette to the scaffold to insure the ascendancy of their faction, appear to me far beneath Robespierre shedding blood in a desperate and terrible struggle with his enemies and those of the republic.

Robespierre shed blood because he thought it necessary, the Rolands because they thought it expedient.

Eagerly desiring to be beforehand with Robespierre, whom they wrongly suspected of an intention to propose the King's trial, the Rolands instigated Valazé and Mailhe to report on the crime, and then on the judgment of the King. They hurried it on, lest somebody else should be beforehand with them.

Valazé made his report, which was a long catalogue of the crimes of Louis XVI.

Danton, eager to gain time, asked that the report should be printed, and, to hide his desire to save the King, spoke of him in the bitterest terms.

The report was ordered to be printed, and the mooted question became the subject of general discourse.

The Jacobins, before wholly indifferent to the King's person, and treating the whole family with contemptuous forgetfulness, became suddenly eager demanders for his judgment.

They saw what the Girondins were aiming at; they knew the man condemned beforehand; and, having no affection or liking for him, resolved not to be outdone in hatred of tyranny by the Gironde. Thus it was they took up in earnest what perhaps their rivals feigned to wish. The promise of the trial and judgment of the King once thrown to the mob, it was utterly useless to resist.

## CHAPTER XLVIII.

### CHARLES.

HAVING given these preliminary remarks, absolutely necessary as the words are to the proper understanding of what follows, I return to Charles Clement.

For several days after the interview with the Countess Miranda and Gracchus Antiboul, Charles Clement remained confined to his room.

His grief had lost much of its first wild and bitter intensity, to remain more gentle and yet more painful.

The whole day was passed in thinking—with a sweet sorrow which fittingly became the memory of one so pure—of Adela. Charles neither read nor wrote as yet. He sat, he lay down, he walked about his room, until towards dinner hour, when Rose came to bid him come down to dinner.

"I would prefer dining alone in my room, if your mistress will kindly allow me," said Charles Clement, rousing himself a little from his apathy.

"I will tell her," replied the affectionate and attached girl, "though she is moping herself to death by herself."

"Does your mistress grieve so much?" asked Charles.

"When Monsieur is not present, she weeps the whole day."

"Ah!" exclaimed Clement, and began to walk about the room.

"Poor girl," said he, after a brief pause, "she stifles her own sorrow to spare me. I am sorry I did not go down. I will go."

And before Rose had reached the saloon, he was behind her, and had entered the apartment.

The Countess Miranda was kneeling by a sofa, on which lay two miniatures. She was gazing at both with an intensity which prevented her from noticing the approach of Charles Clement.

He saw at a glance that they were of himself and Adela.

He changed colour, but, conquering the wild and conflicting emotions which made his heart leap, he spoke.

"I have come to dine with you, dear Miranda," said he;

for really I behave like a *manant* to leave you alone, as I do all day."

Miranda crushed the miniatures together, and rose trembling to her feet, her face ghastly pale.

"I thank you, Charles," cried she, in a trembling voice, "for thinking of me. I am always glad to see you. Besides, have we not our conspiracy? I must talk to you of it; I have much to say to you on the point."

This was said with extreme volubility, as she allowed herself to be led to a chair beside the fire.

"And how feel you to-day?" said she, when, with all a woman's quickness—I had almost said dissimulation—she had effaced every trace of her sudden emotion.

"Weak in body and mind. But I must contend against myself."

"Let us talk politics. I have been reading the *Moniteur*, the *Sentinelle*, *L'Ami du Peuple*, the *Père Duchesne*. I buy everything. So you will hear all the news."

And, with her flowing language, and rich and seductive voice, Miranda narrated rapidly the principal events of the day, quoting, too, the opinions of all parties—Royalist, Girondin, Mountain, and Communal.

Charles Clement listened at first listlessly; but there was something so eloquent in her words, so thrilling in her manner, that it was impossible not to be charmed, and after a few moments he hearkened with breathless interest.

Was it the woman or the politician, the voice or the subject, which made his eye thus sparkle, his cheek flush so warmly?

This is a question I am wholly unable to answer.

Dinner was just served, when Gracchus Antiboul entered, to be warmly and cordially received by both. His quick eye glanced at the pair thus *tête-à-tête*, but the grave and solemn countenance of Charles—Miranda had ceased speaking some minutes—made him involuntarily shake his head.

"The news," cried Miranda, repeating the words which burst, at that time, from the lips of every man or woman who met another likely to be better informed than themselves.

"There is little change, save that the Girondins are eagerly seeking to clutch power, and drive the Mountain to their fastnesses. It is probable the people will have to speak once more."

"More blood! more insurrections!" said Charles Clement, moodily.

"I hope not," cried Gracchus, warmly, who saw the effect of his speech; "but what would you have us do? The Gironde will not work for the Republic with us; they will insist on fixing middle-class supremacy, as hurtful to the nation as any other supremacy."

"But every legitimate and constitutional means must be tried first," replied Clement. "The Mountain have already soiled themselves with enough of blood. What says Robespierre?"

"What he seeks is external peace, when inward dissension will cease. All our evils arise from the power which each party has of accusing the other of being the agents of the foreigner. Robespierre is himself accused of being in the pay of the Duke of Brunswick."

"By whom?"

"By the Girondins, of course."

"Why do they contend against the only man capable of guiding the Revolution?"

"Precisely for that reason. They are intensely jealous of him. Brissot hates him because his incorruptibility is a tacit reproach to the once-hired libeller, Louvet, author of *Faublas*, because Robespierre leads a pure life, which shames his debauched name; the others because the people love him."

"But the trial of Louis?"

"There is no talk of it yet."

"And when will there be?"

"Before long, if peace be not restored. It is the emigrants who are condemning Louis XVI. If his own brothers and the French nobility would keep off the frontiers, he would be quite safe."

"They are mad. But can they not be influenced to make peace for his sake?"

"Not they. They are fighting in his name for their own interests—for their estates, mansions, and power."

"We must wait events," said Charles Clement.

"By the way, Charles, on Saturday there is a meeting in

the section to form a patriotic club, and to select an officer of the volunteers. You must attend it."

"I will," replied Charles, hurriedly, while Miranda looked at him with some surprise.

"I am delighted!" said the Conventionalist, warmly; "at length I see you once more, my friend, likely to become a citizen of the Republic."

"Which I will defend with my life against all its enemies; but, Gracchus, I will aid and abet none of its excesses."

"It is to be hoped none will occur," replied Antiboul. "We have had enough of them."

"Where go you to-night?" asked the Countess.

"To the Jacobins."

"Let us all go," said Miranda, with a sign to Antiboul to insist on Charles accompanying them.

"By all means," added Antiboul.

"I am at your orders," replied Clement. "My friends, I leave myself at present in your hands. What you think wise and proper, I will do, for I am not fit to guide myself."

"Let us dine, then. Sit you down, Gracchus. How is your dear little wife?"

"The same good, excellent creature as ever," replied the young republican.

"And Paul?"

"Happy as an honest man should be."

"And Marie?"

"The happiest little wife I ever saw."

"Bid them all come dine with me to-morrow," added the Countess.

The three friends now rapidly took their meal, as the hour of the sitting of the club was approaching.

At eight at night they went out, Miranda wearing a hood, while Charles and Gracchus, well armed, wore the usual costume of the period.

The streets were deserted and silent; few people as yet ventured out after dark, for the memory of the September massacres was still fresh in the minds of all.

The Jacobin club was quickly gained; but it proved to be a sitting of no great interest, and the party soon left to return home.

They had left the Rue St. Honoré, and were turning in the Rue St. Thomas du Louvre, when a woman suddenly ran against them.

A lamplight was over their heads.

"Lucille!" said Miranda, with surprise.

"Madame la Comtess," cried the woman; and then, checking herself, "*Citoyenne* Miranda, I am glad to see thee."

Miranda, more amused than offended at her familiar tone, smiled.

"It is years since I have seen thee, girl; where hast thou been?"

"Please, I am married," said the girl.

"I hope well."

"Very well," said the woman, with a sigh which belied her words.

"Who is thy husband?"

"The *citoyen* Tison, ex-clerk at a barrier. He is old and cross; but what wouldst thou, *citoyenne?* I was poor, and he never beats me now."

"What is his present occupation?"

"He is at the Temple," said the girl, confusedly.

"Ah!" said Miranda, with a start.

"Art thou employed there?" asked Gracchus.

"We wait on the King since his *officieux** have been dismissed by the Commune."

"I hope," said Gracchus, gravely, "thou wilt do thy duty, *citoyenne*. Remember thy position is a dangerous and responsible one. Let no false pity move thee to join in any machinations favourable to the enemies of the nation."

"*Citoyen*, never fear," cried the *citoyenne* Tison; "my husband is a good patriot; his only fault is, that he treats the *citoyen* Veto too roughly."

"He has no right to do so," added Gracchus. "They are entitled to the same respect which any other prisoners are allowed—no more, no less."

"If I had my will," said the woman, "they should not be ill-treated, as they are by Simon and Rocher. I hate all tyrants, as the *Etre Suprême†* knows; but still I would

---

* Under the Republican *régime*, the word for "servants."
† Under the old Revolution, the word for "the Almighty."

not forget how much they must suffer, changed from the 'Tuileries to the Temple."

"Millions of the ex-subjects of this man," replied Gracchus, moodily, "are worse fed and worse lodged. Pity the millions first, and the few afterwards. *Salut et fraternité.*"

And Gracchus moved on.

"Come to me the first time you can," whispered Miranda, "I wish to see you most particularly."

"I will come in a few days," replied the *femme* Tison; and she hurried away.

Gracchus left his two friends at the door. Just before they parted, there was on his lips something relative to the malevolent interpretation which might be put on the evidence of a young man and young woman being in the same house, almost alone; but he forbore, recollecting both how the idea would pain Miranda, and how many other things the world had just now to think of.

The world is only scandalous when it is idle, which explains the peculiar atmosphere of a watering-place.

----

## CHAPTER XLIX.

### THE MIGHTY ARE FALLEN.

EVERYBODY who has visited Paris has been to the remains of the Temple, the scene of the captivity of Louis XVI. But no one who judges by what they now see can have any idea of what it was in 1792.

A few words of description, and then we will turn to the inmates.

The Temple dated back to the year 1147, though rne building, of which the remains served as the King's prison, was only commenced in 1182.

But we have no time to look at it otherwise than as it appeared on the 24th September, 1792.

Save the Chatelet and the Bastille, which no longer existed, no building was more dismal in all Paris than this old palace. It gave a gloom to the whole neighbourhood in which it was situated.

The old palace, dilapidated and heavy, furnished meanly and antiquely, still remained, and had served recently as an occasional town residence for the Count D'Artois, afterwards Charles X. A deserted and neglected garden surrounded it.

Near this rose the *donjon*.

It was composed of one vast square tower, with a smaller one supporting itself against it. The larger one had four corner towers, with pointed roofs, the smaller two suspended as it were from it. The whole rose in gloomy majesty against the sky.

It is built with stones cut from the vast subterraneous caverns which yawn beneath a great part of Paris—a city resting upon another vast but uninhabited series of chambers, that have given up their solid bowels to erect the one above.

Time had blackened and soiled the building until it seemed one solid tower cut out of rock. Sixty feet high and thirty square, it was sufficiently vast in its dimensions to have a general air of grandeur.

An enormous pile of masonry occupied the centre of the tower, and rose almost to the point of the edifice. This pile, larger and wider at each story, leaned its arches upon the exterior walls, and formed four successive arched roofs, which contained four guard-rooms. These halls communicated with other hidden and narrower places cut in the towers. The walls of the edifice were nine feet thick. The embrasures of the few windows which lighted it, very wide at the entrance of the wall, sunk as they became narrower, even to the crosswork of stone, and left only a feeble and remote light to penetrate into the interior. Bars of iron darkened these apartments still further. Two doors, the one of double oak, very thick, and studded with large diamond-headed nails, the other plated with iron, and fortified with bars of the same metal, divided each hall from the stair by which one ascended to it.

This winding stair rose, in a spiral form, to the platform of the edifice. Seven successive wickets, or seven solid doors, shut by bolt and key, were ranged from landing to landing, from the base to the roof. At each one of these wickets a sentinel and a key-bearer were on guard. An exterior gallery crowned the summit of the donjon. One made here ten steps at each turn. The least breath of air howled there like a tempest. The noises of Paris mounted there, weakening as they came. Thence the eye ranged freely over the low roofs of the Quartier St. Antoine.

The small tower, as I have already said, stood with its back to the large one. It was an oblong square, with also four stories.

On the first story, an ante-chamber, dining-room, and library; on the rest, naked, empty rooms.

The wind whistled, the rain fell, the sparrow flew in, through the broken panes.

After one day's residence in the old palace, the King was sent, with all his family, to the smaller tower, to be afterwards removed to the larger.

On the 24th September there remained in the prison of the Temple, Louis XVI., Marie Antoinette, Madame Elizabeth, the Princess Royal, now Duchess D'Angouleme, and the Dauphin Louis XVII., whose supposed existence in the person of the Baron de Richemont, affords so much annoyance to the Carlist party in France at the present moment.

They were attended on and guarded by Tison and his wife, one Rocher, the eternally infamous Simon, Santerre, and Manuel.

Clery, the King's valet, still remained.

The position of the family was not so bad as some royalist writers have represented it. " Petion sent him (the King) one hundred louis, the alms of a republican to a sovereign fallen into indigence. A list of everything necessary for the royal family was drawn up—and linen, furniture, clothing, fuel, books, were liberally provided at the expense of the Commune, and, through the interposition of its commissaries, all their expenses in suitable proportion, not to the wants of a family, but to the generosity of the nation, and the respect due to fallen greatness. The Republic at this moment exercised its ostracism, with profuseness." *

Simon was commissary of inspection, of labour, and expenses ; Tison was a servant, Rocher, a jailor.

It was twelve o'clock on the 24th September, 1792.

* Lamartine.

The garden of the Temple was filled with National Guards. Sentinels were posted at every door, and almost at every tree.

At the foot of the tower, near the entrance, stood a man, of heavy stature, hang-dog look, and sinister features. Ugly to hideousness, with insolence in every line of his face, grossness in every wrinkle, foulness on his thick, projecting lips, his dog-skin cap, untrimmed beard, hoarse, hollow voice, reeking with tobacco and brandy, a short black pipe never absent from his mouth, all combined to make him the very Cerberus of the fanatic Commune, now wholly directed by Hebert, Panis, Santerre, and the worst of the Jacobin party, who, sincere though they were, partook of the character which we have assigned to the people generally at this period.

A heavy cavalry sabre trailed beside him, which, with a vast bunch of keys, always announced his approach.

Near him were seven men, one of whom wore the rough trappings of a republican general officer, while the others were in civil costume, but with tricoloured scarfs and sabres, with pistols at their belts. They wore also top-boots and slouched hats.

These were Santerre, the commander-in-chief of the National Guard, and the six municipal officers in the service of the Temple.

On a stone, also smoking, sat a man habited in a complete patriotic costume—wooden shoes, tricoloured loose breeches, a *carmagnole*, and huge shaggy hair covered by a bog-skin cap.

This was Simon, the cobbler, the atrocious executioner of the young Dauphin, one of the monsters of the Revolution, whose existence makes one almost feel ashamed to be a republican, when we reflect that there was a day when such men were thought good republicans.

Santerre suddenly made a sign to Rocher, who moved towards the wicket, and entered the house as old Tison came out.

" *Mille boulet rouges!* " cried he, "where is my woman?"

" Making love with some young *citoyen,*" replied a National Guard, with a laugh.

The old fellow glared at the speaker with a look of savage hate.

"With some *valets du tyran*," said another.

"Some *soldats de l' esclavage*," added a third.

"With one of the *lâches satellites des rois*."

Such were the popular names all over France for the emigrants who represented, in all foreign courts, the French people as desiring their return with rapturous expectation.

"*Mille tonnerres!*" cried Tison, "will you be quiet?"

"I think thou saidst *you*," said one gravely.

"I repeat, you," said the old man, furiously, "for I mean you, that is all; not thou, one!"

At this moment an object on which Tison could vent his rage appeared before him.

It was his wife.

"Ah!" he cried, "here thou art, *citoyenne* Tison. Where hast thou been?"

"To carry a letter to the *citoyen* Robespierre," replied she, keeping at a respectful distance.

"From whom?" said the old man, shaking his fist at her.

"Thou hadst best ask him," answered Lucille, the ex-femme de chambre of the Countess Miranda.

The National Guard laughed.

"Silence there," cried the terrible voice of Santerre; "and thou, Tison, if thou beatest thy wife, look out. That's good for days of tyranny; but recollect *mon vieux*, that woman is now something before she is a wife, she is a *citoyenne*."

The National Guard giggled, Tison shrunk away, his wife looked pleased, as women always do when they triumph over their husbands, and, during the confusion, the royal family entered the garden.

The sentinels reversed their guns, lifting the butt-end of their guns on high, in token of contempt.

Next minute they gave the military salute to Santerre, and carried arms to the municipals.

Louis XVI. held the Dauphin by the hand. The contrast of the two was striking. We have already described the King. The only difference in him was in his being paler and stouter, from want of that exercise which was to him a necessity of existence. The Prince reminded one of the effeminate look of Louis XV., while retaining much of the Austrian haughtiness of his mother. He had blue eyes, elevated nostrils, a sharply-defined mouth, projecting lips, chestnut hair, parted on the top of the head, and descending in thick curls on the shoulders, and resembled both his mother and his father.

The lovely princess royal, just bursting into womanhood, walked between Marie Antoinette and Madame Elizabeth.

Madame Tison seemed inclined to advance near to them, but the National Guard pulled her back.

But the young Dauphin had caught the impulse, and made an imperceptible sign to her.

Lucille nodded.

The Dauphin let go his father's hand, caught up a stone, threw it along the ground beside Lucille, and then ran after it.

The stone rolled harmlessly against the foot of the cobbler Simon.

The child hesitated. Some awful· instinct seemed to warn him of what he was to endure from this man.

But the desire to fulfil his scheme overpowered him, and he reached at the stone.

"Little reptile," said Simon, savagely, treading on his hand a she stooped to pick up the stone, "why didst thou cast that stone at me?"

The child's eyes flashed, but he made no reply to the cobbler's cowardly attack.

At the same moment Simon fell like an ox under the blow of the butcher.

Santerre had felled him with his fist.

"Thou art a jailor, not an executioner," said the republican general, severely. "The *citoyen* Capet and his family are little entitled to respect from the citizens of a free Republic; but let me see no more insult or cruelty."

Scarcely had this incident occurred when a beating of drums in the exterior court announced an arrival.

Santerre and the municipals hurried to the gate, while the royal family were told to re-enter their prison.

They obeyed, and were soon in the common room of the tower, where the family was in the habit of assembling.

Another roll of the drums was heard, and then an officer of *gendarmerie*, named Lubin, presented himself, accompanied by Manuel.

He bid the King and Queen go to the window, where they could hear, but not see, what passed in the court.

There was an awful tumult. The voices of a mob rose furious and mad, venting imprecations and insults on the royal name.

Louis XVI. looked curiously at Manuel, who answered by a sign which said there is no danger.

The Queen turned paler than usual, and clutched the hands of the children.

Madame Elizabeth bowed her head in prayer.

"*Citoyen* Louis Capet," said Lubin, harshly, "listen to the voice of retribution."

The drums rolled once more, and then one, in a loud voice, read a proclamation.

It was the official abolition of royalty, and the establishment of the Republic.

Marie Antoinette frowned and bit her lip. Her Austrian pride had revolted, while a look of incomprehensible incredulity crossed her countenance.

This wife, daughter, sister, and mother of kings, could not understand how a nation could exist without this hereditary magistrate.

But Louis XVI. seemed relieved. The crown was a burthen always far above his capabilities, and he seemed to feel it.

"My kingdom," said he to the Queen, "has passed away like a dream, but it was not a happy dream. God had imposed it on me: my people discharge me from it. May France be happy—I will not complain."

It is such phrases as these that have made many persons admire Louis and regret his fall. But a nation cannot keep a king because he is well-meaning.

"Thou art now a simple citizen," said Lubin, "and must be treated as such. These baubles must be stripped off."

And the *gendarme* pointed to the ex-King's sword, and to the insignia of the order of chivalry which adorned his coat.

But Louis did not hear; he was thinking of the tremendous change in his position revealed by the proclamation.

Lubin frowned, and was about to speak more violently, when Manuel stopped him.

"Do not annoy him now," said he; "I will see that those baubles be removed;" and, turning to Clery, the fallen monarch's valet, he bade him take them off when the king undressed.

Lubin, Manuel, Santerre, and the Commissioners, left the room, while, without, tremendous shouts arose.

" *Vive la Republique !* " said some.

" *Mort aux tyrans,*" cried others.

" Death to the *citoyen* Veto."

" Death to the man Capet, to the woman Capet, and to all the little Capets."

The royal family withdrew, shuddering, from the window. They now saw what oceans of wrath a people, oppressed for ages, nurse in their bosoms.

At this moment, when all were alone, the Dauphin opened his hand, and gave a paper to his mother.

*Pour la reine.*    Such was all its address.

Marie Antoinette rapidly opened it, and read—

" Madame,—Though, from conviction, a friend to the revolution, I hate all its excesses, and desire, above all things, the safety of the royal family.  I shall be happy to co-operate with any of your friends in aiding any plan for your personal salvation.  Trust the *femme* Tison with a verbal reply.—MIRANDA del Castelmonte."

" I recollect," said Louis; " one of the friends of those two young men who visited us on the night of the 20th June.  Pity we did not take their advice."

" Though not royalists, they are not our enemies," said Marie Antoinette, stifling the pang which this tacit reproach caused her ; " they may serve us much."

" They had better act in concert with the Chevalier de Jarjais," said Madame Elizabeth.

" But perhaps they will not act with royalists," observed Marie Antoinette.  "We had better wait events; and if our two parties of saviours clash, we can then put them in communication one with another."

" But, if this be a trap ?" said Madame Elizabeth.

" No ! I know the writer.  She is a noble Italian ; and though of the revolutionary party, would not be a traitor."

" We must first sound Tison's wife, "continued Marie Antoinette ; and, sitting down upon a bench, they began to plan their answer.

*        *        *        *        *        *

Meanwhile an explanation had taken place between Miranda and Charles Clement, which somewhat altered their relative position.

"Miranda," said the young man, on his return from the Jacobin Club, "my grief has made me too tender-hearted. I said I would join with you in aiding the escape of Louis. Reflection shows me that I must not.  I am a republican. For me the National Representation is something sacred. They are depositories of the will of the people.  What they decide, I am bound to obey.  If the death of Louis XVI. be considered by them necessary to the well-being of the Republic, I should be a traitor to my country if I joined in any evasion of their decree.  Individually, I wish Louis to escape; but, about to act in public, to assume perhaps a command, to do something for my country, it will be impossible for me to assist you."

"How you have changed," replied the Countess, sorrowfully.

"Dear Miranda," said the young man, "shut up here, I listened only to the dictates of a heart softened by sorrow. I have gone again into the world this night, and recollect my position.  I have aided to impel this revolution.  Publicly, I will do all to restrain its excesses; privately, I cannot conspire.  I would plot against a man, I cannot against a nation."

"After all, you are right," said Miranda.

"But do not tell me what you may do yourself, unless there be danger," continued Charles Clement.  "Be wise and cautious.  Under no circumstances place your existence in peril.  I doubt the possibility of an evasion, if the feeling be strong against the King, as I also doubt a condemnation to death."

"Thank you, Charles; thank you," said Miranda, warmly, "life can have little charms for one so utterly alone as I am; but if my friends wish my presence, I will be careful."

"Are you more lonely than I?" replied Charles Clement, in a low tone, while his eyes were bent on the floor in moody thought.

Miranda made no reply, but, calling Rose to her side, bade her admit Lucille, now *femme* Tison, at any time when she should call, to an immediate audience.

After some further conversation, Charles Clement explained more fully his political reasons for declining to act secretly for the salvation of the King. Still he informed Miranda that it was his design to promote his personal safety, by every means in his power, with the heads of the reoubli-can party.

At midnight they parted.

---

## CHAPTER L.

### JEALOUSY.

CHARLES CLEMENT went out early the next morning to visit his political friends. He called on Robespierre, St. Just, Couthon, Lebas, and all those with whom it was his intention to co-operate in the great work of revolution.

Charles Clement found Robespierre thoroughly determined to avoid any violent course of action—to look only to the salvation, honour, and greatness of France.

"I have received a letter this morning," he said, addressing Charles, "from a friend of my brother, who desires my protection. This letter contains some good ideas. The writer thinks the Republic difficult, but not impossible; but he is particularly anxious that the King should be saved."

"Why?"

"Because he considers it necessary to temporise with England. His name is Bonaparte."

"He is right, this Bonaparte. Germany is enough for us just now; but if we could keep England quiet, we could manage the rest."

"If the Royalists would remain quiet," observed Robespierre, "we could soon organize the country. All I want is internal peace; with that, I care not for all Europe. But disaffection and conspiracy will ruin us. Foreign war will so occupy us, that against internal war we shall have only one arm, and that is death!"

"A terrible weapon."

"But, my friend the only one. Give me external peace;

and I will keep down civil wars by legal means; give me internal peace, and I will despise all the world. But with enemies within and enemies without, conspirators, agents of the emigration in our very bosoms, we have no choice—we must strike!"

"Events alone can tell;" and, shaking Robespierre by the hand, Charles Clement went out.

He returned towards the residence of Miranda. It was, as yet, only eight in the morning, he having gone out at daylight.

The wicket in the *porte cochère* opened as he rung, and he crossed the court. As he entered the house, he ran against a man in a cloak and low-crowned hat, whose face was completely hidden.

"Excuse me," said Charles Clement, drawing on one side.

The stranger muttered some unintelligible words, and hurried out.

"Who can he be?" said the young man to himself; "he has just left the apartment of Miranda."

And a feeling of desolation came, he knew not why, over the heart of the republican.

"Already!" he exclaimed; "already!"

He moved on towards the salon.

"But what is it to me? Miranda may have a dozen lovers, for what I care; and yet, so soon after *her* death, to be thinking on such a subject!"

Charles Clement frowned bitterly; for as he said these words, something whispered to him that feelings he could not explain, and yet which he crushed within him with rage and anger, were beating at his heart—feelings which left him no excuse for blaming Miranda.

"Where is your mistress?" asked he, as Rose came up with breakfast in her hand.

"In the salon," replied the soubrette.

Charles Clement entered and caught sight of Miranda, whose quick eyes detected something gloomy in the air with which the young man saluted her.

"I have had an early visit," said she, in a natural and easy tone of voice.

"Indeed," observed Charles, coldly.

"The celebrated Chevalier de Jarjais called on me; but," added she, "I cannot tell you the secret of our interview."

"And that was the Chevalier I met in the cloak and slouched hat?" asked Charles Clement, in a tone of eager joy.

Miranda did not instantly reply. She gazed at the young man with a vacant air. The expression of his voice had filled her with intense emotion. She wished not to lose a note; she sought to let the very echo of his tones fall upon her heart.

"And so you met," she cried, after an instant's pause. "I dare say now, with the usual good-nature of men, you took him for a lover?"

"Indeed, I did," said Charles Clement, *naïvely*, and colouring violently the instant he had spoken.

"Fie! Monsieur," exclaimed Rose.

Miranda smiled, and turned away, but the expression of her face was very different from what it had been for years. There was something gentle, subdued, and grateful, in her look; as if she thanked God for some gift as unexpected as it was delightful.

"Take care," said Charles, sitting down to breakfast; "this Jarjais has a price on his head. You may seriously compromise yourself. I can ask you no details relative to what you are doing with him; but recollect that if I capture him anywhere, wholly free from your protection, I must give him up to justice. He is a dangerous conspirator against the Republic, and one whom it is my duty to arrest."

"I know it, Charles! I know it! Rely on it, I shall join him in nothing against the Republic. I have particular views; but sooner will I die than do anything against liberty."

"If there were many women like you, there would be some hope for the Revolution; but it is unfortunately true, that women are chiefly on the side of power. Dazzled by its show and glitter, they see not the hideous appendages; they hear not the groans of its victims; and, unwittingly, they support a bad and dangerous cause."

"The education of women explains this. Habituated to

learn only trivial and show accomplishments—embroidery, dancing, music—and adored as the playthings of life, they have no chance of judging correctly. Educate women properly, and they will surely be on the right side."

"And the education of woman must be the grand object of the new organisation. Woman has too much influence on society, and is far too important a feature in the world, to be left to her present superficial education. I would not unsex them, or drive them before the public. But let woman learn something solid—enough of history and politics to judge correctly between two opposite trains of ideas, to guide the infant mind of her children. As sweethearts, and wives, and friends, women are important enough; but it is as mothers that we must chiefly look at them. I detest the theorists who would deprive you of your domesticity, and retiring charms; but neither must you be given up to the vapid tuition of dancing and music masters. Perish those two trivial accomplishments, if, with them, women cannot give their sons right judgment, and correct ideas on the elementary topics of daily and vital importance."

"I expect to see you legislator for the ladies," said Miranda, with a faint smile.

"I know not if I shall ever be legislator on any point," replied Charles Clement. "My ambition has only one great view, that of seeing the Republic safely housed. That once a fact, liberty established, I care not."

"And it will be, Charles, if not in our time."

"But I would live to see it too. 'Tis miserable to have seen the beginning of a revolution, and not its end."

"God's will be done. All is in his hands, and what he wills will happen."

"If God were not above us, I should have little hope indeed. The wickedness of man has been such in this land, that otherwise we were a lost people indeed."

"Where spend you the day?" asked Miranda, as the clock struck nine.

"At the Convention. Gracchus will fetch me presently."

"You will come here late to dine?"

"I shall not fail."

"And you, Miranda?"

"I go to the Temple."

"Miranda! Miranda!" cried Charles, shaking his head; "for Heaven's sake, reflect on the perils you are incurring. I may be able to do nothing to avert them, too."

"I see them all, Charles, and yet I hesitate not. I have entered on a path, and I am resolved to tread it, if need be."

"And am I then to lose you too?" exclaimed Charles Clement, with a despairing accent.

"My loss would be but little, after what you have felt," replied Miranda, in a low tone.

"Miranda!" cried the young man; and then, checking himself, he turned away.

"But how will you enter the Temple?"

"As a cousin of the *citoyenne* Tison."

"Disguises—false names—all terrible dangers. Adieu! I go to join the Republicans. All I can do is to make my influence great, in case you need it."

And Charles Clement retired, with an anxious brow, and a beating heart.

---

## CHAPTER LI.

### THE EX-KING.

TOULAN and Lepitre, two commissaries of the Commune; the Chevalier de Jarjais; Miranda; five of the worst members of the Commune; three servants, Turzy, Marchand, and Chrétien; such were the persons who had joined in the plot to save the life of the King. With these were associated a few hundred National Guards. The plan was simple. These civic soldiers were to be set to guard the Temple some morning; the King, and family, with Toulan and Jarjais, were to escape to Dieppe, and thence to England.

Nothing was wanting to success but unity, and the selection of an appropriate moment for action. There was, however, little time to lose. The Girondins had roused the question of the King's trial, and the Jacobins had accepted it.

Brissot, Vergniaud, and the other great Girondin leaders,

were wholly averse to the execution of the monarch; but having raised the point, they must meet it.

The first question was, " Can the King be judged ?" This was decided in the affirmative.

St. Just, in one of his wild and wonderful speeches, decided the question.

All France seemed on the eve of anarchy. In the departments where corn was abundant, hidden and unknown hands—now known to be reckless royalists—destroyed the staff of life. Flour was thrown into rivers; corn stacks were burnt.

The cross was raised as a standard of revolt; and such was the influence of religion on the minds of the departments, that Danton and Robespierre, to escape from civil war, desired to continue the payment of priests. Besides, Robespierre thus wrote to a private friend.—" Nought now remains in our minds, save those eternal dogmas on which our novel ideas rest, and the touching and sublime doctrines of charity and equality which the Son of Mary formerly taught."

Camille Desmoulins published a journal, with this motto: " There is no victim more agreeable to the Gods than an immolated king."

Suddenly the iron chest was discovered, and Robespierre demanded at once, not the trial, but the punishment of the King !

" But," said he, " to what punishment shall we condemn him? The punishment of death is too cruel, says one. No, says another; life is more cruel still, and we must condemn him to live. Ye, his advocates, would ye, by pity or from cruelty, avert from him the punishment of his crimes? For myself, I abhor the penalty of death. I have neither love nor hate for Louis; I hate nothing but his crimes. I have demanded the abolition of the punishment of death in the Constituent Assembly, and it is not my fault if the first principles of reason have appeared moral and judicial heresies. But you, who have never been of opinion that this relaxation of punishment should be exercised in favour of the unhappy persons whose offences are pardoned and pardonable, by what singular fatality are you reminded of your humanity, in order to plead the cause of the greatest of criminals ! Do you ask an exception from the pain of

death for him who alone could render it legitimate?  **A**
dethroned king in the very heart of a republic not yet
cemented!—a king, whose very name drew foreign hostilities on the nation!  Neither prison nor exile can render his
an innocent existence.  It is with regret I pronounce the
fatal truth.  Louis must perish, rather than a hundred thousand virtuous citizens!  Let Louis perish, that the country
may live."

The *acte d'accusation* was read—the trial appointed.

On the 11th October, Louis XVI. was summoned to the
bar of the Convention.

Paris wore the aspect of a military camp.  All the posts
were doubled, and the muster-roll of the National Guard
was called over every hour.  A piquet of several hundred
men was stationed in the court of each of the eight sections, the Tuileries was occupied by a reserve, and heavy
patrols moved about the streets.

It was the same scene so often witnessed since, up to the
very day I am writing, within a few yards of the theatre of
the above events.

A perfect army of cavalry, infantry, and artillery, surrounded the King, whose rescue, it was well known, had
been planned.  But the conspirators were awed by the
energy of the Convention.

The King was placed at the bar, and his act of accusation read to him.  It contained much truth, and much
exaggeration.

Louis XVI. sealed his own fate, and declared himself
guilty, by denying all knowledge of the iron chest, and putting himself on his defence as wholly innocent.  Had he
boldly avowed what was true in the accusation, and owned
to the papers written with his own hand, his defence would
have been more dignified, if not more fortunate.

The King was sent back to prison; and the Convention
—despite Marat and Billaud-Varennes—voted almost unanimously that the King should choose two counsel.

The King chose Tronchet and Target, the former of
whom alone courageously accepted; to be joined by Desèze
and Malesherbes.

The Convention heard the defence of the fallen monarch
in silence.

Louis XVI. then went out, and the struggle began.

Bazere demanded instant judgment.

Duhem, the *appel nominal*.

Lanjuinais asked for an appeal to the people, but the Convention, determined no longer to temporise, drowned his voice.

" To the Abbaye," cried the Mountain.

" He is a royalist," screamed Duhem.

" He accuses the 10th August," said Legendre, the butcher, and friend of Marat.

" He will soon transfer us into the accused, and the King into a judge," observed Julien.

Lanjuinais replied by saying, " that the enemies of the King could not also be accusers, judges, and jury."

" Down with him!  I accuse him," said Choudieu.

" To the bar!"

" To the Abbaye!"

After tremendous clamour, an adjournment was voted.

The Mountain raised a terrific and tremendous clamour, but the adjournment was persevered in.

On the 27th December, the Debate was renewed.

" If the King be innocent," said St. Just, " the people are guilty.  You have proclaimed martial law against the tyrants of the world, and spare your own.  The revolution only begins when the tyrant ends."

The Gironde, compromised by the iron chest, looked round for some stay.  It was necessary to obtain temporary popularity.  This sealed the fate of Louis XVI.

The Mountain pushed on the condemnation from principle; the Gironde, from interest.

At last the day arrived, and the following questions were put—

*First*—Is Louis guilty?

*Second*—Shall the decision of the Convention be submitted to the ratification of the people?

*Third*—What shall be the sentence?

To the first question, six hundred and eighty replied in the affirmative.

Two hundred and eighty-one voted for the appeal to the people; four hundred and twenty-three against.

Danton now gave up the King.  The vote decided him, and he called for an immediate sentence.

Lanjuinais demanded that a majority, composed of two-thirds of the members, be necessary to condemn the King.

Danton caused this to be rejected.  The Assembly then declared itself permanent until the voting was over.

The names of the members were called over in batches, the members for each department voting together.

At eight o'clock at night this began.

---

## CHAPTER LII

### THE APPEL NOMINAL.

MIRANDA and Charles Clement had obtained tickets for the chamber by the assistance of Gracchus Antiboul, and they had sat it all out.  At six they had left, to return again at eight; and they now took their way, arm-in-arm, to the hall of the Convention.

Paris was gloomy and threatening.  The Commune of the city, but for whom the King would never have been tried, kept the vast metropolis under the pressure of its terror.  All the worst bands of September and August were collected round the Convention.

The cold, wintry night, made the scene doubly dismal.

Threading their way through a countless multitude, Miranda approached the ancient monastery in which sat the Revolution Incarnate, pregnant with fate, and about to hurl defiance in the face of astounded Europe.

The hour, the gloomy passages, the vaults, the cannon with lighted matches beside them in the hands of artillery-men devoted to the Commune, the peculiar costumes of the day, the comings and goings of the members, all added to the wild and savage grandeur of the scene.

The members were going in as our friends came up.

A batch came up amid terrific cheers.  It was Robes-pierre, Couthon, St. Just, and, behind, Marat and Danton.

Robespierre stepped back a moment, and taking Miranda's arm, led her past the sentries.

In a few minutes more, they were sitting in a tribune at the very edge of the Mountain, within speaking of Grac-chus.

It was a scene never to be forgotten.

The Convention hall was not well lighted. The centre only was illumined, while into the corners the glimmer of the chandelier and lamps before the President penetrated not. The public seats were all crammed to suffocation; the front seats being occupied by gaily-dressed young women, with tricoloured ribbons bedecking them.

Miranda and Charles Clement sat at the extreme end of the tribune.

The women talked of indifferent subjects, only stopping to prick with a pin on a card the votes as they were given.

Refreshments, ices, oranges, and sweets, were handed round.

Men stood at the very mouth of the Chamber, to give outside the news.

Each member was called in his turn, and went up to the tribune to give his vote aloud, and with whatever observations he thought proper.

The whole body was agitated: the deputies mingled with the spectators, scarce knowing what they did.

"The stir never ceased but for a moment," says Lamartine, "when the name of some important deputy pronounced by the usher caused all eyes to turn towards him, in order to learn from his appearance, and the motion of his lips, whether he pronounced for life or death. The benches of the deputies were nearly empty. Weary of a sitting of fifteen hours, which was yet to be uninterrupted until sentence was passed, some gathered in small groups, and conversed in under-tones, in attitudes of patient resignation; others, with their legs extended, leaning back on the deserted benches, fell asleep under the weight of their thoughts, and only awoke at the clamour made when a vote was given more energetically than usual. The majority, perpetually driven from one place to another, by the internal agitation of their reflections, kept moving from one back to another. They passed from group to group, exchanging, in low voices, a few words with their colleagues, writing on their knees, erasing what they had written, re-writing their intended vote, and again obliterating it, until the moment when called on by the usher, who, surprising them in their hesitation, snatched from their lips the fatal word, which one minute more would have changed to a contrary decision."

" My God !" whispered Miranda, in a low tone, "how will it be ? "

" The votes are very equal as yet. What thinkest thou, Gracchus ? "

" Death and exile are as yet evenly balanced," replied the Republican. " For my part, I care not much which triumphs. My mind is made up."

"How mean you to vote?" asked Miranda, in a low tone.

"Let me commune with my conscience until the last instant," said Gracchus Antiboul, solemnly. "You will soon hear at the tribune."

" 'Tis curious," remarked Clement; " the votes are almost balanced."

" The Alphabet brings Gironde," replied Gracchus. "When the members for that department have voted, all will be decided."

" Gironde !" said the usher.

Every voice in the vast hall was hushed, as the whole of the deputation of the department of the Gironde moved towards the tribune.

Vergniaud was at their head. His speech against Robespierre was well remembered; besides, the night before, he had promised to save the King.

The great orator's brow was calm, his lips were compressed, his nostrils dilated.

" The *citoyen* Vergniaud ! " said the secretary.

The most intense silence prevailed. Every whisper was hushed. Every eye was fixed on the mighty speaker, who wielded the party of the Gironde at his will.

He walked slowly and calmly up the steps, gazed at the Mountain with a look of courage and defiance, closed his eyes as if reflecting, and then spoke in a low, distinct, and melancholy tone.

" DEATH !"

The Mountain bounded with astonishment—the vast mass spoke not, scarcely breathed. The word was too unexpected—too astounding. All felt that the King was gone.

"They dared not!" said Robespierre, with a smile far more of contempt than satisfaction.

"These are your orators!" muttered Danton, shrugging his shoulders. "All talk. They desert every promise. The party is annihilated."

All the Gironde voted for death, even Sieyes; Condorcet for exile.

"All is over," muttered Miranda, scarcely able to speak.

"Paris!" cried the usher.

Again silence prevailed, and the twenty-one deputies for Paris—Robespierre, Danton, Marat, Billaud—Varennes, David, Gracchus Antiboul, &c.—moved towards the tribune.

Robespierre spoke first.

He repeated his usual protestation against the existence of the punishment of death; but added that, while the Legislature allowed the penalty to exist, it could not be more fittingly applied than to the enemies of the Republic.

"I vote for death!" were his concluding words.

Twenty voices echoed the word death, one after another, including Gracchus Antiboul.

"He, too!" groaned Miranda.

"Hush! Here comes Egalité," said Charles Clement, who was pale and trembling with excitement.

The Duke of Orleans, father of Louis Phillippe, was advancing towards the tribune amid profound silence. Everybody felt that, with the cousin of the King, only one vote was possible. All the curiosity was to hear in what way he would reconcile his democratic with his family feelings.

"Of course," said Robespierre, turning towards Clement, who had spoken to him as the leader of the Mountain took a seat near them, "he must vote for exile."

The Duke unrolled a paper.

"Solely influenced by my duty—convinced that all who have violated, or shall violate hereafter, the sovereignty of the people, merit death—I vote for *death*."

A silence of horror pervaded the Assembly. Miranda covered her face; the Mountain looked at each other with a shudder. Not a man in the whole Convention admired or approved the horrid act. It was not heroism. It was slavish cowardice, to guard his own life.

"The miserable wretch!" said Robespierre. "He had

only needed to have looked to the dictates of his heart, and of nature; he would not, dared not, do so.   The Republic would have been more magnanimous."

The Duke regained his seat, degraded even in the eyes of the most bloody and extreme of the Hebertists.

The voting continued some time longer.

"Have you kept any account?" said Miranda, in a low whisper, while her breath came and went in fitful heavings.

"No! But it is still doubtful," replied Charles Clement.

Morning was approaching, and the voting was declared closed.

Vergniaud took the chair, and, pale and ghastly, rose to proclaim the result.   His hands trembled.

At this instant, a deputy, Duchatel, was carried in on a litter, in his bed-clothes.   He came to vote against death—himself dying.

Vergniaud corrected the figures, and gave them out in a voice of unspeakable agony.

Seven hundred and twenty-one members had voted.

Three hundred and thirty-four voted for exile or a prison until peace.

Three hundred and eighty-seven for death, including the forty-six who voted for death with suspension of the execution.

There was only a majority of seven votes for immediate death.   Take away the Duke of Orleans, Vergniaud, Brissot, and Rolland, and the majority would have been a minority.

Miranda rose, her veil drawn over her face alone concealing her agony, and left the Convention with Charles Clement.

"In how many days will he die?" whispered she, as they gained a street at some little distance from the Assembly.

"In how many hours, ask me rather," said Charles Clement.

"Hours!  My God, what am I to do?  Charles, I must leave you.   I go to meet those who will strive to save him. You cannot accompany me."

"I cannot, Miranda," said the young man, warmly; "but beware what you are doing.   Nothing can save the King.

It is useless struggling. You will only risk your own life uselessly. Take my advice and abstain."

"I have vowed, and I will keep my vow," said the young Countess, who trembled with emotion. "Assist me into this *fiacre*, and then leave me. We shall meet in the evening."

Charles Clement called the coach, put Miranda in it, and then moved away.

On entering the hotel, he found an official letter on his table.

It was an order from Santerre, to take the command of the National Guard at the Temple during the next thirty-six hours.

Charles Clement at once put on his uniform, and, mounting a horse, galloped towards the royal prison, which he entered with the commissioners appointed by the Convention, to announce to Louis his condemnation.

"When?" said the young man, in a whisper, to Santerre.

"In twenty-four hours. That is, to-morrow."

"I expected it."

"And now, citizen," said the commander of the National Guard, drawing Charles Clement on one side, "beware. There are traitors in the Temple. A plot to save Louis exists. He has friends within and without. That rascally Chevalier de Jarjais is at the bottom of it. If they mean to do anything, it will be to-night. You must not let a fibre sleep. The capture of the conspirators is the chief object in view; for, as to any fear of their succeeding, I have none."

"Nor I," said Charles Clement, scarcely able to hide his deep and intense emotion.

"But there is no accounting for these Royalists. The more mad the enterprize, the more they join in it."

"I suspect there are more than Royalists in it. Venal and tender-hearted Republicans are at the bottom."

"I know it. In the Commune itself, the King has accomplices; but they shall be known; and known, they shall all be punished."

And Santerre moved away, to join the commissioners.

Charles Clement remained alone with his thoughts, which were far from pleasant. The danger which Miranda was now about to run was still more evident to his mind, and he was her chief antagonist.

To pass the time, he ordered out the National Guard who were on duty, save those who were sentries.

His eye glanced down the ranks carelessly, and, by a great effort of energy, he mastered his agitation.

In the disguise of National Guard, he recognized M. Brown, Paul Ledru, Duchesne, and some dozen men who were notorious Royalists. He had seen many of them at the Tuilleries on the 10th August.

He sent for Santerre, as if to ask some new instructions.

" General," said he, " grant me a favour, and the whole conspiracy is broken up."

" Whatever it be, my dear Clement, it is granted," replied Santerre.

" Every National Guard in the Temple is a Royalist or a traitor. There are nobles enough to make a court. Order up a sure company, and then march them out. At the door, I will give them a hint which will cool their zeal."

" There are two *sans-culotte* companies in the Rue Vielle du Temple," replied Santerre, astounded. " I will send for them at once. Act as you think best. I give you unlimited command."

In ten minutes more, the drum summoned the National Guard to their arms, to receive some new arrival.

They took up a position in the court ; the gate opened, and the head of a *sans-culotte* column appeared. The National Guard looked wildly at each other.

" Carry arms!" cried Charles Clement.

The National Guard obeyed, and next moment stood in presence of double the number of *sans-culottes*.

" Citizens !" said Charles Clement, severely addressing the National Guard, " I have an objection to commanding a force of so mixed a character as yours. Besides, a rescue of Louis is talked of," and his eye was full of meaning to Brown, Duchesne, and many others ; " and I feel more safety here, surrounded by the children of Paris and Marseilles. You are relieved from your guard."

The National Guard, stupified, made no reply. Charles Clement lost no time. Every sentry was relieved ; and, in a quarter of an hour, the whole body of conspirators were out of the Temple.

# CHAPTER LIII.

### THE DEATH OF LOUIS XVI.

TWENTY-FOUR hours after, a carriage left the Temple, on its way to the Place de la Revolution. In it were four men.

These four men were Louis XVI., two gendarmes, and the last confessor of the unfortunate monarch.

Sixty drums beat loudly at the head of the procession, which was composed of National Guards, the Marseillais, regular troops, both of infantry and cavalry, with gendarmes and artillery.

Not a living soul was allowed to cross the Boulevard, or the streets from the Temple to the Place de la Revolution.

All citizens were commanded to keep within doors on the line of the procession, and not even to show themselves at the windows.

The sky was heavy, with a thick fog in the air.

Pikes and bayonets lined the whole road, while cannon, loaded with grape, guarded the main thoroughfares and approaches.

The terrible Commune of the city of Paris were resolved that nothing should rob them of their prey.

Despite the orders of the municipality, crowds assembled on the line of march, but not a cry, not a murmur, not an insult, was heard. The Paris mob, usually so noisy, were stifled by emotion.

Charles Clement commanded a detachment at the mouth of a narrow street between the Portes St. Denis and St. Martin. He had four hundred sure Republican National Guards under his orders. He had occupied the position from dawn of day.

About six, a body of horse galloped up. At the head of it were several representatives.

Charles Clement recognized Gracchus Antiboul and Robespierre.

"*Salut !*" said Robespierre.

"What news? " replied Charles.

"Be watchful. A rescue will be tried. Our police report that it is just at this spot that that audacious vagabond de Jarjais will attack the procession. We rely on you."

"Count on me," said Clement, firmly. "The will of the Convention shall not be resisted."

"Could not a reinforcement be sent?" asked Gracchus.

"It would excite suspicion, and put them on their guard," replied Robespierre, and he rode off to join St. Just and Lebas, who were examining the other line.

"Until to-night," said Gracchus; and the two young men exchanged a solemn greeting.

Charles Clement remained alone; and, turning his back on the Boulevard, gazed curiously at the houses around.

A house at the corner of the nearest street attracted his attention. He thought he noticed an unusual number of faces at some of the upper windows, while a lad on the roof, looking towards the Bastille, seemed a scout. Besides this, at the end of the street, a number of young men stood in a group.

"March a patrol down yonder street, and disperse that group," said Charles Clement to a serjeant.

The soldier obeyed readily; and a patrol, with a drum beating, soon scattered the crowd, which gave way before it, and disappeared—they could not see how.

Clement felt uneasy. He seemed to know that there was more behind this than he could as yet fathom, while a fear of a terrible and wild nature filled his brain. He moved up and down impatiently, and was only roused from a moody reverie by the arrival of the head of the procession.

The solemn beating of sixty drums awoke all his attention. He formed his men in double line, and prepared to receive the *cortège*.

Behind the drums came General Santerre and his heavy escort. Both the general and his men were silent.

Then came the carriage, at which Charles Clement gazed mournfully, but without remorse, for to him, though regretting the scene, a great act of retribution was being accomplished.

The carriage, which was surrounded by a heavy escort of gendarmes, was just in front of Charles Clement, and was going very slowly down the hill.

" Look out !" cried a sentry from behind the piquet commanded by Charles Clement.

"Help ! those who would save the King," cried a hundred voices.

" *Vive le Roi !*" shouted others.

The Republican turned round. A couple of hundred young men, amongst whom Charles recognized de Jarjais, the Baron de Batz, Devaux, and one or two others, were rushing headlong at the procession; another body seemed ready to guard the street, while more again were unpaving the street.

In half an hour, barricades would have been erected in the name of royalty in Paris streets.

" *Vive la Republique !*" thundered Charles, rushing sword in hand to meet the Royalists.

" *Vive le Roi !*" they replied, raising a cry which for years was to resound no more.

The National Guard had wheeled round, and completely blocked up the way; so much so, that the procession moved quietly on, as if nothing had happened.

The conspirators saw that here all was lost; and as they had many other points agreed on, they gave way.

" *Sauve qui peut !*" thundered the Baron de Vaux.

But the National Guard bore hotly down upon them, and they were compelled to defend themselves. The Royalists fought with desperation. Not one would surrender. Not a shot was fired. Sword, pike, bayonet, did the work. The conspirators blocked up the street, and kept the Republicans bay.

" *Vive la Republique !*" again thundered Charles Clement, urging his men on.

The Royalists replied by their cry as warmly; and though falling before fresh assailants, still held out. At last, not twenty remained. The *sans-culottes* came up. These terrible men went in, pike in hand, to do the work of death.

The small knot had placed their backs against a narrow *porte cochère*, the bell of which one rang furiously all the time.

Clement saw that they had hope of escape, and strove to capture them. He resolved to rush on them and disarm them; but the ardour of the *sans-culottes* was too much for him; he was impelled on; and, in the feverish excitement of the moment, again spoke :—

"*La Republique!   Vive la Republique!*" he cried.

"*La Nation!   Vive la Nation!*" replied a young man, who fought with one hand, while he pulled at the bell with the other.   The voice had a magic effect.

To rush forward, to turn on his own men, to shriek them back, to wave his sword wildly round the youth, to shield him, while he passed through the half-open wicket, by his own body, was for Charles Clement the work of an instant.

" The Royalist has escaped !" yelled the *sans-culottes*.

" Treason !" cried some, waving their pikes over the young man.

" He was alone.   All the rest were dead," replied Charles Clement, coldly.   " I came to fight, not to murder.   I thought I was fighting at the head of true Republicans."

The *sans-culottes* still murmured; but unwilling to lose time, they plunged at the door, and it fell open.   All rushed in, and at their head Charles, who, by his eagerness, regained somewhat the confidence of his men.

They searched the house from garret to cellar, but they found nothing.

" Thank God," whispered Charles Clement, " *she* is safe."

He had saved Miranda from certain death, by recognizing her voice, despite her strange disguise.

After a long search, he re-formed his men; and leaving a piquet in possession of the house, he turned to the Boulevard, and advanced to the Place de la Revolution.

He reached the Rue once Royale, and looked down.

He saw a sea of heads, a hundred thousand upturned faces, and a forest of bayonets, illumined by the faint rays of a wintry sun, and in the centre four upright posts, blood red, and the lofty groove of the guillotine.   Dead silence prevailed.

Suddenly a salute of artillery was heard, a cry of *Vive la Republique*, a huge breath, as if of millions awakening, and the young man knew that the tragedy was over.

Charles Clement turned away to hide a tear.   Much as he hated the King, the race, the system, which had fallen that instant never to rise again, except in a fitful ghostly gust, he pitied the man, and the Republican wept over the grave of the King.

The city, mute with astonishment, went to its home; and that night many a mother kissed her child, and wife her husband, and blessed themselves they were only poor people.

Paris had often enough before rebelled against its tyrants and oppressors, and sent them forth in search of safer quarters; but now, for the first time, the people had calmly put to death a King. Painful as was the act, it was necessary to destroy the king-worship of the people, who, since this day, have admired, feared, loved, obeyed, power; but never worshipped or looked on it as something mystic and divine, which it were sacrilege to touch. The mob of Paris now knew that a king is but a man, and sometimes a very sorry one, worthy only according to his acts, and even more responsible than others; for, of those to whom much is given, much shall be required.

Regicide is as bad as any other murder—no more, no less; but there are periods in the world's history when a link requires to be broken. No monarch ever yet hesitated to let thousands fall to suit his schemes and views; and if once now and then the life of a king be necessary to the people, they take but trifling retribution. Count the millions slain by kings! Count the kings slain by the millions, and judge between them.

Charles Clement went away, silent and moody, towards Miranda's dwelling, impatient to hear news of her escape.

As he entered her street, a dozen *sans-culottes* surrounded him. They had been watching for him for more than an hour.

"Thy sword, citizen," said one.

"To whom speakest thou?"

"To the *citoyen* Charles Clement, whom I arrest by virtue of this *mandat*," said a police agent.

"Of what am I accused?"

"Of Royalism, and aiding the escape of a Royalist."

Charles Clement laughed outright.

"Ay! laugh!" said the *sans-culotte*, "but come, thou canst tell thy story to the *citoyen accusateur public*."

"Thou wilt accuse Robespierre of Royalism next," said our hero, still laughing.

"Who knows?" said one.

"Mirabeau was a traitor," replied another.

"*Citoyen!*" said a gentle voice at his elbow.

Charles Clement turned, and saw Rose, the maid.

"The *citoyenne* Miranda awaits you."

"Tell her," replied Charles, "I was about to visit her, but that the *citoyen accusateur public* has sent for me. Bid her see Robespierre, and tell him of my position, also Gracchus Antiboul."

Rose tremblingly replied she would, and then Charles Clement was marched off to the prison of the *conciergerie* by his republican guard.

---

## CHAPTER LIV

### CHARLES CLEMENT RECEIVES A SUDDEN CHECK.

For more than three weeks Charles Clement remained strictly *au secret.* He neither received communications from without, nor could he himself send forth communications. He saw no one. He was in a cell by himself, knowing of the world only through the fact of his jailor bringing him food at stated hours, but speaking never.

The young Republican remained ignorant alike of the dangers and glories which were crowding round the land. He knew not that war without and treason within were threatening the existence of his land.

Neither did he know the efforts making by his friends for his salvation. Gracchus and Miranda laboured day and night. They demanded interviews of Fouquier Tinville, of Marat, of Danton, of all who had power.

Robespierre refused to interfere, pleading his want of power.

Money, promises, tears, all were used to obtain an interview with him, but in vain.

Letters were sent to him; they never reached him.

At night Miranda wandered like a ghost round the gloomy prison, but in vain.

She attended the Revolutionary tribunal every day.

Never was Paris in such a state. The neglect of Charles Clement by his political friends, was fully to be excused.

Fatal reverses had taken place. Lyons and La Vendee had given the signal of civil war. Custine had been defeated. Dumourier had soiled his previous glorious career by treachery. War had been declared against England, Holland, Spain, and Germany.

The Convention made the danger known.

A black flag was hung on the Cathedral towers.

The rappel beat during twenty consecutive hours in every quarter of Paris, and the people flew to arms.

During this very twenty hours Charles Clement was summoned before the Revolutionary tribunal, presided over by Fouquier Tinville. It was early in the morning, and scarcely a soul was present, save a batch of about a dozen accused, the officials, and a man who passed his days in the court.

This was Paul Ledru ; but by neither sign nor sound did he show that he recognised his beloved master.

" Citizen Charles Clement," said Fouquier Tinville, with one of his hideous smiles—and this wretch was truly a fiend incarnate—" thou art accused of treachery to the Republic. *Mille millions de bombes!* I couldn't have believed it."

" And thou doesn't believe a word of it," replied Charles Clement, quietly.

The gendarmes who stood around looked astonished ; the President pushed back his hair, and the jury laughed ; they were some of the assassins of September, picked out by the atrocious Commune, which did its best to cover Revolutionary principles with everlasting odium.

" What mean'st thou ? " asked Fouquier.

" Thou knowest perfectly well, *citoyen accusateur public,* that I am as good a republican as thyself, if not better ; but thou hast thy instructions ; follow them out."

" *Citoyen,* answer thy accusation."

" I am ready."

" Thy name ? "

" Thou knowest it."

" Thy age ? "

" Twenty-seven."

" Thy profession ? "

" Republican soldier and patriot."

" Wast thou not affianced to an aristocrat ? "

" I was affianced," said Charles Clement, sternly, " to an angel who is now in heaven, with God."

" With the *Etre Suprême*, if thou wilt," said Fouquier Tinville, " but this angel was, I think, a duchess."

" She was, and my cousin."

" Good ! cousin to a duchess, and her affianced husband ; and after confessing this, and it is proved thou aidest the escape of de Jarjais, thou would'st be thought a patriot. Where are thy proofs of civism ? "

" Ask the 14th July.  Ask the 10th August," replied Charles.  " Ask Robespierre."

" All very good, but proving nothing," said Fouquier Tinville.  " On those two days thou mayest have done thy duty, to be a traitor afterwards, and the *citoyen* Robespierre may have been deceived."

" He may," replied Charles, " and probably he was. Since thou hast made up thy mind, *citoyen* judge, 'tis useless asking further questions."

The sanguinary Draco of the Revolution smiled grimly, and turned towards his jury, who smiled too, and nodded their heads.

Five minutes after, Charles Clement was condemned to death, and ordered for execution at daybreak on the following day.  He made no reply, but made way for the next victim, who had a better fate.

It was a young girl, whose arrest having been proved to be the act of private revenge, the accuser took her place, and was sent to prison for two years, the man narrowly escaping the guillotine.

When their political passions were not excited, these men were always just.

Paul Ledru had quitted the hall the instant after the condemnation of Charles Clement, who was shortly after removed to a vast cell, in company with those who were to be his comrades in the morning.

They were nine in number, and himself made

They were all men, and one of them was a priest.

They came in sullen, and sat down on the heaps of straw which lay on each side, and on which so many were yet to lie, to await a bloody rising.

The priest alone sat not down, but lifted up his voice and prayed aloud.

"Silence," said one, a middle-aged man, condemned to death for exciting a mob to pillage a baker's shop; "we have had enough of that croaking all our days."

"Hush," replied Charles Clement, sternly; "you do not mean what you say. We are all about to die, and to meet our God with our sins upon our heads. Think you, scoffer, that you will die less happy, because a minister of his word has offered you comfort?"

"I don't know," said the man, sullenly.

"I am pleased to meet one," said the priest, meekly, "who has respect for heaven and its will. This man who scoffs is a Royalist too ——"

"But I am a Republican, but none the less a believer. My condemnation is the result of a mistake. But I murmur not. My country is in trouble enough, without caring about me."

"You are a Republican, and believe in God?" said the priest, surprised.

"It is because I believe in God, in his goodness, in his mercy, that I am a Republican, Monsieur the *curé*. As I understand sacred history, God created man to enjoy the earth and its fruits. I find kings and nobles occupied solely with one object, and that is, to take unto themselves as much as possible, leaving to the many as little as is convenient. As this is unnatural, and against the manifest will of the Almighty, I have sought for something more just in the eyes of God than the association of a few for the injury of the many, and I have thought that the association of the many for the benefit of all is something likely to be pleasing to Him. Hence I am a Republican."

"You may be right, and you may be wrong," replied the meek priest, "but now is not the time to discuss this question. Let us pray together, forgetting alike our differences of belief, of opinion, and of faith."

Charles Clement bowed his head, and the priest prayed.

For a while some lay sullen, or sobbing, but presently they roused up, and before many minutes, the Cell of Death was a chapel of adoration.

Prayer over, the victims cowered on the straw, or walked about, or talked. Some slept, and even heavily, dreaming of green fields, and young days, and happy hours, and waking with a start, to know that life was nearly over. The Royalist agent of the *émeute* walked about in a towering passion.

"To be caught working for a cause I hate, for money," he growled. "Curse the day I quitted my section to take Royalist gold. Ah! Pitt, I wish I had you here. Dog! I would crush you. And Brunswick, how I would throttle him."

"Adieu! wife! child! world! all!" murmured a young man, pale, and yet calm, "'tis hard to leave them. I would not care perishing in battle against the foreigner, but the guillotine"—and he buried his face in his hands and said no more.

---

# CHAPTER LV

### THE END.

An hour passed, and Charles Clement remained lying on the straw in deep thought. He feared not death; but he regretted not being able to bid adieu to those friends for whom he felt so much affection. Miranda, Gracchus, Paul Ledru, their two wives, all he would have gladly seen once more.

"*Citoyen* Charles Clement," said the jailor, in a deep hoarse voice,

"Already!" he murmured.

"Already," repeated the nine other victims.

The jailor made no reply, but bade the young man move quickly and not keep a public functionary waiting.

He followed the turnkey into the passage.

It was lined with gendarmes of the Republic.

They made way for him.

"Go in there," said the jailor.

Charles Clement saw a narrow door before him leading into a chamber; he went in. The door closed behind him.

"Saved!" muttered a voice.

He raised his eyes. Robespierre stood beside him; and behind Gracchus, Miranda, and Paul Ledru.

"Citizen," said Robespierre, quietly, "I never forgot you; but appearances were against you, and my power was not sufficient to save a *suspect*. I dared not affront the Commune."

"And now?"

"Now, citizen Clement—why, I have come to save you out of desperation. This *citoyenne* leaves me no peace. At my own door I meet her every day; at the Convention gate I meet her at night."

"Never mind," cried Miranda; "he is safe; 'tis to thee we owe his life."

"Nay, to thee. This morning she came to my room, forced her way in, told me, before St. Just, the story of her disguise, and how you became suspected. I saw at once that no political motive actuated you, and I determined to ve you."

"Thanks!" cried Charles—"Thanks to all."

"But, citizen," said Robespierre, "a word with you. Remember we are in terrible times, in times when we cannot be moderate; be tight of tongue, and firm of act, and judge not the Revolution hastily. Nor do you judge me too quick. The emigrants and the coalition have thrown defiance, and war, treason, and myriad spies at us. We must, above all, save the Republic. If we lose, while so doing, our lives, and even our fame, it matters not. What boots it I am thought a ruffian, so my principles live? Be firm, honest, and true to liberty, and we shall go hand in hand."

"The Republic before all," replied Charles. "But are we not about to leave?"

" Nay, there is a condition imposed on your liberty," said Robespierre.

" A condition ! " cried Miranda.

" A condition ! " repeated Charles.

" Yes ! a condition.   It is a fancy of my own, but one which shall be accomplished ere you leave this prison, or I abandon you to your fate.   You love Miranda ? "

"I love Miranda ! " said Charles, starting back.

" You love this young man ? " continued Robespierre, turning to the Countess.

" I love Charles ! " exclaimed she, blushing, turning pale, and staggering.

" You love one another; but reasons I well appreciate keep you both silent.   But for me, months would have passed ere your secret would have been told, because you were scarce conscious of it.   But I know it, and my condition is, that you marry on the spot, in the prison."

" But we cannot," said Charles.

" It is impossible," murmured Miranda.

" I and Gracchus are good witnesses ! "

" But I cannot marry without a priest," said the Countess, faintly.

" There — is — one — in — the — Hall," — stammered Charles.

" Then you wish this marriage ? " cried Miranda.

" Believe, friend, Robespierre is right; I love you."

Miranda fell weeping in his arms.

Robespierre sent for the priest, who came readily, and the civil and religious contract was speedily passed between them.

The condemned to death was the husband of the lovely Countess Miranda ; and the devotion, love, and friendship, of our heroine were at length fully rewarded.

When the ceremony was over, Robespierre bade them come away, for he was engaged.

Clement drew him aside, took his hand, pressed it to his lips, pointed to the priest, to Miranda, to the chamber of death, and implored—

" It cannot be," replied Robespierre, who held in his

hand the pardon of Charles Clement, which came from the Commune.

"But 'tis my wedding, *citoyen représentant!*"

"Charles Clement and his supposed accomplices," said Robespierre, reading off the paper. "It can be done. They are all free, save the agent of the foreigner. He deserves his fate, and must die. Besides, I dare not save him. The rest are obscure criminals. He was caught distributing gold, and urging on a mob to pillage."

"I give him up. Receive my thanks for the rest."

Robespierre called the jailor, countersigned the pardon, included the eight supposed accomplices, and sent for the seven who were yet absent. They came, and the wretched man was left alone.

They came with fear and trembling to the room, where the husband and wife, scarce yet able to understand the truth, stood waiting for them. They saw at a glance, by their faces, that there was no bad news.

"My friends, thanks to the generous clemency of the *citoyen* Maximilien Robespierre, your innocence is recognised. Thank him, and cry with me *Vive la Republique!*"

Loud and warm was the response of the reprieved, who crowded round and embraced the knees of the great revolutionist.

"I have but expressed the wishes of the Commune," said Robespierre, pushing them away; "and now let us depart. Time presses, the Convention is sitting, and I must join my colleagues."

The prisoners readily obeyed, and, a few formalities complied with, the whole party left the prison.

Robespierre hastened with Gracchus to the Tuileries.

Charles and Miranda moved, arm-in-arm, in silence towards her residence.

The prisoners dispersed after all had thanked our hero.

The pair moved on, I have said, in silence. They were thinking. They could scarcely understand the change.

"Miranda!" said Charles, in a low whisper, "is it true you love me?"

"I loved you," replied his wife, looking him sweetly in the face, "from the first hour that I saw you."

Charles Clement was silent with surprise. A world of mystery was thus cleared up to him, and many hints from Gracchus were now understood.

They reached the Rue St. Thomas de Louvre, where Rose received them rapturously.

"And Monsieur is come to stay again," said the soubrette.

"Rose!" replied the Countess, blushing, "Monsieur Charles Clement is now your master and my husband."

"My God!" cried the girl, "what has happened?"

"We were married an hour ago," said Charles, with a smile.

Rose made no reply, but looked at her mistress with ineffable delight, and clapped her hands.

"Come, dear child. They have starved him in prison. It is your task to restore your master."

Charles gazed at himself in a glass, and he was truly gaunt, pale, and thin.

They remained alone, and the emotions of a month found vent in words. His sufferings, his tortures, hopes, fears, schemes, were all told over and over again, and then, without forgetting the dead, they spoke of their love and their affections.

And they were really **happy**, for they were worthy of one another. Miranda ever remained as devoted and fond a wife as she had been sincere a friend. Charles never forgot Adela, the more fondly remembered when he knew her wish that he should wed Miranda; but he never ceased to adore his wife, whose virtues were rewarded by faithful and attached affection.

Paul Ledru and Gracchus Antiboul lived long to witness the happiness they had done their utmost to promote.

And when the 9th Thermidor came, and a wretched gang, furious at the intention of Robespierre to put an end to the terror, overthrew his power by a trick, they all turned out to support him and the Revolution.

But Robespierre refused to fire a gun, and the Talliens and other refuse of the Mountain prevailed but for an hour. Though, when they tried to double the number of daily victims, the people bade them stop; they had overthrown

Robespierre under the pretence of stopping blood, and the Parisian populace told them to keep their word.

He died, and never was he forgotten by his friends. They knew that he had faults, great faults, but they never forgot that he loved his country, and that to them he had been more than a friend.

And thus endeth the eventful narrative of the life of Miranda del Castelmonte, who, noble-born as she was, lived and died a devoted admirer of the great French Revolution, which did much evil, but far more good.

THE END.